SAFE HARBOR

Tymber Dalton

MENAGE AMOUR

Siren Publishing, Inc.
www.SirenPublishing.com

A SIREN PUBLISHING BOOK
IMPRINT: Ménage Amour

SAFE HARBOR
Copyright © 2010 by Tymber Dalton

ISBN-10: 1-60601-665-2
ISBN-13: 978-1-60601-665-7

First Printing: April 2010

Cover design by Jinger Heaston
All cover art and logo copyright © 2010 by Siren Publishing, Inc.

Printed in the U.S.A.

PUBLISHER
Siren Publishing, Inc.
www.SirenPublishing.com

DEDICATION

This one's for Steph. She knows why.

AUTHOR'S NOTE

For any reader who's curious about them, Ray, Oot, and kitten also make an appearance in *Love Slave for Two: Beginnings*.

SAFE HARBOR

TYMBER DALTON

Chapter One

Someone—she couldn't remember who—once told Clarisse Moore how lucky she was to have Bryan Jackson as her boyfriend.

If they could see me now.

Clarisse huddled deeper in her seat in the bus station lobby, her legs curled under her to keep her feet warm. The denim jacket she wore over her hooded sweatshirt proved no match for the cold Ohio January breeze that flooded the depot every time the door opened. Which at this time on an early Tuesday morning seemed remarkably frequent and made her even more nervous.

The bus wasn't due in for another twenty minutes. Clarisse couldn't help but scan the parking lot for Bryan's car. No way he'd let her leave without a fight.

Literally.

If not for his fists, she could deal with the rest of it. Mrs. Moore didn't raise her daughter to be a punching bag. The first time, he got a freebie because she was too scared to report him. That time, he apologized and reined in his anger for a few months, until he gradually returned to his old, angry ways. Over the past few months, his rages had increased until he snapped yesterday morning.

He wouldn't get a third chance.

By now, Bryan had already found all her things gone. She'd stashed her stuff in a storage space on the west side of Zanesville.

Raquel would care for Bart, her dog, until she got settled and came back for him and her belongings.

Clarisse figured Bryan would be angriest about the bank account. At least she'd left him a hundred bucks—more generous than she should be, considering how he'd blown through her inheritance. She'd ended up with ten grand out of the original hundred thousand, nine of which she'd already deposited in a new bank account. She had a thousand in cash on her.

She couldn't risk using credit cards.

Raquel had begged and pleaded for Clarisse to file charges this time. Reluctantly, she did.

He had beaten the crap out of her Monday morning. They didn't arrest him because there were no witnesses or proof he did it beyond her word against his. He claimed his innocence. The police opened a case file and took her statement. She got an emergency restraining order against him, and the department put him on paid administrative leave.

Against her, the fact that Bryan's father was best friends with the chief of police—Bryan's boss. Late that afternoon, an unidentified man called her cell phone and threatened her unless she dropped the charges. She refused. Clarisse had been sitting on Raquel's couch when the call came in. After she hung up, she smashed the phone with her foot. It was in Bryan's name. Why the hell would she want it when he could probably track her with it?

Then she found "FAT FUCKING BITCH" deeply keyed into her car door when she returned to the house later that evening. She'd only been inside ten minutes. Clarisse had stopped by to drop off the car and take one last look around for anything she couldn't bear to leave. Raquel had been following only minutes behind her. Clarisse raced inside the house, then out the back door and through a small patch of woods in case anyone had been watching the street.

Yes, she felt that paranoid. Justifiably so.

He'd registered the car in his name, even though her inheritance

had paid for it—let him get it repainted. Served him right. She also
didn't want him following through with his threat to report the car
stolen if she ever left with it. She didn't know if he really could do
that or not, but she wouldn't risk it.

It was easiest this way. New start, new life. No more being
screamed at for not folding his shirts just right. No more merciless
harassment about her size sixteen frame.

That had been his favorite target lately, the one thing she'd not
been able to immediately rectify about herself to curb his anger. Her
hips would always be round, her thighs would always be full, and she
would always be a little broad across the beam. At five-six she wasn't
obese, just amply rounded and curvy, but still no match for Bryan's
hulking two-hundred-plus pounds of muscle once he unleashed on her
for talking back to him and telling him to fuck off.

As Raquel had said, he'd bitch no matter what, so the fewer
reasons she gave him, the more he had to invent. Then their argument
gave him a prime reason, so he claimed.

Still, she knew she had to get away fast. The restraining order
would only protect her for a little while. He'd always teased that he
could kill her and no one would know it, that his dad would get him
out of trouble, that she could never outrun him or find a place to hide
where he couldn't find her. Maybe he'd be in jail by the time she
came back for Bart and her stuff.

She patted the key ring in her jeans pocket, the keys she'd
frantically searched for and finally found buried in a small box full of
mementos. A cherished memory of an old, nearly forgotten life. Three
keys, hopefully ones leading to her freedom.

The bus pulled in. She hefted her bags and painfully made her
way outside. After the driver stowed her luggage, Clarisse boarded.
Relieved, she sank into her seat and tried to relax.

Clarisse always thought of herself as relatively smart, which made
it even more inexplicable to her that she fell for someone as
controlling, manipulative, and dangerous as Bryan Jackson.

* * * *

By the time the bus pulled into a station in southern Ohio, Clarisse was ready to jump off to use a real bathroom. When the driver assured her that she had time, Clarisse raced inside. With relief, she finished and washed her hands.

She flinched when she caught sight of her reflection in the mirror. The shiner looked horrible, the eye still nearly swollen shut, both her blue eyes red from crying. Thank God he hadn't broken her nose. The split upper lip hurt like hell. She knew without looking that the black-and-blue bruises over her kidneys would take time to fade—as would the marks on her thighs and chest where he kicked her when she curled into a ball on the floor.

She pulled her baseball cap lower on her head and didn't bother threading her long, black hair through the back. She could keep her head down. Her hair hid the worst of her wounds from others.

Back on the bus, she settled in her still-warm seat. Fortunately, no seat mate. She pulled the hood of the sweatshirt she wore under her jacket over her head, over the baseball cap, and stared out the window as the bus rolled south throughout the morning.

Her last look at the Midwest. No more brutal winters. She'd miss Bart like crazy until she could get him, but getting out fast was her priority.

Getting out alive.

She'd thought about flying. Bryan might have called the airport, so she didn't. She didn't know how that worked, only that he had threatened he could track her no matter what and prevent her escape in anything other than a body bag. He knew that she despised taking the bus. She'd sworn she'd never ride one again after a less-than-stellar cross-country trip with two of her friends after high school.

Maybe it would stall him. He might be a cop, hopefully soon to be *ex*-cop, and yes, he worked in the computer division, but he wasn't a freaking psychic. Armed with her mom's old driver's license, using her name and paying cash for the ticket might slow Bryan a little more. Thank goodness she'd held on to that. She'd found it in the box with the set of keys.

Clarisse tried not to think about her mom and dad. It hurt too much. She left knowing that unless Bryan went to jail, she couldn't risk visiting their graves one last time.

Despite her exhaustion, she couldn't sleep. Instead, she watched the miles and country flow past the window as the day rolled into evening and the bus drew closer to Columbia, Virginia.

She spent the six-hour layover for the bus to Myrtle Beach counting the number of snack packages in one of the vending machines.

Blessed numbness had settled in. Emotional detachment.

Exhaustion.

At least it marginally overrode her pain.

Then she realized she couldn't sleep. Every time a car pulled alongside the bus and stayed there for any length of time, she nervously waited to see if Bryan or one of his buddies was driving.

By the time the bus reached Myrtle Beach, Clarisse's exhaustion had carried her into the realm of jittery, paranoid anxiety. The term "sleep-deprivation psychosis" swam through her mind as she stood waiting her turn at the ticket counter with her bags at her feet and her mom's driver's license in her hand. The black eye and split lip proved an asset at this point. She resembled her mom closely enough that the ticket clerks didn't question her.

She patted her pocket to ensure the keys were still there.

They were.

That had quickly become a nervous, calming habit. She didn't dare take them out of her pocket for fear of dropping and losing them. Stupid to think they'd even work, but it was her only chance.

At least she'd had the sense not to buy her entire trip at once. She didn't want Bryan waiting for her at her destination. Yes, he could track her if he got that far, but hopefully he'd be running around Rapid City looking for her.

Clarisse had taken the time before she left to use the house phone to call an old high school friend who lived in Rapid City. She'd warned her old buddy that Bryan might come looking for her. Clarisse said she might head out that way, possibly to Spokane where another old friend lived.

Red herring. Isn't that what they called it?

She closed her eyes and startled awake when the clerk called out to her.

Clarisse shuffled forward. "Tallahassee, please." One more leg. She'd checked the boards. Take a bus to Tallahassee or wait five more hours for one to Miami. The bus to Tampa left in three hours, but that was too close to her final destination for her comfort.

How many hours, days, since she left? Time blurred. She didn't know for sure what day it was, only that she hadn't slept in the twenty-four hours from when Bryan beat the crap out of her early Monday morning, until she stepped aboard the bus in Columbus early Tuesday. Or more than catnaps since. That meant it had to be at least late Wednesday.

She thought she dozed off on the bus. Either that or her mind had gone. On the last leg of her journey, exhaustion claimed what little fight remained in her.

"Where to?" the Tallahassee ticket clerk asked.

"Do you have anything to Tarpon Springs?" Clarisse swayed on her feet while the girl looked it up.

"I do, a bus going to St. Petersburg stops there on the way. It's leaving in two hours."

"Perfect."

* * * *

Clarisse hoped Uncle Tad still docked at the same marina. She didn't dare use the disposable phone yet. She'd bought it on the way to the bus station in Columbus, wanted her calls slower to trace. Now, some time after midnight Thursday morning, Clarisse could barely speak due to exhaustion. The cabby dropped her off at the marina.

Clarisse sobbed with relief when she spotted the Dilly Dally docked in its berth. The fifty-foot fishing trawler was a beautiful sight.

Maybe the most beautiful sight in the whole world.

Oh, thank you God!

She didn't have a plan B. This was her *only* plan, and it belatedly hit her she could have called the marina from Ohio.

It didn't matter now. She was here, and so was the Dilly.

Clarisse slung her duffel bag and purse over her arm, yanked the handle on her large rolling bag, and carefully made her way down the familiar dock. She struggled with her bags, somehow muscled them on board without dropping them into the drink. Her hands trembled as she fished the keys out of her pocket. She studied the wheelhouse door lock.

Please, please, please...

She needed both hands to fit the key in the lock. Then she closed her eyes, and...

It turned.

Clarisse cried. She quickly dragged her bags through the door and into the wheelhouse and closed and locked it behind her. All the while, tears coursed down her cheeks. She pulled her stuff downstairs through the main cabin to the small bow V-berth cabin she used to use. Despite the tight fit, she wrestled her stuff inside and shut the door behind her. Cold inside, but warm compared to Columbus. She didn't want to risk turning on lights or cranking the generator or engines to start the heater. Clarisse didn't know if the Dilly was hooked to shore power, and, frankly, she felt too tired to look.

Apparently Uncle Tad had become a better housekeeper than he used to be. Otherwise, not much else had changed.

Clarisse left her jacket and sweatshirt on, fell onto the bunk, then sank into immediate darkness.

* * * *

Her dreams took her back to high school, when she spent summers and weekends with Uncle Tad and Aunt Karen, learning how to shrimp, fishing, working on the boat, and enjoying herself. Before she moved to Columbus with her mom and dad.

Before she met Bryan.

Before Aunt Karen and then later her parents died.

She hadn't heard anything from her uncle in nearly two years. She worried maybe he'd moved or sold the boat. Calling him wasn't an option because Bryan tightly controlled and monitored the home and cell phone bills. Before leaving Columbus, she'd risked calling Uncle Tad's old phone number from Raquel's cell phone. She received a disconnected number message.

She hadn't told Raquel that, afraid her friend would talk her into not going to Florida on a potential wild-goose chase.

But the Dilly still sat here in her old slip.

At least something had gone right for her, finally. If she'd stayed in Columbus, anywhere within a thousand-mile radius of Bryan, he'd kill her. She believed that with every sore bone in her body.

Clarisse slept throughout the morning and straight through the day. She never even stirred when the boat gently rocked as two men climbed on board a little after five o'clock that afternoon.

Chapter Two

"So, *Captain*, what's on the agenda?" Sullivan Nicoletto playfully asked his partner.

Brant MacCaffrey arched an eyebrow at him. "You're a real ballsy guy for someone who's stepping into *my* domain, aren't you?"

Sully grinned. "You know I enjoy it, Mac."

"You try to yank my chain, I might find a few new interesting ways for you to spend the weekend on the water." He grabbed a box of groceries off the dock and handed it over the side to Sully.

"As long as I can pay you back on dry land, we're copacetic." Sully winked, his grey eyes twinkling.

Mac cranked the diesels and let them idle. Fifteen minutes later, with everything stowed in the galley and their familiar routine complete, Mac checked the gauges and set the GPS. "Okay, go ahead and cast off. I want to be at the head marker before low tide hits."

Sully untied the lines, neatly coiling and stowing them. Then he took his usual position on the gunwale as Mac smoothly steered the boat out of the berth.

"Clear?" Mac called out.

Sully kept his eye on the final piling. "Okay, now."

Mac used the bow thrusters to turn them in the marina basin. They cleared the marina and idled down the Anclote River channel toward the Gulf of Mexico. An hour later, they motored into open water and watched the sun set on the horizon in front of them. With the closest vessel in sight more than several miles away, they were virtually alone. Mac set the autopilot and radar guard alarm before he turned to Sully.

"Well?"

"Well what?"

Mac held up a leather collar. "Don't make me tell you."

Sully rolled his eyes but reached for the collar.

"Oh, don't even do the eye roll, buddy," Mac playfully warned. "That'll earn you another ten."

When Sully had the collar fastened around his neck, he turned so Mac could affix a small, silver lock to the buckle. "Now what?" Sully asked.

Mac pointed to the wheelhouse door. "You know what I want."

Sully walked outside to the railing and bent over, placing his hands on it and spreading his legs. "Like this?"

After grabbing a couple of straps from a storage nook, Mac stepped behind Sully. "Damn straight." With fluid, practiced movements, he securely bound Sully's wrists to the railing.

Sully looked over his shoulder at Mac. "It's cold out here."

Mac pressed his body against Sully's ass and gripped his lover's hips. "Yeah, but you're damn hot, buddy." He reached around, unfastened Sully's jeans, and shoved them down his hips. Sully had gone commando. His bare ass prickled with goose bumps in the chilly evening air.

Mac ran his hands over Sully's ass and squeezed his cheeks. "Gonna warm that up for you real fast." He stepped to the side and spanked him, leaving the skin red and warm.

Sully tightly shut his eyes. "Don't fucking tease me, man," he groaned.

Mac laughed and ground his hips against Sully's ass. "Payback's a bitch, and so am I." He reached around the other man again. This time he grabbed Sully's hard, throbbing cock and squeezed it. "Doesn't seem like the cold air's bothering you too much." Sully tried to rock his hips against Mac's hand, but Mac squeezed even harder, which drew a pained moan from Sully. "Uh-uh. No you don't. You get to come when I say so, and I'm not ready to let you do that yet."

Sully groaned again.

* * * *

Clarisse realized three things immediately upon awaking—the engines were running, from the way the boat rocked she knew they weren't at the dock anymore, and that her entire body hurt like a motherfucker.

She groaned as she slowly sat up and scrubbed her face with her hands, then glanced at her cell phone to check the time.

Holy crap.

The fact that she'd slept more than twelve hours shocked what little sleep remained right out of her system. Despite protesting muscles, she opened the door to the small bow cabin and looked around below decks. No one in sight.

She started to mount the galley stairs to the wheelhouse when through the open wheelhouse door she caught sight of two men on deck. Neither her uncle. The one man...

Oh, shit.

She ducked, her heart racing and her muscles screaming at the sudden movement. In the dim light she couldn't see them well, but they both looked hunky. A shorter, brown-haired one bent over the rail with his jeans shoved down past his ass, and the other...

Oh, baby!

Was that a *collar* around the brown-haired man's neck?

The blond man ground his hips against the other's bare ass. Then he unzipped his jeans and reached for something. She watched as the blond man slicked his cock with lube before sliding it inside the other man. Her throat went dry as she watched his firm, tight ass clench and relax as he thrust into his partner.

"Jesus, you feel like you've got bigger," the man on the receiving end said.

Blondie laughed. "You just haven't been fucked enough lately.

You need to get out on the boat more often with me." He leaned in close and pressed his still-clothed torso against the other man's back. "I take your cock without a second thought. I sure as hell don't complain. Don't tell me you're whining?"

The other man bucked his hips backward to impale himself even more deeply. "I can take anything you dish out, buddy. Bring it on."

Blondie grinned. "I hoped you'd say that."

Clarisse realized that she stood out in the open. As much as she wouldn't mind watching the two handsome hunks go at it, she realized that might not be a good idea.

She turned and started toward the front bow cabin. She spotted, in its usual place, the familiar blue plastic envelope where the boat registration and documentation papers were kept. Clarisse grabbed it, raced to the front cabin, and softly closed the door behind her. Unfortunately, one thing hadn't changed—the latch on the cabin door still didn't work. It would stay closed, but she couldn't lock it. She jammed her suitcase into the space between the bunk and the bottom of the door. Wedged against the base of the bunk, it would slow someone down for a few minutes, at least. Not that the thin cabin door would hold if one of those buff guys wanted to kick it in.

She risked turning on the small reading light. With trembling hands, she opened the envelope.

State commercial fishing licenses and permits, vessel registration and documentation papers, captain's license paperwork, and other official permits and documents.

The Dilly's new owner: Sullivan Nicoletto, forty-two. The captain: Brant MacCaffrey, thirty-eight. PO Box address in Tarpon Springs.

She wondered who was who. Well, one of them had to be MacCaffrey, because the captain's and commercial fishing licenses had been issued in his name.

With the situation fully striking home, Clarisse closed her eyes and fought another round of tears. It'd been a long shot, sure, but when she'd seen the Dilly in her slip, Clarisse thought her luck had changed for the better.

Where is Uncle Tad?

Even over the deep throb of the twin diesels below decks, Clarisse heard one of the men shout something. She shoved the paperwork into the envelope and shut off the light.

Hopefully they won't be interested in me. A nervous giggle escaped her. That absolutely had to be stress. Not a damn thing funny about this situation.

Maybe exhaustion had finally gotten the better of her. She'd been physically and emotionally beat to hell and back. No catch in the looks or sex department himself, Bryan had accused her of infidelity enough times she'd been tempted to go out and actually do it for real, if she could even find someone interested in a "big girl" like herself. Standing there watching those two guys...

Yum.

Clarisse curled up on the bunk. The cabin felt warmer than it had earlier. They must have turned on the heater.

Why were they out on deck?

Not as cold as Columbus, but still chilly enough out there. Why not take advantage of the warmer below-decks area?

Hopefully they wouldn't discover her. The master cabin had a much larger bunk where two big, hunky guys could easily...

Cripes.

She shook her head to clear it. She hoped she'd be safe in the tiny bow cabin. Except now, she had a problem.

She had to pee.

Holding her breath, she moved the suitcase and carefully peeked out the cabin door. No sign of the men below decks.

With the forward head door right there, she ducked inside. Keeping the light off, she relieved herself and started to reach for the flush lever when she stopped.

Dammit. They might hear.

She cracked the head door open. She caught a glimpse of Blondie's ass, still on deck.

Clarisse flushed and washed her hands.

Well, if they were still busy, she might be able to take care of another need—her stomach. She crept back to the galley where she checked the fridge and pulled out two bottles of water. From a box on the counter, she snagged a couple of packages of peanut butter crackers and three bananas before scooting back to the bow cabin.

* * * *

Mac considered untying Sully and stripping him, but it was a tad too chilly for that. Instead, he reached under the front of Sully's shirt, found his nipples, and twisted them hard.

From Sully's sharp, hissing breath, Mac knew he was close.

"Don't you fucking come," Mac growled at him. He thrust his cock deep inside his lover, his own release rapidly approaching.

Sully threw his head back against Mac's shoulder. "Goddamn, where did you learn that?"

"You."

"Oh, yeah." Sully laughed. "You're a good student."

Mac nipped the side of his neck. "My Master's a damn good teacher. You can schmooze all you want. You still can't come yet."

"Fucker."

Mac released Sully's nipples and grabbed his hips. "You betcha." He thrust hard and fast, slamming his cock home until he cried out as he came. He wrapped his arms around Sully as he caught his breath. "I'm gonna fuck your brains out this weekend."

"I thought you had to fish?"

"Who says I can't do both?"

Sully wiggled his hips against Mac, whose softening cock was still planted in his ass. "Thank God I brought a few pairs of sweatpants. Otherwise I'd be freezing my butt off."

"I should have modified them and cut a hole in the ass." Mac dropped his hand to the other man's still-hard cock. "You've got thirty seconds to come or you have to wait until the next time I feel like doing this." He started stroking as Sully's eyes dropped closed, his hips working against Mac's hand. The action immediately revived the interest of Mac's cock, which started inflating again.

"Mmm, yeah, I get seconds," Mac said. He wrapped his fingers tighter around Sully's cock and pumped his fist up and down his shaft.

Sully fucked himself back and forth between Mac's cock and hand, groaning as he struggled to make it. Just when he thought he never would, his climax rocked him, coating Mac's hand with his juices. "Fuck yeah!" he groaned.

Mac gave him a few seconds before he grabbed Sully's hips again and pounded his cock into him. "You lucky bastard, you barely made it. This is what happens when you torture me before we get on the goddamned boat. You left me fucking horny this morning...ah!"

He leaned against Sully for support again, trying to catch his breath. After a moment, he withdrew and slapped Sully's ass, hard. "Be right back."

"You're leaving me here?"

Mac laughed. "Gonna clean up. I'll take care of you in a minute." He walked around the sorting table. "Hey, at least it's too cold for me to hose you down."

"You wouldn't?"

"I might. My boat, my rules. That's the deal." He grinned. "I told you, payback's a bitch and so am I." He didn't bother zipping his jeans. He walked below decks to the aft head and cleaned up. Then he zipped, washed his hands, and walked over to the box of supplies on the galley counter. He reached in, hesitating before he pulled out a banana. He returned to the deck.

"Hey, you been into the food already?" he asked Sully.

Sully glanced at him. "That's a weird tangent."

Mac didn't bother untying Sully. He lounged next to him in the deepening gloom and peeled the banana. "There's only three bananas left. You been into them? I thought I grabbed a larger bunch than that." He broke off a piece and fed it to Sully after taking a bite himself.

Sully shook his head, chewed, and swallowed. "Nope."

They finished the banana. Mac tossed the peel overboard. "Well, whatever." He caressed Sully's ass. "You're feeling a little chilly there, buddy."

"No shit."

Mac started slapping his ass again until Sully's flesh turned warm and pink. Only then did he relent and untie his hands. "Go clean up." When Sully turned from the railing, Mac grabbed the front of his sweatshirt, pulled him close, and crushed his lips with his. "I'm gonna love using your ass this weekend. You're gonna be gone a lot next month. That's not fair."

"Life's not fair." Sully grinned. "You'll just have to get creative."

* * * *

Clarisse huddled in the V-berth and prayed they didn't find her. How would she find Uncle Tad? Maybe the marina would know.

Worse, where would she go? She still had more than five hundred dollars in cash, but she wouldn't be able to access the other funds in the new account for several days. She'd been gone from Florida for so long that she didn't know anyone else here but Uncle Tad, unless some of the regulars still had slips in the marina.

Now she'd have to call Raquel and admit this was a dead end. She felt so tired, bone-dead tired, exhausted mentally, physically, and emotionally.

Maybe she should have just stayed and let Bryan kill her. No more struggle, no more fighting. She'd be with her dad and mom, right? Hopefully.

She closed her eyes and rested her head on a pillow. No, definitely exhaustion speaking. She didn't want to be dead. She wanted to be free, and it'd been so damn long since she'd been free that she'd forgotten what it felt like.

Her eyes snapped open. She must have slept again because she saw through the tiny port window that night had fallen. She didn't hear the men, just the sound of the diesels.

What woke her?

Her heart raced. Something had awoken her. Her instincts from all the time she spent on board kicked in.

She closed her eyes and listened, trying to pick out old, familiar sounds. The diesels—they sounded smooth, no problems there. But something...

Then she heard it again and immediately recognized it. The auxiliary aft bait tank circulation pump had clogged or sucked air, jamming the automatic kill switch open. That happened sometimes. She waited, anticipating one of the men would go below decks and unplug it. Usually Uncle Tad didn't bother using the auxiliary pump unless absolutely necessary.

The minutes ticked by. *What the fuck are they waiting for? How could they not hear that?* If it overheated, it could short-circuit and cause a fire in the engine compartment. At the very least, it would ruin the pump.

She sat up and waited, chewing her nails.

The sound grew more shrill.

She heard a noise from the master cabin and realized why the men hadn't reacted.

Didn't anyone tell those assholes you have to have someone on watch?

She waited for several minutes. Unable to take it any longer, she yanked her suitcase out of the way and pounded on their cabin door as she ran past. "Get up! The pump's burning up!"

* * * *

Mac jumped, startled by the pounding on the door. He whacked his head so hard against the bulkhead that he yelped in pain and dropped to the berth, swearing and gripping the back of his head.

Sully yanked on his restraints. "Who the fuck is that?"

"I don't know!" With one hand on the rapidly swelling goose egg on the back of his head, Mac used the other to unclip Sully's wrist cuffs and grab a pair of sweatpants. The men tumbled out of the cabin as they pulled on clothes. By the time they reached the main cabin hatch, they saw the engine room cover was up and caught a glimpse of a woman's head disappearing through the opening.

"Shit!" Sully growled. He took the lead, ripping off the leather wrist cuffs as he ran. He raced down the ladder ahead of Mac. The woman had the engine room light on and was already buried headfirst in the far alcove behind the port engine where some of the electrical junctions were located.

Mac reached for the protective earmuffs he kept hanging inside the hatch and found them missing.

What the fuck?

Then he heard the screeching noise, what he didn't hear before. Okay, so he'd been distracted, but still.

Sully started to go after the woman. Mac caught his arm and shook his head. Sully wouldn't have heard him over the engine noise anyway.

After a moment, the screech stopped. The woman emerged. Yes, she wore the earmuffs and held a flashlight. The flashlight that also hung by the hatchway.

Who the hell is she?

* * * *

Clarisse had found the connector and, with no time to waste, yanked as hard as she could on the wire. When it broke loose at the junction box connector, the auxiliary pump shut off. Flipping the switch in the wheelhouse wouldn't have done any good, because when the float switch stuck it overrode the on-off switch. It would have taken twice as long to find the damn fuse and yank it, but that would have killed both pumps. Uncle Tad had always sworn he never should have let his brother-in-law install the damn thing. He'd meant to rewire it properly to eliminate the problem, hence why he rarely used it when the other pump usually sufficed.

Old habits died hard. Even though she wasn't thin and hadn't set foot on the boat in years, Clarisse had no problem carefully wiggling her way out of the alcove. She maneuvered around the back of the port engine and avoided the exhaust manifold. Even with the earmuffs on, it was still friggin' loud.

The two men looked stunned. She glanced at them only long enough to shove past them, her face turned away. She replaced the flashlight and earmuffs before scrambling up the ladder to the deck.

Fear set in. She raced for the V-berth cabin, hoping to get there first. Maybe she could talk to them through the door and they wouldn't press charges against her for being a stowaway or breaking and entering or whatever since she'd saved their asses.

* * * *

His initial shock waning, Mac raced after her. He managed to grab her jacket and yank her back. "Stop! Wait, who the hell are you?"

She fought, hard and viciously. In the narrow passageway, he had to wrap both arms around her and drag her back to the main cabin area. She still managed to land a few good strikes to his shins with her heels. Fortunately for him her sneakers didn't cause him much damage.

"Stop fighting! We're not going to hurt you!" He muscled her into the galley and forced her to sit in the booth table. Sully pushed in, blocking her escape. She cringed away from them, her long hair obscuring her face.

"I'm sorry! Please don't call the police!" She curled into a tight ball against the bulkhead wall.

"Are you on the run from the cops?" Sully asked.

She shook her head.

The men exchanged a glance. They still couldn't see her face.

With Sully keeping her penned in, Mac slowly slid into the other side of the booth. She cringed. Jesus, she seemed so familiar—

Then it hit him. Betsy. She acted a lot like his little sister had the last time he saw her alive.

Before her husband killed her.

Sully started to say something else but Mac held up a hand. His Joe Friday cop routine wouldn't fly right then. "What did you do? In the engine room?"

She still wouldn't look at them, her hair concealing her face. "The auxiliary bait tank pump. You can't use it. It gets stuck because the wiring's messed up. I yanked the wire, that's all. I heard it going. If it'd burned up, it could have short-circuited the panel and caused a fire."

Mac felt Sully's eyes burning into him, but he refused to look at his partner. Only someone with intimate knowledge of the boat could know that. He'd stupidly forgotten it, even though Tad had warned him about it and suggested calling an electrician to fix it.

"Look at me," Mac softly commanded.

She cringed again, but she tipped her head just enough he spotted one eye through her hair. Still not enough to see her face.

"Thank you," he said.

The girl froze. "You're welcome," she finally said.

Mac grabbed her wrist, firmly but not painfully. He reached for her chin and hesitated when she flinched.

"I'm not going to hurt you," he said. "I promise, neither one of us will hurt you." When she relaxed, he tilted her chin so she had to look at them. Mac heard Sully's sharp intake of breath when they got their first good look at her face—and her injuries. Someone had beaten the crap out of her. No wonder she was hiding and scared.

"Who did this to you?" Sully growled.

Mac felt her tremble. He released her chin, but laced his fingers through hers.

"Bryan. My boyfriend. Ex."

Her soft, scared voice ripped at Mac's heart. He wanted to wrap his arms around her, protect her, never let her go.

And he didn't even know her name. Dammit, she looked familiar though, like he'd seen her somewhere before.

"You're not going back to him," Sully growled. With Sully, Mac knew that was a command, not a request or even a question.

At least they were on the same page.

She vigorously shook her head. "No, but I have to return to Columbus at some point in the next few weeks to handle the legal stuff and get my things."

"I'll go with you," Mac immediately volunteered. *What the fuck?* His reaction surprised even him.

Sully arched an eyebrow at him over that outburst. Okay, that would cost him some stripes back on dry land, but it'd be worth it.

The girl shook her head and slowly pulled her hands back. "No. That's okay. I'm sorry, I didn't know you guys owned the Dilly now." She dipped a hand into her jacket pocket and withdrew a ring of three familiar-looking keys, laid them on the table, and cautiously slid them toward Mac. "You'll want these."

He looked at the keys but didn't reach for them. "Let's back up. Who are you? How did you get keys to my boat?"

"Clarisse Moore. My Uncle Tad used to own her." She finally glanced around, her gaze quickly skipping over Sully, briefly landing on Mac, before she looked at the table again. "I spent a lot of time here growing up. I didn't know where else to go. I didn't have anywhere else to go where Bryan couldn't find me. I knew it was a long shot. I'm sorry."

He realized why she looked familiar. Tad had shown him pictures of her. "I'm Brant MacCaffrey. You can call me Mac, everyone does. This is Sullivan Nicoletto, my partner."

"Sully," he said from where he stood.

"I'll leave as soon as we return to the marina. I'll work while I'm here, earn my keep. I can do everything—fish, shrimp, sort, take watches." She sighed. "I don't suppose you know how I can get in touch with Uncle Tad, do you?" The men exchanged a knowing glance. "What?"

"We wrote you a couple of times," Sully said. "Tad gave us your address. He's in a nursing home. He had a stroke."

No way could she have faked the shock on her face.

"When?"

"Last March," Sully told her. "You never got our letters?"

Clarisse shook her head. "No." She closed her eyes and swore. "Bryan probably got them and threw them away. Is Uncle Tad okay?"

Sully must have felt it safe enough to sit. He slid into the booth next to Mac. "He's partially paralyzed on his right side. He can get around, but he's very weak. He had to sell the boat, and we offered to buy it from him. We go see him all the time. We were friends with him before he had the stroke."

She felt a little hope—and a lot of guilt. "Is he close by?"

"Nice place, just south of Tarpon."

She buried her face in her hands and slumped over the table as she sobbed.

Mac reached across the table again and gently patted her arm. "It's okay, Clarisse. He's got a lot of years left in him. He likes where he's at. We can take you to see him when we get back."

This time, she didn't flinch away. When she finished crying a few minutes later, Sully offered her a roll of paper towels and she gratefully accepted it. She blew her nose and took a deep breath. "I'm sorry. I fell asleep. When I woke up, we were underway and I saw you guys on deck." Her face reddened. "I didn't mean to barge in like that. God, could I have messed up my life any worse?"

"Let's back up," Sully said. Mac sat back and let him handle the situation now that she'd calmed down. "Where did you come from?"

"I just spent a couple of days on buses from Columbus, Ohio. What day is it?"

"Thursday night."

"I left there on Tuesday morning, early." She looked at the keys, which still lay on the table. Mac hadn't pocketed them yet. "I guess that means I got here late last night or early this morning. I really lost track of time."

"You didn't have anyone in Columbus to stay with? Parents? Friends?"

"My parents died in an accident a couple of years ago. My only friend Bryan didn't run off, Raquel, she's got a baby. I didn't want to put her family at risk. He would have found me there anyway, probably the first place he looked."

"Did you file charges?"

She nervously shredded the paper towel. "Yeah." She snorted. "They took my report. Fat lot of good *that'll* do. We lived outside of Columbus, in Maxwell, close to Zanesville. He's a cop there. Computer division."

"In Maxwell?"

"Yeah."

Mac spoke up. "Well, kiddo, you absolutely ended up in the right place. Sully used to be a cop—" He stopped at her shocked, fearful expression. She pulled away from them and drew tight into the corner again, trying to melt into the bulkhead. "Whoa, what's wrong?"

She anxiously shook her head. "I saw the looks on their faces. His dad is best friends with the police chief. Two of his cousins work there, too. I don't hold any hopes of him going to trial. They put him on 'paid administrative leave' after they arrested him. That's bullshit cop slang for they'll lose my paperwork and give him a pass. Again."

Her angry gaze fixed on Sully. "Cops always stick together. They did the first time, they will this time. When his cousins saw my black eye the last time, they'd both sort of smiled and turned the other way." She snorted in disgust. "He told me they wouldn't believe me if I pressed charges that time."

Mac exchanged a look with Sully. "Clarisse, trust me, you're safe with us," Mac assured her.

She wouldn't take her eyes off Sully. "No, thank you for the offer, but I'll find somewhere to go when we return to port. I'm sorry I ruined your weekend."

Sully slowly leaned back, trying to open a little space for her. Mac suspected he'd seen this before, the overwhelming fear and anxiety in a victim. "Clarisse," he softly said, "I promise you, if your ex shows up, I'll be the first to put a bullet in his brain if he tries to lay a finger on you."

She burst into tears. "He said he's going to kill me! He told me if I ever left him, he'd hunt me down and kill me and nobody would stop him or prove he did it! That he'd done it before and got away with it!"

Mac nudged Sully. Sully climbed out of the booth, out of Mac's way. Mac changed places and sat next to her, drew her into his arms. At first she resisted. Then she slumped against him and cried harder.

"It's okay, honey," Mac said. "I promise we won't let him hurt you. I swear. We can take care of ourselves and protect you and keep you safe."

After ten minutes, she cried herself to sleep in his arms. Sully sadly stared at her. "Fuck," he whispered. "She's out of her mind."

"You would be, too," Mac shot back.

"I didn't mean she didn't have a reason. She's spent days on the run, in fear, looking over her shoulder. She's past the point of exhaustion."

Mac carefully brushed the hair away from her face. Fuck, if her face looked this bad, he wondered what other injuries she had.

As if reading his mind, Sully said, "Brant, she's not Betsy. You can't save her if she decides to go back."

Mac set his jaw. "Save your goddamn psychology bullshit." He carefully slipped out of the booth and gathered her into his arms. "Go open the V-berth cabin door, please."

It was a tight squeeze, but Mac managed to tuck her into the bunk without whacking her head against the wall or hitting his own again. Sully fetched a blanket for her from their cabin. Then they closed the door behind them and returned above decks. Mac closed the engine room hatch and checked the autopilot and radar. He'd only planned to be below for ten minutes, more than enough time to play. Fortunately, their path remained clear.

Still shirtless, he shivered as he disengaged the autopilot, punched new numbers into the GPS, and turned the boat around. Sully emerged from the cabin. Fully dressed, he carried a shirt and jacket for Mac.

"Thanks." He took them and dressed.

"We going in?" Sully asked.

"Uh, yeah. Duh, I think we have to, don't you? We need to get her to a doctor."

Sully fell quiet for a moment. "You don't know she'll want to see a doctor. Or if she can afford it."

"She has to!"

Sully eyed him, his voice calm and quiet. "Calm down and back down. *Right* now."

Mac glared at him. "Don't you *dare* fucking start with me. You can beat the shit out of me for this when we get home, but dammit, I'm not letting her walk off and get killed! Take it out of my money if you have to, but she's going to see a fucking doctor and get checked out."

Sully studied him for a long while. When he spoke, his voice sounded firm. "You're talking back to me, slave. You realize you're getting too emotionally involved with someone you don't even know. She's an adult. Keep in mind she'll probably be freaked out by what we do."

Mac slumped in his chair as the full impact of Sully's words slammed home. He reached for a lanyard hanging on a hook. From it dangled a small silver key. "I'm sorry, Master." He waved him over. "I know we're still on the boat, but you're right. I'm too emotional about this. You need to handle this."

Sully leaned over so Mac could unlock the collar and remove it. Then he cupped his hand around the back of Mac's neck, touched his forehead to Mac's and pressed a kiss to his lips. "We're in agreement about protecting her," Sully told him. "But we can't overwhelm her."

"I still want to go with her to get her stuff."

"Let's deal with that when it's time. It's too soon to decide that."

"Please?"

"If it gets to that point, yes, I'll let you."

Mac hugged him, burying his face against Sully's shoulder. Mac struggled not to think about Betsy, about how she'd looked when he'd found her, almost dead and beaten beyond recognition.

Sully whispered in his ear, "Just keep reminding yourself, she's not Betsy. She's Tad's niece, and we'll protect her. We won't let anything happen to her, but you have to let me deal with this. Okay?"

"Yes, Master."

* * * *

Near dawn they heard her moving around. They were still three miles from the head marker. Sully worked in the galley, cooking breakfast. He walked to her cabin and knocked. "Do you want some scrambled eggs and sausage? We've got plenty. I made extra."

After a moment came her tentative reply. "Yes, please. Thanks. I'll be out in a minute."

He hated that when she emerged she warily eyed him, like a child watching a dog that's bit them before but still has to be around it.

He kept his voice soft, steady. "How do you take your coffee?"

"Milk and sugar, if you have it. If not, I'll drink it black."

He poured her a cup and set it on the table, not so close that she had to approach him to reach it. He left the milk and sugar on the edge of the table after she sat back.

Mac stuck his head through the doorway. "Good morning! Did you sleep okay?"

"Fine, thank you."

Clarisse watched both men. Last night, when she'd collapsed, they'd both been shirtless. Mac stood a little taller and beefier than Sully, both men obviously in great shape, and Mac had nipple rings. But this morning, Sully's neck no longer had a collar locked around it.

She suspected the collar most likely meant Mac ran their weird little relationship. That made her feel safe somehow, even if it was stupid to feel like that about someone she just met. Maybe it was how his sweet brown eyes seemed to pull her in.

She didn't trust Sully, though. Not a cop. She couldn't trust a cop. Mac, however…something about him settled her.

"You come home with us," Mac said. "Grab a shower and change, and we'll take you to see Tad."

She started to tell them no, to resist their help, then realized what an asinine idea that was. She had no place to go and no idea where her uncle lived. If they'd wanted to hurt her, they could have done it in the middle of the Gulf and then disposed of her body, not haul her back to shore just to molest her at their home. Besides that, they were obviously gay from what she witnessed.

"Okay, thanks." She tried not to flinch when Sully set a plate of food in front of her. "Thank you."

Mac returned to the wheelhouse. Sully took a plate to Mac, then returned and sat across from her with his breakfast. She stole glances at him. Brown hair, a little grey around the temples. Piercing grey eyes. He didn't try to coax her to talk, something she felt extremely grateful for.

After fifteen minutes, he spoke. "So how much did you see last night? Of us on deck?"

She looked up, startled. He wore a smile she could describe as playful.

She blushed and glanced away. "Enough. I'm sorry."

When he gently touched the back of her hand, she forced herself not to pull away.

"I hope we didn't scare you. Seeing us like that."

She shook her head. No, she hadn't been scared. She tried to fight the sudden throbbing in her nether regions. What a totally inappropriate response to her memory of the sight of the two hunks…

Yowza.

"You didn't scare me," she managed. "I mean…" She had to swallow to form spit. "I'm scared, but not of you guys." She closed her eyes. "I just feel so freaking stupid for not leaving him the first time."

His fingers slipped around her hand. He gently squeezed before letting go and withdrawing his hand. "We meant it when we said we'll protect you." He paused. "We have a very large house, plenty of room. If you don't mind our relationship, if that doesn't bother you, we can work something out."

Before she could reply, he stood and took his empty plate to the sink.

Tempting. *So* tempting. Why did he have to be a damn cop?

"Mac's sister was murdered," Sully said from where he stood at the sink. He turned and leaned against the counter. "He might come off as overbearing in some ways. I just wanted to tell you why he's latched onto you. Her husband murdered her. Mac found her, she hadn't died yet. The guy beat her to death. They pulled life support after several days."

He left her chewing that over as he climbed the stairs to the wheelhouse.

She finished her breakfast and washed her dishes. Then she

hunted down her toothbrush and toothpaste and went to the head. In daylight, she realized how horrible and pitiful she appeared. Her eye wasn't as swollen, but the awful purple and green bruises looked almost worse. The split lip hurt. Thank God she still had all her teeth. She peeled down her jeans so she could use the toilet and noticed those bruises also starting to fade although they still looked ugly.

She changed clothes, felt marginally better, and applied copious amounts of deodorant to take care of the worst of her stench. When she returned to the main cabin, the men were still in the wheelhouse. She remembered to replace the envelope of paperwork, then climbed up to join them.

Both men offered friendly smiles. She noticed they'd passed Anclote Island. At idle speed, it'd take another half-hour to reach the marina.

She edged around the men so she stood on Mac's far side, with him separating her from Sully. She watched their eyes, how they studied her injuries.

Their pity.

"We want to offer you a deal," Sully said. Mac stayed silent. "Please, hear us out. You can stay with us. There's only a couple of things I'll require."

She tensed again. "No, I'll go somewhere. I'll—"

"Can I finish?"

She nodded.

He ticked them off on his fingers. "As you've seen, Mac and I have an unusual relationship. We only demand respect, not endorsement or participation from you. You will see things that might disturb you, but they are consensual. We don't expect you to do any of it, just let us live our life. We expect you to respect our privacy and not talk about our private life with others. We'll protect you, but you can't have contact with your ex. You'll have to listen to us and do what we say in regard to handling that situation. You must give us total honesty, because that's a firm, unbreakable rule in our home.

Absolutely no lying allowed."

She waited for him to continue. When he didn't, she asked, "That's it?"

"That's the important and nonnegotiable stuff. You can pay rent, or you can work for us. You don't bring people over without letting us know first so we're not..." He arched an eyebrow at her. "Obviously so we're not outed, so to speak. You're free to come and go as you please, but if you're going out, you keep in touch so we know you're okay. It only makes sense for you to stay with us. You should be close to Tad, and we have the room."

"Work for you?"

"Help Mac on the boat. You already know the ropes." He smiled. "No pun intended. Help me at home, too. I could use an assistant. We'll pay cash and trade room and board for chores."

"Chores?" she nervously asked.

Sully smiled. "Yeah, chores. You know, washing dishes, doing errands, vacuuming. Not like blow jobs."

She finally let out a tired laugh before returning his smile. "Okay."

Sully stuck out his hand. "Deal?"

She nodded and hesitantly shook hands with him. "Deal. Thank you."

Chapter Three

They returned to dock. Clarisse seemed to fall into her old patterns. She climbed onto the port gunwale as Mac eased the Dilly backward into her slip. She kept watch to make sure they didn't hit, grabbed lines, jumped onto the dock, and deftly wrapped the line around the cleat. Sully grabbed the starboard side.

Sully offered her his hand as she moved to jump down to the deck. He didn't miss her hesitation before she finally reached out and took it. As soon as she'd regained her footing, she pulled her hand from his.

Still scared.

Beautiful despite her injuries, she had blue eyes and long, black hair halfway down her back that, combined with her sweet rounded curves, made his cock stand up and take notice. He'd never preferred skinny women. Despite his honest reassurances, his ex-wife had struggled with her weight, constantly working out and dieting, usually miserable and grouchy the entire time, never happy with herself.

Clarisse was a beautiful woman. A real woman.

A woman terrified of him.

Mac helped her with her luggage. After securing the boat and connecting the Dilly to shore power, they headed for Mac's truck.

She had to ride between them. Sully didn't miss how she tended to stick closer to Mac's side of the seat while he drove. Sully tried to observe her out of the corner of his eye as they rode toward the house.

They lived in a small, private, gated community. Their waterfront house on Spring Bayou, a large, sprawling one-story stilt home on a huge double lot, sat near the end of a cul-de-sac. Mac parked next to

Sully's Jaguar sedan and shut the truck off.

Clarisse stared, stunned. "You guys live *here*?" She knew location alone meant the house had to be expensive.

Mac smiled. "Be it ever so humble and all that crap."

Clarisse noticed Sully didn't help Mac with her bags. She started to grab her duffle bag, but Mac waved her off. "I've got it, sweetie. That's my job. You go on upstairs with him."

Sully had already climbed halfway up the stairs. A large enclosed room filled the space beneath the house. "Utility room, exercise equipment, and storage," he explained, pointing at the downstairs room.

She nodded and followed.

Sully unlocked the door and ushered her into the foyer, where he deactivated the alarm. Unpretentious decor, but the furnishings weren't crap, either. These men lived well, obviously didn't flaunt it, and the house seemed spotless. A textured Berber carpet, white walls with earth-tone accents, beautiful photographs on the walls. A lot of landscapes, but a few of the men together. A very masculine feel overall.

When Mac walked through the door with her bags, he looked at Sully.

"Take them to the larger guest room," he told Mac. "The one with the bathroom." He walked over to a pass-through kitchen counter and laid his keys down. "Can I get you anything to drink or eat?"

She shook her head and slowly walked around the large living room. These men had built a nice life for themselves. Pictures of the two of them showed a happy couple very much in love.

In one, Mac sat on a fence while Sully stood next to him. They looked at each other, blatant love in their gazes…

Clarisse stifled a sob. She'd never felt like that before. Damn sure never felt that way about Bryan.

She tried to rein in her emotions. Exhausted and beat half to death, she felt barely sane and needed a shower.

Mac returned from wherever he'd taken her bags. Clarisse turned to speak to him, then realized his full attention had focused on Sully.

She glanced at Sully and found him staring at Mac. After a long, nearly awkward moment, Sully spoke in a quiet, firm voice. "Don't make me tell you."

When Mac's gaze nervously flicked her way, a horrible feeling washed through her. Maybe she'd terribly misjudged these men.

Without thinking, she edged a step backward, closer to the front door.

Mac finally spoke. "Please?"

Sully leaned against the counter and crossed his arms. "All right, fine. Just remember it has to happen sooner rather than later. Shorts if you insist, but that means you owe me five strokes."

Mac nodded before disappearing into another room.

Sully smiled. "We warned you, we have a…different lifestyle." He walked into the kitchen. She heard him rummaging around, then water running, followed by a coffeepot gurgling a moment later.

She didn't move. "Different how?" she finally asked. Her voice sounded way too weak for the cavernous cathedral ceiling.

He stared at her from across the counter. "How open-minded are you?"

She felt some of her new anxiety fade. "Consenting human adults. If you're not trying to coerce me into it, I probably won't object."

He smiled again. While she didn't trust him, she had to admit that the way his lips curled softened his face and crinkled the corners of his grey eyes in a playful way. "Girl after our own hearts then." He disappeared into the kitchen where she couldn't see him.

Movement out of the corner of her eye caught her attention. Mac had returned to the living room. He wore shorts and nothing else.

Almost nothing else.

Something in her heart fluttered at the sight of his bare chest. Yes, he had nipple rings, gold ones. She also realized his chest was completely bare, shaved. That wasn't the unusual thing.

The custom-tooled leather collar around his neck with a small silver lock attached to the buckle caught her attention.

Sully stepped out of the kitchen. "And?"

Clarisse looked at him. "And what?"

"Not you, sweetie." He looked pointedly at Mac.

Mac knelt on the floor. That's when the situation hit her. Whatever their relationship, Sully was in control, not Mac, regardless of what she'd witnessed on the boat.

Sully walked over to Mac and stood beside him, brushed his hand through Mac's blond hair. "Mac and I have a complex relationship. I'm his Master, he's my slave." Sully's hand remained on Mac's head, his fingers twined through his hair. "So we're partners, lovers, and more than that. It's consensual. We've lived this way for several years."

As she stared at them, trying to decide what to say, she watched Mac lean in, close his eyes, and rest his head against Sully's thigh. She realized both men wore matching bands on their left hands, like wedding bands.

"It's okay, Clarisse," Sully assured her. "You can freak out now if you want."

"That's not funny, Master," Mac mumbled.

Clarisse noticed a change in Mac's voice, like he'd suddenly relaxed.

Sully must have noticed her expression. "Sorry. I don't want to freak you out, but since you'll be living here, you need to understand who we are. Usually no one outside the lifestyle sees us like this. As you can see, he enjoys this as much as I do."

Her mind whirled. She didn't know what to say.

"What you witnessed on the boat," Sully continued, "is just one aspect of what we do. I own the boat. Mac is the captain. I decided that as captain, we could play by his rules when I went out with him. I don't get to go out with him all the time. Sometimes it's fun for me to sit back and let him have fun. He enjoys topping on occasion. It mixes things up."

Clarisse stared.

Sully gave her a moment, obviously realizing she was still processing information, before he continued. "As I said, we will never expect you to join in this with us. Although if you were curious and wanted to learn more, we would be happy to answer questions or help you out. Hopefully, after a few days, you will be more comfortable with this. Of course, we expect you to not say anything to anyone about this aspect of our relationship."

She nodded.

"Normally I would have told Mac we'd act vanilla. Under the circumstances, because you'll be with us for the foreseeable future, I'd rather be up front about this from the start instead of hiding what and who we are." He patted Mac's head. "Show her to her room, get her anything she needs. Then you and I need to shower and get dressed so we can take her to visit Tad."

He stood and flashed her a smile. "I already laid stuff out for you. Come on, this way."

He led her down a hallway to a bedroom. At first, she thought maybe they'd walked into the master suite. The house she'd lived in with Bryan hadn't had a master bedroom this large.

Mac walked over to the bathroom door and flipped the light on. "I got you Epsom salts to put in the water. That'll help with the soreness. I put out towels and some shampoo and conditioner for you. I'll get with you about a shopping list, things you like and want, so I can buy them next time I go. I also put a disposable razor in there, and some shaving cream." He gave her an apologetic smile. "Don't have any shaving gel, sorry."

She felt numb, in a good way. "That's okay. That'll be fine." Anything to shave and quit feeling like a filthy Sasquatch would be a blessing.

"Just leave your dirty clothes and the towels on the floor for me," he said over his shoulder as he walked out.

"What?"

"I do the laundry," he said from the bedroom. "And most of the cooking. The cleaning." He paused. "I need to talk with Sully. He'll probably want to let you do some of it. Anyway, we can work that out later. Tad's going to be so glad to see you. He's really missed you, talks about you all the time."

With that, he walked out and softly closed the bedroom door behind him, leaving her feeling guilty as hell.

Uncle Tad was her only living relative besides a few distant cousins she didn't even know. She should have stood up to Bryan, kept in better contact. He never should have had to go through this alone.

Well, bitching and moaning wouldn't get her there any sooner. She sorted dirty clothes from clean ones in her bag and dumped them in the bathroom. That didn't feel right though. She felt guilty again, this time over saddling Mac with her laundry. She tried to tidy the pile a little.

Must be exhaustion.

She gave up, stripped, then turned, and studied herself in the bathroom mirror.

What a mess.

Turning, she saw the huge purplish-green swaths of bruises around her kidneys in addition to all the others.

That dealt the final blow to her psyche. She burst into tears, loudly sobbing. How had she let her life get so out of control as to reach this point? What was that stupid line, relying on the kindness of strangers? Had she really sunk to that?

A knock sounded on her bedroom door. It opened a crack and Sully softly called to her.

"Clarisse? Are you okay, honey?"

Mac had even hung a robe on the back of the bathroom door. She grabbed it and pulled it on. "Yeah," she called out as she sniffled. She wiped her face with her hands.

"Is it safe to come in?"

"Yeah." She walked out to the bedroom.

He stuck his head in. "Are you really okay?"

She started to say yes, then burst into tears again and crumpled onto the end of the bed. He walked in and sat next to her. Despite her earlier hesitation, she let him put his arm around her as she cried against him. Mac appeared in the bedroom doorway.

"We promise he won't hurt you again," Sully quietly said. "I swear."

"I'm sorry. I…it's just that…it's horrible. I look like a punching bag."

"I'm going to make a suggestion. Please keep in mind I was a cop for over ten years."

"Okay."

"Did anyone get pictures of your injuries? Did you go to the hospital?"

"My friend Raquel took some. The cops took some. I don't remember if the hospital did or not."

"Do you want me to take another round for backup? Just in case you need them later?"

She didn't want to, even though she knew it was a good idea. But she feared the file and the evidence getting lost and Bryan getting off, no matter how much they had assured her that wouldn't happen.

He continued. "I can give you the roll of film to have developed. I don't even have to see it after I take them."

She took a deep, shuddering breath. "It's probably better someone else has them. In case."

Mac stepped into the room. When he spoke, his voice dropped in anger. "I'm telling you, if your boyfriend shows up, we'll fucking kill him, I swear we will. We won't give him another chance to hurt you."

Sully flashed him a look that obviously meant *shut up*. "I'll go put in a fresh roll of film. We can do it right here. Mac will get you a large towel so you can stay covered."

She nodded.

He gently patted her thigh before leaving the room.

Mac fetched a large towel from the bathroom and turned on all the room lights. She felt touched that he held the towel and averted his eyes as she slipped the robe off and pulled the towel around her. When he saw the bruises on her thighs, he sucked in a sharp breath.

"Son of a bitch," he whispered. "That motherfucker."

She couldn't meet his gaze. Instead, she kept her eyes on the collar around his neck. "They don't hurt as much as they did the other day." Then again, she suspected her exhaustion had masked a lot of her pain.

Sully walked in while adjusting the camera and pulled up short when he saw her bruises. It shouldn't have shocked him, considering what he'd seen as a cop, but it did.

A surge of rage welled inside him. The asshole that did this to her would not get away with it. It pissed him off that any man would do this to a woman.

It brought back his own nightmares.

She lifted her gaze to him, briefly, then her focus skittered away again. He took a deep breath to steady his voice.

"Let's start with your back. Sit on the bed and you can let the towel fall open, okay?"

She nodded. Mac stepped back, holding her robe ready to put on her as soon as they finished.

Bless Mac's heart. Sully could easily see where this would lead Mac if she spent any length of time with them. Wanting to prevent the past from repeating itself.

Sully took the pictures, fighting through his own anger as he saw the bruising on her back. The digital readout on the camera confirmed the shots. He would save a backup of each picture while still committing them to film. He did each arm, then her legs. He focused on her sweet blue eyes through the viewfinder.

Her crippling fear bubbled just below the surface, he suspected.

Then came time to photograph her torso.

"Where did he bruise you? Maybe we can keep you covered and not expose anything."

Her face reddened. "Everywhere."

He knelt in front of her. "If you don't want me to—"

"It's okay." She took a deep breath. "If it'll help later, help nail him."

"I'll make it fast. I promise."

"Okay."

"Let me focus first, before you drop the towel." He prepared as best he could, then told her to move the towel. Shooting quickly, he fought back the bile in his throat. From the dark purple of some of the bruises over her breasts, he suspected they'd been nearly black when fresher. "Okay, that's it."

She wrapped the towel around herself while Mac swooped in to drape the robe over her. Sully spotted the tears in Mac's eyes.

So did Clarisse, apparently.

That finished her. She broke down crying again. This time Mac consoled her. When she composed herself, Sully tried to offer her a comforting smile, although he suspected his anger had given him a harsh look.

"Go take a nice hot bath, take as long as you want. Do you want any Tylenol or anything? We've got hot tea."

She nodded. "That'd be great. Thank you."

Mac jumped up and raced to get them, leaving Sully alone with her. He knelt in front of her again. "Take your time. We can visit until eight tonight. We'll see if we can eat dinner with him."

"Okay."

He left her alone.

Clarisse sat there for a moment before willing her legs to stand. She figured why close the bedroom door? They were gay, what difference did it make?

Maybe she could trust Sully one day. Not right now. Not this soon. She sensed he wasn't an ax murderer. Still, it made her uncomfortable baring her soul to him.

Mac was a different story. She trusted him, instinctively sensed he would die before he let anyone hurt her. Considering the men were all she had, she was willing to trust that much.

She'd crawled into the tub, comfortably immersed in the water, when Mac knocked on the bathroom door.

"I have your Tylenol and your hot tea."

"It's okay. Just bring them in."

"Are you sure?"

"Yeah."

He opened the door and cautiously stuck his head in. "I didn't know if you wanted sugar in your tea, so I brought some." He walked in and set everything on the counter. He handed her two capsules and a cold bottle of water. When she downed the medicine, he took the bottle back and handed her the tea. "Sugar?"

"No, that's okay." He sat on the edge of the huge tub after he handed her the mug. She didn't bother trying to cover herself or sink lower in the water. It was too exhausting, and, frankly, she didn't want to expend the effort and feel her muscles scream.

He looked like he wanted to say something but caught himself.

"What is it?"

"Can we take you to the doctor? We'll pay for it."

She blushed and shook her head. "I let them look me over at the ER before I checked myself out. They x-rayed my ribs, said I wouldn't die. It would have been stupid to waste time sitting in a hospital when I could have been moving."

"Aren't you hurting?"

She laughed, setting off pain in her ribs. "Yeah, worse than I ever have in my life. I've got a high pain tolerance, though. It's okay. I once smashed my hand in the rigging. When Uncle Tad wanted to turn around and head to dock, I wouldn't let him. I just stuck it in ice for a few hours and kept sorting. My mom was pissed, but my dad was proud of me." She studied her left hand as she flexed it.

A light scar traced across her palm. "Did that when I landed a lemon shark one night. Took ten stitches to close it when we got back, but I used butterfly bandages on it and didn't let Uncle Tad see how bad the shark got me."

Mac gently caught her hand in his, kissed it, and gently traced his fingers over the scar. "How long has he been hitting you?"

She didn't pull her hand away. "Verbally? From day one. Physically, this is only the second time he laid his hands on me. And the last."

"You won't let me take you to the doctor?"

"No, but thank you. I appreciate it."

Mac released her hand and stood. "You're not going to go back to him, are you?"

"Hell, no." She sighed. "I need to get Bart, though."

"Bart?"

"My dog. My friend Raquel is taking care of him for me." A horrible thought hit her. "He's little and he's crate trained. Will Sully let me bring him back?" Then she did start to cry. "He's my baby. He's the only reason I stayed sane. Bryan let me get him after the first time he hit me. I think he used him as a peace offering. He's a really good dog."

"Yeah. I'll take care of it, honey. Don't worry." He started for the bathroom door. "Take as long as you need. Don't rush." He pulled the bathroom door partially shut behind him.

Clarisse sipped the tea and closed her eyes. She was safe and relatively secure here. She wouldn't even try to say she was sane at this point, because she still felt like an alien in her own body. Partly due to the exhaustion and stress and pain, partly due to fear.

She set the mug on the edge of the tub and slowly sank deeper into the water.

Chapter Four

After their showers, Sully and Mac waited for Clarisse to emerge from her bedroom. Mac heated her some soup and fixed her another mug of hot tea. She sat at the counter, not looking at the men, her damp hair tucked behind her ears. It made the bruises look worse.

"Do you have any makeup?" Sully asked.

She shook her head. "He wouldn't let me spend money on it even if I did wear it, which I usually didn't." She blushed. "I had some cheap powder and lipstick, but I didn't bring it. I didn't want to waste the space in my purse when I left. It wouldn't have done any good on this anyway."

Mac and Sully had changed into pullover shirts and jeans. Mac no longer wore his collar. In its place lay a heavy silver necklace. Sully reached into his back pocket, pulled out his wallet, and handed Mac a credit card.

"Run to Walgreens. They've got a makeup counter. Tell the clerk your little sister has a pale complexion and she needs some basics. Get good stuff. Spend whatever you have to. Make sure to get a heavy concealer too. Tell her she's got a burn scar or something that needs hiding."

Clarisse started to protest. Sully overruled her. "If Tad sees you looking like this, he'll be really upset. I'd rather not spring that on him. Hopefully he'll be too happy to see you to realize how badly you're hurt." He looked at Mac. "Waterproof mascara."

Mac nodded, grabbed his keys, and disappeared out the door before she could object again.

Clarisse stiffened in fear. She intellectually knew Sully wouldn't hurt her. Emotionally, she didn't want to be without Mac's comforting, safe presence.

Sully leaned against the opposite counter and gentled his voice. "I'm sorry to take over like that, but you'll see I'm right. If you're acting like a beat dog while trying to hide your injuries, it won't be good for Tad."

He was right, of course.

"I'll pay you back," she said.

"No, you won't." He left her alone in the kitchen to finish her soup. An hour later, Mac returned with a plastic bag full of cosmetics.

"I'm not much into makeup." She picked up a bottle of concealer. "I don't know how to use most of this stuff."

"Don't worry. The lady at the counter was very helpful and explained to me how to tell you to apply it." He spied the receipt and snagged it before she could look at it. Sully returned to the kitchen, and Mac handed him the receipt and the credit card. Then Mac took her into her bathroom and supervised while she carefully applied everything. He helped her a little, examined the result, and called Sully in when she finished.

He nodded in approval. "You can still see it, but it's not nearly as bad." He handed her a pair of sunglasses. "You can use these, too. They're mine. Let's go."

They took Sully's Jag. She felt a little embarrassed when Mac insisted she sit in the front seat while he took the back. Sully drove. Fifteen minutes later, they pulled into the parking lot of a very nice-looking nursing home complex.

Mac jumped out, opened her door, then raced around, and opened Sully's for him. Sully waited for her to step close to rest his hand on the small of her back. She cringed but forced herself not to draw away.

"It's a really nice place. You'll see." He walked her inside while Mac flanked her. They stopped at the front desk where the nurse on duty flashed Sully and Mac a broad smile.

"Hey! I thought you were going out fishing this weekend." She frowned a little as she studied Clarisse.

Clarisse felt heat creep into her face, knowing the makeup and sunglasses didn't hide all her injuries. She studied the spotless tile floor.

"We were," Sully said, "but we ended up with an unexpected visitor. Mandy, this is Clarisse Moore, Tad's niece." Clarisse looked up.

Mandy's eyes widened in surprise. Clarisse witnessed the nurse's mistrust immediately transform to pity. "Oh, honey! He's gonna be so glad to see you! Go on back, guys. I think he's in his apartment."

"Thanks." Sully led her from the desk and down a hallway. The light and airy facility faintly smelled like oranges. "Tad's got a small efficiency apartment. He cooks some meals still, when he's not busy flirting with his nurses."

Clarisse couldn't help but laugh. That sounded like Uncle Tad.

They wound through the facility and stopped in front of a door numbered 125. This wing resembled an apartment building more than a hospital. A nursing station sat at the entrance, but other than that, nothing overtly identified it as a medical facility. Sully knocked.

"Goddammit, I told you I don't feel like playing bingo! They're running a *Dukes of Hazzard* marathon on TV this afternoon!"

The door opened. Clarisse didn't know who was more shocked, her or Uncle Tad. He looked thin, drawn, one side of his face frozen in a lopsided droop.

After a stunned moment, he whispered, "Son of a bitch!" and then engulfed her in a weak hug she was afraid to return too strongly for fear of hurting him.

"Hi, Uncle Tad," she lamely said.

He held her at arm's length, frowning for a moment, then smiling. "Please tell me you left the son of a bitch."

She sniffled. "Yep."

He hugged her again, then gripped her hand and led them inside to a small sitting area. He slowly lowered himself to the sofa, pulling her down with him. Mac and Sully settled into two chairs. The apartment was small but tidy. A four-person dinette sat near a window, and an open doorway led to a small bedroom. Another revealed the bathroom.

"Reecie, you scared the heck outta me, little girl." He raised his hand to her face as if to stroke her cheek, then lowered it. "It doesn't matter anymore. You'd better be telling me you're moving here."

Sully spoke up. "She's living with us."

Clarisse noticed he said "living" and not "staying."

Tad nodded. "Good." He grinned. "These boys are the best, but you've probably already seen that."

They sat and talked with him all afternoon. Near dinner time, he handed Mac a wad of bills. "Why don't you take Reecie to Plaka's and get us some dinner? I bet she missed their gyros."

Mac tried to refuse the money, but Sully shot him a look. "Go on. I'll stay here with Tad."

Clarisse suspected her uncle wanted a few uninterrupted minutes to talk with Sully about the circumstances of her arrival. She didn't resist when Mac laced his fingers through hers and helped her up from the couch. "You want the usual, Tad?" he asked.

"Yep. Go by Hellas, too. Get us something for dessert from their bakery."

* * * *

After they left, Tad turned to Sully, his face hard. Sully suspected the older man wanted to talk with him alone.

"Promise me, boy," Tad said. "Promise me you'll make the bastard pay."

"I will."

Tad leaned back and closed his eyes. "She never wears makeup. Your idea?"

"I didn't want to shock you."

He snorted. "Takes a lot more than that to shock me. I'm just glad she got out alive. I always worried that asshole would kill her. Fucking mean son of a bitch. Damn bully. She really gonna live with you?"

"As long as she wants. You have my word."

Tad arched an eyebrow at Sully. "She already know about you two?"

Sully laughed. "Yeah. We told her the basics. Needed to, don't you think?" They hadn't told Tad all the details of their pastimes, but he knew Sully and Mac had more than just an average relationship.

Tad slowly pulled himself up from the couch. "I suppose." He started for the kitchenette to get plates. Sully stood to help him. "You know," Tad said, "you two could be good for her, long term. Security. Safety. Someone to rely on."

Sully took several plates from him and laid them on the table. "What are you getting at?"

He turned. "I'm just saying there's something to be said for a girl having a couple of strong guys in her life." His eyes twinkled. "If you get my drift."

Sully was afraid he did, but he let the subject drop. Tad apparently felt content to leave his piece said at that.

* * * *

Clarisse stared out the window as Mac drove them to Dodecanese Boulevard and found a parking spot. It'd been years since she'd last visited the Sponge Docks. Much to her surprise, many of the restaurants and shops still bore the same names and signs and even merchandise, in some cases. He led her to Plaka's where they placed their food order. Then, while they waited, they walked a few doors down to Hellas and bought several items for dessert from the Greek bakery there. He sat her in a booth and bought her a Coke. After he sat, he handed her two Tylenol.

"Take these, sweetie. You need them. You look like you're hurting."

She didn't fight him, gratefully took them, and washed them down. "Thanks."

He gently squeezed her hand. "Let us take care of you, okay?"

"I don't think I can get used to having a slave, Mac."

He grinned. "Well, don't think of it that way, honey. Think of it as having a guy Friday."

Clarisse glanced over at him, loving his friendly, easy smile and twinkling brown eyes.

Safe.

She glanced around before studying the table again. Her hair hung in curtains beside her face, which helped her feel a little more secure about her appearance in public. "I promise I'll pull my weight. Please tell Sully I mean that."

"Hey, honey, we don't care. We told you we'll figure something out."

"I can get a job, at least part-time somewhere, to pay rent."

"Clarisse."

Her head snapped up at his firm tone, fear tensing her body.

He squeezed her hand again, his voice gentling. "Stop it. Don't worry. It's okay."

She'd glimpsed a hint of Mac on the boat, the way he'd handled Sully.

In charge.

After she finished her Coke, they picked up their order from Plaka's. Mac insisted on carrying everything, juggling the food to open the Jag's door for her.

"Listen," he said when she protested, "Sully'd kick my ass in a bad way, he catches me slacking. Unless I can't do it, you don't open your own doors, girlie."

She blushed. "I'm not an invalid."

"Despite rumors to the contrary, I am a gentleman." He grabbed her hand, brought it to his lips, and kissed it. "And I take care of *my* lady."

Another pleasant flood of heat raced to her face and down her body at the possessive tone in his voice. If only he wasn't gay, she'd gladly be his lady. Meanwhile, she would be happily content to have him in this way, at least.

It didn't matter. She had no intention of getting into another relationship for a long, long time. If ever.

A blue VW bug had parked next to them. Mac caught her looking at it. "What?"

"I've always loved those little cars. I'm going to save my money and buy me one in a few years. I wanted one, but Bryan hated them. He bought me a Chevy, said it was practical."

Mac studied the car. "Practical, huh?"

"Yeah. He despises foreign cars. His dad owned a Chevy dealership before he retired." She stared at the car until he started the Jag. "Now I can get whatever the hell I want." She laughed. "Well, I have to get whatever I can afford. But when I can afford one, I'm getting one."

When they reached the nursing home, Clarisse checked and refreshed her makeup in the car before they returned to Uncle Tad's room. They had a great dinner and a nice visit. By the time they left, Clarisse felt exhausted and close to collapse. At home, she bid the men good night, went straight to her room, and closed the door behind her.

* * * *

The men made sure Clarisse was sound asleep before they headed for their bedroom. Sully closed and locked their door, hooked his MP3 player to the stereo in their bedroom, and set it to a mix he liked to play to. He tweaked the volume up just a smidge.

"Do I need to use a gag?" he asked Mac.

Mac had already stripped and replaced his silver necklace with his collar. He'd fetched the rattan punishment cane and knelt on the floor, head bowed, waiting for Sully. "No, Master," he quietly replied.

"How many do you owe me?"

"Five for letting me wear shorts, Master. Then my outburst on the boat, talking back to you on the boat, and my outburst in her bedroom."

Sully studied him. "It shocked both of us. I commend you for wanting to protect her. How many do you think I should give you?"

"Normally you give me twenty-five for talking back. So that would be seventy-five in addition to the five."

Sully was glad Mac had bowed his head and couldn't see his eyebrows arch in surprise. "Why that many? Explain your rationale."

"I talked back. The outbursts are the same as talking back."

"So you're willing to take eighty strokes?"

"I will take as many as Master gives me."

"What if I say I'm going to give you a hundred?"

"Then maybe we do need the gag."

Sully picked up the cane and touched it to Mac's exposed ass. Mac didn't flinch, didn't tense. Sully knew he expected it to start at any time and was ready for it. "On the bed, ass over," Sully softly commanded.

Mac immediately complied.

Sully waited, drawing it out. Then he quickly delivered eight viciously hard blows in rapid succession, harder than he would normally strike, impacts that immediately raised welts on Mac's ass and came damn close to drawing blood.

Mac tensed, but he didn't cry out.

Sully walked over to the dresser, picked up a bottle of cucumber lotion, poured some into his palm, then sat on the edge of the bed and lovingly applied it to Mac's flesh.

"That's all you're getting."

"Thank you, Master."

"Do you want to know why I gave you only eight?" He knew Mac wouldn't ask, but he had to be curious. Usually when Sully told him he should give him a certain number, that was the number he finally delivered.

"Yes, Master. Please."

Sully gently worked the lotion into Mac's skin. "Five for the shorts. And five every day you decide to wear clothes at home, automatically, until you decide you should go naked again. One stroke for talking back, one for the outburst saying you'd go with her to Ohio without asking me first, one for the outburst in her bedroom. Hard because you were willing to take a hundred for your actions. Fast because I didn't want to torture you." He applied more lotion, feeling Mac relax under his hand as it soothed his flesh. "I'm proud of you for wanting to protect her. I just want you to be careful. You know I won't let her get hurt. You have to trust me on this. She's not Betsy."

"I know, Master. I'm sorry."

"That's okay." He capped the bottle. "Done."

Mac gingerly rolled over, wincing a little but not complaining. He would never complain. He never had complained.

Mac also never extracted payback for punishment while on the boat. Sully had anticipated he might and was willing to take it if he dealt it, but Mac's enjoyment of his limited top time came mostly in the form of sexual enjoyment, not sadism.

Sully used the bathroom, turned their stereo and lights off, and settled into bed with Mac. Not many things drove Mac to tears outside of a scene. Not even punishment, usually. That night, Sully sensed Mac needed more than a Master.

He needed his lover and friend.

Sully wrapped his arms around Mac. "Let it out, Brant," he ordered. "Don't hold it in."

At first Mac tensed, and then he relaxed against Sully as his tears flowed.

"She's not Betsy," he whispered in Mac's ear. "Keep saying that to yourself. She's not Betsy, and she's not going to die. We won't let that happen."

Mac clutched Sully, crying, shaking with the force of his anguish. "Fuck, Sul. He beat her to a pulp."

Sully knew how difficult it had been for Mac, keeping his emotions in check around Clarisse all day. He knew better than anyone how hard this was on Mac, seeing her bruised and battered, helping her with the makeup, trying to maintain appearances in front of Tad.

After twenty minutes, he finally cried himself to sleep. Sully closed his eyes and pressed a kiss to his forehead. If someone had told him years ago that he'd love this man the way he did, he'd have decked them. People asked how he could explore complex and fluid gender roles in relationships in his books in such a realistic way. It was easy for him.

He lived it.

* * * *

The nightmare played out the same every time. Knowing it was a dream didn't help Mac escape it. He'd talked to Betsy earlier that day, confirmed he'd be by at six to help her move. Her husband was going out of town for the weekend on a fishing trip to the Keys with a buddy of his. By the time the asshole returned late Sunday, Betsy would be safe at Mac's apartment.

When he arrived at five to six, the lights were all off but her car sat in the driveway.

He tried the door, found it locked.

Fear sent his heart racing as he tried calling her, heard the phone ring counterpoint somewhere inside. Then he tried her cell.

He faintly heard it ringing through the door too.

Shit.

He pounded on the door. "Bets! Open up, honey. You're scaring me!"

He circled the house. All the blinds were drawn and the back gate locked. Highly unusual.

Hoping he was wrong, that it would prove to be a false alarm, he returned to the front door, called 911, and told them he was breaking down the door.

Despite the dispatcher advising him to wait, Mac kicked the door in and screamed when he found Betsy face down on the living room floor in a puddle of blood.

He yelled at the dispatcher to send an ambulance and then checked her pulse. Jesus, she was still breathing.

Barely.

She moaned.

"Oh, honey," he cried. "Please hang on! Bets, you gotta hang on, they're coming." It looked as if someone had taken a baseball bat to her, her face unrecognizable, her hair matted with blood, the house ripped apart.

Unlike every other dream he'd had reliving that horrible afternoon, tonight when he cradled her in his arms, she opened her eyes. It wasn't Betsy's brown eyes, but Clarisse's blue ones.

* * * *

Sully felt Mac startle awake. He'd lain there unable to sleep, expecting this. It'd been months since Mac's last nightmare about Betsy. He'd suspected Clarisse's unexpected entry into their lives might trigger a return of Mac's flashbacks. Sully wrapped his arms around his lover as the other man started crying.

"It's okay, buddy," Sully soothed. "Let it out."

Mac eventually cried himself back to sleep, which finally allowed Sully to relax and close his eyes. Mac never dreamed it twice and always slept the rest of the night after waking up. They both had their demons.

His appeared some nights in the form of a woman, who looked like she wasn't even legal drinking age, pulling a 9mm semi-automatic on him during the drug raid and shooting him in the gut before he blew out the back of her skull. Jason shot and killed her boyfriend, but not until after the guy put a bullet in Sully's leg. Had Sully not pulled the trigger, the woman's next shot likely would have killed him.

He never felt guilty about killing her, because she'd also been carrying a .38 in her purse, along with more than three grand worth of crack. His only choice had been to shoot. That still didn't stop the dreams.

Only the feel of Mac's body in his arms did that.

Chapter Five

Clarisse awoke just before dawn the next morning, feeling disoriented, in pain, and frightened out of her mind. She'd been trapped in a nightmare where Bryan had found her and was torturing her.

She sat up, crying, trying to remember where the hell she was.

Mac.

As soon as she thought of him, her world went calm, a feeling of security returned. With a pained grunt, she slowly swung her feet over the edge of the bed and carefully stood.

Everything hurt. Not as bad as the day before, but it hurt. A full night's sleep in a good bed had helped a lot.

She used the bathroom and pulled on the fluffy robe before quietly opening her bedroom door. The house lay dim and quiet.

Chiding herself for not asking Mac where he kept the Tylenol, Clarisse silently padded out to the kitchen and started rummaging through the cabinets as quietly as she could.

* * * *

Mac slipped out of bed at his usual time and headed for the bathroom. When he returned, he slipped on a pair of shorts. Sully sent Mac a pointed look.

"I'll take the five, Master," he quietly said.

Without another word, Sully headed for their bathroom. Mac silently opened and closed their bedroom door, not wanting to disturb Clarisse. No doubt she'd be asleep for hours yet. With some surprise, he rounded the corner into the kitchen and nearly walked into her, scaring both of them.

The look of sheer terror on her face as she screamed broke his heart. When she realized it was him, she sobbed and collapsed against him. He wrapped his arms around her and held her, trying to soothe her. Drawn by the noise, Sully quietly appeared in the doorway. With her back to him she didn't know he was there.

Sully frowned, then looked sad. He held up three fingers.

Mac gratefully nodded. Sully nodded in reply and disappeared again.

Mac scooped her into his arms, carried her over to the couch where he held her, consoling her while she got the nervous tears out of her system. Only three strokes? He'd take a hell of a lot more than that to ease her through this. Sully must be feeling generous this morning. Mac had fully expected at least ten, if not more, to allow him this kind of unapproved, unnegotiated contact with her.

After ten minutes, she sniffled in his arms. "I'm sorry I'm such a pain, Mac."

"You're not a pain. Why are you apologizing?"

"I shouldn't be imposing on you guys like this."

He tipped her face back so he could look into her eyes. Even with her wounds, it was all he could do to not lean in and kiss her.

The sudden urge scared him.

"You're not imposing, sweetie. You'll live with us, and we'll take care of you, and you can be near Tad. Quit stressing." He helped her to her feet after planting a chaste kiss on her forehead. "I'm sorry I scared you."

"Did I wake you?"

"No. I always get up this early."

"On a Saturday?"

He led her to the kitchen. "Every day. I don't sleep in. What were you looking for?"

"Tylenol."

He smiled, opened a cabinet she hadn't checked yet, and handed her the bottle. "It's all in there. You ready for coffee and breakfast?"

She blushed as she shook out a couple of capsules and took an offered glass of water. "You don't have to cook for me, Mac."

With a gentle touch, he used his finger to tip her chin so he could look into her eyes. "I want to."

She sat at the counter and talked with him while he cooked. He took a mug of coffee to their bedroom for Sully. When Mac returned, he explained. "He likes to be alone when he first wakes up. Helps him think, helps with his writing. Clears his head."

She sipped her coffee. "What does he write?"

"Lots of things. Fiction and nonfiction. He travels quite a bit too. He gives law enforcement and author educational seminars on several topics."

"What kind of fiction?"

"Mysteries, thrillers, procedurals, erotica."

The last raised her eyebrows. "Erotica?"

"Yeah. He uses a pen name for that stuff, but it's not a secret he's the author. The irony is that's where he makes a goodly chunk of money long term."

Mac set her food in front of her when she heard their bedroom door open. Sully emerged wearing jeans and a T-shirt and carrying his coffee mug. She watched Mac bow his head when Sully walked in. Sully cupped his hand around the back of Mac's neck, his hand on Mac's collar, and whispered something to him that she couldn't hear.

She didn't miss the smile that lit Mac's face as he softly replied, "Yes, Master."

Sully handed Mac his mug, which Mac refilled for him. Then Sully turned to her and offered a friendly smile.

"How do you feel? Did you sleep well?"

She hesitantly nodded, still trying to process the intimate exchange she'd just witnessed. Innocent, but obviously full of meaning to the men. "I'm okay. Sore."

"You sure we can't take you to the doctor?"

"That's okay. I'm fine. Just look like hell, that's all." Relieved that Sully decided to sit at the far end of the counter away from her, she rushed the rest of her meal and excused herself to her bedroom.

Sully sadly watched her departure, then looked at Mac.

Mac knew what he thought. "Yeah, it's going to take her a while to not be afraid of you."

Sully finished eating. "Take her with you today, if she feels up to it, to visit Tad and shopping."

"Master?"

Sully arched an eyebrow at him. "Was I not clear?"

Mac reddened. "It's okay?"

"I'm going to shut myself in the office and work today since we're not out on the boat. It'll be easier on her if I make myself scarce." Leaving his dishes on the counter for Mac to take care of, Sully stepped around and softly said, "I mean it. For today and tomorrow, the five still apply for the clothes, but except for the three you're taking for earlier, I'll give you a pass until Monday. We'll revisit the issue then." He gently squeezed Mac's shoulder before he left the kitchen.

Mac ate his breakfast before washing the dishes. One of their ironclad rules of conduct stated Mac couldn't do more than shake hands with people, or friendly hugs with only certain, preapproved people they knew, unless Sully was present or had given prior permission. By comforting Clarisse the way he had before Sully arrived, Mac had earned himself three strokes, which surprised the hell out of him because normally Sully would have demanded at least ten for that infraction.

It was a rule Sully strictly enforced after Mac's habit of friendly, innocent hugs had led to a girl at one of the clubs they frequented wanting to get a little too friendly and causing them problems. In the years since the rule's inception, Mac had never breached it.

Until now.

Mac took a shower and dressed and did his usual chores while he waited for Clarisse to emerge. He didn't really think she would want to go shopping with him. At least, not that morning. Not while she still looked like hell. He imagined she would want to visit Tad.

An hour later, he drove her to Tad's and walked her inside. He stayed for a moment to say hi, then left her with a promise to return in two hours.

* * * *

Uncle Tad smiled as he draped a frail arm around her shoulders. "You have no idea how glad I am to see you're safely back, sweetheart."

She inwardly cringed. "I thought you were friends with Mac and Sully?"

He looked startled, then laughed. "Honey, I trust them with your life. I meant you're back in Tarpon." She loved how he said it, like the old local he was, pronounced "Tar-pawn" instead of "Tarpin" as others said it.

It finally sank in that she'd made it home.

An angry glare shadowed his face. "How bad did the asshole hurt you?"

She blushed and looked away. "I'm okay, Uncle Tad."

He snorted in disgust. "You don't need to wear makeup on my account. I talked with Sully about it yesterday. You kids think I'm gonna pop a gasket if I get excited or something. You're as bad as those boys are."

He leaned back on the couch and muted the TV. "Let me tell you something. Maybe I'm not as strong or fast as I used to be, but there's not a thing wrong with my mind. If you even so much as think about leaving Sully and Mac, I'll hunt you down and kick your ass myself, little girl. Do I make myself clear? Promise me you'll stay with them."

The heat in her face blossomed to supernova proportions. "Yes, sir. I promise."

He laughed. "Good. Glad to see you still listen to me. You have breakfast yet? What am I saying, of course you did. Mac woulda made you eat something." He sighed. "Wish I could give you a better homecoming, little girl."

She didn't mind the endearment. It was what he and Aunt Karen had both called her, because they didn't have kids of their own.

They talked most of the morning until a soft knock on his door interrupted them.

"Come in, goddammit!" he hollered.

Clarisse giggled, glad to see her beloved uncle's spirit still firmly intact even if his body failed him.

A young woman opened the door. "Mr. Moore? I've got that paperwork ready for your niece to sign. Can I borrow her for a few minutes?"

"Hi, Cindy." He poked Clarisse's shoulder. "Go with her. They've got the forms ready adding you as my next of kin and stuff. I'll be here."

Clarisse followed the friendly, chatty clerk down a series of hallways to the administrative wing, where Cindy led her to a cubicle and indicated the chair in front of her desk. She pulled out a sheaf of paperwork and showed Clarisse where to sign. Some of the paperwork had to do with guaranteeing payment. Clarisse noticed Sully had already filled out and signed some of it.

Clarisse blushed. "Can you explain this to me? What happens if his insurance or whatever runs out? I'm not working yet. Is there a government program or something that would pay his bill?"

"Oh, I doubt that'll be an issue. It's mostly a formality."

"You don't know my luck."

Cindy frowned. "I figured Mr. Nicoletto discussed this with you already."

"Discussed what?"

"Your uncle's insurance pays only a portion. Mr. Nicoletto pays the rest. He paid the apartment lease fees up front when your uncle moved in, and he takes care of the difference in expenses every month."

Clarisse's hand felt numb as she shakily signed the paperwork. "He does?"

"Yes. Oh, and he asked us not to tell your uncle that. Mr. Moore is under the impression his insurance and Medicaid pays for it all."

* * * *

Mac returned for Clarisse a little after noon. She'd already eaten with her uncle, had fixed them both BLT sandwiches while she struggled to hold a conversation under the weight of her new knowledge. She had asked Cindy for a look at her uncle's records, since she was being added as secondary guarantor of funds.

Sully and Mac were the ones who found this place for Tad and got him admitted. By her best guess, Sully had spent more than fifty grand on the initial apartment condo fee, guaranteeing that her uncle in essence "owned" his little efficiency, in addition to fifteen hundred dollars in care expenses he paid every month. That meant around one hundred thousand dollars to date.

How would she ever earn that kind of money to repay him? And how the hell would she ever find a job that paid good enough to support herself as well as pay for her uncle's care?

The thought overwhelmed her. She struggled not to cry. She felt guilty that Sully had spent all that money on her uncle when she should have been living here with him, taking care of him. Her inheritance would have paid for the apartment fees and some of his care.

If Mac noticed her disquiet, he didn't mention it. She offered to help him schlep the groceries upstairs, but he refused. She disappeared to her room and closed the door behind her to think in private.

* * * *

Sully walked downstairs to talk to Mac when he realized Clarisse had closed herself in her bedroom. "How is she?"

Mac shook his head. "I don't know. She seemed awful quiet when I picked her up."

Later that evening, before dinner, Sully left his office door open. He sensed Clarisse's presence in the doorway even before she spoke.

"Am I interrupting you?" she quietly asked.

He turned and smiled. "No, sweetie. That's okay. Come on in."

She didn't move from the doorway. "Can I speak to you alone?"

"Of course."

Hesitantly, she stepped just inside and pulled the door shut and leaned against it, but she didn't approach him. It killed him that she couldn't trust him but he knew he couldn't force it.

"I wanted to say thank you. For taking care of Uncle Tad."

He mentally swore. He'd meant to tell Cindy not to reveal the payment arrangement to Clarisse. It had totally slipped his mind. "Tad's like family."

She wouldn't look him in the eye. "I'll figure out a way to pay you back somehow. I promise."

He struggled to keep his tone soft and steady despite his aggravation threatening to break through. Goddamn her ex for destroying her trust. "You don't need to do that. I don't want your money."

She shook her head. An edge of anxiety crept into her voice. "No. He's my uncle. He's my responsibility."

Sully didn't have the heart to correct her, to remind her she had jack shit and a raging case of PTSD to overcome. She was in no condition to take care of herself, much less Tad. "Clarisse, honey, it's okay. Don't stress it. Please. Tad will always be taken care of. I promise you."

Her hair hid her eyes, but he didn't miss the tears rolling down her cheeks. "I *will* pay you back," she softly promised again before she slipped out the door.

Before he made it to the office doorway, he heard her bedroom door softly close. When he walked down the hall with every intention of knocking and talking to her, he heard her muffled sobs on the other side.

Mac, his instincts finely tuned as ever, quickly appeared in the hallway entrance, a dark frown on his face. "What's wrong?"

Sully shook his head, lifted a finger to his lips, and waited until he led Mac downstairs to talk about it.

Mac sat on the bottom step, his head cradled in his hands. "Dammit. I want to help her. I want to strangle the son of a bitch with my own hands. What do we do?"

"Nothing, for now. I just wanted you to know what's going on with her. That's why she acted so quiet when you picked her up." He started to mount the stairs, but Mac reached out and touched Sully's leg.

"When you said she could stay with us as long as she needed, you meant that, right?"

Sully sat on the riser next to Mac and draped an arm around his shoulders. "Yes, I meant it. It'll be good for Tad to have her around." He gently shook him. "And I don't have the patience to have you running back and forth a dozen times a day to wherever she might move to make sure she's okay."

Mac snorted with laughter and leaned into Sully's embrace. "Point taken, Master."

Sully kissed the top of his head. "I don't mind that you care about her. It's natural. If you want the truth, I care about her, too." He rested his chin on top of Mac's head. "As long as we're clear where your priorities lay?"

Mac bowed his head and tucked it against Sully's shoulder.

"Master always comes first in my life."

Sully closed his eyes and, relieved, drew in a long breath. No matter how many times Mac said or swore it, it still gave him the same feeling, engendered the same emotions. Mac wanted him, wasn't ready to break free.

Yet.

"You will always be my first responsibility, slave. Always." He kissed the back of Mac's neck and untangled himself before climbing the stairs.

Clarisse didn't reappear until Mac softly tapped on her bedroom door and called her out for dinner. As soon as they finished dinner and after Mac refused her help with the dishes, she disappeared again.

Sully walked up behind him and laid his hand on Mac's shoulder. "Give her time to adjust and decompress," he softly said before returning to his office.

An hour later, Mac walked into Sully's office, closed the door behind him, and knelt on the floor next to Sully's chair. He didn't speak, simply bowed his head and waited.

Sully finished the paragraph he was writing and saved the file before laying his hand on Mac's head. "Yes, slave?"

"May I respectfully request something?"

"Of course."

"Can we go downstairs? Now? I…need it."

Sully expected he knew exactly what Mac needed. With Clarisse's fragile mental state, Sully didn't want to risk freaking her out. Witnessing them and their normal ways without prior explanation would definitely freak her out in her present state of mind. They couldn't use their playroom or she'd hear them. Downstairs, in the exercise room, would be better.

"Do you want punishment or release?"

"Can we do both?"

If Mac was asking for that, combined with his formal request, he was in serious emotional pain. Sully nodded. "Are all your chores done for the night?"

"Yes, Master."

"All right. Meet me downstairs in ten minutes. You may go."

Sully waited until Mac's departure to let out a huge breath. He'd found early on that Mac's deep masochistic streak was both a blessing and a curse. Sully soon discovered his own streak of sadism, which dovetailed nicely into their dynamic. Even more important, Mac wasn't just a pain pig, although he did enjoy it. He also used physical pain to help him process emotional pain.

Mac didn't normally ask for a heavy scene unless he deeply hurt inside, even though he could and would willingly take one without question or complaint. Part of Mac's willing submission in their relationship was that he rarely asked for things like this, only when he truly needed them. Otherwise, he felt asking for things equated to topping from the bottom, something he hated doing. The only reason he asked at all was because Sully ordered him to never ignore his deepest needs.

Sully walked to their bedroom and grabbed a duffel bag. Even though he was only going downstairs, he didn't want Clarisse to accidentally spot him carrying what he'd need. He took his MP3 player, the punishment cane he kept in their bedroom, Mac's wrist cuffs, the bottle of cucumber lotion, towels, and a light blanket. After checking that Clarisse was in her room, he walked down the hall to their playroom and quickly punched in the lock code.

They hadn't shown her this room yet, and would not show her until he had a chance to sit and talk with her. Inside lay their well-stocked private dungeon. He quickly strode over to the tall cabinet and selected a riding crop, another cane, a light flogger, a severe flogger, and ankle cuffs. He also took several straps he needed to convert the weight bench, as well as some first-aid supplies.

After a little thought, he added a large ball gag. Mac would want him to use a whip for the sting, but that would be too loud. He'd have to stick with the canes, which meant he'd most likely cut him.

He stopped by Clarisse's bedroom door. "Are you okay?" he called to her.

He heard her sniffling. "Yeah. I'm fine."

"Mac and I are going downstairs to work out. Can I get you anything?"

"No, I'm okay."

He brushed his fingers over the doorknob. He wanted to walk inside and hold her, to comfort her the way Mac could.

He knew he couldn't, that he had to let her decide to trust him in her own time. "We'll have the door locked. I'll leave my cell number on the counter, because we won't be able to hear you over the music. I'll see my cell ring." Well, that was close enough to the truth to not be a lie. She would assume they were really working out or having sex.

Not that he was beating the shit out of Mac.

"Thanks, Sully."

He jotted the number on the notepad and left it by the phone on the counter. He shivered in his short sleeves as he descended the stairs. Inside the workout room, Mac had already closed all the blinds and bumped up the thermostat a little to take the chill out of the air. Naked, he waited, kneeling on the cold tile floor with his head bowed.

Sully saw his flesh pimpled with goose bumps. "Stand up. You'll make yourself sick."

Mac complied while Sully locked the door and hooked up his MP3 player. He found his heavy scene playlist, a selection of songs that would help him quickly drop Mac into subspace. With the player plugged into the stereo he cranked the volume loud enough that Clarisse wouldn't be able to hear anything over the music, but the neighbors wouldn't complain. It only took him a few minutes to prepare the weight bench, turning it into a makeshift bondage bench.

He stood in front of Mac. "Look at me, slave," he softly commanded.

Mac lifted his head. His eyes had already started glazing over. It always amazed Sully how quickly Mac dropped into subspace, faster than anyone he'd ever met since their time in the lifestyle.

"Wrists," Sully commanded.

Mac lifted his arms as Sully fixed first one leather cuff, then the other around them, including the small padlocks.

He pointed to the bench where he'd laid a towel. "Face-down, slave."

Mac complied without hesitation. Sully quickly attached his wrist cuffs to the straps, the angle spreading his arms wide and tight. Then he knelt behind him, affixed the ankle cuffs, locked them, and hooked them to another set of straps. Spread, his legs were immobilized, leaving his ass an open and easy target.

Sully stroked Mac's ass. He still bore stripes from the evening before, bruises that would normally heal within a few days. Then he drew back his hand and smacked him hard, on the left ass cheek.

Mac didn't jump.

Sully leaned in close so he didn't have to yell over the music. "Where are you, slave?"

"Green, Master." Mac's eyes had closed. Sully knew that he'd already started his withdrawal into his deep place, as they'd dubbed it, where he could let go and deal with whatever troubled him.

It was the only way he could.

Sully quickly stripped his shirt off and grabbed a small rubber ball out of the bag. He pressed it into Mac's left palm and closed his fingers around it. "Safety, slave."

"Yes, Master."

Sully fitted him with the large leather ball gag, an expensive one Mac could safely bite down on and scream through and still be able to breathe without much additional effort. When he finished adjusting the straps, he stroked Mac's hair. "Where are we?"

Mac rotated his left wrist, their signal for green.

Sully took a moment to stretch and loosen his arms. Then he picked up the mild flogger and started on Mac, from shoulders to ass and back again. As far as their ritual had already sunk Mac into subspace, Sully could have started heavier and Mac would have been okay, but he preferred staying with their usual routine.

After ten minutes, the skin of Mac's back, ass, and thighs had turned pink. Sully switched to the heavier flogger and continued. Before long, just from watching Mac's breathing, he knew Mac had flown over the edge to his deep place.

That's when Sully picked up the pace. He used the springy riding crop along the back of Mac's thighs, alternating between slaps with the flapper and stokes with the shaft. Then he laid the punishment cane across Mac's ass and tapped him lightly with it in warning. With his free hand firmly pressing on Mac's lower back to hold him in place, Sully delivered the eight punishment strokes, viciously, as hard as he could, two of which drew thin lines of blood.

He immediately switched back to the heavier flogger, focusing on Mac's shoulders and back, swinging lighter over his kidneys to prevent injury, then down the backs of his thighs and calves while avoiding the injured flesh of his ass. After twenty minutes of this, Sully switched to the other cane. Avoiding the injured flesh, he escalated the power and tempo of his strokes as the music grew heavier and faster until his last several vicious strokes were timed to fall with a crashing crescendo of deep, resonating notes.

The next song was a step down, which allowed Mac time to breathe and recover, a guarantee that if he could make it to that point, he knew the scene would wind down.

Sully would normally use the light flogger, but Mac's clenched hands and the tears running down his cheeks told Sully that wasn't necessary. Using his hands and starting with Mac's arms, Sully slowly massaged his lover, using firm strokes, from shoulders down his back, to his hips. He skipped over his ass to his legs, first one, then the other. Then he unclipped and removed the ankle cuffs and dragged the duffel bag over.

He took his time gently dabbing at the wounds with gauze and antiseptic. Everywhere else in that region, where the brunt of the strokes from the stricter implements had landed, he soothed the hot, reddened flesh with the cucumber lotion. That finished, as the songs turned quieter and gentler, he draped the blanket over Mac and unhooked and removed his wrist cuffs before removing the ball gag.

Carefully, he helped Mac off the bench and onto the floor, where Sully sat cross-legged with Mac curled and lying halfway in his lap. He took the ball from his left hand.

"How are we, slave?"

Mac shivered and rotated his left wrist, too overwhelmed to speak yet.

Sully held Mac tighter, his arms around him, consoling him as yet another round of tears incapacitated him. It had been a long time since Mac needed a session like this.

They were still sitting there nearly half an hour later. Sully thought his ass would go numb on the tile floor even through his jeans, but he wouldn't make Mac move until he was ready. Finally, Mac sniffled and drew the blanket a little tighter around him.

Sully twined his fingers in the man's hair. "You okay, Brant?"

"Yeah." He rolled over. "Did I get the eight?"

Sully's mouth curled in a playful smile. "Yeah. Early on."

Mac blew out a long, deep breath before Sully helped him sit up. "I don't remember it."

"I can believe it. You went harder and faster than normal."

Mac's eyes searched his. "What about you?"

"What about me?"

Mac arched an eyebrow at him. Sully loved that inquisitive expression. "I'm not so out of it I can't tell that my ass hasn't been reamed, *Master*." He added a pinch of sarcastic tone to the last word.

Sully shrugged. "The weight bench isn't the right height for me to fuck you like that. You want to have to haul me to the ER while you're trying to recover from subspace because I throw my back out?"

With the blanket wrapped around him, Mac sat back on his heels. "Then let me do something else," he quietly suggested.

Sully eyed him, trying to decide if he'd recovered enough or if it was just endorphin-fueled bravado. He stood and unzipped his jeans. Mac leaned forward and pulled Sully's cock out, which had grown stiff at the thought of finally seeing a little action. Sully closed his eyes as Mac's hot mouth wrapped around his shaft, slick as satin and knowing exactly where every pleasure point was located. His tongue stroked and teased him as Sully fisted his hands in Mac's hair and started pumping deeper.

Mac stayed with him, taking him deep into his throat without gagging. The blanket slid down Mac's back and puddled on the floor behind him as he gripped the back of Sully's thighs and held on for balance.

Sully fucked his mouth, harder as his release drew closer. Mac added just a little scrape of teeth, which triggered Sully's climax.

"Now, slave." Mac sucked him deeply and swallowed every drop while Sully's flesh throbbed in his mouth until it finally relaxed, softening.

Sully took a few breaths to regain control, then tapped Mac on the head. "Very good, slave. That's enough."

Mac released him with a *pop*, then sat back and smiled. Sully read the exhaustion in Mac's eyes even though Mac tried to put on a good show. Sully held a hand out to him, helped him stand, and retrieved the blanket for him.

"Wait for me by the door," Sully ordered.

He tucked his cock away and zipped his jeans, pulled on his shirt, then quickly gathered their supplies and Mac's clothes and jammed it all into the bag. He turned off the stereo and lights, locked the door behind them, and slipped an arm around Mac's waist to support him up the stairs.

"Let's get you to bed, buddy."

Mac didn't argue. Sully sensed Mac's post-scene crash setting in.

A normal play scene made Mac hornier than a college frat boy set loose in an adult theater. A heavy scene like this emotionally and physically drained him, which is why he'd asked for it.

Tomorrow morning, however, Mac would be ready for action.

He got Mac inside, locked the front door, and guided him to their bedroom. He pulled the covers down before Mac carefully crawled, face-down, onto the mattress.

Sully stepped away from the bed. Mac was softly snoring before Sully finished crossing the room. He quickly stripped and decided to deal with the rest of the bag's contents in the morning. After using the bathroom, he carefully slipped into bed with Mac and pulled the covers over them. After settling his arm over Mac's back, avoiding the broken flesh, he quickly dropped into an exhausted sleep of his own.

Chapter Six

Sully knew Mac wouldn't dream that night. He never did after a heavy session. The flood of endorphins sent him into a deep, heavy crash that allowed him to sleep uninterrupted.

And himself too, by default.

He awoke early the next morning to the feel of Mac's lips wrapped around his cock. Sully smiled and fisted his hands in Mac's hair. "Did I give you permission to do that, slave?"

Mac made an "uh-uh" sound, but didn't stop what he was doing.

As he'd predicted, Mac woke up hornier than hell. He always did after a heavy scene despite his body being sore and achy. Sully wished their boat trip hadn't been interrupted. He'd been looking forward to letting Mac top him and still had an erotic itch their normal activities didn't scratch.

Mac kept him on edge, holding him back, reading his body, and not letting him come. Finally, he crawled up the bed and kissed Sully. "Shower?"

Sully hooked a leg around Mac's and rolled him onto his back, pinning him beneath him with his arms over his head. "What do you want," he growled. "Tell me and quit dicking around." He suspected he already knew what Mac wanted.

Mac's stiff cock rubbed against Sully's hip. "Just for this morning? Please, Master?"

"Maybe I should make you beg for it." It'd been a long time since he'd let Mac top him anywhere but on the boat.

"If that's what you want, I will."

Sully smiled and sat up. He grabbed Mac's nipple rings and

twisted them. "I should make you pay for asking out of turn."

Mac eagerly nodded.

Sully laughed and swung off him. "Go get the shower ready, you horny slut." He waited for Mac to walk into the bathroom. Then he rummaged through his dresser drawer and found one of Mac's old play collars—one that could get wet. When he walked into the bathroom, Mac was examining his ass in the mirror. Clearly delineated black and blue lines crossed his cheeks and upper thighs.

"Damn. You got me good, Master."

Sully handed him the collar and went to use the toilet. "You ask, you receive." When he finished, he faced Mac. "Well?"

Mac grinned and crooked his finger at Sully. Sully smiled and turned, dropping his chin so Mac could fasten the collar's buckle at the back of his neck. Sully grabbed the key from the counter, unlocked Mac's collar, and removed it. "Happy?"

Mac grabbed him and kissed him deeply, his tongue plunging into Sully's mouth. "Not yet, but I will be once my cock is buried in your sweet ass."

Sully closed his eyes and took a deep, sated breath. He wouldn't deny he enjoyed this, being able to trust Mac enough to let him take over for short periods. Mac spun him around to face the mirror. "Hands on the counter," he growled.

As steam drifted through the bathroom, Sully complied. "Like this?"

Mac shook his head, then nudged Sully's feet farther apart. "Like that." He reached between Sully's legs, palmed his sac, and gently squeezed and rolled the soft weight along his hand. He pressed his chest against Sully's back. "You want my cock inside you?"

Sully, his eyes still closed, let his head drop. "You know I do." His stiff cock wouldn't let him lie about it anyway.

Mac's hand slid up along the seam of his ass, one finger pressing against the puckered ring of flesh without penetrating. "I had a lot of plans for you this weekend."

"I'm sure you did. You're pretty creative."

Mac snickered and swatted Sully on the ass. "Shower. Now."

Sully didn't bother concealing his smile as he stepped across the bathroom. Mac grabbed a bottle of lube and followed him into the shower.

"Against the wall."

Sully complied.

Mac slicked his cock with lube and then worked some into Sully with his fingers to loosen him. "You like that?"

Sully's eyes dropped closed. "Would I let you if I didn't?"

Mac chuckled. "Nope. You'd make my life miserable." He pressed his cockhead against Sully's dark hole. Both men groaned as Mac slowly seated himself inside Sully. With his cock buried to the hilt, he grabbed Sully's hips and slowly thrust. "I hadn't even got started," he whispered in Sully's ear. "Had a lot more I wanted to do. What am I gonna do if she's on the boat with us, hmm?"

"You want to fuck or talk?"

With a hard bump of his hips, Mac thrust deep. "What do you think?"

Sully tried to hold back, his own cock throbbing with every stroke of Mac's shaft along his gland. After a few minutes, Mac slowed his pace and reached around Sully's waist. He wrapped his fingers around Sully's cock and stroked. "Make it fast, man."

Pushed past the point of conscious will, Sully worked his hips back and forth, between Mac's talented fingers and his lover's stiff cock.

"Come now!" Mac growled.

It pushed him over the edge. His hands clenched into fists against the tile wall as his climax washed over him. Mac took that as his cue. He grabbed Sully's hips again and pounded into him until he came with a cry, his cock pulsing inside the other man. Mac didn't move for a moment, leaning against Sully for support and trying to catch his breath. Then he withdrew, turned Sully around, and embraced him as they stepped under the water.

Mac rested his head on the shorter man's shoulder. "You didn't have to put a collar on," he softly said, reverting to gentle Mac.

Back to slave.

Sully closed his eyes and held Mac. "I know you like it."

After a moment, Mac grabbed the soap. He sank to his knees and, working the soap around Sully's groin and ass, lathered and washed him before taking care of himself. Once satisfied, he reached for the collar. "Maybe we should take that off."

"Why?"

Mac shrugged, but wouldn't meet Sully's gaze.

Sully grabbed Mac's chin and forced him to look at him. "Why?" he quietly but firmly asked.

"It doesn't look right."

Sully let him remove it and toss it out of the shower. "But it's right on the boat?"

"That's different."

"It didn't used to bother you before."

"I'm not used to seeing you like that at home anymore."

Bless his heart, Mac was a creature of habit. It didn't matter that he was a "strong" man. He was, in his heart, a slave. He'd embraced it, eagerly, and enjoyed living for his Master. Mac liked clearly defined rules and roles, enjoyed his limited time in charge because it felt natural to him to be in charge on the Dilly.

At home, however, it was a different matter since their routine had changed over the years.

"Turn around," Sully commanded. "Let me look at your ass."

Mac snorted in amusement even as he complied. Sully skimmed his hand down Mac's flesh. The welts he'd opened last night were healing over. While bruised, he saw no sign of infection. "When we get done, let me put some ointment on that before you get dressed."

Mac stepped under the spray to shampoo his hair. "Thank you for that, by the way."

"Anytime." He poked him in the stomach. "You'll have to bank your punishment strokes over the next couple of days. I don't want to give you new ones until you've healed more."

Faltering only a little, Mac barely missed a beat in his reply. "You too chicken to hit me?"

"No," Sully growled. "I don't like to break my toys."

Mac froze, then burst out laughing. "Yes, Master."

"You don't have to take them, you know. You can renegotiate that boundary so there's no punishment."

The expected answer. "No, Master. Thank you, but I'll take them. I don't like to change the rules."

"I thought you'd say that." Mac was, if nothing else, sweetly predictable.

It didn't hurt he was a masochist.

* * * *

After their shower, Sully retreated to his office. Mac brought him coffee.

Clarisse still slept.

Mac cooked Sully breakfast and brought it into the office for him. Sully was already engrossed in his latest manuscript. "Thank you," he mumbled as he studied his laptop screen.

Mac hesitated, then knelt beside Sully's chair, waiting.

Sully hoped his sigh wasn't audible. He saved his file and twined his fingers in Mac's hair. "Yes, slave?"

"What do you want me to do today?"

Poor Mac, he really felt out of sorts with their plans upended. "Chores around the house, take Clarisse to see Tad, stay there with her. Maybe take her out to dinner if she feels up to it."

Mac looked up, startled. "What about you?"

"What about me?"

"Leave you alone all day?"

He moved the breakfast plate out of the way and tapped the corner of his desk. "Talk to me, Brant."

Mac perched on the corner of the desk. The forced equality when in slave mode always knocked Mac mentally off balance. "I'm trying to wrap my head around it. I admit I need to let you be in charge of this, but it's hard for me to not think about Betsy."

"I know. Clarisse trusts you. She needs that in her life and I don't begrudge it. I'm not jealous. I trust you."

Mac laced his fingers together in his lap. "Thank you, Master," he quietly said. "For helping her."

"Why would you think I wouldn't?"

He shrugged but didn't respond.

"Brant, she's Tad's niece. There's no way I wouldn't help her, just on that basis alone. Yes, it pisses me off she's scared of me, but I understand why and don't blame her. I still wouldn't walk away from the situation."

Mac took Sully's hand, lifted it to his lips, and kissed it. "Thank you, Master." He slipped off the desk and left the room, quietly closing the office door behind him.

Sully leaned back in his chair and laced his fingers behind his head. What a mixed bag. Why *was* he doing this? He could have easily contacted the police yesterday morning as soon as they returned to port, helped her file a report, and got her set up at a cheap motel nearby within walking distance of Tad. That would have been more than generous. And Mac's life wouldn't have been completely upended, nightmares from his past returning to haunt him.

He closed his eyes and thought about her terrified blue gaze. He'd be lying if he denied he wanted a chance to erase her fear.

He'd also be lying if he said he wasn't attracted to her.

Too late to back out now.

* * * *

After finishing his breakfast, Sully engrossed himself in his writing again. Just when he'd hit a groove, he heard her moving around in her bathroom next door, heard the toilet flush, the sink run. Then her bedroom door opened and almost immediately Mac's voice greeted her, full of forced cheer. He had expected Mac's refusal to renegotiate the daily punishment strokes for wearing clothes. It didn't mean it didn't surprise him.

He waited a few minutes before carrying his empty coffee mug and plate out to the kitchen. He took great pains to circle around her to avoid where she sat at the counter. "Good morning, Clarisse." He risked a glance at her.

"Good morning." She didn't look at him, studied the coffee mug and plate of food in front of her. Her hair hung loose, hiding her face.

She reminded him of a beat dog.

His sudden anger surprised him. If Bryan Jackson appeared on his doorstep, he would kill the fucker. Working hard to keep his rage in check, he slowly set down his mug and walked around the end of the counter to where she sat.

She didn't turn her head, didn't look at him.

He sensed Mac's sudden tension and ignored it.

"Sweetie," Sully softly said, "please look at me."

He waited her out. After a long moment, she tilted her gaze toward him but didn't fully lift her head.

He slowly reached out, hating that she flinched. He watched her tense, fight or flight instincts warring for control.

Undaunted, he swept her hair back and carefully tucked it behind her ears. Then he caught her chin. She didn't resist when he tipped her face, her frightened blue eyes darting past him to Mac.

Again he waited her out, until her gaze settled on him and didn't leave.

"May I ask a favor?" he asked.

She barely nodded.

"Would you please wear your hair back? For me? You have

beautiful eyes." He brushed the tip of her nose with his finger. "I've always been a sucker for blue eyes."

Finally, the hint of a smile.

Mac snorted behind him. "I thought you loved my eyes."

Sully's gaze didn't leave hers. "I love your ass, Mac. Yes, your eyes are nice, but hers are pretty. Do you really want me calling you 'pretty eyes'?"

A little more of a smile. Her bruised flesh crinkled around the corners of her eyes.

Bingo.

"She has *very* pretty eyes," Sully repeated.

Mac walked over, apparently understanding what Sully was trying to accomplish. "Yes, you're right, Master. Her eyes are definitely prettier than mine."

"I mean, I can make you wear a dress, if you really want me calling you pretty—"

"No, that's okay, Master."

Amused, she snorted a little. Sully read her posture, sensed her slight relaxation.

That's when he gave her a broad, beaming smile and stepped back, out of her personal space. She didn't drop her head, kept her eyes on him.

"I don't know, Clarisse. You think I should make him wear a dress?"

A little more of an amused curl to her lips. "I think he's more a tight jeans kind of guy. He does have a nice ass." She blushed a little but didn't look away.

"Score one for the girl," Sully teased as he picked up his mug. Mac had refilled it. He turned to Mac and lifted an eyebrow at him. "Lucky for you, I'm feeling charitable. Go find the tightest pair of jeans you can squeeze yourself into. No underwear."

Mac looked startled, but went to do it while Clarisse actually laughed.

He'd guessed right—she had a beautiful, clear laugh. On that sweet note, he returned to his study but left the door cracked open.

* * * *

Over the next hour or so, he heard them talking, the occasional laugh from Mac or Clarisse, the front door opening and shutting as they went outside, probably so Mac could show her around. Five minutes later, movement in the yard caught his eye through the window. Sure enough, Mac and Clarisse stood at the seawall, looking out at the bayou. Mac pointed to something. Clarisse nodded.

Sully smiled. She'd pulled her hair back into a low ponytail. *Good girl.*

He wouldn't force her, wouldn't rush her. But maybe that tiny breach in her defenses would be enough to start her on the road to trusting him.

She said something, because Mac laughed. Then a moment later, he frowned and pulled her to him.

Sully forced himself to stay seated and watch, fought the urge to race downstairs.

To help Mac console her.

Her entire body shook with the force of her sobs as Mac guided her down to the grass, where he held her cradled tenderly against him. Sully felt pain in his palms and realized he'd clenched his fists, his nails digging into his flesh.

She'd been deeply wounded. Her physical injuries were already healing but how long to heal her psyche? To restore her trust and get her to a point where she could be a fully functioning human again?

Would she ever stop flinching when he moved toward her? Would there ever come a point when a stern voice wouldn't set into motion an ingrained series of protective responses?

Tad's implied suggestion came back to him. It was far too soon to entertain any ideas along that line. Unfortunately, with the idea planted in his mind, it had quickly taken root and sprouted no matter how impractical it sounded.

Tad knew they weren't gay, had teased the men many times about their almost identical head pivots as they followed a pretty woman's progress with their eyes.

Not to mention the fact that after what Clarisse had been through, the last kind of relationship she'd probably ever want would be the only kind they could give her.

He watched as Mac pressed a kiss to the top of her head before she sat up and wiped at her face. He said something, prompting a nod from her.

Did he miss women? Yes. Not Cybil, not after what she'd put him through. There were nights he'd lie in bed with Mac sleeping soundly next to him and wish for the soft curves of a feminine body.

Not that he'd ever admit that to Mac.

Another thing he'd never admit—he was scared to ask Mac if he missed women too, not sure if he'd like the answer.

* * * *

Sully closed his office door before they returned. He heard them talking in the living room. Then her bedroom door opened and shut, the sound of the shower coming on in her bathroom.

A soft knock sounded at his door.

"Come."

Mac walked in. "We're going to see Tad after she gets her shower."

Sully reached into his back pocket for his wallet. He handed Mac a credit card. "Use this if you need it."

Mac took it. "Thank you, Master." He didn't leave.

"What?"

"Are you really okay with this?"

Sully felt a cold thread of fear slowly wind its way through his soul. "Why wouldn't I be, slave?"

"Because I don't want to do anything you wouldn't approve of."

He studied Mac. He knew Mac went out of his way to walk a narrow path with him, not because he demanded it, but because Mac had helped him through the emotional aftermath of his shooting and divorce and wanted to keep his trust. "I have every confidence that you won't disappoint me."

Mac leaned in and kissed him. "Thank you, Master." He left, closing the door behind him.

Getting back to his writing wasn't easy. He heard the shower shut off, then her bedroom door open a few minutes later. The sound of them talking in the living room before the front door opened and closed. Silence descended. Then the sound of Mac's truck starting and pulling out of the driveway.

Alone.

He tried to throw himself back into his manuscript.

* * * *

Around three-thirty, he heard Mac's truck return. The front door. Voices. Her bedroom door opening and closing. Bathroom noises. Then...

Nothing.

Sully looked up from his computer and waited.

Five minutes later, he walked out to the kitchen. Mac sat at the counter, a cookbook opened in front of him.

"You guys are back early."

"She's tired. She didn't feel like going out to eat. I told her to lie down and take a nap."

He watched Mac, how he massaged his forehead, a sure sign of stress. Sully walked around the counter and rubbed his shoulders. "You okay, Brant?"

"Yeah."

"Really?"

"No. I want to kill the fucking bastard. Is that normal?"

Sully snorted with amusement. "Yeah. I'd worry about you if you didn't."

Mac prepared one of Sully's favorites, a savory chicken casserole he hadn't cooked in a while. At dinner time, Sully heard Mac tap on Clarisse's door.

Nothing.

He tapped again, then finally opened the bedroom door and stepped inside when he received no response.

Sully left his chair and walked down the hall. He stood just outside her doorway and listened. Clarisse's low voice sounded sleepy. Mac's soft, warm chuckle. Then Mac reappeared, nearly running into him.

Sully led him to the kitchen. "She okay?"

He looked sad. "Yeah. She was sound asleep, poor thing. It's caught up with her."

She joined them at the table a few minutes later. She'd remembered to pull her hair back. That pleased Sully. Mac held her chair for her, which seemed to surprise her.

"Did you have a nice nap?" Sully asked.

"Yes, thank you."

Mac kept up a nervous running conversation. Sully spotted the deep exhaustion painted on her face. When they finished eating, before she could offer to help with the dishes, Sully stood and grabbed his plate and hers. "Sweetie, you go chill out, seriously. We'll clean up. You need to rest."

Without a word, she slowly returned to her room. The men sadly watched her go. Mac took the plates from Sully.

"Good show, Master," he snarked.

Sully smiled and picked up the casserole dish. "Maybe I was planning to help you."

Mac snorted, laughing. "Since when do you do dishes?"

"Whenever I want. I'm the Master."

Chapter Seven

Monday morning, Sully left Clarisse with Mac. Mac would take her to visit Tad.

His own destination—the sheriff's office. He parked in the public lot. It felt weird returning here as a civilian.

He walked in and didn't recognize the receptionist.

"Detective Callahan, please. Tell him it's Sully."

She picked up the phone as he waited. A moment later, she smiled. "Go on back. He said you know the way." She handed him a visitor's pass and had him sign in.

"Thanks."

He did know the way. Jason occupied his old office, although it was arranged differently now. He knocked on the open doorway, and Jason looked up. "Hey! There you are!" He waved Sully inside.

Sully closed the door behind him and hugged Jason, then sat in one of the visitor's chairs. He set the roll of film on his friend's desk. "I need a favor, Jayce."

Jason frowned. "What's up?" Sully told him the short version of the story. "Holy fuck." Jason shook his head. "You're worried the paperwork might disappear?"

"You know it. If it hasn't already. Can you stop by tonight and take her statement?"

"You don't want to bring her in?"

"It's not like we'd have jurisdiction here anyway. Besides, I don't think Brant and I together could carry her into a police station right now. She'd fight us tooth and nail. She's terrified. She's even scared of me because I'm a cop."

Jason sat back. "Wow." He looked thoughtful. "You don't want her officially in the system, either."

"Of course not. If his buddies have her plugged in and are keeping an eye out for her, he'll be down here looking for her. I want unofficial official paperwork on her in case something else happens."

"I wouldn't do this for anyone but you, you know."

"I know. I appreciate it."

Jason fell quiet for a moment. "So…how is Brant?"

"We're good. Doing fine."

Jason snickered. "I heard Cybil filed for divorce from number five."

Sully slowly nodded. "I heard."

"Did you ever stop to think maybe she did you a favor? Even as shitty as it was?" He shrugged. "I mean, you know me, my brother's gay. What people do doesn't bother me. But…" He shrugged again. "I'll be honest, I don't think I ever saw you as happy with her as you have been with Brant."

"I know. I wasn't."

* * * *

Sully stopped by Publix on his way home and bought a few things for dinner that night. He didn't want Mac to have to leave and stress Clarisse out even more by her being alone with him. Jason and his wife, Katie, would come over for dinner. Having another woman to talk to might help Clarisse relax and open up. Mac was in the kitchen making lunch when Sully returned. He leaned in and kissed him.

"I've got groceries in the car for you to unload. Where is she?"

Mac looked sad. "She's asleep again. I got her to eat a little breakfast, and then she went to lie down after we got back from Tad's. When I checked on her, she was out."

"Jason and Katie will be here at seven for dinner. He'll talk to her, take her statement. Just a precaution. Any luck talking her into seeing a doctor?"

Mac shook his head. "She won't do it. I told her if she showed any signs of a problem, I would force her to go."

"Maybe we should call Dr. Elliot and get her an appointment."

Mac frowned. "Your old shrink?"

"You said it yourself, she's got PTSD." Sully took a deep breath, prepared for Mac's objection to his next comment. "I've decided that starting today, until we know she can handle things the way they normally are around here, you should stay dressed around her. No punishment. I'll catch up the ones you still owe me in another day or so."

Mac's jaw clenched, his lips pulled taut into a thin line. "I don't get a say in this?"

"You really think I'm wrong here, Brant? It's in her best interest. Frankly, I don't like beating you for something you shouldn't be punished for. That's not fair to *me*, you know. If you want a session, all you have to do is ask and I'll gladly give it to you, you know that."

Sully knew he'd pulled a double-pronged argument out of his ass that Mac couldn't counter. "When do we go back to normal?" Mac finally asked.

"When I'm sure it won't scare her."

He retreated to his office and ignored the way Mac slammed a few things around on the counter. Mac hated it when he made a sudden change to loosen the rules like that. Mac thrived on the strict service and obedience aspect of their dynamic as much as he did the sadomasochism. In this case, Mac would just have to adapt.

* * * *

Clarisse awoke a little after two. She walked out to the kitchen, and when Mac heard her, he went to help.

"Hey, you feeling better?"

She nodded but wouldn't look at him. He noticed she'd donned sweatpants and a long-sleeved shirt despite how warm the house felt. She did, at least, have her hair pulled back into a ponytail.

"Let me make you something, sweetie. What would you like?"

"I can do it."

He smiled. "It's okay. I'll—"

"I can do it!"

Mac took a step back at her shrill tone. Sully hurried into the kitchen. "What's wrong?"

"Nothing's wrong!" she insisted. Then she leaned over the counter and started crying again.

The men walked over to her. Sully hung back while Mac gently wrapped his arms around her and held her. "Shh, you're okay. You're safe."

"How did my life get so fucked up?" she sobbed.

Sully left the kitchen. As much as his heart ached for her, he knew his presence wouldn't help. She needed Mac, the safety she felt with him. Sully knew he topped her automatically mistrusted list. He hoped that after a few more days or weeks with them, she'd change her opinion.

He returned to his study but left the door open in case Mac needed him. He could hear them softly talking in the kitchen, then heard Mac cooking something for her.

Her soft laugh.

Out in the bayou, the guy across from them headed out on his boat, probably a trip to Anclote Island with his grandkids who were visiting from Michigan.

Sully closed his eyes and tried to push away that thought. Kids. Thank God he didn't have any with Cybil. Yes, he'd heard about Cybil's divorce. Straight from her own goddamned mouth two Saturdays ago at Haslam's, when he'd been there for a book signing. Mac had been out fishing. She'd cornered him at the end of the appearance and not-so-subtly hinted that she would soon be single again and asked if he would like to get together for coffee or, wink, more? For old time's sake?

He snorted in amusement. She wouldn't last five minutes with him now. Cybil wanted a guy she could push around and milk for every last cent and ounce of energy until she tossed him and found a replacement. How had he not seen through her before? Yes, it'd emotionally destroyed him when she left him the way she had, finding out about her months of screwing around on top of the divorce while he fought for his life.

Thank God for Mac.

Sully would admit the evil satisfaction of watching her jaw drop and her face blanche when he leaned in and whispered exactly what she'd have to do, in addition to hell freezing over first and the Bucs winning five Super Bowls in a row, before he'd even think about taking her back.

It had felt damn good walking away and leaving her standing there in shock.

He grinned.

He felt a little guilty testing the waters when Mac returned home the next evening, telling him that she had shown up and watching Mac's face to see what he thought. The joyful thrill that ran through him when Mac looked scared before he clamped down on it, and then Mac's relief when Sully reassured him and repeated the conversation.

The more eager than usual way Mac begged to be used that night once they went to bed.

No, he'd never get rid of Mac for Cybil or anyone else, for that matter.

He turned back to his laptop and tried to write.

* * * *

About an hour before Jason's scheduled arrival, Mac walked into Sully's office and quietly closed the door behind him. "How do you want to handle this?" he asked.

"Tell her a friend and his wife are coming for dinner. Don't tell her he's a cop yet."

"Me?"

"Yes, you."

Mac frowned. "I'm not lying to her."

"How is that lying?"

"Not telling her he's a cop. She'll never trust me again."

Sully swore under his breath. Mac was right. "Where is she?"

"She's watching TV in the living room."

Sully stood, pushed past Mac, and silently swore again at her startled flinch when he entered the room. He offered a smile. "Sweetie, a friend of mine and his wife are coming over for dinner tonight."

She'd been channel surfing. At his words, she put down the remote and started to stand. "Okay, I'll just eat in my room."

"No, honey, that's not what I meant. I want you to meet them." He sat in one of the other chairs. "He's my former partner. I want you to talk to him, tell him what happened."

He hated that her scared rabbit look returned. She shook her head. "No, that's okay. Mac can run me over to Uncle Tad's—"

"Clarisse." Mac's stern voice from behind Sully startled him. He glanced over his shoulder, but Mac's gaze had focused on her. "Honey, Jason is a good guy. He's going to help us nail that son of a bitch to the fucking wall. I promise."

She'd gone white, like she teetered on the edge of another breakdown. At Mac's firm tone, she hesitantly nodded. "Okay," she softly said.

"Good girl," Mac soothed, moving to sit next to her on the couch.

Sully watched them for a moment before he quietly left the room and returned to his office. He shut the door behind him. Even through the door he could hear them eventually moving to the kitchen and the sound of pots and pans rattling, the aroma of cooking food drifting to him.

Her laugh.

Since getting together with Mac, he'd never felt deep fear over the possibility of losing him.

Until now.

He closed his eyes. Despite their dynamic, Mac could come and go as he pleased. If Mac fell hard and fast for this girl, he couldn't—wouldn't—stop him from leaving.

Even if it ripped his soul out in the process.

* * * *

Jason and Katie arrived right on time. Katie was a sweet, soft-spoken librarian. Sully had seen her charm a roomful of rambunctious, sugar-high ten-year-olds without raising her voice. He had no doubt she could relax Clarisse.

Clarisse hovered around Mac, almost using him as a human shield. Sully would have found it amusing except he knew how terrified she felt.

Mac artfully seated her between himself and Katie. As their meal progressed with no mention of taking her statement, Sully watched Clarisse relax. When they finished, before Mac could stand to clear the table, Sully stood. "You all talk. I'll do the dishes."

Mac shot him a glare but didn't argue. They moved out to the living room where Sully listened while Jason carefully steered her toward the events of the attack. As they talked, Sully sneaked a peek. Jason had taken out a notepad and jotted information as she quietly related what happened. By the time Jason and Katie were ready to leave, Clarisse had marginally relaxed again.

Sully escorted his friends downstairs, leaving Mac with Clarisse. Both Jason and Katie looked angry.

Jason blew out a deep breath. "Goddamn, that poor kid's totally fucked up." Jason and Katie had a daughter just a few years older than Clarisse.

"You see why I had you come over."

"She can stay with us if she'd be more comfortable," Katie offered.

"Thanks, Katie. I'll pass that on, but from one cop's house to another, she'll still be frightened. She's latched onto Mac."

"How about I take her out to dinner one evening when she's feeling better? Girls' night out?"

"That would be good for her. Thanks."

They said good-bye. When Sully returned upstairs, Mac was sullenly cleaning up what Sully had missed in the kitchen. "Where is she?"

"She went to bed." He threw down the dishtowel and turned on Sully, but before he could lay into him, Sully held up a hand.

"Brant, listen to me. She needs to come first. Don't hassle me on this. She's going to be taking over some of your chores anyway, so what difference does it make if it's me or her doing them?"

He started to reply, then dropped his gaze. "That's different. It's not right you doing stuff. You're my Master. It's *my* job."

Jesus, I so don't need this tonight.

Bless his heart, Mac was pretty set in his way, had his oddly skewed sense of duty and pride when it came to protocols. "You have to take care of her first and foremost. Do what's best for her. Your job is what I tell you it is. Quit topping from the bottom, goddammit."

He couldn't have slapped Mac and elicited the same shocked look. Mac bowed his head. "I'm sorry, Master," he quietly said.

"Good. I did leave you stuff to finish, by the way." He stalked to his office, quietly closed the door, and locked it after thinking about it. His nerves were on edge, partly from Clarisse's tension throughout the meal, partly from Mac's unwillingness to back the fuck off protocol. He understood why it was so important to Mac. The income disparity aside, Mac seriously considered it his job to take care of him. It made Mac feel like a failure when he didn't do it. Sully totally got that.

It didn't mean that it didn't exasperate him, especially considering the situation.

Around their normal bedtime, he heard Mac try the office door knob. That was a clear, silent sign to Mac that he wanted to be left alone.

He put his headphones on, cranked his MP3 player, and wrote until nearly four in the morning, until words swam across his laptop screen and he spent more time correcting errors than he did typing.

When he opened his office door, he nearly tripped over Mac. The man had fallen asleep sitting in the hall, his head resting against the wall.

On one hand, it irritated Sully. On the other, it warmed him. If a third hand were available, it would have been holding a bucketful of guilt that Mac had spent all those hours waiting for him. He should have anticipated it and ordered him to bed.

He knelt beside him and touched Mac's chin. Mac's eyes snapped open.

"Hey, buddy," Sully whispered, hoping they didn't wake Clarisse. "Ready for bed?"

Mac nodded and followed Sully to their room. Within minutes, they were in bed and Mac was already dozing again. Where Sully thought he'd fall asleep immediately, he found his troubled mind wandering. Mac was a strong man, a tough man, but whenever he felt emotionally vulnerable his slave side took over, sometimes to an annoying degree.

Mac didn't like to talk about his feelings even though he was a sensitive man. He preferred to present a solid, silent, stoic façade to the rest of the world, a holdover from his childhood. An abusive, alcoholic father who had left his mom and the three kids when Mac was eight. Not until after he'd beaten the shit out of Mac, Betsy, and their mom plenty of times first though. Only Mac's younger brother, Jim, escaped the abuse, born four months after David MacCaffrey's departure.

When Sully tried to talk Mac into counseling, he'd refused. Sully didn't want to stoop to ordering him to go because then it wouldn't do him any good.

He drifted to sleep, trying not to think about Clarisse's mistrustful stare.

Chapter Eight

Clarisse didn't hear anyone stirring when she awoke early Tuesday morning. The dinner had been stressful, but she really liked Jason's wife. She found it easier to put her mistrust for Sully and Jason aside, but it would take some time.

Intellectually, she knew her mistrust was neither warranted nor fair, considering they'd been nothing but nice to her.

Especially considering what Sully had done for Uncle Tad.

Emotionally was another story. She checked herself in the bathroom mirror. Some of the bruises had faded to ugly greenish-yellow clouds on her skin instead of the deep, angry purples and blues. Her eye almost looked normal, and her lip had nearly healed.

Stripping, she turned to look in the mirror again. Along her back and thighs, those bruises were also fading—thank God—and the worst of the pain had abated. Several nights in a damn good bed without worrying about dying had helped.

After her shower, she dressed and started for the kitchen when she realized she hadn't pulled her hair back.

Okay, so she didn't mind doing that for Sully.

Pretty eyes. The way he'd said it...Yes, it sent a warm, sweet thrill through her that she'd never felt before.

Even though her hair hadn't dried, she pulled it back and loosely bound it at the nape of her neck. Hell, it was the least she could do. One simple request from a man who had twisted himself inside out to take care of her and her uncle when she'd done nothing but mistrust him.

At the very least, she owed him this simple gesture until she felt more comfortable calling him friend.

The house sat dark and quiet. She guessed the men must still be asleep. Having spotted where Mac kept the coffee and filters, she fixed a pot and walked downstairs to get the paper while it brewed.

She shivered in the chilly air and wished she'd put on more than jeans and a T-shirt. Not quite six-thirty, the neighborhood lay still and quiet around her.

There were worse places to live. Far worse. She felt guilty she had uprooted the men's lives and knew she'd have to save her money and get her shit together so she could get a place of her own no matter what she'd promised Uncle Tad. Wouldn't be nearly this swanky, but as long as it had A/C and no roaches or rodents, she'd survive.

She needed a job. She couldn't do that until she got her driver's license changed. But to do that would put Bryan on her trail.

No car. Very little money.

She missed Bart.

The last thought finished her. She sat on the bottom step and cried with her head in her hands. That was another thing—she couldn't control her fucking emotions! Mac had warned her to expect mood swings considering all she'd been through, but this was freaking ridiculous!

She cried for ten minutes, then angrily chastised herself to pull it together. She didn't want to cry in front of the men, didn't want to look like a total damn moron. After taking a deep breath, she returned upstairs with the paper but realized she still felt too unsettled to stay inside. She pulled on a sweatshirt and jacket and took the paper and a mug of coffee downstairs to sit by the seawall.

Faint tendrils of steam floated off the bayou's calm surface. A beautiful view, very relaxing. Next to her aunt and uncle, she'd missed the water most of all when she'd to moved to Ohio. There was nothing more beautiful than a quiet morning on the water, watching the world come to life. Plenty of times Uncle Tad had let her sleep alone on the Dilly in the marina. She'd claimed it was so she could sleep a little later in the mornings before a trip. The truth was she didn't know how to explain, without feeling like an idiot, how the water calmed her. Soothing. The sound of the rigging chiming as the boat rocked in its slip, the calls of seagulls, the deep, warm throb of the engines, all of it.

No words could adequately describe it.

The paper lay unread in her lap as she sipped her coffee and stared across the bayou. Beyond it lay the Gulf. She'd love to work on the Dilly again. Hard work, sure, but nothing compared. Being stuck on dry land in Ohio made her miserable. When her parents told her of the move she'd sobbed, begged to stay behind. Uncle Tad and Aunt Karen had offered to let her live with them and finish high school, but her mom stood her ground, not wanting to be away from her "baby."

Truth be told, Clarisse's mom had never liked her brother-in-law, had looked down her nose at Tad Moore.

Mac was so sweet, and he tried so hard to make things good for her. And Sully...

She closed her eyes and thought about his grey gaze. He was a handsome man, they both were, in different ways. How ironic Mac had a few inches and several pounds on Sully, yet Sully had the "Master" role.

I've got to try harder.

It would only be fair for Sully to toss her out on her ass if she couldn't be a little kinder to him.

The sun lifted over the tree line, warming her back and shoulders to the point where she shed the sweatshirt and put the jacket on again. She sat there for almost two hours, completely finished the paper. About the time she'd planned to return inside, she heard the front door open and shut, followed by a single pair of footsteps on the stairs. From the sound, she recognized Sully's lighter step.

Clarisse tensed.

A car door opened and closed. Then Sully's Jag started and pulled out.

When she turned, he was already down the road.

She hadn't even tried to call out to him, to say good morning or thanks for helping her out.

She'd hunched down, praying she wasn't noticed.

She gathered everything and returned to the house. Mac offered her a broad smile when she walked into the kitchen.

"Morning! You hungry, kiddo?"

She nodded and slid onto one of the stools at the counter. She wanted to ask about Sully but didn't. It wasn't her business where he went or what he did.

Mac kept up a mostly one-sided conversation with her while he cooked. When he slid a plate of bacon and eggs in front of her, he laid his hand over hers. "Are you really okay?"

"It's just hitting me, that's all. And I really miss Bart." She almost successfully fought the urge to sniffle. "I've never been away from him before. I know it sounds dumb, but he's like my baby."

"We'll get him back for you, sweetie. One way or the other, and you won't have to go alone. I promise."

"I can't ask you to go with me."

His face and voice grew firm, commanding. "You aren't asking. I'm telling you, I'm going with you."

"Will Sully let you?" She wished she hadn't asked it.

He squeezed her hand before moving back to the stove. "He won't dare say no."

* * * *

Mac didn't offer Sully's whereabouts and she didn't pry. Mac took her to Tad's and dropped her off while he ran errands. When he picked her up and they drove home, she managed to snag two grocery bags out of the truck before he could stop her.

"No, I'm helping." She stuck her tongue out at him, daring him to take the bags away from her.

He laughed. "Okay, fine. Carry the damn bags, you stubborn brat."

She paused at his playful tone of voice. Normally, comments like that would cause her to bristle or shoot back with a scathing reply. But...

It felt different coming from Mac. She couldn't explain it.

Sully returned home before dinner. Clarisse suspected from Mac's puzzled look that he didn't have any idea where Sully had been. Sully kissed him, then turned to her.

"Did you have a good day?"

She fought her body's instincts. She could do this, dammit. He was a nice guy. "Yes, thank you."

He held out his hand. "Come with me. I want to show you something."

Clarisse hesitated before placing her hand in his.

He smiled, full of playful, teasing mirth, and led her to the front door with Mac trailing behind. "Mac, cover her eyes, don't let her see. Clarisse, use the handrail. I won't let you fall."

Like that, they helped her down the stairs. She didn't know what waited, only that halfway down, Mac suppressed a laugh.

They led her across the driveway. She could tell by the feel of the gravel under her feet. When they stopped, Sully gently squeezed her hand before pressing something into her palm. "Open your eyes, honey."

A bright green VW Bug sat next to Sully's Jag in the driveway. She looked at what he'd put into her hand—a keychain.

Numb shock hit her, followed by a wave of tears. She felt Mac slip his arm around her shoulders. "Well, how about that?" Mac said. "Go on. Let's see how you look in it."

"Mac, did you know he was going to do this?"

He smiled and shook his head. "Nope. But now I know what he was up to all freaking day long."

She turned to Sully. "I can't accept this."

He stepped forward and gently took her hands. "You can, and you will. This is a gift. It's not new, it's six years old, but it's in good shape. I had my mechanic go over it. It'll get good gas mileage and it'll last you for several years. I put it in my name for now. I'll pay the insurance for you until…things settle."

She wiped the tears off her face and forced herself to hug him. "Thank you." She relaxed against him, allowing herself to rest her head on his shoulder. "You've been so nice to me and I'm such a bitch."

"Stop." He made her look at him. "You've been through hell. You're not a bitch. Don't make me spank you." The curl along the edges of his mouth belied his words.

She laughed. "Okay. Thank you."

Mac walked ahead and opened the driver's door for her. Sully climbed into the passenger side. "Want to take me for a quick spin?"

"Sure."

Mac stuck his head in the driver side. "Dinner's almost ready."

"We'll be right back," Sully assured him.

They buckled up and drove to the end of their street and back. When they pulled in, he started to unbuckle his seatbelt when she reached over.

"Sully…really. Thank you. You've been nothing but good to me. I'm sorry I'm…difficult."

"You're anything but difficult." He brushed a finger along her chin, sending a warm flutter through her core. "We need to get upstairs before we ruin Mac's dinner and make him mad."

* * * *

Sully let her climb the stairs first and tried to keep his eyes off her ass as he followed. She was cute. She was also totally off-limits for several reasons, the first and foremost being the man who slept in his bed every night. The second, she was in no way, shape, or form someone he needed to even think about in that way due to what she'd been through. Despite Tad's persistent hints, while Sully wasn't adverse to a poly situation, Clarisse most likely wouldn't want to join them in their relationship. Especially when, back to point number two, she'd been beat to hell and back.

Sully stayed up late working that night. When a story called, it called. He'd long ago learned to write when the words flowed. A little after midnight, he heard a noise from Clarisse's room. By the time he reached her door, she was screaming.

Without hesitation and realizing he'd reached for a gun he no longer wore, he burst through her door to find her alone in bed.

A nightmare.

By the time he reached her side and pulled her into his arms, she was sobbing and clung to him.

"Shh, it's okay. Just bad dreams." He stroked her hair as she cried, trembling from fear and adrenaline.

Mac ran in carrying a baseball bat. "What happened? What's wrong?"

Sully smirked. "Stand down, slugger. She had a nightmare."

He put the bat down and joined them in bed, sandwiching her between them until she calmed.

She made no attempt to pull away from Sully.

He closed his eyes as he nuzzled her hair, smelled her shampoo, breathed her scent. "Why don't you come sleep with us tonight, sweetie?"

Without a word she nodded, still shivering in his arms.

Fuck.

She was terrified. Whatever the dream had been, it did more than scare the crap out of her. It had probably triggered flashbacks of the attack.

Mac hovered, worried, as Sully helped her out of bed. Sully kept his arm around her, snugged her closely to his side, and led her to their bedroom. A few minutes later, she curled in his arms in their bed while Mac lay beside her and held her hands.

"Thank you," she whispered.

Sully kissed her shoulder. "It's okay. You're softer to cuddle with than he is."

"Hey," Mac protested, but he smiled.

She looked over her shoulder at Sully, a wan smile on her face. "I'm sorry I'm a pain."

"Stop," he firmly said. "You're not a pain. Go to sleep and have good dreams. That's an order."

* * * *

Clarisse found she couldn't resist that command. Being protectively snuggled in Sully's arms, Mac's comforting presence there…

She felt loved.

Well, maybe not loved, but it felt a hell of a lot better than the terror she'd awoken to.

In the lonely, stormy sea her life had become, these two men provided a safe harbor.

She closed her eyes and tried not to think about the nightmare. About the feel of Bryan's fist shooting out and punching her as she'd turned from the stove after telling him to fuck off.

His angry voice as he kicked and punched her, then the terror as he wrapped his hands around her throat and threatened to choke the life out of her.

When he finally quit beating and kicking her, how he'd knelt in front of her.

"I want meatloaf for dinner. I'll be home at the usual time. Have a good day." His tone sounding light, as if he hadn't just beaten the crap out of her.

The slamming of the front door and the sound of his car pulling out of the driveway, heading for work as if he hadn't just threatened to kill her.

She'd lain on the cold kitchen tile for nearly thirty minutes before she could stand and call Raquel. Raquel had raced over, taken one look at her, and called 911 despite Clarisse's protests.

She hadn't seen Bryan Jackson face to face since. He'd claimed she was fine when he left the house, hence why he was put on administrative leave and not immediately fired. He'd acted like the desperately worried boyfriend wanting revenge against whoever had beaten his beloved girlfriend. He'd been wearing driving gloves when he attacked her, because of the cold morning, so there were no marks on his hands. No surprise, he'd denied he'd worn gloves on that morning.

He said, she said.

Not to mention Bryan's father's pull with the chief of police.

She tried to push that all out of her mind as she focused on the comforting feel of Sully's body against hers.

Could she trust him?

It occurred to her that maybe the question should be could she afford *not* to?

Chapter Nine

Clarisse made a pointed effort to get closer to Sully over the next few days. Mac told her Sully would leave early Friday morning, flying to California for a conference. As her bruises faded, she needed less makeup to hide them. She stepped into Sully's office doorway on Thursday night, hesitant to interrupt him.

He offered her a soul-melting smile. "Hi, sweetie, come on in. What's up?"

She didn't mind the endearments from either man. Maybe it made her weak to enjoy the warm fuzzies, but she didn't care. She felt more welcomed with two practical strangers than she had in the years she spent with Bryan. She stepped forward, closer to him. "If I don't see you before you leave tomorrow morning, I just wanted to say have a safe trip." She took a deep breath. "I'll miss you."

He smiled. "I'll miss you, too. You starting to feel a little more stable?"

"That's an understatement."

"When I get back, we can talk about the details of your arrangement. This weekend, let Mac spoil you. I know he's planning on taking the boat out. I'd prefer you go with him. I don't want you here alone."

"I'll be okay by myself."

He leaned back in his chair. "I would prefer not to leave you alone right now."

She felt herself falling into his grey gaze. "You're worried Bryan might find me?"

"Let's not take any chances. The longer we go without hearing anything from him, the better I'll feel. If you don't want to go out on the boat, Mac can stay here."

A chance to be out on the Dilly again, alone with Mac?

"No, that's okay. I'll go." She took a chance and leaned in, hugged him. "Thank you for everything, Sully. Really."

He patted her on the back before releasing her. "It's okay. I hope you aren't planning on leaving any time soon."

"No. Uncle Tad would spank me."

He winked. "Maybe I would, too."

* * * *

She pondered his comment as she prepared for bed. She suspected Sully and Mac hadn't shown her all the aspects of their relationship, most likely out of fear she'd run away, screaming and terrified. A few days ago, she would have agreed. Now she felt safe enough with them to know they were men of their word. Neither had acted even remotely improper with her, and the night she'd spent in their bed had been nothing but platonic.

Besides, they were, after all, gay. The fact that Uncle Tad felt secure with her arrangement went a long way to settling her mind.

The next morning when she got up at six, Mac was making coffee and Sully had already left. Mac flashed her a bright smile. "Ready to get back on the water, kiddo?"

"Yeah." She took the offered mug. "When do we leave?"

"I figured we go see Tad, hit the store, then pull out around four, catch the tide."

A thrill of excitement washed through her, the first time she'd felt it in…years.

Getting out on the boat.

By three o'clock, they unloaded gear and supplies at the dock. When she stepped out of Mac's truck, she closed her eyes and took a deep breath. Marina salt water, diesel fumes, bait.

Home. God how she'd missed it! She reached into the back of the truck to grab her duffel bag.

Mac touched her arm. "You'll need these. Why don't you go unlock the boat?"

Her Dilly keys dangled from his hand.

She smiled as she took them. "You're giving them back?"

"They're your keys."

"It's your boat."

He laughed as he handed her the bag. "Technically, it's Sully's boat. But you're part of the family, so to speak."

They loaded and she fell into the familiar routine as if she'd never missed a trip. There were a few different boats in the marina and two of the covered slip sheds had been expanded. Other than that, not much had changed. She cast off the lines and stood watch as Mac deftly guided the boat out of the marina and down the channel.

Despite the warm afternoon, wind off the chilly Gulf soon forced her to don her hoodie. She stood next to Mac in the wheelhouse and watched the Gulf waters slip past. He hooked an arm around her shoulder.

"Feeling okay?"

She instinctively leaned in to his firm, warm body. "Yeah. Better than I have in a long time."

* * * *

She cooked them dinner while he set the autopilot and kept watch. Not much had changed on the Dilly Dally in her absence other than newer electronics and a new autopilot.

She brought their plates to the wheelhouse and ate with Mac.

He smiled. "You look relaxed."

"I am." The sun dipped in the sky, painting the horizon in fiery reds and oranges. "I can almost forget."

He didn't break the silence for a while. "What are you thinking?"

The answer that popped out of her mouth surprised even her. "What's really in the other room? The one that's locked?"

He choked on his soda and took a moment to regain his composure. He laughed. "You don't waste words, do you?"

"No."

He took another drink to buy him some time. "How much do you want to know?"

"How much should I know?" She indicated his neck, the padlocked collar. He'd changed it out before they left home, wearing the heavy silver necklace. Then after they pulled the Dilly out of the marina basin, Mac had put the leather collar back on. "It has to do with all of that, doesn't it?"

"Yeah. It does." He turned to her. "You want the full and honest truth, or a bullshit euphemism?"

"The full and honest truth."

"Sully and I are into BDSM. We have our own dungeon."

She blinked. "Say again?"

Mac's lips twisted into a wry smile. "We have our own dungeon. Playroom. I like it when he ties me up and whips me."

She sat back. He intently stared into her eyes, not letting her gaze wander. "Whips you?" she whispered, all strength in her voice gone.

"Yep. Like we told you, we'll never ask you to participate in any of that." He set his plate on the dash. "We do, however, sometimes host parties, have friends over who are also in the lifestyle. Play parties. I haven't talked to Sully about that yet. We're supposed to host one next weekend. I need to find out if he wants to cancel."

Her mouth had gone dry. "You let him *beat* you? Why?"

"It's complicated. I don't expect you to understand."

"But you're bigger than him!"

"So?"

Her brain felt like it had short-circuited. Comfort drained from her soul.

He stood and took her empty plate. "Can you stand watch?" he asked. "I'll go wash up."

She numbly nodded.

When he returned to the wheelhouse twenty minutes later, she felt a little more stable. "So what's in the room you didn't want me to see?"

"You won't let up, will you?"

"No."

"I'll be happy to show you when we get home, if you really want to see."

"Why the lock?"

"We tell people it's Sully's private office. We don't want people wandering in there who don't belong. We do have vanilla friends who come over on occasion."

"Jason and his wife?"

"Yep. He probably suspects Sully's in charge in our relationship, but he doesn't know everything."

What trust she'd built for Sully slipped away like the boat's wake. Did she believe he would he hurt her? No. Had he taken care of Tad and been more than generous with her? Absolutely. Had he made her feel welcomed and safe? Definitely. Would she let him get any closer to her?

Probably not. Not if he was doing something like that to someone as sweet as Mac.

She turned away from Mac and stared out the front windows. Tried to reconcile the warmth, affection, and security she'd felt while nestled in Sully's arms with this new truth.

"What's wrong?"

"Nothing." She wanted to keep her thoughts to herself. What Sully and Mac did in their private life was just that—private. She had no right to inject her opinions into their relationship. But throughout the evening, as he set their drag patterns into the GPS and they started their shrimp run, every time her eyes fell on Mac's collar, she wanted to cringe.

Poor Mac.

What had Sully done to him to talk him into such a relationship? Faced with the reality of their truth, she found it difficult to maintain the open-minded mindset she'd prided herself on.

She sorted shrimp in silence. At break time, she retreated to the bow cabin to lie down and rest. Unfortunately, her brain wouldn't shut off.

Her thoughts drifted back to that first night. Despite her exhaustion and confusion and fear, she remembered her body's reaction while watching the men.

Why did it feel different for her now knowing it was really Sully in charge and knowing what Mac let Sully to do him?

Knowing it was an irrational way to think didn't make her any more able to change her mind.

Clarisse closed her eyes and tried to sleep.

* * * *

Mac stared out at the dark water. No boat lights in sight, only the stars and moon. He'd screwed up and he knew it. He'd felt Clarisse's emotional withdrawal after admitting what lay behind mysterious door number three.

He should have waited, let Sully handle it. No way he could have lied to her, even if he'd wanted to. Lying felt alien to him after his years with Sully.

He had enough shrimp on board to fulfill his obligation to the bait wholesaler at the dock. He baited a few lines and set the rods in holders on deck. Not much else to do, it kept his mind off the sick feeling permeating his gut that he might have driven Clarisse away from them.

Before dawn she emerged from the cabin. He forced a smile and fixed her a cup of coffee. "How'd you sleep?"

She sounded guarded. "Good."

He couldn't stand it any longer. "Can we talk about this?"

"About what?" From the way she ducked past him on her way to the wheelhouse, he knew his assessment was spot-on.

"What we talked about last night. I know it sounds weird, especially considering what you've been through. Believe me, what Master and I have together, it's okay. I want it this way."

"That's between you two. I'm sorry I asked. It's none of my business."

From her tone, he knew better than to press her.

I'm sorry too. For being a dumbass and not waiting for Master to handle this.

* * * *

Mac hated the cautious mask she wore all weekend. Fearing he'd do something else to scare her, he walked on eggshells around her. By the time they headed back to Tarpon on Sunday afternoon, he prayed that he hadn't done irreparable damage to the trust he'd established with her.

She sat in the passenger seat and wore Sully's sunglasses against the bright glare.

He couldn't stand it any longer. "I'm sorry," he said.

"For what?"

"Scaring you."

Finally, she turned to look at him. He wished she'd take the sunglasses off so he could see her eyes. "You didn't scare me, Mac."

Her tone sounded measured. He clearly heard it in her voice, the way she weighed every word before speaking.

"You've pulled away from me, hon. Don't deny it. I can feel it."

"What you two have is private between you." She picked at her fingernails. "I'll get another job and save money so I can move out and get my own car once this mess with Bryan is sorted out. Then you guys can get back to normal without worrying about me."

His heart dropped. He stepped over to her and gently grabbed her wrists. "Clarisse, you can't leave us. Please." His desperation reflected back to him in the sunglasses. She couldn't leave. He couldn't—wouldn't—let her. He had to protect her.

The way he'd failed to protect Betsy.

"Mac, I'm cramping your lifestyle. You shouldn't have to hide who you guys are because of me. It's not fair to you."

"Would you please promise to stay at least six months? See how it is between Master and me. You'll understand better. You haven't seen us together the way we normally are."

"You can't be together the way you normally are with me around."

He released her wrists. She was right.

"You promise me at least six months, and Master and I will show you how we normally are. You'll see it's okay. Please?"

* * * *

Clarisse stared at him, grateful for the minimal shield the dark sunglasses offered. Mac was so sweet, how could she stand watching Sully beat him?

Realistically, how would she take care of herself?

Six months. If she could tolerate years of Bryan's verbal, mental, and emotional abuse, she could deal with six months of retreating to her room when the two men did whatever it was they did. It's not like they'd be doing any of it to her.

Six months to get her shit together.

"Okay. Six months."

He threw his arms around her and hugged her tightly to him. She wouldn't deny *that* felt nice, comforting. More than a brother or friend.

Clarisse sat back, not wanting to follow that mental trail.

"Thank you, sweetie," he said. "You won't regret it. You'll see, at the end of six months you'll feel like part of the family. You won't want to leave.

That's what I'm afraid of.

* * * *

Sully closed his eyes and let his mind drift as the car drove him home from the airport. His leg hurt like a son of a bitch. He hadn't taken his cane or his heavier pain meds with him, not needing either in months, but the weekend had been long and exhausting with a lot more time spent on his feet than expected.

He rubbed his hand over his left thigh, just above his knee, and tried to massage the ache. He couldn't wait to get home, fall into bed, and let Mac work over his muscles with his talented hands.

He wondered how the weekend had gone for Clarisse. He hadn't called, knowing with them out on the boat that Mac's cell probably would be out of range anyway. If there'd been any emergencies, Mac would have used the satellite phone to call him, even from the water.

As his leg throbbed, he tried to distract himself with other thoughts. By the time the car dropped him at home a little after midnight, he felt nearly sick from the pain. He pulled himself up the stairs and left his bags inside the front door for Mac to take care of in the morning.

He rummaged through the kitchen cabinet for the bottle of OxyContin, relieved to see he still had eight left. He took one, swallowing it with a glass of water.

"Master?" Mac stood in the kitchen doorway, naked except for his collar. When he spotted the bottle of pain pills on the counter, his face turned worried. "Are you okay?"

Sully shook his head. "A lot of pain. Help me to bed, please."

Mac swooped in, slipping his arm around Sully's waist, draping Sully's arm around his shoulders. He carefully helped him limp into their room and gently lowered him to their bed. He knelt in front of him and removed Sully's shoes.

"How long have you been hurting?"

"I woke up this morning and limped into the shower, stood there until I could walk again. I've been eating Tylenol all day. I haven't hurt this bad in months."

"Lie down."

Sully did. Mac helped him slide his slacks off, then retrieved a tube of ointment from the bathroom. He worked it into Sully's left leg, his fingers knowing exactly what muscles to focus on, where to press, where to rub.

Sully grunted both in pain and relief as Mac's attention, in combination with the drugs, started to relieve the worst of the pain.

"Is that helping, Master?"

Sully's eyes closed. "Yeah. Don't stop."

Mac worked on his leg for nearly half an hour. Sully unbuttoned his shirt as he lay there with his eyes closed and tried to hold on until the pain diminished enough for him to move again.

"You need to take it easy this week, Master. Should I call the doctor?"

"No. He'll want to put me back in physical therapy. I overdid it and didn't take my cane. I've spent too much time sitting at my desk instead of working out." He cracked open an eyelid. "How's Clarisse?"

Mac's hands hesitated for a moment. "She's okay."

He propped himself on his elbows despite the pain it caused. "Slave."

Mac sighed and related the conversation. Sully lowered himself to the bed, silently swearing. He hadn't left Mac with any explicit instructions, hadn't considered them necessary. He wouldn't punish him for telling her the truth, but he suspected what little trust Clarisse had gained in him sailed overboard at the revelation.

"Master?"

"It's okay. You did the right thing to tell her the truth."

"Why doesn't it feel okay?"

"It's okay." Mac lifted Sully's leg, helping him flex at the hip and knee. "That really helped, thank you."

Mac helped him sit and remove his shirt. "Do you want the heating pad?"

"Might not be a bad idea." The drugs started to take hold in his system. He hated using them, but under the circumstances, he'd make an exception.

Mac got him situated, propped himself with a few pillows to read, and tucked his body against Sully's to hold Sully in a comfortable position. Sully knew Mac would stay up, waiting until after he'd fallen asleep so he could put away the heating pad to prevent him from getting burned.

As Sully drifted into sleep, he realized he'd forgotten to go through their usual greeting routine, the pain taking precedent. He drowsily reached back and patted Mac's thigh. "Thank you, Brant."

Mac kissed his forehead. "You're always welcome, Master."

Chapter Ten

Sully awoke in pain early the next morning, but not as bad as he'd felt the night before. Mac was already out of bed, but had left the heating pad on the mattress where he could reach it. Sully grabbed it, turned it on, and wrapped it around his thigh.

Fucking leg. Then again, he should consider himself lucky he still had a leg. The bullet had shattered it above the knee. He supposed some pain on occasion was a small price to pay.

But dammit, he hated paying it.

Mac walked in with his coffee, a glass of water, and a pain pill. "You'll want this, Master." He handed him the water and the pill.

Sully nodded, no arguments. He needed to get on top of the pain sooner rather than later. He could spend the rest of the day on over-the-counter pain meds if he knocked the pain back now. After this kicked in, Mac would draw him a hot bath to soak in and work on his leg to loosen the muscles.

"I'm sorry I couldn't go through our routine last night," Sully apologized.

Mac smiled. "It's okay, Master. No infractions."

Sully realized Mac was naked. "Where's your clothes?"

Mac blushed. "I think I should go ahead and let her see the way we really are. She promised me six months."

Sully hurt too badly to argue. "I'll overrule you if I think it's necessary."

"Yes, Master."

Mac worked on Sully's leg, then drew him a hot bath. Sully would soak in there for a while. After another round with Mac's hands, maybe he could function. As Mac helped him ease into the hot water, Sully grabbed his lover's hand. "Hey." Sully tugged, drawing him closer.

Mac smiled, leaned in, and kissed him. "I missed you."

"Missed you, too. Let's see how I feel later and maybe take her out to dinner tonight."

"Okay. Yell if you need me. Don't you dare hurt yourself getting out." Mac left the bathroom door partially open so he could hear if Sully called for him.

Sully closed his eyes. How had he lucked out? Their relationship wasn't anything that had ever raised the blip of a possibility on his future radar. Dammit, he was grateful for Brant's presence in his life. Especially in times like this.

He settled back in the water, slowly flexing his leg to work some of the stiffness out of it.

* * * *

Clarisse smelled coffee and rolled over. Sully should be home, but she hadn't heard anyone moving around or talking.

She could dash into the kitchen for her coffee and then retreat to her bedroom, hopefully avoid Sully until he locked himself in his office, but she knew that wouldn't do her any good long term.

She had to face him and his whacked-out relationship with Mac sooner or later.

After pulling on her robe, she quietly opened her bedroom door. The house was dark, but the over-counter lights were on in the kitchen. When she rounded the corner into the kitchen, the sight of Mac's naked ass stopped her in her tracks. He must have heard her shocked "eep!" because he turned and offered her a smile before she could retreat.

"Good morning. You ready for breakfast?"

She stared, unable to take her eyes off his body. The gold nipple rings that she wanted to play with. The…

Holy crap, he was well-hung.

He arched an eyebrow at her. "You all right?"

"Um…uh…yeah. Okay."

He leaned against the counter and crossed his arms over his broad chest. "Six months, sweetie. That's what you promised. If it really bothers you, I'll go put on shorts."

"Um…yeah…I mean, no, it doesn't bother me. I just wasn't expecting…" What? What wasn't she expecting? Mac in full slave mode?

He laughed and reached over for the mug she always used, poured her a cup of coffee, and offered it to her. "To see me naked?"

"Yeah." She took the mug and held it in both hands, hoping he couldn't see how they trembled. He was…*goddamn*, he looked gorgeous!

She forced her eyes up from his groin to his brown eyes. "Does Sully walk around naked too?" That could be a blessing and a curse. If he was hung half as well as Mac…

Ohmigod.

They're gay…they're gay…they're gay…

"No," Mac said with a smile. "Not usually. Sometimes I make him do that on the boat. Otherwise, he's usually dressed." He pointed to the counter. "Go ahead, sit. I'll make breakfast."

There were far worse views than Mac's firm and well-shaped ass as he stood at the stove and made French toast. "Is Sully eating with us?"

Mac shook his head. "I'm making him stay in bed this morning."

Clarisse blushed. Even though Mac didn't turn, he must have realized how that sounded because he cast a glance at her over his shoulder.

"His leg is really hurting him this morning. He came home last night barely able to walk."

"Oh. What'd he do to it?"

"Old injury. He didn't take his cane with him."

After a moment, Clarisse realized she wouldn't get any more information from him. Cane? She hadn't seen Sully use a cane, although come to think of it, he did have a noticeable limp.

Sully didn't make an appearance before she finished her breakfast. Mac sat at the other end of the counter, a towel on his seat.

She realized by the time she finished eating it almost felt...well, not normal, but she'd managed to grow more accustomed to seeing Mac running around naked. She shouldn't complain. If he was fine with it, why not? At least she got one hell of a great view out of it. Just because he was gay didn't mean she couldn't enjoy the scenery.

She took her shower. When she finished and returned to the living room on her way to refill her coffee, she found Sully on the couch with Mac fussing over him, getting him arranged with his left leg propped on pillows.

"I'm okay," Sully insisted.

"No, you're not. You could barely walk and you're going to stay put. Whip my ass if you want, but I'm not budging on this." Mac moved the coffee table close to the couch. "I'll bring your laptop out here. You take it easy." He disappeared down the hallway.

When Sully's gaze landed on her, she stifled a laugh. He looked absolutely miserable. He shrugged as if to say, "What can I do?"

Despite her reborn mistrust, she smiled. "I'm sorry you're not feeling well."

"Thanks. It's my own fault for overdoing it."

"Mac said it was from an old injury?"

Sully's face darkened. "Yeah. I got shot. Line of duty."

She didn't know how to respond. Before she could, Mac reappeared with the laptop and a lap desk for Sully. "All right, what else do you need?"

"A new body?"

Mac smiled. He'd pulled a pair of sweatpants on, but was still shirtless. "I've got to run downstairs for the laundry. If you need something, have Clarisse get it for you or wait for me. Do *not* get off that couch, you hear me?"

Sully glared, but snapped him a mock salute before Mac left.

Clarisse circled the couch. "Can I get you anything?"

"The remote, over there, please."

She handed it to him and sat in one of the chairs. "Is that why you retired? You were shot?"

His face darkened again. "Yeah. Not my best day. I wasn't supposed to be there, got called in at the last minute when I was off-duty and not at home. Only damn day I didn't have a vest on, I get shot." He flipped through channels before settling on MSNBC. "Nearly died. Lots of rehab." He rubbed his left leg, above the knee. She spotted the pale, twisted scar that started at his knee and ran up his thigh, disappearing under his shorts. "One here, one in the gut."

"I'm sorry."

The hint of a smile. It turned his hard face sexy and conflicted her in ways she didn't understand. "Why? It's not your fault I got shot."

"I'm still sorry." She stood, walked to the kitchen, and poured a cup of coffee. She tried to delay her return to the living room. In reality, there wasn't much else for her to do.

Maybe that was the answer.

She returned to the chair. "Before you get involved in your work, can we talk?"

"Sure." He set the lap desk and computer on the coffee table. "What's up?"

"Our arrangement." She cleared her throat. "What I should be doing. To help out."

"Why don't we discuss the elephant in the middle of the room first?"

She blushed. He still wore that sexy smile. "What do you mean?"

"The talk you and Mac had on the boat this weekend."

She felt more heat pulsating in her face. "I told him that's between you two."

"No, as someone who lives here, it involves you, too." Mac opened the front door and walked in carrying a laundry basket. Sully called out to him, "Slave, put that down. Now. Come here."

Looking confused, he set the basket down and walked over.

"Help me up." When Mac started to protest, Sully silenced him. "Don't argue with me, slave. I want this conversation over with so we can get on with life." Mac helped Sully stand. Then he handed him a walking cane that had been leaning against the end of the couch. "Follow us, honey," Sully said to her.

With her fingers firmly wrapped around her steaming mug of coffee, she followed the men down the hall. At the locked door, Sully punched in a code and turned the knob. "Zero, one, one, three. His birth date," Sully explained. "January thirteenth." He pushed the door open and limped inside where he flipped a light switch.

When Clarisse hesitated at the doorway, Sully turned and waved her in. "It's okay," he said, his tone gentle.

She stepped inside. The large room, approximately the same size as her bedroom, didn't have an attached bathroom. Separated from her bedroom by Sully's office, it was the last room at the end of the hallway. Several large pieces of equipment were pushed against the black walls, and a large cabinet took up one corner. A window shade muted the bright sunlight outside. She spotted several eyebolts screwed into the ceiling in strategic locations.

Sully followed her gaze. "They're screwed into the roof trusses, so they can bear weight."

"How much weight?"

He shrugged. "At least four hundred pounds. They're reinforced with metal plates." He pointed to one X-shaped structure. "St. Andrew's Cross." He explained how it was used, then worked his way around the room naming the devices and basic uses. He could have been holding a seminar on decomposition rates or blood spatter patterns for a group of fellow cops, not BDSM furniture.

He finished. "Well?"

"Well what?"

"Want to know more?"

She glanced at Mac and didn't miss the desperate look on his face. He worried she'd be scared off, that much was blatantly obvious. "Do I need to?"

Sully hobbled over to one of the benches and heavily sat with a pained grunt. "Here's the thing. We were going to have a party next weekend, but I don't mind canceling it if it's too soon for you."

This wasn't her house. "I won't tell you what you can and can't do under your own roof."

"That's not the point," Sully countered. "I don't want you to feel uncomfortable."

"As long as nobody's doing anything to me, don't cancel your party on my account. I'll turn my TV up and lock my door."

Mac looked worried. Sully nodded. "Okay." He studied Mac's attire. "Why are you still dressed?"

Mac blushed but stripped off the sweatpants. It was Clarisse's turn to blush. Okay, so maybe there were major perks to this arrangement.

"If you have any questions, you're always welcomed to ask," Sully assured her.

"Why do you have to beat him?"

"I don't *have* to."

"Then why do it?" They said ask questions? By God, she'd ask.

Mac didn't wait for Sully to answer. "Because I like it," he softly said, glancing at Sully as if for reassurance.

"How can anyone enjoy getting beaten?"

"It's not as simple as that," Sully interjected. "Only by seeing it over time can you understand. Punishment isn't the same as play. It's not all about pain, a lot of it is sensual."

She shivered and gripped her mug more tightly.

Sully wasn't finished. "Mac always has the ability to stop anything he doesn't like. He can call red." He glanced at Mac. "That brings me to another point. We don't want to force our lifestyle on you. You are, however, welcome to watch if the door is open. Or if something happens you aren't comfortable seeing, speak up and we'll take it behind closed doors."

"Does my uncle know what you do?"

"No, not really. He suspects I'm in charge, but that's it." He motioned to Mac, who helped him stand. "I'm not mentally at my best today, between the pain and the painkillers. So I need to give you a rain check on going over what I want you to do to help me out. Basically, you'll be my administrative assistant. As far as household duties, you and Mac can split them as he sees fit." Mac started to protest, but Sully hushed him. "You *will* split your duties with her, slave. That'll give you more time to work on the boat, keep your paperwork up to date, stuff like that. You said you wished you could take the boat out more often. Now you can."

Mac finally nodded, but he didn't look totally happy. "Yes, Master."

With Mac's assistance, Sully limped down the hall and back to the couch. "You'll help Mac on the boat as he needs. Mac will come up with a reasonable pay scale for that. For what you'll do around the house and for me, I'll pay you two hundred a week cash, and you'll get free room and board and the car on top of that. I'll also pay your insurance. Is that okay?"

She numbly nodded. "Yeah, that's fine." A minimum of eight hundred a month, free and clear, in addition to whatever Mac paid her.

Add that to what she still had in savings, it wouldn't take long to build a nice nest egg. After six months, she'd have more than enough to afford a small apartment and buy a cheap car of her own.

"I'll pay you cash so Bryan can't track you. Once that situation's handled, I'll adjust your pay so your after-tax income is still the same."

"Thanks."

Mac helped Sully rearrange himself on the couch. Mac started to hand him the lap desk, but Sully waved him off. "No, I think I need a nap." His face appeared pinched with pain. "Let the pain meds kick in." He shot a serious look at Mac. "Make a chore schedule of some sort by the end of the day. Doesn't have to be elaborate, but you will let her take turns with chores."

Mac reddened. "Yes, Master."

Clarisse followed Mac into the kitchen. Then he spotted the laundry basket still sitting on the floor. "Well, you could help me with that." He changed course and she followed him into their bedroom, where he dumped the clothes onto the bed.

It didn't look like a monster lived here. As she helped Mac fold clothes, she snuck glances around, trying to spot anything out of the ordinary.

That sighting came when he opened the door to their large walk-in closet and flipped on the light. In the corner stood a small umbrella stand. Inside it, an umbrella, two more walking canes, several thin lengths of wood, and a few things that if she had to identify them, she'd swear they were riding crops.

She gulped.

Mac followed her gaze and smiled. "Punishment canes. Rattan." He pulled one of the thin, whippy rods from the stand and showed it to her. "Depending on how it's used it can feel fantastic, or slice the skin open and flay flesh right off the bone."

"How can that possibly feel good?"

"Turn around," he softly said.

She eyed him.

"I won't hurt you," he promised.

She reluctantly turned.

She forced herself not to flinch when he touched her right shoulder, between her neck and arm, with the cane. "Don't move." He started a gentle but firm bouncing rhythm with the wooden rod that didn't hurt at all. In fact, it felt more like a massage than a maiming. As she relaxed, he increased the force a little, until she closed her eyes and reached out to the closet doorway for support. After a few minutes, he switched to her other shoulder and repeated the same process until she relaxed so much that her eyes popped open when he stopped.

She turned. "That's it?"

He slid the cane into the stand. "Did it hurt?"

She shook her head. Hell, it actually felt pretty good there at the end as she'd relaxed and her muscles loosened.

"Maybe one day he'll let me work you over with a heavy flogger. When I finish, you'll think you had a spa massage." He winked.

She helped him finish putting clothes away. As she opened one drawer, the sight of leather cuffs and a few other intimate odds and ends greeted her.

He noticed her expression. "Sorry, should have warned you about that drawer."

When they returned to the living room, Sully was already asleep. Mac retrieved his sweatpants from the playroom and led her downstairs to the utility room to show her where everything was. She stared at the exercise equipment. Maybe she could make use of that now that her body didn't hurt. Work off a little of her excess physical baggage.

"Can I use this?"

"Of course. Help yourself. May I ask why?"

She rolled her eyes. "You're kidding, right?"

He frowned and leaned against the washer. "No, I'm not. You don't need to work out."

Clarisse snorted in disgust. "You know, I appreciate it, and it's sweet of you, but cut the bullshit."

"Clarisse." His firm tone, the one she thought of as his "boat voice." "I meant it when I said it. You're beautiful the way you are. You don't need to work out. Want to? That's fine. Don't you dare let me catch you driving yourself crazy dieting and working out."

The intensity in his voice made her blush. "Whatever," she

mumbled self-consciously.

He caught her hands and made her look at him. "Sweetie, you are beautiful. I don't lie. I don't like getting my ass whipped for that. Exercising to be healthy, fine, I'll go along with that. If you try to turn yourself into some skinny little anorexic waif, I'll force feed you rice pudding."

"Rice pudding, huh?"

"Yeah. One of my specialties." He pulled her to him for a quick hug. "I make it with heavy whipping cream." She snorted, in amusement this time. He laughed when he realized what he'd said. "Haha, very funny, girlie."

* * * *

Another reason Sully hated the painkillers—the dreams. He usually experienced really vivid ones when in the narcotic's grip. Mostly bad dreams that left him sweating and trembling as he relived the shooting.

As he napped on the sofa, his dreams turned slightly more distant. Standing nearby while Jason questioned a man with sandy blond hair who sat on the back bumper of a rescue wagon. The ambulance carrying the man's sister had just pulled out. Gauging from the blood patterns on the guy's clothes, he'd been the one to find her, not harm her.

"Please, can I go? I need to be with her!" Tears rimmed his brown eyes, but there was no spray of blood on his face or in his hair to declare him guilty.

"I'm sorry, Mr. MacCaffrey. I'm almost done," Jason said.

Sully listened as Jason quickly ran through the standard questions. One of the crime scene techs took pictures of the guy and scrapings from under his fingernails.

"I'm sorry, sir. I'll need to take your shirt as evidence."

The man stood and removed it. One of the EMTs brought over a bottle of saline to rinse the blood off his hands and arms.

If Sully hated anything about his job, it was this, the grieving kin. Not dealing with them, but struggling against his own memories, demons, and nightmares as he tried to help them through the process.

"I'm going inside, Jayce," Sully said. Jason nodded. Sully walked to the front door and showed his badge to the uniformed deputy standing guard.

He pulled up short at the large pool of blood on the floor. Scanning the house, Sully fought to contain his rage. Young female victim, attacked by the husband, most likely. Lots of pictures on the walls, many showing a woman he guessed would turn out to be the victim. Quite a few of them including the man being questioned outside.

He couldn't stand it. He returned to Jason, who was finishing with MacCaffrey. "Mr. MacCaffrey, give me your keys. I'll drive you. My partner can follow us."

Jason arched an eyebrow at him.

The man fumbled in his jeans for his keys and handed them over with a trembling hand.

"Are you sure you don't want to have the EMTs transport you to the hospital?" he asked. "Get you checked out?" He suspected the man was close to shock.

"No. I want to be with Betsy."

Jason nodded. "Go ahead. They transported her to Harborside. I'll catch you there."

The man led Sully to his truck, grabbed a duffel bag from behind the seat, rummaged around and found a shirt, and pulled it on. From the look of his tan and firm, natural muscles, he was used to hard outdoors work. He climbed into the passenger seat and waited for Sully.

Sully noticed the stacks of collapsed boxes and other moving supplies in the truck bed as he opened the driver side door. He threaded the truck between emergency vehicles and marked patrol cars as he pulled out of the driveway.

"Why do you think it was her husband, Mr. MacCaffrey?" he quietly asked.

"Because the bastard's been beating on her for years. I told you guys, I was moving her out tonight." He closed his eyes as tears rolled down his face. He punched the dash. "I should have made her leave him sooner. Dammit!" He broke down sobbing. "This is my fault! I should have been here for her!" He stared out the window. "She met the fucker while I was in Iraq. If I'd been home and not in the fucking Army, I never would have let her marry the bastard. Or I would have killed the fucker myself the first time he hit her."

"She's an adult. You can't force someone to do something if they don't want to."

"She's my little sister!" He moaned. "Aw, fuck. I've got to call my baby brother."

"Baby?"

"Well, that's how I think of Jim. I'm the oldest, I'm twenty-eight. He's twenty."

"Do you have other family?"

"No." He slumped against the door. "My mom died last year. It's just us three kids."

Sully sympathized. His own mother had been murdered by her boyfriend when he was only seventeen.

MacCaffrey pulled out his cell phone, called, and broke the news to his brother. When he hung up, he stared out the window again.

"I can't lose her, man. She's my life, they both are. They're all I've got."

Sully stayed with Brant at the hospital, using his badge to get them faster access to information and doctors than might normally be available. Sully was on a first name basis with Brant by the time his brother arrived. Within three hours, the prognosis was known and it wasn't good. Sully called Jason to update him and have him inform the state attorney's office the charges would most likely be updated to murder within a few days.

He knew he was getting personally involved when he shouldn't, but he couldn't help it. He saw too much of himself in the younger man.

He sat with the brothers all night as Betsy was taken from surgery and moved into the SICU. He stayed with them for their first visit with her, offering them support and helping them navigate the quagmire of red tape.

Jason tried to get Sully to go home, but he wouldn't. "I can't leave them. Not like this. They need someone."

Jason shook his head. "This isn't your mom all over again. You need to maintain your distance."

"Fuck that, they need someone to lean on." It's not like Cybil would miss him.

If she was even home.

Better to focus on helping someone else through their pain than having to face his own. At least something good could come of it.

Sully listened to the brothers tell stories about their sister and comforted them when the doctors made their final grim prognosis. By this time, Jason had gone home. Sully stayed with the two men. A uniformed deputy had been assigned to stand watch in the SICU in case the husband showed up. He hadn't been apprehended yet.

"Brant, let me take you home so you can get a shower and change clothes." He needed one too. "They won't let you back in until morning." The man seemed emotionally numb, trapped in the denial stage of his grief. His younger brother had left for home an hour earlier to shower and change clothes and would be back soon.

On the ride north, Brant slumped in the passenger side. "Why are you doing this for us?" he hoarsely asked. "Not that I'm complaining, seriously."

Sully gripped the steering wheel and fought his own demons. "Because I need to."

"How do I get through this? I can't lose her. She's my little sister."

"You keep putting one foot in front of the other. That's all you can do. Don't look ahead. Just focus on the next step."

Over the days that followed, Sully used some of his personal days to stay with the brothers, console them, sit with them. When the brothers made the final decision to discontinue Betsy's life support, Sully kept a supporting arm around each man as they watched her life end. He helped them plan the funeral and sat with them through the service.

Despite the horrible circumstances, he considered Brant a friend and knew he was one of the few people who could honestly say he truly understood exactly what Brant felt. The anger, the guilt, the what-ifs.

The *I should have been there and done more* self-loathing.

The sound of pots and pans in the kitchen awakened Sully. When he glanced at the cable box, he realized he'd napped two hours away.

Damn. So much for working.

Mac heard him trying to sit up and hurried out to help him. "Do you want another pain pill, Master?"

Sully studied his lover's worried face, his dream of their past fresh in his mind. He smiled as he reached out and, taking Mac's hand, accepted his help. "No, I'm okay. Let's try the regular stuff. I'm just really stiff." Mac helped Sully limp to the bathroom, then grabbed a tube of ointment on their way back to the couch. Clarisse stood in the kitchen entrance and watched as Mac worked on Sully's leg.

Clarisse moved a little closer. "What does that do?"

Mac didn't look up from where he knelt on the floor, his hands working the tight muscles in Sully's leg. "The PT showed me what to do, warned me this could happen from time to time." He shot Sully a stink-eye look. "Especially when someone doesn't exercise or work their leg like they're supposed to so the muscles don't tighten up."

"He's worse than any drill sergeant," Sully quipped. "You sure can tell he was in the Army."

"Hey, I don't hear you complaining over the naughty nurse game."

* * * *

Clarisse felt her pulse skip when Sully smiled and reached over to tousle Mac's hair. "Okay, you've got me there, *Nurse* Brant."

Mac's beaming smile stirred something in Clarisse's heart. He obviously doted on Sully, loved the man. Who was she to judge what they did in their relationship?

She wouldn't deny a twinge of jealous envy. Bryan had never shown appreciation to her. Especially not the way Sully did with Mac. Sully appeared to love Mac as much as Mac loved him.

Sully tipped his head back and met her gaze. "Watch out. If Mac gets his hands on you for a backrub, he'll have you melting into the carpet. He's great."

Mac blushed. "Thank you, Master."

* * * *

Sully spent the entire day on the sofa, working, napping, and talking with Clarisse. They ordered a pizza for dinner. At bedtime, Clarisse retired for the night and the men returned to their bedroom. Mac surprised Sully when he brought the punishment cane out and presented it to him, then knelt on the floor next to the bed and bowed his head.

"What's this for?"

"I owe Master strokes."

Sully tried to replay the day in his mind, as much as he could remember through the medication, pain, and naps. "Okay, I give. For what? You ditched the clothes."

Mac related his earlier exchange and demonstration with Clarisse and the cane.

Sully considered it, letting Mac sit and stew for a moment. "You didn't actually touch her though? Just with the cane?"

"Just with the cane, Master."

"She enjoyed it?"

"Yes, Master."

Sully fought the urge to laugh, knowing that would hurt Mac's feelings. Mac had done more to win back her trust with that short demonstration than he realized.

"Stand up and bend over."

Mac complied. Sully didn't stand. He lined up the cane from where he sat and laid only one stroke across Mac's ass. "That's all."

Mac frowned. "Master?"

He immediately gave Mac a second one. "That's for questioning me."

Mac took the offered can and returned it to the closet. Only when they were situated in bed did Sully explain. "I only gave you one because you felt you needed it. You didn't break any rules. You didn't hurt her. In fact, that might have helped change her perceptions in a good way. You know why you earned the second."

"Sorry, Master."

Over the years, during the bad times they'd found the best position for Sully to lay propped against Mac, the larger man's body supporting his leg at the perfect angle to help relieve the pain. Snuggled like that, with Mac's arm around him, Sully settled in and tried to sleep. It not only helped with his pain, but the contact with Mac's body also helped keep the bad dreams away.

His safe harbor.

"Thank you for taking such good care of me, Brant," Sully said. "I appreciate it."

Mac rubbed his chin across the top of Sully's head. "Thank you for allowing me to serve you, Master."

Chapter Eleven

On Wednesday afternoon, Mac vocally protested when Sully wanted to go downstairs to work out.

"You need to rest your leg another day or two, Master."

Sully still heavily relied on his cane. "Not exercising is what got me in trouble."

"Master, I don't want you to hurt yourself again. Just relax today and—"

"Stop, slave."

Clarisse looked up at Sully's sharp tone. Mac's face reddened before his gaze dropped to the floor.

"Go bring it and meet me in the playroom," Sully ordered. "Now."

Mac disappeared to their bedroom and returned a moment later carrying a punishment cane. He followed Sully to the playroom.

They left the door open.

Clarisse heard their voices. Curiosity got the better of her. She quietly walked down the hallway and peeked through the open door.

Mac knelt on the floor, his head bowed.

"What have I told you about talking back, slave?"

"I'm sorry, Master. I'm worried about your leg."

"What is the proper way to express your opinion?"

"I ask to talk with you."

"And did you?"

"No, Master. I've earned twenty-five."

"Over the bench. Now."

Mac complied. She gasped when he stood and she realized despite that the fact he was about to get smacked, his cock stood proud and rigid.

Holy crap!

Mac leaned over one of the benches, where Sully quickly delivered the blows. Red stripes crisscrossed Mac's ass and upper thighs, but not once did she hear him cry out.

Pain in her fingers made her realize she'd grabbed hold of the door frame and was hanging on for dear life. She couldn't bring herself to leave.

Sully walked across the room and picked up a tube of lotion, then returned to Mac and applied it to his flesh. Clarisse didn't know how to reconcile the tender gesture with the punishment she'd just witnessed.

When Sully finished, he gently patted Mac on the back. "Finished."

Mac rose from the bench, then knelt in front of Sully again. "Thank you, Master."

Sully's fingers twined in Mac's hair. "Feeling better?"

"Yes, Master." Mac nuzzled his forehead against Sully's thigh.

"I'm going downstairs to work out. You may come with me to keep an eye on me, if you want. I promise I won't overdo it."

"Thank you, Master. I will."

"Then put this away and get some clothes on."

Sully handed Mac the cane. Mac stood. When he spotted Clarisse by the door, he smiled. She ducked into the hallway and leaned against the wall, trying to catch her breath. Mac appeared, carrying the cane.

"You all right, sweetie?"

She nodded. She couldn't look him in the eye, but when her gaze dropped to the floor, she found herself staring at his erect cock.

Clarisse swallowed hard and looked up at Mac's smiling face.

He winked. Then he turned and walked down the hall. The angry red stripes prominently crisscrossed his ass.

"Are you okay?"

Sully's voice startled her. She turned. "Yeah."

He leaned against the door frame, his arms crossed over his chest and holding his walking cane. "Want to talk about it?"

"It's between you two."

He pushed off from the wall. "You live here. I do care about your feelings."

"I don't have any say in the matter." She turned to go, but he reached out and touched her arm. Not grabbing, yet the gesture stopped her anyway.

"Clarisse," he softly said, "you have to understand it's who he is. What he needs."

"I don't know if I can." She returned to her room and shut the door. A few minutes later, she heard the men go downstairs. Then the faint sound of music filtered through the floor.

She couldn't get the sight of Mac's erect cock out of her mind. How could punishment *excite* him? Yeah, she understood the theories behind what they did, but it didn't make it any easier to digest.

She also didn't understand why it was suddenly so important to her that she do.

* * * *

The next afternoon she drove the Bug and visited Uncle Tad by herself. She tried to visit him every day. With the worst of her bruises fading, it was a relief not to pancake makeup on her face. He welcomed her in, and they settled on the couch to talk.

"What's on your mind, little girl? You doing okay? You look worried."

Clarisse forced a smile. "I'm fine."

He scowled as much as he could with his face half frozen by the stroke. "You'd better not be considering moving."

She blushed. "What do you mean?"

He gripped her hand with a strength she didn't think he could possess. "Sully and Mac are good men. I've known them for years. Dammit, I don't want to worry about you being on your own and falling for some asshole who's gonna beat your brains out and finish what Bryan started!"

"Uncle Tad—"

"No!" He pulled himself to his feet and turned on her, shaking his finger at her like she was a child. "You were so all-fired worried to protect my feelings? Then you listen to me. You don't even *think* about moving out of there, or I swear to Jesus I'll have another stroke just to spite you!"

Clarisse tried not to laugh, but she couldn't help it. "All right, Uncle Tad. I promise I'll stay with them for now."

"No, not 'for now.' That's bullshit. You stay with them until I say otherwise, got it? Don't make me guilt trip you."

"All right, all right. Fine. I promise." Was it a promise she could keep?

She'd spent the night before dreaming of Mac tying her up and spanking her before making love to her—not exactly something she'd expected. Agreeably a damn sight better than her nightmares of Bryan trying to kill her, but when she awoke she was left with a dull, empty ache in her heart.

Not to mention an uncomfortably erotic throbbing and dampness between her legs.

Tad smiled, apparently knowing he'd won the battle. "That's better."

* * * *

Saturday, the morning of the party, Clarisse helped Mac in the kitchen with preparations. She still didn't know how she'd handle the night. Sully invited her to watch and mingle if she wanted. If she felt more comfortable, she could close herself in her room for the evening.

Either way, their guests had already been informed of her presence so there would be no misunderstandings.

Mac loaned her his MP3 player and Sully's noise-cancelling headphones he sometimes used while working. Between those and the TV, there would be no way she could hear anything…if she so chose.

By eight o'clock that evening, Mac had rearranged the living room. He moved a couple of the benches from the playroom out to the living room and locked Sully's office door.

Mac looked handsome in jeans and a black button-up shirt. He still wore his leather collar. Sully had dressed similarly, only in a white shirt.

She'd had the Mac dream several more times, each ending the same way, with Mac's sweet cock plunging into her eager body. That would never happen in real life, duh. Despite his sweet reassurances that he thought she was pretty, he was—*hellooo*—gay.

Add to the mix his blatantly obvious devotion to Sully and she felt a little jealous for a whole bunch of irrational reasons she couldn't explain or deny.

The house phone rang at a quarter to nine. Sully answered, then buzzed the gate code to allow the caller in. Mac pulled Clarisse in for a hug.

"The first guests are here. You're welcome to stay or go. It's up to you."

Curiosity had gotten the better of her. "I'll stay for a little while, at least." She'd pulled on sweatpants and a baggy T-shirt of Mac's that hung nearly to her knees.

Mac left her in the kitchen and walked downstairs to greet their guests. Sully had turned the TV off and put on music. "Curious?"

She blushed. "Yeah."

He limped over. "You do realize I love him and would never do anything I thought would harm him, right?"

She nodded as his grey gaze impaled her. An unquenchable need to understand Mac's relationship with Sully had taken over. She'd gladly escaped Bryan's abuse. Why would anyone willingly subject themselves to punishment?

Why did he trust Sully so much?

Why couldn't she?

And why the *fuck* did it matter so much to her?

Mac returned with their guests, a man and a woman. Mac carried a large duffel bag. The woman wore a trench coat, impossibly high stiletto heels, and a black leather collar around her neck. The guy wore blue jeans, a chambray shirt, and a brown leather vest. They both looked like average people.

Sully introduced her. "Clarisse, this is Bob and Jenna."

She shook hands with them and exchanged greetings before Sully led them into the living room. Jenna slipped off her coat, which Mac took for her. Beneath it, she wore a black leather corset that pushed her breasts up and left her nipples exposed. Her frilly short skirt testified to the fact that she hadn't worn any panties, just a garter belt and stockings. She reminded Clarisse of a pornographic ballerina.

Clarisse understood why Mac had laid decorative throw covers on all the furniture.

As other guests arrived, Mac helped them with their things. A husband and wife couple, Alex and Doreen, with Doreen obviously submissive to her husband. Again, Alex wore slacks and a button-up shirt and could have been on his way to dinner. Doreen wore knee boots and a full skirt that skimmed her knees. She'd unbuttoned her loose blouse to her waist to expose the black bustier she wore underneath. Around her left wrist, she wore a silver charm bracelet with small bells that tinkled every time she moved.

The last couple, the woman was in charge. The man, Mike, wore a high leather collar that kept his chin up and looked uncomfortable.

Clarisse stayed in the kitchen as she listened and observed, feeling critical and curious at the same time.

The woman, Yvette, had short, spiked, bright orange hair. She gave Mac a huge hug and left her arm draped around him while she talked with Sully. Then she looked at Mike. "What are you doing standing there, boy?"

"Sorry, Ma'am." He started unbuttoning his shirt.

"That's better." Yvette returned her attention to Sully and Mac as the man stripped, neatly folded his clothes and laid them on top of the rolling suitcase they'd brought, and then knelt before her.

He wore a leather harness that circled his waist and passed between his legs and...

Clarisse tried not to stare. She couldn't help herself. The wicked metal cage, composed of several rings, encompassed his balls and cock.

Yvette hooked her arm through Mac's. Clarisse wanted to walk over and push her away from him.

Then Sully caught Clarisse's eye from across the room. "Mac, bring me something to drink, please," he ordered.

Yvette released his arm and he headed to the kitchen. Sully still talked to the woman, but his gaze never wavered from Clarisse.

Mac walked into the kitchen and fixed Sully a drink. "You okay, sweetie?"

"Yeah. Just going to stand here and stare for a while," she tried to joke, her gaze still locked on Sully, unable to look away.

He patted her on the back before returning to Sully's side. Sully took the drink, thanked him, then ordered him to kneel on the floor next to him. With that, he lifted an eyebrow at Clarisse before returning his full attention to Yvette.

Clarisse blushed.

If she didn't know any better, it was as if he'd read her mind, had sensed her jealousy seeing the other woman acting that friendly with Mac.

Clarisse fixed herself a plate of food and leaned against the far counter to eat, out of sight of the living room. A moment later, Jenna walked in carrying a bottle of wine and looking for a corkscrew.

Clarisse helped her rummage through drawers, found it, and

handed it to her. "Here you go."

"Thanks." She set the bottle on the counter to open it. "You've never seen a party like this, I bet."

Her friendly smile couldn't be denied a reply. Clarisse reached over to help steady the bottle as Jenna worked on the cork. "No, can't say as I have."

"We don't bite." She giggled. "Well, actually Yvette does bite, but only people who want to be bitten."

"I'll pass."

As Jenna made progress with the cork, they shifted the bottle to give her a better grip. "So do I. I'm a sensual slut, not a pain slut," she said and giggled again. The cork gave way with a *pop*. Jenna handed Clarisse the corkscrew. "Thanks for the help. Feel free to ask me anything, I like to talk about the lifestyle. Bob and I host the local Munch." At Clarisse's obviously confused look, Jenna smiled. "It's like a vanilla dinner where we get together and eat and talk."

Weird. This wasn't scrapbooking or bowling. This was whips and chains. "Thanks, I'll keep that in mind."

Jenna returned to the living room while Clarisse finished her food.

Stay or go? She felt plain, frumpy and underdressed—overdressed, actually—in her sweats and T-shirt. The women all looked beautiful, hair and makeup and nails done. All she'd done was run a brush through her hair and pulled it back into a ponytail.

She ducked outside through the back sliders and walked around the porch to the stairs. She had a load of laundry in the dryer that should be finished. She took her time sorting and folding, and then she grabbed paper towels and spray cleaner and started wiping down the washer and drier even though they didn't need it. She cleaned the downstairs bathroom. She ran a bucket of mop water and started on the tile floor when she heard footsteps on the stairs.

The door opened. "You in here, sweetie?" Sully called.

She tensed. "Yeah, I'm here."

He closed the door behind him and walked into the laundry

alcove. "You don't have to do this tonight," he softly said.

Clarisse opted for forced chipperness. "That's all right. No one will be down here tonight. I meant to do it today and got sidetracked."

"It doesn't need it."

"Still has to be done."

"Clarisse," he firmly said.

She tensed and forced herself to keep breathing slowly and steadily. "What?"

"Please look at me."

She turned. If only he wasn't so ruggedly handsome. His good looks differed from Mac's easy, open charm. Sully's hard face spoke of determination and an iron backbone, his smiles warming his face when he chose to use them.

"Answer me truthfully. Are you okay?"

"Yeah. I'm just…easing into things."

"I won't let her touch Mac again."

She blinked.

Sully smiled at her obvious surprise. "You looked like you wanted to rip her arm off."

Clarisse blushed, grabbed the mop, and busied herself swabbing the floor. Not knowing what to say in reply, she kept her mouth shut.

* * * *

Sully watched her, knew better than to push her. He hadn't been sure he'd read her reaction correctly until he said that.

Without another word he returned to the party, an idea forming in his mind. She felt jealous, had feelings for Mac. He stifled his envy that those feelings weren't for him.

He could, however, use it to his advantage.

By the time Clarisse returned upstairs, Sully had stripped Mac while Yvette tied Mike to one of the benches in the living room and started warming him up. Sully didn't say anything to Mac about his brief talk with Clarisse. An hour later, while Doreen talked with Clarisse, Sully ordered Mac to fetch his wrist and ankle cuffs.

Doreen squealed. "Ooh! Sully's going to play with Mac! I love watching them play!" Doreen had shed her blouse, but her bustier didn't expose her breasts the way Jenna's did. Like a high-heeled force of nature, she latched onto Clarisse's arm and led her to the playroom, following Sully and the others.

Sully had counted on Doreen's enthusiasm, from the way she'd befriended Clarisse, to get Clarisse into the playroom. If that hadn't worked, he'd been prepared to play with Mac in the living room despite how it would change their routine.

Mac fetched the requested implements as Sully unbuttoned his shirt and draped it over a chair. He didn't look at Clarisse, but caught glimpses of her standing off to the side, listening to Doreen's nonstop, golf-whisper narration of events. He plugged his MP3 player into the small speaker system in the room and set it to one of his favorite scene mixes.

When Mac lay face-down on the bench, Sully clipped his wrist cuffs to it and knelt next to him so he could whisper in his ear. He knew Clarisse couldn't hear him between the music and Doreen.

"I want you to call red tonight."

Mac already wore his ball gag and looked at Sully with confusion clearly visible in his expression.

"Don't question me, slave. When I switch from the cane to the singletail, give me a few strokes and then call red. Understand?"

Mac hesitated, then rotated his left hand, their signal for green or yes.

Patting him on the shoulder, Sully ignored the questions in Mac's eyes and his arched eyebrow. He clipped Mac's ankle cuffs to the bench and grabbed a light flogger to start their warm-up.

He fought the urge to hurry, hoping Mac didn't sink so far into subspace he couldn't remember his command. He took his time, checking in frequently while knowing that he'd owe Mac an apology and a make-up play session later. He paused at one point to reach between Mac's legs and squeeze his balls.

Mac's hips bucked against him, wanting more, wanting release.

Sully slapped him on the ass. "Not yet, slave. Later."

* * * *

Clarisse couldn't tune out Doreen's soft voice as she watched Sully play with Mac. There remained no doubt in Clarisse's mind that Mac enjoyed it, but reconciling that with common sense and her own experiences still troubled her.

Sully's back muscles rippled with every stroke as he alternated between using the flogger and sensuous strokes from his hands. Her breath caught in her throat.

"They look beautiful together, don't they?" Doreen whispered. "He gets Mac so deep into subspace it's amazing. I wish I could do that, go deep like Mac does."

Sully put down the flogger and picked up a cane similar to the one he used on Mac before. She winced as every hard stroke landed, but she watched how Sully alternated hard strikes across his ass with lighter ones, reminiscent of how Mac had demonstrated on her, across his shoulders and the backs of his thighs. After ten minutes of this, Sully switched to a four-foot whip.

Clarisse cringed. Correctly interpreting her reaction, Doreen patted her on the arm. "Mac loves this part. That's his favorite one."

Sully took a few practice strokes in the air, gauging his distance and stroke, before stepping in and nailing Mac in the ass several times in quick succession. Then Mac raised his left hand as far as the cuff would allow. He rapidly shook his fist up and down.

Sully immediately stopped. He removed Mac's ball gag and bent in. Clarisse couldn't hear them over the music. Sully looked at her. "Please go into our bathroom and grab that tube of ointment off the counter, the one Mac uses on my leg."

Clarisse raced to do it. By the time she returned, Sully had Mac's right leg unclipped and stretched out, massaging it, but Mac's ball gag was back in place.

She handed Sully the tube and watched as he squirted ointment in his hand and spent several minutes working on Mac's calf. How did she reconcile that tender treatment with the sadistic scourging he'd administered him?

After several minutes, Sully lowered Mac's leg. "Better, slave?"

Mac rotated his left hand.

"Do you want me to continue playing or stop?"

Mac rotated his hand again.

Sully rehooked Mac's ankle cuff and picked up a flogger.

Clarisse returned to her place next to Doreen. After a few minutes, Sully leaned in and whispered something to Mac. Mac's ass had started gyrating in the air by this point, his rigid cock desperate for release.

Whatever Sully said to Mac, it made the bound man moan loudly enough Clarisse could hear him over the music.

Sully returned to his place behind Mac, but as he did, he let his gaze knowingly settle on Clarisse for a moment before he turned and reached under Mac's hips with his right hand. With his left hand, he started spanking Mac. Heat filled Clarisse's face as she realized what he was doing—jerking Mac off.

"How did Sully know to stop?" Clarisse asked Doreen for an excuse to take her attention off the two men.

"Mac called red," Doreen said. "Which is really rare. He must have cramped bad. That thing Mac did with his hand, that's their code. I think that's only the third time I've ever seen Mac call red, and they get pretty intense."

Clarisse digested that while Sully finished Mac off. Mac tensed, his back arching as a loud moan escaped around the ball gag. When he finally went limp on the bench, Sully got a towel and cleaned him up. He applied a different lotion to Mac's reddened flesh, then unclipped Mac and rubbed his arms and legs for him before letting him sit up. He wrapped a blanket around the other man and stood there holding him while Mac sat on the bench and leaned against Sully, his eyes closed.

For the briefest of moments, Clarisse wished it was her wrapped securely in Sully's arms as she remembered the night she spent with them.

Or better, in Mac's.

Alex caught Doreen's eye and, crooking his finger at her, motioned her outside. She grabbed Clarisse's arm. "Want to watch us?"

Clarisse glanced back at Mac and Sully. Sully's eyes had also closed, his face buried in Mac's hair as he whispered something.

She wanted to stay. She wanted to be a part of them.

And part of her couldn't stand to watch them without being a part of it.

She didn't really want to watch Doreen play, but it was a good excuse to leave. She followed Doreen out of the room.

* * * *

When they were alone in the playroom and Sully knew Mac had regained most of his senses, he left him sitting on the bench and turned off the music. Mac's brown eyes followed him.

"What?" Sully asked.

Mac sent one eyebrow skyward. "Far be it from me to question Master."

Sully walked to the playroom door, glanced down the hallway to make sure the coast was clear, and shut it. "I wanted to prove a point. I also didn't want to force you into telling her a lie."

"So *you'll* lie to her?"

Sully shrugged. "I haven't lied. She hasn't asked me what happened. Pretty obvious I took care of a leg cramp though, right?"

He winked.

Mac laughed and shook his head. "Son of a bitch, you're a sneaky fuck, aren't you?"

"Excuse me?"

"You're a sneaky fuck, *Master*."

Sully held up three fingers.

"It's worth it," Mac said. "You want to give them to me now or later?"

"In the morning. Go clean up. You can put on a pair of shorts if you want. Doreen should be begging her head off in a few minutes."

* * * *

Clarisse returned to her spot in the kitchen where she could look over the counter and watch the events in the living room from a safe distance. Alex used several ropes to bind Doreen, who had stripped, in a kneeling position on one of the benches. He started warming her up with a good spanking.

Sully reappeared first and poured himself a glass of iced tea. "You all right?" he asked Clarisse.

"Peachy."

He smirked before he returned to the living room.

When Mac emerged from their bedroom, he had removed the cuffs and donned a pair of shorts. He walked into the kitchen and stood next to Clarisse. "You all right?"

"I'm fine!" She realized how short she sounded. "Sorry. Sully just asked me." Sully was helping Alex do something to Doreen. When Sully stepped to the side, she realized he held a vibrator in his hand, which he'd shoved between Doreen's spread and bound legs.

Another irrational wave of jealousy—or was it envy—washed through her.

"What's he doing?" she whispered to Mac.

Mac slipped his arm around her shoulders. "Sully helps out like that. Not everyone, just a few friends. Makes it more intense for the sub."

Alex stood in front of Doreen, pinching and twisting her nipples as she wriggled against her bonds.

Then Sully's stern order. "Don't you dare come yet. You haven't been given permission."

Doreen squealed in frustration and started begging. "Please, Sir? Please let me come!"

"No. You don't come until I tell you to."

Tears ran down the woman's face as the two men mercilessly tormented her. Sully said, "Hold it until I say so."

"I can't—"

"You will, or your Master will whip your ass."

She bucked her hips, trying to escape the vibrator Sully kept pressed against her clit. "Hold it," he ordered.

Clarisse instinctively pressed closer to Mac, unable to sort through the emotions and desires rolling through her.

"Please, Sir! Please let me come!" Doreen's begging fell on deaf ears as Sully continued to torment her.

Finally, he said, "All right, come *now!*"

Doreen screamed, sobbed as her back rounded and an explosive climax ripped through her. Sully didn't relent, keeping the vibrator pressed against her. "Again, come now!"

She screamed again, sobbing and wriggling, trying to get away from the devious device, but Sully and Alex weren't through with her yet. Alex helped hold her down as Sully pulled the vibrator away and replaced it with his other hand. "Come again, now!"

Her screams dissolved into ragged sobs as he made her come four more times in quick succession before he stopped. When she limply collapsed onto the bench, Sully left the room. Alex stepped in and took over, draped his arm across her back and whispered to her.

Clarisse, her brain swirling, realized she was stiffly standing against Mac.

Mac gently shook her. "Fry your brain?"

"Did she really come that many times?"

Mac laughed. "Oh, yeah. She loves to play like this, especially with her job. Gives her a way to release her stress."

"Why? What does she do?"

"She's a criminal prosecutor with the circuit court. Alex is a family law attorney."

Clarisse tried to absorb that information. "Where'd Sully go?" She felt like she could barely talk.

"Washing his hands, probably."

Ew.

Okay, that finished her off. She disengaged herself from Mac, mumbled an apology, and returned to her room. She shut and locked the door behind her.

What the fuck?

She turned on her TV and, for good measure, used the MP3 player and headphones. She couldn't focus on anything but the sights and sounds of the evening.

Mac.

The way Sully made Doreen beg to come.

The jealousy she'd felt over Mac.

Okay, fuck, yes, the jealousy she'd felt watching Sully with Doreen.

It didn't make sense. None of it made sense. She should be sickened or at the very least unmoved, shouldn't she? Not...

Horny.

She closed her eyes and pulled a pillow over her head. At some point she drifted to sleep, but she dreamed of both Sully and Mac taking turns fucking her while she was bound to a bench. When she woke up and removed the headphones, she couldn't hear anything but the TV. The clock read three-thirty, and when she shut off the TV, the house sounded quiet.

Cautiously, she unlocked her bedroom door and peeked out. The house stood empty, dark, silent. Apparently, they'd already cleaned up, because the living room had been put back to normal and the slip covers removed.

Clarisse closed her door and undressed before slipping under the covers with her mind a swirling mass of confused emotions.

Chapter Twelve

The next morning, Clarisse leaned against the kitchen doorway and watched Mac wash dishes. Weird. What did it say about her that she'd quickly come to see a naked man in a collar washing dishes as a normal fixture in her world?

"What's on your mind?" he asked, startling her.

"What?"

He turned from the sink, that playful smile on his face. "What's rolling around that pretty brain of yours, kiddo?"

From the heat in her face, she knew she was blushing. "Honestly?"

His smile faded. He dried his hands on the dishtowel and leaned against the counter. "Always. Total honesty, you know that. It's law in this house."

She tried to keep her eyes off his cock and her mind off how she'd dreamed about it plunging deep into her...

Clarisse sat at the table. "How can you let him do this to you?"

"Do what?"

"Treat you the way he treats you?"

Mac pulled out his chair, the one he kept a towel on, and sat across from her. His voice softened. "Treats me how?"

With his cock safely out of sight under the table, she met his eyes. "You're his slave."

A hint of a smile returned to his face. "That's sort of the whole point. You hadn't guessed that by now?"

"How can you do that? Let him run your life."

"I love him."

"How do you know he won't throw you out one day?"

Mac shrugged and leaned back in his chair. "I don't. I don't know that any more than he knows I won't up and leave one day. I'm not held hostage, if you haven't noticed. I'm here willingly. We trust and love each other."

With the questions coming, she couldn't stop. "The things you let him do to you, like at the party and even the everyday stuff. Doesn't that make you feel...used?"

He grinned. "Again, that's sort of the whole point. For me, at least. I want to serve him."

She didn't know what worried her more, that he seemed so okay with it or that of late her fantasies were of letting Mac tie her up and do some of them to her. "He beats you!"

"Not nearly hard enough sometimes, doll."

At her shocked silence, he grinned. "I love this. Don't you get it? I trust him. Including last night, I think I can count on one hand the times I've had to safeword for something other than equipment issues. Sully, he'll call a scene a lot faster than I will. He doesn't go nearly far enough for my liking sometimes. He's a worrywart."

More stunned silence from her.

He leaned forward, his elbows on the table, hands clasped. "I like the pain. Haven't you noticed how sometimes I'll goad him so he'll have to punish me?"

She nodded. She'd watched Mac's eyes twinkle all the times Sully held up fingers denoting strokes after an infraction. It had been her suspicion, but she hadn't wanted to voice it, didn't know if that was a taboo subject or not.

"He knows I do it. Sweetie, I love him. More importantly, I trust him. There's been times he's taken me further than I thought I could stand and I didn't safeword and I'm damn glad I didn't. Usually if I safeword, it's because of an equipment malfunction or I get a cramp or I know something's seriously wrong. I rarely safeword because of what he's doing to me."

"But he hurts you."

"Yeah. Isn't it great?" His playful smile melted her.

She shivered. He reached across the table, just enough his fingers brushed the back of her hand. "Not everyone gets off on pain. Like Doreen last night, she's not a pain slut, she likes the bondage and forced orgasm play. I enjoy pain. Vanilla sex doesn't do it for me. He gets off on the control. He needs it. He gives me what I need, and I give him what he needs. It works for us. Every person in the lifestyle is in it for a different reason and practices it in a different way."

He leaned back again, withdrawing his hand. "I mean, I like my turn in the driver's seat every once in a while, too. That's why he decided to let me have him when we're out on the boat. He trusts me as much as I trust him, and every so often he digs doing that."

"But he's *using* you!"

"Fuck yeah, in a good way. It's what I want. He's using *only* me. He's not going around getting his rocks off with just anyone. He needs me as much as I need him."

"What about last night? Doreen."

He shrugged. "He helped out. That doesn't bother me. It gets me off knowing he trusts me as much as I trust him, which is why he lets me be in charge on the boat. I'm the only person he trusts like that. And it mixes it up, gives him some downtime in a way he can safely enjoy it."

"Why not at home? Why don't you take turns?"

Mac's expression turned sad. "He's been hurt in a lot of ways, and not just the shooting. It's not my place to tell his secrets. I can say he's had a damn good reason to not want to trust. I don't blame him. I was there for him to help pick up the pieces, and I was lucky enough to prove to him he could trust me." He looked at her. "He trusted me enough to believe me when I offered myself to him."

She couldn't process that. "You *asked* him to make you his slave?"

"Yeah."

She still found that difficult to believe. "You've got nothing."

"I have Sully. He's my Master. That's everything I need. He's all I need. If I have him, he'll take care of the rest. That's all I need to know." The look on her face must have showed her disbelief. "Besides, you've seen for yourself not everything we do is Master/slave stuff. A lot of it is normal. Do you know what he bought me for our first Christmas together?"

She shook her head.

He smiled. "I got up that morning, and yes, we were full-on slave and Master at that point, and there's a Corvette sitting in the driveway. Not new, but in great shape."

"But whose name was it in?" She struggled to understand, to reconcile the new longing in her soul with the stubborn balking in her mind.

"His. He owns me. Everything that's mine, so to speak, is his. Here's the thing, I never asked him for a new car. We'd been at a car show the weekend before and I saw one there. I was looking at it. I never said I wished I had one, never offered an opinion on it. I spent a few minutes looking at it, and while I knew in my heart I wished I had one, I never told him."

Confusion set in. "So how did he know?"

Mac grinned. "That's the point! He knows me better than I know myself sometimes. He knew from watching me that I wanted one. I didn't even consciously do anything. He just knew."

She thought about the VW in the driveway. "Is that how he knew about the Bug?"

"Naw, that was me. I'll admit I gave him the idea. I knew he'd been planning on getting you a car, and I told him what you'd said about them."

Part of her felt uplifted that the men cared enough about her to do that for her. Part of her felt...disappointed. Sully hadn't read her mind after all.

She shoved that last twinge out of her thoughts. "What if he kicks you out with nothing?"

He shrugged. "He could, but he won't. Legally we have an agreement that if we separate I'll get certain things."

"The Dilly?"

"That's one of them."

"It doesn't scare you?"

"Why should it?"

Wrapping her head around the issue wasn't happening as she hoped it would. She stood and paced the kitchen. "How do you know? How do you know you won't get screwed? In the bad way," she added.

"I don't."

"So you're perfectly okay with him having all this control over you? Faced with the very real possibility of having to start over?"

He shrugged. "I can always get a job, go back to school for my master's degree, something."

It struck her how little she knew about the men. "You went to college?"

"Yeah. Sully made me take advantage of my GI Bill bennies. I had no interest in going to college. He ordered me to. I enlisted in the Army the week after I graduated from high school, went to boot camp a few weeks later. I had no interest in college."

"What's your degree in?"

"Marine biology. Sully said I could pick any major I wanted, but I had to earn a degree in something." He smirked. "So you see, I'm not some poor, dumb asshole without options. I was offered an internship at Mote Marine. I turned it down despite Sully wanting me to take it."

"He *made* you go to school?"

He grinned. "Yeah, how horrible is that? Fuckin' sadist."

Clarisse tried to process that. "You're a marine biologist?"

He lifted an eyebrow. "No. I'm a slave."

She blinked, trying to make sense of that. "Why would you give up a career to do that?"

"I trust him. This is what I want to do for the rest of my life, to serve him." He studied her. "Have you ever really trusted anyone?"

She started to answer, then stopped, thinking about it.

He picked up the conversation. "I trust him to blindfold me, strap me to a cross, and whip the shit out of me and not let anyone else touch me. I trust him to pay the electric bill and buy me food. I trust him not to sell the Dilly out from under me. I'm not saying that level of trust magically appeared overnight. We didn't start out from day one the way we are now. We started out with pretty elaborate boundaries. Eventually, over the years, we dropped almost everything and replaced it with safewording. At some point you have to take the leap and trust you're going to be caught. In exchange for that, I'm perfectly happy to serve him."

The war waged within her. "He was a cop. How do I ever trust one of them!" An old argument and one she knew wasn't valid anymore, but it remained her mistrustful brain's fallback position.

One her mind could comfortably wrap around even while her heart disputed the truth of that belief.

"Not all cops are like Bryan," Mac said. "Most of them aren't. Most of them are decent, caring guys dedicated to their jobs. I'm not saying they're not human and don't make mistakes, but the majority of them don't hurt people."

She crossed her arms in front of her. "He's still a fucking cop. They stick together. Sort of like the Mafia, isn't it?" Any excuse, any lie she could tell herself to deny the new and conflicting feelings struggling to take over.

Anything to stall having to admit the truth to herself.

Mac sadly shook his head. "No, babe. Not even close. Not like that." He closed his eyes. "If Sully could have killed Betsy's husband with his bare hands, he would have. It ripped him up nearly as badly as me when she died. He didn't even know me then. I was the victim's brother. He came to the hospital every day and sat with me and my brother, talked with us. When we finally took her off life support, he stood there with us when it happened. He was there for us during the trial and the asshole's conviction."

He opened his eyes. She noticed they looked too bright, like maybe he was close to tears. "Maybe that's the answer to your question. How can I trust him? Because he walked through hell with me when I was still just part of the job to him. How can he trust me? Because when our positions were reversed, I walked through hell with him and refused to let him give up."

He pushed away from the table and left the kitchen.

* * * *

Sully departed early the next morning for a conference. Although Clarisse didn't revisit the topic, her brain still struggled to make sense of it. Modern women were supposed to be strong and independent and not want to be under anyone's thumb, right? She'd struggled for years under Bryan's anger, chafing under his control and abuse.

So why did she want to throw herself at Mac?

And Sully, to a lesser extent.

By the next day, she couldn't take it anymore. After lunch, she sought Mac out in the study off the living room, where he sat in front of his computer—naked, of course—working on paperwork for the Dilly.

Mac looked up as she walked in. She felt a cautious mask descend. Something she'd never felt from him before.

"Can I interrupt you?" she quietly asked.

He nodded.

"I want to understand. About you and Sully. Why you can do this with him."

"Does it matter? Sully's told you, you can stay here with us as long as you want. When he says that, he means it. I agree with him." He laughed. "See? He *did* ask my opinion on that."

She took a deep breath. "I want to understand what you two have.

I want to be able to get it."

"Why? It's between me and him. We've already told you we'll never force you to be part of us like that. As long as you let us do our thing, respect what and who we are, it's okay."

Her face felt hot, flushed, throbbing as her pulse pounded. "I want to understand," she carefully said, "because I don't understand it. But I want to."

He watched her for several long, silent moments. Her face heated even more under his steady gaze. "Close your eyes," he softly commanded.

She did.

"Don't open them," he said in that same soft, steady voice.

She heard him push his chair back and stand. She tried to listen for him, but his lack of clothing made it impossible.

Then she felt his breath against the back of her neck. When he whispered near her left ear, she flinched. "Trust doesn't happen overnight." He stepped away.

Her breath came in ragged gasps she struggled to control. Where would he be next? What would he do?

Then in her right ear, "Do you trust me not to hurt you?"

She nodded.

His fingers softly brushed up her left arm, making her shiver.

"Don't move," he whispered. "Don't speak until I say so."

His fingers disappeared. Then he repeated the action along her right arm and withdrew his fingers.

For a long moment, nothing. No sound, no movement, no hint of breath.

She jumped when she felt the gentle caress from his lips, warm and moist, along the back of her neck, above her neckline.

Her pulse thrummed in her throat.

His mouth disappeared.

"What do you feel?" he asked. "Tell me."

She struggled for an answer. "I don't know. What am I supposed to feel?"

"I can't tell you that. What do *you* feel?"

"Horny." She blushed even deeper, but his soft, amused chuckle warmed her further.

"I imagine you do." Then he caressed both arms with his fingers. She fought the urge to moan. "What else?"

"Scared," she blurted out.

His fingers hesitated. "Of me?"

"No."

"Then what?"

"I don't know."

"That's a good place to start then, isn't it?" His fingers disappeared, and she sensed him step back. He next spoke from in front of her. "Fear prevents trust. You have to learn to trust, even if it's only one step at a time." She heard him sit. "You can open your eyes."

He now sat at the computer again and stared at the monitor. She felt frozen, incomplete, on the edge of something and she didn't know what.

"That's all?"

"What do you mean?"

There should be more, shouldn't there? "You didn't...there wasn't..."

He grinned. "I already earned myself ten with the cane."

Clarisse fought and lost against her frustration. "Dammit, I want answers, not fucking Yoda!"

He leaned back. She glimpsed a frown, a hint of the expression he wore on the boat. "You have to learn when to appropriately trust. You can't have everything your way. I'm not saying trust everyone all the time or even in the same way."

He turned toward her. "If you're saying you want me to take you to bed and fuck your brains out because you're horny, I can't do that no matter how badly I want to. Sully and I have boundaries in our relationship. We don't cross them without discussing and agreeing first. That's part and parcel of having trust in each other."

Fuck her brains out? She swallowed to form spit. That's *exactly* what she wanted him to do, God help her, and the fact that an immediate flood of moisture pooled in her sex confirmed it. "I didn't ask you to do that," she said. But dammit, she wanted him to.

He smiled, a slight, knowing curve to his lips. "You didn't have to." He turned back to the monitor. "When you can trust—really, deeply trust—then maybe we can talk more."

"Can't you be my...whatever? My Dom? Can't you play with me the way Sully played with Alex and Doreen?"

"Is that something you want?"

She couldn't say it. She nodded.

"Maybe one day."

He didn't say anything else. From the way he focused on his work, she realized the conversation was over. On shaky legs, she walked to her room and closed the door.

* * * *

After she left, Mac leaned back and let out a deep breath. His cock throbbed, harder than ever. He didn't dare touch it, not even to scratch, for fear of exploding. That would earn him an extra twenty-five in addition to the ten he'd get for what he had done with her, for kissing the back of her neck.

He'd like nothing better than to walk into her bedroom and order her to strip and spread her legs and spend all night there with her.

He closed his eyes and took several long, deep breaths to steady himself. Because he wanted to, that's exactly why he couldn't. He wouldn't risk what he had with Sully.

They had trust. He wouldn't betray it.

Sully called from the airport a little before midnight. When he walked into their bedroom shortly after one o'clock, Mac was waiting, naked, on his knees, the cane on the floor before him.

Sully pulled up short as he closed the bedroom door behind him. "What's going on?"

Mac didn't lift his gaze. "I owe Master ten strokes."

Still watching him, Sully walked around him and started removing his shirt. "What did you do?"

Mac inwardly winced at the cautious tone in Sully's voice. The guarded fear. He closed his eyes and related his discussion with Clarisse. How he'd kissed the back of her neck.

Well worth ten. Hell, it was worth twenty-five to do it again. It wasn't, however, worth putting Sully emotionally on edge over it.

Nothing was worth that.

Sully's voice sounded soft and firm. "On the bed. Ass over the edge."

Mac rushed to comply. He'd barely moved into position when Sully struck him, hard, across the ass with the cane.

He closed his eyes and anticipated the second stroke, but it didn't come. Instead, Sully's hand, warm and gentle on his flesh, stroking the mark. "That's all that happened?"

"Yes, Master—" *Whack!*

Mac braced himself. The strokes felt harder tonight, but not as fast. Sully would draw it out.

Sully's hand again, stroking. "How did that make you feel, kissing her like that?"

"I couldn't touch my dick for an hour, I was so fucking hard."

Whack!

The way his cock rubbed against the bedspread now didn't help either.

"Are you hard, slave?"

"Yes, Master."

Whack!

Six to go and his eyes already stung with tears. *Damn!*

"You could have taken her to bed right then, couldn't you?"

"Yes, Mast—" *Whack!*

Mac struggled to control his breathing and his willful cock. Dammit, he was so fucking horny he could barely stand it.

"You want to come, don't you?"

"Yes, Master!" He tensed, anticipating, but the strike didn't come.

"Stand up."

Mac didn't have time to consider the change in routine. He complied.

"Grip your cock. Both hands."

He did.

"Start stroking, but you don't come until I tell you or you'll get an extra fifty."

Mac fisted his cock, trying to keep his eyes on Sully.

Sully stepped behind him and took another stroke. Mac's rhythm faltered as he struggled to hold back.

In quick succession, the rest of the strokes fell. "Now," Sully ordered.

Mac's climax exploded, his juices coating his hands as the pain in his ass drove him over the edge hard and fast.

Sully stood beside him. "Show me."

Trembling with exhaustion and release, Mac lifted his hands.

"Lick them clean, slave."

Mac did, wishing it were Sully's come and struggling not to get hard again.

Sully reached over and tugged on one of Mac's nipple rings, then the other. "You've been a good boy for me, have you?"

"Only that, Master. What I told you."

Sully stroked Mac's cheek in a softly tender way. "That pleases me. You know honesty is always rewarded." He stood in front of Mac and unzipped his slacks, freeing his cock. "I know what you want. Go ahead. On your knees."

Mac fell to his knees, grabbed Sully's hips, and greedily sucked his cock. The feel of his lover's hands tightly fisting in his hair, holding on as he fucked his thick cock down his throat only intensified Mac's already growing need.

"Swallow every drop, slave," Sully ordered.

Sully fucked his face, hard, ramming his cock into Mac's mouth. Mac stayed with him, not missing a beat, careful not to hurt him with his teeth and finally giving up the fight to keep his own cock soft.

Mac closed his eyes and enjoyed every second. Harder and faster until he sensed the change in Sully's pace.

"Now, slave."

Mac sucked, hard, swallowing, moaning at the taste of his Master in his throat. Sully fell still, the hard, firm grip in Mac's hair changing, loosening, tender strokes along Mac's scalp as Sully's thick member softened against Mac's tongue.

Mac would kneel there all night like that if Sully let him.

No, Clarisse wasn't even close to understanding why he could give himself to Sully. He strongly suspected her submissive needs came nowhere close to his. He also knew she wasn't a switch. She would want soft and snuggly, easy sensual play that slipped into cuddling when all was said and done.

Could she ever truly live the way they lived? Were they even capable of giving her what she wanted and needed?

Sully finally patted the top of Mac's head. "Very good. Good boy. Release me."

Reluctantly, Mac did, giving his cock one last kiss before sitting back on his heels and looking at Sully.

"How will you explain the marks?"

"The truth, Master. I already mentioned to her that I'd earned myself ten."

"But not why?"

He shook his head.

Sully's eyes dropped to Mac's lap, where his stiff cock bobbed in the air. Sully smiled. "Go get your wrist cuffs."

A surge of excitement raced through Mac as he jumped to do it.

Sully finished undressing, put the cane away, and turned off the lights. Moonlight filtered through the blinds, enough to see by. It only took Mac a moment to securely cinch the cuffs around his wrists and stand at the end of their bed.

"Lie down. On your back." Sully held something behind him.

Mac had been too distracted by the unexpected command to fetch his cuffs to notice what Sully had picked up. Once Mac was secured on the bed, Sully showed him the vibrator. Not the largest, but enough.

His cock throbbed.

Sully laughed as he knelt between Mac's legs. "You know what I've got in store, don't you?"

"I hope so, Master."

Sully grinned. "You know damn well honesty is always rewarded. You've been a very good boy. You could have easily not told me what happened. I never would have known. But you did, knowing I would punish you." He thumbed the control and the vibrator clicked to life. Mac's breath caught as the hum filled the room. "I never want you to have a reason to not tell me the absolute truth."

Sully cupped the top of Mac's rigid cock in his left hand as he used his right to apply the vibrator to the sensitive spot on the underside of the head. Mac's hips involuntarily jerked, but he didn't take his eyes off Sully.

"You may come," Sully softly said.

Mac closed his eyes and threw his head back as the sensation overwhelmed him. Sully knew damn well Mac never could hold back very long like this, and as Sully worked the vibrator along the underside of Mac's cock, his release rapidly built.

"Tell me when you're coming," Sully ordered.

Mac's eyes squeezed tightly shut, his world ending at the feel of his cock lying in Sully's warm hand and of what the vibrator did to him. In another minute, he was there. "I'm coming, Master!" he gasped as the explosion ripped through him. Sully pressed the vibrator tightly against the underside of the head, drawing another cry from Mac as his climax seemed to increase, double in size. After what felt like forever, the pressure relented until Sully finally withdrew the vibrator and shut it off.

Drained, spent, Mac lay gasping on the bed. Then the feel of Sully's palm against his lips. He opened his mouth and licked his lover's hand clean without opening his eyes. As Sully pressed his fingers between Mac's lips, Mac lovingly sucked them, working his tongue over Sully's hand as if it were his cock.

After a moment, the hand disappeared, but he felt Sully unsnap his cuffs from the bed. Then Sully's arms encircled him and pulled him close. Mac cuddled tightly against his side, the cuffs still around his wrists.

"I love you, Brant," Sully whispered.

Mac squeezed him in a tight hug. "I love you too, Sul. Jesus, you have no idea how much I love you."

A soft breath escaped Sully. Mac interpreted it as relief. He knew Sully still struggled with his own fears sometimes. He also knew he'd do whatever he had to, for the rest of their lives, to keep proving to Sully he would never betray his trust.

Sully kissed the top of his head. "Let's sleep in a little tomorrow, okay?"

Mac smiled. "Okay."

Chapter Thirteen

Late the next afternoon, Sully went to take a nap. His leg still bothered him off and on and he needed to rest. Mac uncapped a beer and walked into the living room. Clarisse sat, reading, in one of the chairs. Mac settled at his usual place on the sofa, seated on his towel. On the coffee table, he placed a red folder.

He nodded to it. "Go ahead. I've already talked with Sully. You need to see that. It might help you understand."

When Clarisse realized the folder was full of personal paperwork—wills, powers of attorney, other such items—she immediately closed it. "I can't look through this. This is your private stuff."

"Read it," he softly said. "Please."

She didn't want to. It felt like she was intruding on the most private and intimate part of their lives.

Then she chided herself. How could it be more private than what she witnessed on a daily basis or at the party?

Mac watched as she opened the folder.

Sully's will sat on top. She glanced through it and faltered as she realized everything he had—quite a considerable amount—totally went to Mac in the event of Sully's death, with a provision to care for Tad, if he was still alive. The power of attorney paperwork covered medical as well as financial decisions and again gave Mac total control of everything.

The folder contained similar paperwork for Mac, ceding power to Sully. A huge life insurance policy on Sully naming Mac as the sole beneficiary. The cars and properties had been set up in a trust with the two men as the sole beneficiaries. Deeds for the house and several rental and commercial properties listed Mac as co-owner through the trust. And a sort of pre-nup, a private contract between them, notarized, specifying how they would divide their assets if they ever split, regardless of who wanted the "divorce."

With Mac getting quite a considerable amount. Then she noticed a number that concerned her. "Why would you only get twenty-five percent of your bank account?"

"Because I only contribute approximately twenty percent. He was generous. I was willing to settle for a flat sum, or even something like ten percent. He wanted to make sure we split it fairly. Between his pension, benefits, writing, and speaking engagements, he makes a helluva lot more than I do in a good year, sugar."

"What's all this stuff mean?" She closed the folder and set it on the table.

"I wanted you to see that this isn't all it appears to be on the surface. He went through a lot of trouble to make sure I was protected. That's why he got the life insurance. Again, Sully did that, not me. He wanted to make sure that if something ever happened to him, I was protected and no distant relatives could swoop in to try to take over. That's the only reason I'm on the properties and the trust. I didn't want to be. I wanted him to totally own everything, but the lawyer said with properties that it would be better if we were both on them because it would save the other on IRS crap in case one of us died, and it would help prevent any other issues."

"Relatives like who?"

"Sully's ex-wife, for one. She's friends with a cousin of his. I wouldn't put it past them to try something. Fucking bitch." His expression darkened as he took another pull on his beer. "My brother's cool with it. He wouldn't try something."

"Ex-wife?" She didn't realize Sully had been married.

"Yeah." He leaned back, crossing his legs. "She presented him with divorce papers while he lay in the hospital after the shooting.

Could barely open his eyes, and she forced him to sign everything. Fortunately, I helped him get that overturned because he wasn't coherent."

Rage built inside her. Despite her stubborn, lingering reservations about Sully, the fact that someone would take advantage of him like that boiled her bacon.

Mac hadn't finished. "He told me I could tell you about how we got together," he softly said. "I think you should hear it."

Clarisse nodded.

"It started almost nine years ago."

* * * *

Mac sat at the lunch counter with the paper opened to the want ads. His mood darkened with each failure. He didn't want to reenlist, even if the Army would take him back. He'd end up in the brig after punching some CO out, without a doubt. Since Betsy's death, he struggled every day just to get out of bed, and then it was a fight not to kill someone until he went to bed every night. He couldn't get rid of the anger.

The guilt.

The waitress, Lisa, walked over and refilled his coffee. "Real fucking shame, isn't it?"

If she wanted to bust his balls, today was not the day to do it. "What is?" he growled.

She gave him a strange look. "Didn't you hear?"

He slammed his pen onto the counter. "Hear *what*?"

Her eyes widened. "Oh my God! You haven't." She set the coffee pot down, her mood totally changed. "Sweetie, there was a shoot-out last night. A drug bust at some bar went bad."

A chill washed down Mac's spine. He didn't want to hear, but he asked anyway. "What happened?"

"That detective friend of yours. The one who worked your sister's case. He's in Harborside's ICU. They don't know if he'll make it."

Mac didn't remember the drive to St. Pete. He knew the way to the ICU and fortunately recognized two of the officers standing vigil outside the unit. They found their supervisor, who spoke to the nursing staff and got Mac in. HIPAA be damned, Sully was a cop, one of their brothers, and they wouldn't take no for an answer.

There was no one else there, no family, no friends. One of the other detectives walked in with him, a friend of Sully's, and explained the basics.

Mac remembered how hollow, nearly dead he felt as he forced his feet across the room to stand beside Sully's bed. Unconscious, on a ventilator, tubes, and IVs and monitor leads all over him.

For a moment, he flashed back to when Betsy lay in a bed in this very unit, then he shoved that away.

Mac didn't want to admit what he felt. He'd meant to call Sully several times over the past few months, just never got around to it. He'd thought about him a lot, especially over the past several weeks as the anniversary of Betsy's death drew near. They'd talked all the time in the beginning, several times a week, sometimes several times a day after Betsy's funeral. Then Mac let things drift, didn't return all of Sully's calls.

Didn't want to admit he struggled with his anger, grief, and guilt. Didn't want Sully to think he was looking for a handout or pity.

And here he lay in a bed with fucking tubes and wires in him. The only person who seemed to understand him, who'd had the right words, and *knew* what he had gone through because he'd lost a loved one in a similar way. The anger.

The guilt.

Love. He wanted to break down and cry and hold Sully's hand and confess that yes, maybe it was weird and strange, but he loved him. The detective who stood on the other side of the bed while helpfully droning details about Sully's condition made that impossible.

So did the wedding band on Sully's left hand.

Mac didn't even know what that meant for him. He wasn't gay, yet here lay a man he'd gladly spend the rest of his life with if given half a chance. A man who'd talked him out of killing himself, who'd spent more than one night sitting with him, watching him until he sobered up. The man who'd called 911, rode with him in the ambulance to the hospital, and stayed there three days with him, then drove him home and stayed a week with him after he'd decided to chase fifty Tylenol PM with a bottle of Jack Daniel's following Betsy's husband's conviction.

A man who'd given him hope. Friendship.

Who had faith in him even when his own had shriveled and died.

After their fifteen minute visitation ended, the detective led Mac back to the waiting room. He asked to speak to Sully's wife, he thought he remembered her name was Cybil, but he'd never met her. After some of the officers exchanged uncomfortable looks, they told Mac she wasn't there and probably wouldn't return.

Protective rage surged within Mac. He pulled Sully's partner aside to talk with him privately. He'd been helpful with Betsy's case but Mac didn't feel a fraction as close to him. "What's going on?"

The detective, Jason Callahan, glanced around and lowered his voice even more. "She's on the way out, okay? He didn't know it, but she was planning on filing for divorce next week. She's met someone else." He looked disgusted. "She told us all of that while we waited on him to make it through surgery. Once he was out and stable, she took off. We got the impression she's hoping he doesn't pull through because it would make her life easier. Bitch."

"Who's taking care of him?"

He shrugged. "We're here for him."

"That's not what I mean."

"He doesn't have any close family, if that's what you mean."

"Can I stay and help? Please?"

Jason's expression softened. He knew Sully and Mac were close friends. "He wouldn't expect you to do that."

"Please?"

"Okay. We'll talk to the staff for you."

Jason convinced Cybil to sign permission forms allowing Mac to be there in her absence, to help care for Sully.

To make things easier on her, he'd explained. So she could work at her business and not have to spend all day at the hospital.

Mac admired how Jason skillfully handled the bitch. She'd signed the paperwork, glad to have one less burden. Mac found out from Jason that she was ten years older than Sully, and he was her third husband. Her first two, much older than herself, had both died of natural causes, leaving her fairly well off.

The seemingly endless hours marched on until four days later, when Sully finally opened his eyes.

Mac sat at his side. Despite what it might look like to others, Mac openly wept and held Sully's hand. Sully couldn't speak because of the ventilator, but he looked at Mac. When Mac squeezed his hand, Sully squeezed back.

Mac rarely left his side. Good thing he could crash on Tad's boat, because he'd basically lost everything and had to vacate his apartment since he didn't have a job. When Cybil had waltzed in one afternoon and demanded Sully sign the divorce papers, Mac had wanted to stop it but couldn't at the time. She'd threatened, as Sully's wife, to have Mac removed from the room and banned from the hospital.

She could have done it.

Mac thought fast enough to have a nurse and doctor come in and witness everything so they could testify Sully wasn't competent to sign the paperwork because of his medication and physical condition.

As Sully grew stronger in body, he withdrew emotionally. The stunning shock of being served with divorce papers put him into a tailspin that Mac didn't know how to pull him from. But damn, he sure could sympathize.

One evening, once Sully's cop friends left after their daily visit, Mac pulled his chair over to Sully's bed. The nursing staff let Mac stay bedside since Sully had been moved to a regular room. Sully had asked them to allow it, especially after Cybil's bombshell.

"You okay?"

Sully's grey eyes appeared dead and distant. Mac knew it wasn't just because of the pain meds. "I want it over. It's all fucking bullshit. Why bother?"

Mac wanted to confess and knew he couldn't. Sully had quit wearing his wedding ring, but Mac didn't know if Sully would ever want him the way Mac wanted him. "You told me life goes on, one step at a time. That's what you told me."

"I was wrong. It's all fucking bullshit."'

"No, it's not." Mac wanted to cry for him. He'd seen the depths of Sully's compassion and love for others, his emotions, his selflessness. This man was an empty wasteland. "You can't give up on me, man."

"Doesn't matter. Don't have a home. Don't have a wife. I can't take care of myself. Can't be out in the field anymore, I know that. They'll offer me a desk job if I'm lucky, probably disability, retirement, and benefits, shuffle me off." He looked at Mac. "What difference does it make?"

"I'll take care of you. I'll help you get better." His need approached desperation. How could he prove it? "Please, Sul, you were there for me with Bets. Let me help you through this. You didn't give up on me. I won't give up on you, I swear."

Two months later, after extensive rehab and rounds with a lawyer to protect Sully from Cybil, Mac helped Sully walk through the door of their new apartment. They'd gotten the divorce settlement overturned. Cybil had to pay Sully half the value of the equity in the house. That would help him. Mac, along with Sully's lawyer, had gone in with a court order, deputies, and Jason Callahan, and retrieved as many of Sully's personal effects as they could.

Sully was still a broken shell. Worse, he'd sunk into anger.

Mac didn't take it personally. One evening, while Sully lay on the couch watching TV, he fell trying to stand by himself. He pitched an angry tantrum that dissolved into nearly hysterical tears. Mac held him, his heart breaking for this man, his friend.

His soul mate.

And he couldn't even tell him.

"Let me lie here, Brant," Sully cried. "Like the fucking trash. That's all I am."

Mac forced him to his feet, one of Sully's arms around his shoulders, and into bed. He helped him undress as he usually did, while Sully still ranted and railed, vacillating between anger and anguish.

Finally settling on rage, he screamed at Mac. "Leave me the fuck alone!"

Mac turned on him. "No! I'm not going to sit by and let you waste your fucking life. You're going to get better and when you do, you'll figure out where to go from there. When will you get it through your thick goddamned head that I'm your friend and I love you and I'm not going anywhere no matter how much you tell me to?" His breath caught in his throat. It was as close as he'd ever come to confessing.

Sully's evening meds had kicked in, adding to an already bad mood. He grabbed his crotch through his boxers and screamed, "Fuck you! You can suck my dick. Life sucks. I wish they'd let me fucking die!"

As good an invitation as any, Mac didn't have time to consider the consequences. He pinned Sully's wrists to the bed. "You're telling me to suck your cock, Sul?"

"Yeah!" Sully sneered. Sully's pupils had dilated, the pain medicine mostly in charge at this point. "You want to fucking stay here with me? Well make yourself useful and suck my goddamned cock, asshole!"

Mac grinned. "Okay." He'd never done it before, but had to admit he'd fantasized about it plenty of times while helping Sully with his bath or going to the bathroom. Before Sully could protest, Mac yanked down Sully's boxers and greedily sucked the man's cock.

Sully went silent and still. Mac, not releasing Sully's cock, changed position to kneel between the man's legs so he could look at him. Shock, disbelief, and…more than a twinge of lust painted Sully's face.

After a few minutes, Sully's head dropped to his pillow and he started working his hips in time with Mac's mouth. When Sully's hands tangled in his hair, Mac closed his eyes and slowed his movements, trying to think about how he loved getting a blow job and what girls did to him and doing that to Sully. He didn't feel at all squeamish about it.

He'd consider the consequences later.

After a few minutes, Sully started muttering, "Fuck, fuck, fuck," under his breath. Mac grabbed his hips and held on as Sully's body tensed, then Sully moaned as his climax hit. Hot seed pumped over Mac's tongue. Again he didn't have time to consider it as he swallowed every drop. It felt right.

It felt good.

Sully didn't move his hands, left them resting on Mac's head. From the ragged sound of Sully's breath, Mac knew he was still awake. Mac finally released his cock and rested his cheek against Sully's hip. He didn't move, was almost afraid to breathe.

Sully still didn't move his hands.

After long, anxious minutes, Sully whispered, "I've never done that before."

Mac laughed. "Well join the club. Neither have I." He felt that maybe it was safe to lift his head and look. "I'm not going to apologize for it either. You're the first guy I've ever been with. I don't know why you, why I love you, but I do. So you're stuck with me for a while. If you want to tell me to get the fuck out, fine, I accept that. At least let me stay with you until you're on your feet again. I owe you that much for keeping me going and not letting me die. If you tell me never to do that again and want to pretend it didn't happen, fine, I accept that, too. I'll even apologize if you want. I won't lie and say I didn't enjoy it when I did."

Sully's grey eyes settled on him. For once, they seemed less dead than they had for the past several months. "You love me?"

"Yeah. I thought I was only into girls. I still like girls. But I love *you*. So gay, bi, whatever that makes me, I don't care. All I know is I love *you*." He took a deep breath. "Do you want me to go?"

Sully slowly shook his head. "No," he finally whispered. "I don't want you to go."

Mac felt a relieved sigh escape him. "Good, because I don't want to go."

* * * *

"Then what happened?" Clarisse asked.

Mac shrugged and took another swallow of his beer. "We went to sleep and woke up the next morning, both of us sort of uncomfortable. His painkillers had worn off and I thought, 'Oh shit, I hope I didn't screw things up.' We talked, kept talking. It was a long road between then and now. A good road. Not a perfect one. We're like anyone else with a relationship. There's good and bad times. In our case, very few bad and minor compared to many people's problems. The good always makes it worth it."

Mac looked normal, natural in a collar, nipple rings, and nothing else. He damn sure had the body for it. "How did you become his slave?"

"That happened early on. I ran naked out of the bathroom one day to grab the phone and he joked that he liked the look on me. I started walking around naked." He smiled as he took another swallow. "That led to more interesting things."

"But how did you know you were submissive?"

"How do you know you're a girl? I'm not like this with everyone, if you haven't noticed. Only him. Even then, we switch it up a little. On the boat, I top and he bottoms."

"You mean he's your slave."

"Fuck no. He's always my Master. Top and bottom can be different from Dom and sub or Master and slave. He lets me top on the boat. I get to call the shots. Like the day we found you, he's still my Master and I defer to him. He would never try to get his way while we play when I'm topping. That goes back to trust. That lets me get my needs taken care of to be in charge, lets him relax and turn over control in a safe way."

She scrubbed her face with her hands. "I don't understand why you only want to be in control sometimes."

"When we didn't have the boat, we had a different arrangement, like one weekend a month or something, we'd switch. I like that structure, knowing that in certain cases, this is what I am and do and the rest of the time it's all him. I loved that about the Army, the protocol, the procedures. I hated some of the assholes I worked under and getting my fucking ass shot at. Master gives me what I need and want."

"That didn't answer my question about how you knew."

He shrugged. "I loved taking care of him, being there for him. I didn't want to stop. As he healed, I started doing other things for him. Let him focus on his writing and, later, the classes he taught. It made me happy. It made him happy. Hell, if you'd told me a few years ago I'd be happy doing this, I'd have said you were nuts. Much less that it was with a guy." His brow furrowed in concentration.

"Master and I...fuck labels. They're just that, better for clothing or food contents than people. We're not gay. We don't go lusting after guys. If we see a cute guy, yeah, sure, we might make a comment to each other. It's not like my dick hardens. A beautiful woman walks by, honey, my dick stands up. So does Master's."

He met her eyes as she felt molten heat pool between her legs. "I look into Master's eyes and I want to drop to my knees and beg him to fuck me. He's the only guy that does that to me. You walk by and my dick screams for attention and tries to talk me into fucking you.

Believe me, I wish I could, because I would in a heartbeat." He finished the beer before standing and walking out to the kitchen.

His words rang in her ears. They weren't gay.

Numb shock washed through her system. When a wild-assed hope from far left field popped its head up and screamed for attention, she beat it back. She didn't want to go there. She didn't want to hang her hat on impossible hopes and have her heart broken. Sully and Mac were devoted to each other. Only a moron could miss that.

She wished they felt like that about her.

* * * *

Sully felt his BlackBerry vibrate next to him on the bed, rousting him from his nap. Without looking, he fumbled for it and answered. "Nicoletto."

"Hey, Sul. It's Jason."

Sully flexed his leg. It hurt, but not as bad as the other day. "What's up?"

"You know me, can't mind my own business. I've been doing some digging."

"What?"

"I found out something interesting about Officer Bryan Jackson."

Sleep left Sully's system. "What?"

"Ed and Lorraine Moore died in a tragic hit and run accident three years ago. Their car plunged off an embankment one evening. Paint scrapes showed another vehicle was involved."

Sully rolled over. Jason had his full and undivided attention. "Clarisse's parents?"

"Yeah. That same day, about an hour before the accident scene was discovered, Officer Jackson reported his car stolen. Never recovered."

Sully chewed that over in his mind. "Son of a bitch."

"Yeah. Get this. I requested the accident report from the Licking

County sheriff's office up there. One witness reported a car the same color as Jackson's car leaving the area about the time the accident would have happened, but it was dark and they didn't get a tag or make-model or see the accident happen."

"He killed them?"

"He had an alibi. He was sitting in the station, filling out a report on the car. Before that, he's on surveillance video shopping at Wal-Mart, complete with a time-date-stamped credit card receipt. His car was stolen from the lot, also caught on video, but the perp was never identified."

"No one ever thought to put that shit together?"

"Jackson's father and the police chief of that charming little hamlet went to school together."

Sully closed his eyes and pinched the bridge of his nose. "Clarisse received a hundred-grand life insurance payout when they died."

"He might have known that since they dated for a couple of years before."

"Most likely. Son of a bitch."

If she'd stayed, how much longer until Clarisse would have met with an "accident"? More importantly, how much danger was she in now that she'd pressed charges against Jackson?

* * * *

After dinner, Clarisse curled up on one end of the couch to watch TV. Sully emerged from his office. "Mind if I join you?"

"It's your house."

He settled on the far end of the couch. "You okay?"

"Yeah." She tried to focus on the show and not Sully's presence. After a few minutes, Mac finished cleaning up the kitchen and joined them. Instead of sitting on the couch, he sat on the floor by Sully.

Clarisse felt her heart skip as she watched Sully tenderly stroke Mac's hair. Mac's eyes dropped closed as he settled against Sully's leg.

She wanted that. The bond, the closeness. The tenderness.

The love.

She found it difficult to focus on the TV show. Part of her wanted to crawl across the couch and snuggle with Sully.

When the show ended, Sully tapped Mac's shoulder. Mac startled. He'd been asleep. "Bedtime, buddy," Sully said.

Mac sleepily nodded and stood. "Good night, sweetie," he said to Clarisse.

"Night."

Sully offered a smile. "See you in the morning." Mac followed him to their bedroom, leaving Clarisse alone with her own conflicted desires.

She headed for bed with a book. *Chances Taken,* by one S. N. MacCaffrey.

She smiled. Sully wrote under his own name too, for his nonfiction and some of his fiction. For the erotica, however, he used the pen name. This was the first chance she'd had to read any of his books. It touched her that he used Mac's last name for his pen name.

Three hours later, Clarisse yawned, but she was so engrossed in the book she couldn't put it down. It wasn't just erotica, but a gut-wrenching, emotional, beautiful, and sexy romance between two men who loved each other, yet life and circumstances kept them apart. Fortunately, it had a happily-ever-after ending. From the depth of the writing, the skill used to weave the story around the intensely erotic scenes, she knew Sully's still waters ran deep, so to speak.

When she closed the book, she was surprised to find it almost five in the morning. She closed her eyes and drifted to sleep, thinking about the book and wondering if she'd ever find *her* happily-ever-after.

Chapter Fourteen

The next day, before lunch, Sully called Clarisse into his office. He handed her a new cell phone.

"What's this for?" She examined it, an expensive phone with all the bells and whistles.

"It's in my name. If caller ID picks up, it shows me. I'm warning you, it's got a GPS tracker in it I can access from my computer."

Fear crept in. "Why?"

"I prefer to know we can find you. When the phone's on, I can track it. If you didn't have the issue of Bryan hanging over your head, it'd be different. I'm paying for it and you're free to use it as much as you need. I do, however, insist on the ability to find you. You're my responsibility. Tad would kill me if anything happened to you. Go get dressed. Jeans, nothing fancy."

"Why?"

"You and I are going out."

When Sully met her in the kitchen a few minutes later, he carried a metal briefcase.

This outing was apparently news to Mac as well. Mac's eyebrows arched. "What's going on?"

"I'm taking Clarisse out for a couple of hours. We'll grab lunch while we're gone. Come on, babe."

Mac stared. "Did you want me to come?"

"You've got a lot to do, including finishing your month-end trip ticket paperwork, don't you?" He held the door open for Clarisse.

"Yes, Master," Mac said.

Clarisse followed Sully downstairs where he held the passenger door of the Jag open for her. He locked the briefcase in the trunk before getting behind the wheel. She noticed he'd brought his cane with him.

"Where are we going?" she asked.

"You'll see." A playful smile curled his lips. He winked. "Nervous?"

"Should I be?"

He gently caught her hand and laced his fingers through hers before bringing it to his lips. He kissed the back of her hand. "I promise you I would die to keep you safe."

A deep shiver ran through her at the depth of his voice, the emotions in his words. She instinctively knew he meant it.

If she could only force her brain to accept the memo.

The XM radio in his car was tuned to the sixties channel. As they pulled out of the driveway, Sully put his sunglasses on. "Feel free to change the channel if you want."

"No, that's okay. It's fine." She didn't know what to talk about but didn't feel a need to fill the silence between them, either. She had the same kind of rapport with Mac, could work side by side with him on the boat or in the kitchen without needing to talk.

Only with Mac she felt free to have a playful relationship with him, to bump hips or to spontaneously dance with him when a favorite song played on the stereo.

She wasn't sure she should have that kind of interaction with Sully.

Then again, maybe she should tone it down with Mac, too. They weren't her men, could never be anything but friends. To lose her heart to them, especially knowing they weren't gay, would only cause her pain in the end.

Clarisse settled in her seat and watched the scenery pass. Thirty minutes later, they pulled into the parking lot of a gun store and shooting range in New Port Richey.

Nervous tension filled her. She suspected what the metal briefcase held. "What are we doing here?"

Without removing his sunglasses, he turned to look at her. "I need you to be able to defend yourself."

"Why? What have you heard?" Sully had taken over and contacted the detective in charge of her case in Ohio. She knew Sully was planning for her to return to Ohio soon to speak with them, but she didn't know any of the details.

She didn't want to.

"Nothing. I don't trust the slimy son of a bitch. I won't feel comfortable giving you access to my guns without knowing you can safely handle them."

"How many do you have?"

He smiled. "Enough."

He walked around the front of the car to open her door for her. She noticed he limped and put his hand on the hood and fenders to steady himself. He retrieved his cane from the backseat before getting the briefcase and a duffel bag out of the trunk. Inside, the man behind the counter smiled when he recognized Sully.

"Hey, Sul. Haven't seen you in a couple of months."

"Been busy, Gus." He laid the briefcase on the counter, unlocked it, and opened it. Inside, nestled in protective foam, lay three handguns. She knew enough to recognize one was a revolver and the other two were semiautomatic pistols, but beyond that, she had no clue.

The clerk brought Sully three boxes of ammunition and several targets and rang him up. "Take your pick, they're all open."

"Thanks."

Sully carried everything and led the way through a door to the shooting range. "Have you ever shot one of these before?"

"When I was a kid, Uncle Tad taught me how to shoot a pellet gun."

"So the answer would be no?" He turned. The curl to his lips belied his words.

She smiled. "No."

His smile widened. "Okay." He removed two pairs of protective glasses and shooter's ear muffs from the duffel bag. Then he clipped one of the targets to the line and ran it down to the end of the range. Before he even removed the trigger locks from the guns he explained them to her. One was a 9mm, the other pistol a .45, and the revolver a .38. He explained the safety mechanisms, how to load them, how to shoot them. Then he unlocked them and demonstrated.

"I'm sure Tad explained to you to always treat any gun, even an unloaded one, as if it was loaded."

"Yeah."

He loaded the 9mm's clip and put on his safety glasses and muffs. "Put those on," he ordered, nodding toward hers.

She did.

He told her where to stand, out of the way. Then he emptied the clip into the target. Most of the shots lay close to or inside the bull's-eye. "Did you watch how I stood and held it?"

"Yeah."

He removed the clip and handed it and the gun to her. "Load it."

With trembling hands she did while Sully offered encouragement when needed. When it came time to put the clip in the gun, he laid his hands over hers.

"Remember to breathe. Then hold your breath before you pull the trigger."

He stepped behind her and put his arms around her as she readied the gun. Clarisse fought against the urge to lean back against him, into his embrace. He helped her position her hands and arms correctly before stepping out of the way.

"Okay."

She flicked the safety and took a deep breath, fired. The kick startled her more than the noise. The way Sully shot made it look easy. She glanced at him where he stood to the side, leaning against the partition wall with his arms crossed over his chest. He nodded his approval.

She took a deep breath and over the space of a minute finished the clip, then ejected it, and laid it and the gun on the counter.

Sully nodded again and stepped in to take the gun. "Good job, sweetheart."

Her hands throbbed. He ran the target back to them. Her shots were clearly distinct from Sully's because hers never hit the center of the bull's-eye. He hung a fresh target.

"What do you mean good job? My aim sucks."

"You hit the target. I'm not entering you in the Olympics, kiddo. I want you to be able to safely handle a gun."

"Why didn't we bring Mac?" The look on his face when they left had bothered her. Like he felt left out.

Sully frowned, his hands hesitating only a second as he loaded the clip in the .45. "Mac hates guns."

"He doesn't like to shoot?"

"Flashbacks." Sully glanced at her. "He spent three years in Iraq."

There was a lot she didn't know about the men. She knew Mac had been in the Army for a while, but hadn't asked him any questions about it, sensing he didn't like to talk about it.

"Why don't the two of you catch a movie tonight?" Sully suggested.

"What?"

"Make it up to him for leaving him alone."

"That's freaking spooky."

"What?"

"You reading my mind like that."

He motioned for her to step back as he assumed a shooting stance. "What can I say? It's a Dom thing." His mouth curled into an amused smile.

She watched as he emptied the clip. Again, all of his shots hit near or on center. He helped her load the .45 and watched her shoot it. When she finished, she laid it on the counter.

"Do me a favor, sweetie. Please pick up the shells. My leg's bothering me."

"Okay." While she did, he reloaded the .45 for her.

"You don't like the Sig, do you?" he asked.

"What?"

"The nine millimeter."

"No."

"You acted scared of it."

She shrugged as she put the shells on the counter. He had her shoot three more clips with the .45 before switching to the revolver. She didn't like it much more than the 9mm, but by the time their hour ended, she realized she felt closer to Sully and more relaxed around him than she ever had before. As she helped him relock the guns and put them away, it occurred to her she hadn't once felt nervous around him since their arrival.

He tucked a stray hair behind her ear. "How about we have a standing once-a-week shooting date?"

She grinned. "Date?"

He slipped his arms around her and pulled her to him. "Mac gets to spend most of the time with you. Maybe I'd like the pleasure of your company once in a while."

She sensed something deeper in his grey gaze than simple friendship. Or maybe just wishful thinking on her part? "Okay. I'd like that."

He kissed her forehead. "I'm thinking all this is overkill on my part, but it would kill me if something happened to you because I didn't teach you what you need to know to keep yourself safe and we weren't there to protect you."

She allowed herself to relax in his arms, rested her forehead against his chest, and closed her eyes. Her mind drifted back to the play party, to the way Mac surrendered to him, to the trust he had in him.

How could she ever admit to him that she wished she could have that, too?

"Thanks, Sully."

"Let's go eat." He released her and slipped his sunglasses on before gathering their things. Moment over.

* * * *

Sully thought back to Jason's call. He didn't have any proof. He instinctively knew Clarisse wouldn't have had anything to do with her parents' deaths, and she probably didn't suspect Bryan Jackson did either. When they were seated at a table in the restaurant, he decided to test the waters. After chatting with her for a few minutes, he sprang the question.

"So how did your parents feel about Bryan Jackson?"

"They hated him. I actually broke up with him twice before we got back together for good." She looked sad. "I should have listened to them."

"Why did you get back together with him?"

Clarisse's gaze fell to the table. He didn't miss the tears that filled her eyes. "He personally came to break the news to me about their accident. He was at the station when it happened." She sniffled and wiped at her eyes with her napkin as her voice dropped. "He insisted on being the one to tell me. I...I fell apart. He picked me up and kept me together, helped me plan the funeral and the arrangements."

She took a deep breath and forced a smile. "It was like I saw a different side of him, right? That's before he hit me the first time, obviously. He acted so sweet. He didn't try to be romantic with me or anything, just...he was there."

She met Sully's gaze. "He would stop by to check on me, make sure I was okay. Then after a few weeks, I invited him over for dinner and we got back together. I thought I'd seen a changed man. I thought maybe he'd gotten a handle on his anger. He said he'd been working really hard to change. He acted different for a while. After six months or so, the old Bryan reappeared. Slowly, little things here and there. By the time I realized he hadn't really changed, I wasn't strong enough to make him leave again. I put up with it."

Sully nodded and traced his fingers through the condensation on his glass. "That's understandable." It also confirmed his suspicions that she had no involvement in her parents' deaths.

"No, it's not," she angrily shot back. She glanced around and lowered her voice. "I acted fucking *stupid*. I let him take me for everything, and by the time I felt ready to go back to school and finish my degree, I couldn't because I'd let him control me and take control of everything. He wouldn't give me the money to go to school. Then when I told him I'd kick him out, that's when he hit me and threatened me the first time."

"You're *not* stupid, Clarisse."

"Stop it. I am stupid. I'm stupid and I was scared I couldn't make it on my own, and then I was scared he'd fucking kill me. Who else would have wanted me anyway? Fucking fat chick, all I can attract is a psycho cop for a boyfriend—"

Sully reached across the table and grabbed her chin. "Stop," he whispered. "Don't you *dare* let me hear you talk about yourself like that ever again. So help me, girl, I will spank that attitude out of your gorgeous hide." He placed one finger over her lips. "I don't give a shit what that asshole told you. Who are you going to believe? A lying psychopath or someone who's willing to put a gun in your hand?" A playful smile teased his lips.

She finally smiled. When she did, he touched the end of her nose before settling in his chair again. His gaze bored into her. "Baby, I will tolerate a lot, believe me. But I mean it, if I hear you talk like that again, I *will* haul you over my lap."

She looked shocked for a moment, then smiled. "Promise?"

He laughed and took a sip of water. "You'd better believe it."

After their food arrived, she nervously studied him. "Mac told me about how you guys got together."

"I told him it was okay. I want you to understand there's a lot more to what we've got than it appears. I love him, he loves me."

"I read *Chances Taken*."

He smirked. "What did you think?"

"What came first? Your relationship with Mac or the writing?"

He shrugged and leaned back in his chair. "I've been writing since high school."

"The erotica?"

"That came after I got together with Mac."

"It's good. Very emotional."

"I'm glad you liked it."

"Can I ask you something personal?"

"Sure."

"How did you end up with a guy if you're not gay?"

He shrugged. "Just happened. I can't explain it. Sometimes you have to admit it when you love someone and not worry what the hell anyone else thinks." He turned his pointed gaze on her. "It is what it is."

* * * *

When they returned from their afternoon together, Sully went upstairs to clean the guns and sent Clarisse to find Mac. She found him in the backyard doing yard work.

"Hey. Did you guys have fun?"

She watched his eyes. "Sully took me shooting."

She didn't miss the cloud that passed through his expression. "I figured, when I saw the gun case."

"He suggested you and I go catch a movie or something tonight. Together."

The cloud lifted, his eyes shone. "He did, did he?"

"Yeah."

"How about you help me cook dinner and we stay home and

watch a movie? We can shout lines at the TV without pissing everyone off."

Clarisse giggled. She'd discovered she had that in common with Mac one evening when they both started doing it, their snarky commentary cracking Sully up in the process. "Okay. That sounds good."

She returned to the house and changed clothes to work out. The elliptical was both her favorite and her most hated machine. After twenty minutes, Sully appeared, also dressed in workout clothes. "Mind if I join you?"

"Of course not."

He set up the weight bench and started working on his legs. He didn't wear a shirt, which allowed her to stare at the scar on his abdomen. She hadn't noticed it during the party, her attention more on Mac than on Sully that night.

"Why do you want to work out?" he asked her.

She blushed, paused the timer on the elliptical, and used the break to get a drink of water. "Please don't start. Mac already gave me the 'don't kill yourself to get thin' lecture."

Sully glanced over at her. "He's right. You're beautiful the way you are."

Her face felt even hotter. "I'd be prettier if I was thinner."

The weights clanked as he stopped and sat up. "Why do you say that?"

Clarisse shrugged and climbed back onto the elliptical. "Because it's the truth."

"Is that more of Bryan Jackson's bullshit talking?"

"No," she shot back. "It's me knowing the truth. I'm fucking fat." She got off the machine and angrily stalked toward the door.

Sully intercepted her, caught her arm, and spun her around. "Listen to me, what did I tell you about you talking like that?"

Her eyes widened. "You wouldn't!"

He swatted her ass, not hard enough to sting, but the shock of his action stunned her. His voice dropped to a low growl. "I never lie about what I'm going to do, honey. That was a warning shot." He pulled her closer. "You *are* beautiful, and Bryan Jackson is a fucking moron. End of subject, got it?"

She still couldn't believe that he'd swatted her on the ass. She nodded.

He smiled and enveloped her in a hug. "We think you're beautiful, sweetie," he murmured in her hair. "As Mac told you, we do appreciate a beautiful woman when we see one." He kissed the top of her head before releasing her and returning to the weight bench. "You going to finish your work out?"

She took a moment to catch her breath before she returned to the elliptical machine, her mind whirling.

After dinner, Sully disappeared to his office to work. Mac left the choice of movie to Clarisse. She picked a thriller she hadn't seen yet from their considerable DVD library.

An hour later, she cuddled on the couch next to Mac—who'd donned shorts—jumping at the scary parts and adding their own snarky comments to the dialogue.

As the credits rolled, Mac hugged her. "We should do this more often."

"Maybe this could be our date-night thing?"

He smiled and planted a kiss on her forehead. "Sounds good to me."

Chapter Fifteen

Over a month after her arrival, Clarisse seemed to have settled in. Sully knew she still had reservations about him, but she'd quit flinching around him and had even started spontaneously hugging him.

It gave him hope.

He didn't look up when Mac quietly walked into their bedroom one evening and knelt beside his recliner by the window, where he'd been reading. He reached out and stroked Mac's hair. "What's up?"

"May I talk with you, Master?"

Sully sat back and studied Mac. Formal kneel, hands on knees, head lowered. "Go ahead," Sully told him. His gut clenched as he expected the worst. *I want out,* or *I'm moving out with Clarisse.* The first would break his heart.

The latter would crush his soul.

He knew Mac had a much closer relationship with Clarisse than he did, but he'd hoped that after their afternoon together, maybe she would eventually come to trust him the way she trusted Mac.

Maybe time had run out for that to happen.

"I love you, Master."

Sully closed his eyes, dreading it. *Here it comes.*

"I want to spend my life with you," Mac continued. "So I hope this doesn't make you mad, but you told me to be honest."

Get it over with, Brant, Sully thought. *Please, don't drag it out.*

"I'm in love with Clarisse."

There it was. Mac wasn't finished, however.

"I wanted to know if you would consider letting me tell her."

Huh? "What?" Had he heard him right?

Mac cringed. "Please don't be upset! I still love you, and if you say no, I understand—"

"Wait. Whoa. Back up. She doesn't know how you feel?"

Mac shook his head. "I knew I had to talk to you first."

Sully studied him for several long minutes. "What if I say no?"

Mac's shoulders dropped a little. "Then that would be your will."

"And if I say yes?"

He heard Mac's breath catch. "That is also your will."

Sully stood. "Take your collar off and come here." He sat on the end of their bed while Mac scrambled to comply. When Mac was seated next to him, Sully looked at him. "What do you want, Brant?"

"Honestly? I'd love for the three of us to be together. If she'll have us like that. Both of us."

"*Both* of us?"

Mac nodded.

Sully took a moment to compose his thoughts. "You wouldn't be jealous?"

Mac shook his head, a sly smile crossing his face. "I know you love her, too. I can see it in your eyes."

"You're not ready to get rid of me yet?"

"Fuck no!" Mac looked horrified at the very thought. His reaction lifted Sully's soul. "I love you! I can't lose you."

Sully studied him. "She'd have to agree to our way of life. I can't stop being who I am for her. Neither can you. And I won't give you up."

"I want you to marry her," Mac said.

Well, that was a surprise. "Really?"

"Yes." Mac reached out and touched his lover's knee. "You own me. You'd own her, too. That's the way it should be. It's the way I want it." From the way Mac's cock started to inflate, Sully knew he told the truth.

"You've thought this through."

"It's all I can think about." He met Sully's gaze again. "Sul, when we agreed to do this, I meant it for life." He laced his fingers through Sully's. "I belong to you. When I gave myself to you, it was for as long as you'll have me. She won't change that."

Sully considered it. "Here at home, it would be me over you both. Boat rules still apply."

Mac threw his arms around him. "Thank you!"

"Don't thank me yet. You don't know she'll say yes."

"I feel it, Sul. She wants to be with us as much as we want her here."

"I'll take the lead."

"Okay!"

"Put some shorts on. Leave your collar off."

Mac's eyes widened. "Now?"

"Yeah. Why?"

"I mean…right now?"

"Now."

"Are you sure we won't scare her off?"

"Scare her now or scare her later. I would rather get it out of the way. I don't want to spend the next few months loving her from a distance to lose her because she leaves and doesn't know how we feel." He sighed. "That would hurt too much."

Mac broadly grinned. "You *do* love her! I knew it!"

Sully stroked the other man's face, left his fingers resting on his chin. "I loved you *first*. I don't ever want to lose you."

Mac caught his hand, kissed Sully's fingers, and nuzzled his hand against his cheek. "I can't lose you. You're the first one, the only one who's ever understood me. The only one I've ever trusted."

There weren't many truly warm and fuzzy moments in their relationship, but this was one of them. Sully leaned in and kissed him, then hugged him. "We're in agreement that we have to come first, right? I don't want to jeopardize what we've got over her, no matter how we feel about her."

Mac hugged him harder. "Absolutely."

Sully touched his forehead to Mac's and closed his eyes. "I was afraid you were going to tell me you were leaving."

Mac harshly laughed. "No fucking way, dude. You're stuck with me for life. You don't get rid of me that easily."

Clarisse had been curled on the sofa, watching TV when the men walked out to the living room. She nervously eyed them as she sat up. "What's going on?"

"We need to talk," Sully said, taking a seat on the opposite end of the couch. Mac sat on the coffee table.

"Talk?" Clarisse felt fear settle inside her heart. Here it was. They were going to ask her to leave, or tell her it wasn't working out, just as she'd started to relax and feel like maybe she could be a part of their lives in some small way. She swallowed back the nasty cold, metallic taste in her throat. A taste she knew well and hadn't experienced since leaving Bryan.

Fear.

Mac and Sully exchanged a glance. Sully leveled his grey gaze at her. "Do you like living here? Honestly?"

Unable to speak through her fear, she nodded.

"Do you have any intentions to leave?"

She shook her head.

His lips curled into the sexy smile that melted her every time. "Good, because we don't want you to leave. In fact, we want you to stay. Permanently."

She couldn't have heard him right. "Permanently?" Mac looked desperately hopeful. He nodded. She returned her attention to Sully. "What do you mean?"

"I know you're not in love with me. I understand that. I'm not asking for your love, only for your trust. What Mac and I have is different even by unconventional standards. We want to offer you the chance to stay with us permanently."

She tried to digest that. "Permanently?"

"Yes. Mac has something he needs to tell you."

Mac looked shocked, like he hadn't expected Sully to pass the ball to him. He took a deep breath. In a soft voice that didn't sound like him, he said, "I love you, Clarisse."

She smiled. "I love you too, Mac."

"No, I mean I'm *in* love with you."

She was sure she didn't hear him right. "What?"

"He just told me." Sully waited for her response. She studied his face, then Mac's, then back to Sully. He didn't look mad. In fact, truth be told, he looked...

Happy?

He finally spoke again. "We're a package deal, sweetheart. You get one, you get the other. I'll never try to force you to love me, no matter how much I love you. I only ask for your trust. In return, I swear to you that we will never let you down."

Still stunned, Clarisse tried to process Mac's confession. "You're in love with me?"

"Yes," he softly said.

She stared at Sully, unsure what to say.

He spoke. "There's no reason to give us an answer tonight. We will never force you to do what we do. However, Mac will always be my slave. Nothing changes that unless he decides he doesn't want it anymore. We love each other, and while we want you to be a part of our lives, we won't give each other up. If you feel you can accept that, and want to be a part of us, we would welcome you with open arms."

"I need some time with this." In reality, she wanted to jump into Mac's arms and say yes.

"Of course."

She stared at Sully, then at Mac. "If I said yes, what would that mean?" Her heart thumped in her chest as she met Mac's hopeful brown gaze. She did love him, and she'd be lying to deny it.

"That's something we'd have to discuss. Mac will always be mine, for as long as he chooses to be. Whether you can handle being second in his life to me—that's something only you can decide."

One of her dreams about the men taking her together came back to her with crystal clarity. She forced herself to speak loudly enough they could hear her. "What if I wanted to be involved with both of you? Or if both of you wanted to be involved with me?"

The men exchanged a glance she couldn't interpret. "You have to be able to trust me before that can happen," Sully said. "You and I both know I don't have that from you yet."

"I trust you."

He arched an eyebrow at her.

"I know you won't hurt me."

He didn't speak.

When she finally dropped her gaze, she twisted her hands together in her lap. "I *do* trust you."

"Not in the way you'd have to trust me to have a relationship with me like Mac does."

"What if that's something I want?"

"Do you think it is?"

She shrugged.

Mac quietly spoke. "There's the play party this weekend. We could take her. I haven't cancelled our RSVP yet."

Sully studied him for a moment, then nodded. "Okay. Then I propose this. You come with us to the play party this weekend. Take a chance in our world. See if you really think you can fit in with us before you commit to anything. I promise I won't injure you, just give you a taste of what it could be like."

He sat back. "Something else you need to understand, I will not take our relationship to the next level until you can fully trust me and commit to me."

"What does that mean, exactly?"

He leaned forward again, his grey gaze intense. "Mac doesn't get to fuck you unless I get to first. I won't fuck you unless or until you're married to me. I marry for love. And I won't marry you unless

I know you truly love me in return first. Do I make myself clear?"

She swallowed hard. "Yes."

"Honestly, I can't tell you how this will work between you and Mac. I'm still trying to sort logistics out myself. Let's table the topic until after the play party this weekend. If it's still an issue, we can talk more. I will promise you this—you *always* have a home with us. Forever. Even if nothing changes in our relationship from the way it is right this minute. The only thing that would make me ask you to leave is if you lied to us or if you got involved with another man. You can stay as long as you are ours and ours alone, even if only in our hearts and not our bed. No strings attached. Understood?"

"Okay."

Sully stood and left them alone. Mac's eyes searched her face. "I love you, sweetie. But he's my life and I can't lose him. I'm sorry. If you can put up with us, I promise we'll make you happier than any woman alive."

"I would be sharing you with him."

He smiled. "Not really. It'll be him sharing you with me."

She shivered, but recognized the feeling as desire, not fear.

He reached out and tucked a stray hair behind her ear. "I know it's strange, but think about it. Please? Ask questions. Talk to us." He leaned in and kissed her, sweetly, lovingly. When he leaned back he wore a smile. "Worth every stroke," he whispered before standing and following Sully to their bedroom.

* * * *

Clarisse needed time to process the new information. She spent a long sleepless night replaying the conversation in her mind.

Thought about Mac's kiss.

Truth be told, she loved Mac, too.

And maybe even Sully.

The next morning, she headed to Uncle Tad's. As soon as she

walked in, he nailed her. "What's wrong?"

"What do you mean?"

"I know that look, little girl. You've got something percolating in your brain. What's going on?"

How did she talk about *this*?

Tad surprised her again. "You'd better not be thinking about moving. You promised me."

She laughed. No, *that* wasn't the problem. "I know. I'm not thinking about moving."

"Then what the hell is going on?"

She blushed, not sure how to approach it. Not sure he'd approve. When she couldn't admit it, Tad laughed. "Please tell me one or both of those boys made a pass at you?"

Her eyes widened in shock as she stared at him. "What?"

He grinned. "Oh, come on. They're both crazy about you, admit it."

Clarisse remained silent.

Tad leaned in close. "Listen to me. Life's short. If they love you, then enjoy it and to hell with what anyone else thinks."

He dropped the topic, to her immense relief. She stayed a little longer, but it was blatantly obvious from his pleased smile and twinkling gaze that he would absolutely be unable to render impartial advice.

Before she returned to the house, she detoured by Howard Park and drove all the way out to the beach. A windy, chilly, overcast weekday meant she had the place to herself. She found a bench facing the Gulf and stared out at the choppy, grey water.

A chance for her dreams to come true.

For her very own happily-ever-after.

Was she brave enough to take it? Could she live that way? Voluntarily turn herself over to someone else when she'd struggled so hard to be free? What *was* freedom?

Was it fighting for every dollar she had to earn and living alone and on her own, or was it allowing herself to be taken care of, albeit unconventionally, by two men who would no doubt make sure she never wanted for anything.

Why couldn't it have just been one of them? Either of them...

She realized what she'd thought. Mac or Sully.

But they weren't asking her to make a choice. Maybe Sully didn't love her the way Mac did, but he still wanted her around. That was something, right?

Still confused and unsure what to do, she returned to the Bug and drove home.

Chapter Sixteen

Mac took her shopping on Friday afternoon, to an adult store in Clearwater that sold sexy club and dance clothes in addition to novelties and movies.

She stopped at the doorway. No prude that's for sure, but she'd never been in one of those places before.

Mac noticed her discomfort. He laced his fingers through hers and squeezed. "Trust me?"

She nodded and let him lead her inside.

It took every ounce of will she had to fight the urge to turn around, walk out, and demand he take her home. There were a few mannequins dressed—to use the term loosely—in form-fitting and skimpy wear she knew would look horrible on her. Her body was too large and round to ever wear anything like that.

A friendly sales clerk walked up. Mac took the lead. As Clarisse could do little more than stare at the store's offerings, Mac told the woman what he wanted and she showed them several racks of clothing.

Mac consulted with the woman and picked out several things, then handed them to Clarisse. "Go try them on. What shoe size are you?"

"What?"

"What shoe size?"

"Eight."

He turned to the clerk. "Stiletto pump, black, basic."

"I can't walk in stilettos!"

"Have you ever tried?"

"Mac, look at me. I'm too—"

"If you say 'fat,' I'll spank you right here, so help me I will."

Her mouth snapped shut. That's *exactly* what she was going to say, but she wouldn't give him the satisfaction. "I was going to say clumsy. I've never worn tall heels before. I damn near kill myself in flats."

"Then it's time you learn how."

The clerk returned with two shoe boxes and showed the contents to Mac. He pointed to one. "Perfect."

Clarisse looked at the items he'd picked for her to try on. "I don't know how to put these on," she finally admitted.

The clerk smiled. "I'll help you." She ushered Clarisse into the changing room while Mac took a seat and waited for the show to start.

The first corset looked beautiful. The clerk laced the back for her. It forced her to stand up straight. As she turned and looked at herself in the mirror...

Her mouth gaped. Not thin, but the garment gave her a shape she never realized she had. "Wow!"

"That looks gorgeous on you," the clerk said. "You've got a perfect waist, an hourglass figure. I wish I had your hips."

"I'll give them to you. I wish I had less of them."

The woman shook her head. "No, you wouldn't look good skinny. Your proportions are perfect." She grinned. "Your man doesn't seem to mind your figure. He practically drooled while he picked out those outfits for you."

Clarisse's blush deepened. The woman helped her into a leather skirt and the shoes. The shoes fit, but she nearly fell over on the five-inch heels. With the clerk offering a steadying arm, Clarisse tottered out to show Mac.

He stood at her appearance, his jaw gaped in shock.

She knew it. It'd been stupid to think she could pull this off. She—

He covered the distance between them in two strides, pulled her into his arms, and deeply kissed her with an intense passion that not only took her breath away, it felt like he'd sucked her soul out from the very ends of her toes. Stunned, she nearly fell over when he released her until he grabbed her to hold her steady.

The clerk laughed. "I take it you'll want these?"

"Yeah," Mac hoarsely said. "Probably the rest too, if she looks this good in them."

Clarisse couldn't pull her gaze from his. "How many strokes did that just cost you?" she whispered.

He grinned. "I don't care."

He kissed her again before sending her back to the dressing room. By the time they finished an hour later, he'd bought her seven different outfits she could mix and match, and two pairs of shoes. He smiled as he produced a credit card for the clerk to ring up the sale.

When they were back in the car, he couldn't stop grinning. "You looked positively miserable in there, sweetie." He leaned in and kissed her again. "But you also looked drop-dead gorgeous."

Clarisse couldn't stop thinking about the first kiss. Especially since her panties had grown considerably damp as a result. "Three kisses. He'll beat you black-and-blue for that, won't he?"

"I sure hope so."

* * * *

Sully insisted on a modeling session when they returned. He sat on the couch and Mac helped her negotiate the walk from her bedroom to the living room in her heels. She wasn't sure if Sully's expression meant he liked them or not until she modeled the final outfit. Then he stood and walked over to her.

"They're all gorgeous. I think you should wear this one at the party tomorrow."

She blushed. "Why this one?"

"I think you'll be most comfortable in it." While the least restrictive of the outfits, she felt practically naked in the short

Spandex skirt that barely covered her ass and the leather halter top that pushed her breasts up and made them look two cup sizes larger.

"Comfortable?"

The corner of his mouth curled in a smile. "Unrestricted. But wear the first corset and the leather skirt in the car on the way there. They're street legal, so to speak. You can change into this after we get there." Then he leaned in and gently kissed her on the lips. Not in the same deeply passionate way Mac had, but it still lit fires inside her.

Mac had another surprise for Clarisse. He made her sit on the couch and gave her a long, sensual foot massage before he painted her toenails.

He wore shorts, yet she didn't miss the firm bulge poking out in front.

"I think this color looks sexy on you," he said as he painstakingly painted her toes.

The deep metallic red did look pretty. When she didn't reply, he looked up, worried. "You like the color, don't you?"

She managed a smile. "Yes, I like the color."

That relieved him. "Master said this could be a special little routine between you and me, before play parties."

Fine with her, the foot rub had made her exceptionally horny while also nearly putting her to sleep.

When Sully said goodnight to Clarisse that evening, he cautioned her to get a good night's sleep. In their bedroom, Mac was already kneeling, the punishment cane on the floor in front of him.

"How many?"

Mac didn't raise his head. "I kissed her three times. Twice in the store and once in the car. I'm sorry, Master. She came out of the dressing room and... I'm sorry. There's no excuse." He sighed. "But it's worth it."

Sully smiled as he unbuttoned his shirt. Had he been there, no doubt he probably would have done the same thing, if not taking her against the wall the dressing room.

"I'm going to do something I haven't done before, slave."

"Master?"

"You get three strokes tonight. One for each kiss. I don't want to stripe you and then waste a good play party because you're too sore to play. I'll take the rest out of you tomorrow night." He dropped his shirt into the hamper. "Or, you can take them all tonight and you don't play tomorrow night. Your choice."

Mac blinked in confusion. "Master?"

"Your choice," Sully repeated.

After a moment, Mac said, "May I ask you a question?"

"Sure."

"I thought you were going to play with me hard at the party anyway."

Sully sat on the bed after stripping off his slacks. "That's not a question, but you're right." Sully watched Mac ponder that.

"Not that I'm complaining, and yes, I'll take the strokes at the party, but why?"

"Have I ever deliberately set you up to fail, slave?"

"No, Master."

"Have I ever put you in a situation where you couldn't help but earn punishment?"

"No, Master."

"I told you to take her shopping. I should have gone too, but I wanted to work since tomorrow will be a lost day. Had I thought it out a little more, I probably would have anticipated this. Therefore, I don't feel like punishing you for something that was ultimately my responsibility. Understand?"

"I understand, but I don't agree. I could have not kissed her."

Sully grinned. "Yeah, like *that* could have happened." He pointed to his cock, which had grown stiff. "Get over here and take care of me. I'll give you your stripes after you're done."

Mac eagerly complied as Sully relaxed on the bed. Mac knelt on the floor between Sully's legs and slowly laved his tongue along Sully's cock. Sully reached down and tightly gripped Mac's hair. "That's it, slave. Suck my cock."

Mac's efforts increased. He worked his lips over the shaft, slowly, drawing it out for Sully the way he knew he liked. Over the years, he'd become an expert at reading Sully's body, knowing where to lick, when to suck, how to time his efforts just right to maximize the man's pleasure.

He took pride in his work.

He palmed Sully's sac, gently stroked his balls, licked them, felt the tension of impending climax build in Sully. He backed off a little, just enough to prolong the pleasure before deep throating him, triggering his release.

His hips bucked against Mac's face as he came, moaning as his hot juices pumped down Mac's throat. After a few moments, Sully's grip on his hair relaxed. Mac released his cock, rested his face against Sully's thigh, and waited for him to recover.

Sully eventually patted his head. "Very good, slave. Excellent. Get the cane. Ass over the bed."

Mac complied as Sully sat up and took the cane from him. Then without fanfare, he quickly laid three strokes across his ass, stingy blows that didn't break the skin. He put the cane away and got the lotion. Mac didn't always need it, but the aftercare had become a familiar and comfortable part of their routine.

Mac's stiff cock brushed against Sully's thigh as they curled together in bed.

"Are you horny, slave?"

"Yes, Master."

"Good. I want you good and horny for tomorrow night. Go to sleep."

"Yes, Master."

* * * *

The next evening, they loaded into the Jag. Mac drove, and an hour later, they pulled into a gated driveway. The area was rural, the property heavily wooded, neighbors scarce. Mac spoke to someone through the intercom. A moment later, the gate rolled open and they drove through.

Clarisse felt another bout of nerves threatening. Could she do this? Really? Despite Sully's assurances that he would respect a safeword, she felt renewed doubts creep in.

This was a chance to make her fantasies come true, and one she wouldn't willingly give up until she'd had a chance to see them through. Sully and Mac looked darkly handsome. Both wore jeans and black button-up shirts. Mac wore his leather collar, padlocked shut.

The driveway wound through the woods until they reached a large cleared area. From what she could see of the woods, she suspected it was a tree farm. Several cars were already parked outside a large building that looked like a barn. Windows in a nearby house appeared dark.

Clarisse waited for Mac to open the back door for her and help her out. She nervously eyed the expanse of grass she'd have to navigate in her heels between the car and the barn. Sully walked around the car and, without fanfare, scooped her into his arms and carried her.

She looked into his eyes, felt her heart thumping at his amused expression.

"You ready for tonight, baby?" he murmured.

She nodded, her mouth suddenly dry.

Mac followed them after getting a few things from the trunk. They'd brought a covered dish, as had everyone else, and two duffel bags full of items Sully deemed necessary for the night's play, including the outfit Sully wanted her to change into.

Sully set her on her feet when they reached a concrete pathway leading to a small door at the end of the barn. He kept his arm around her waist as she tottered toward the entrance. Mac had spent time helping her practice walking in the heels, but she felt far from steady. A man holding a clipboard greeted them outside, checked their names off a list, and welcomed them.

A woman sat at a desk in the small entryway and checked them in. Sully took Clarisse's arm and led her through a curtained doorway into a large dressing room.

Lockers lined the walls and several people were changing clothes. A few of them greeted Sully and Mac by name. Clarisse tried not to stare and failed miserably. People were in various stages of dress and undress—bustiers, corsets, fishnets—and that was just a couple of the men.

Mac stowed their gear in a locker while Sully led her through to another room. Mac followed, carrying the casserole he'd made. A few people already stood around a buffet table set up in one far corner.

The huge play space boggled her mind. The enormous building had been turned into a dungeon. There were a few curtained-off areas, but much of the space lay open where anyone could watch.

What have I gotten myself into?

Sully guided her over to a chair in a quiet corner, made her sit, and knelt in front of her. Mac stood behind him, watching. "I'm going to collar you for the evening, sweetheart. Just a formality."

Fear gripped her. "Why?"

He smiled. "Nothing will stop a jerk from hitting on you if he's determined, but most of the people here, if you're wearing a collar, it'll send them a message that you're taken. It's not a locking collar. It's one of Mac's old play collars."

It belonged to Mac? Somehow, that made the notion more comfortable. She nodded.

Mac handed Sully the collar, and he fitted it around her neck. It was way too loose, even on the smallest hole. He removed it, pulled out a pocket knife, poked a new hole in it, then tried again. Not too tight, not too loose.

The pleased grin on Mac's face wiped away all fears in her heart.

"Is that okay? Is it comfortable?" Sully asked.

She nodded and, feeling it with her hand, noticed a small tag attached to the collar. She couldn't read it, but she fingered it. "What does that say?"

Sully smiled, his grey gaze holding her captive. "Mine."

She gasped. The possessive way he'd said it took her breath away.

"Another thing," he said. "For tonight, you'll address me as 'Sir' when talking to me. I will call you 'girl.' That's the only formality I'll insist on. Do you understand?"

"Yes, Sir. Why don't you want me to call you Master like Mac does?"

If she didn't know any better, she'd swear he looked…sad. He reached out and gently stroked her cheek. "Because I'm not your Master, sweetheart. You're not my slave. Tonight is just to see how you'll like it. I take the relationship and responsibilities I have with slave as his Master more seriously than a marriage. It's not just a role-playing game to us. Understand?"

Emotions spun through her. She nodded.

He smiled, erasing the sad look from his face. "Good girl." He offered his hand and helped her stand. "Let's go introduce you around."

Doreen and Alex arrived. When she spotted Clarisse, Doreen squealed with joy and enveloped Clarisse in a hug that nearly knocked her off her feet. Fortunately, Sully stood there with his hands on her waist, keeping her upright.

"I'm so glad you made it! You're going to have a blast tonight!"

Clarisse wasn't sure if she'd remember anyone Sully introduced her to. Maybe if reminded what they wore, because that's what stuck in her mind. If so, they could jostle her memory with descriptors such as "painful looking metal cage on his cock man" or "the woman with the pierced nipples and bells strung on them." Everyone was friendly and welcomed Clarisse. As the arrival window closed and the party's official start time drew near, more people changed from street clothes into a wide variety of fetish wear from relatively tame to totally naked with accessories.

Frequently hung from pierced body parts.

She wondered if Sully would make Mac change, but he didn't. Yvette and Mike showed up, as did Bob and Jenna. Yvette had Mike naked and hunched over. Yvette grinned at Clarisse's puzzled expression. "Bet you've never seen one of these before, have you? Turn around, boy. Show her your pretty ass."

Mike shuffled around so his backside was visible. Across the backs of his thighs lay a long wooden clamp, with a hole in the center, through which were clamped his...

Clarisse felt a sympathetic pain in her own nether regions. The device tightly squeezed his balls and cock. Yvette had clipped his cuffed wrists to each end of the thing.

"It's a humbler," Yvette gleefully exclaimed. Then she spun him around, caught his head with her arm, and pulled him up. He winced as his cock and balls were stretched by the device. "He's my good boy, aren't you?"

"Yes, Ma'am!" he gasped.

She let him return to his hunched over position. "He talked back to me on the way here. Normally I don't make him wear it this soon in the evening, but I gave him a choice of this, or I was going to let Ray and Oot have their way with him and spit roast him. He chose this."

"Ray and Oot?"

"You haven't met them yet, girl," Sully said. He spotted someone at the other end of the building. "In fact, there they are. Let's go introduce you before they start playing."

Yvette stopped Sully. "Hey, can I play with Mac later?" She grinned. "I brought an extra humbler."

"Sorry. I have plans of my own for him tonight."

"Damn. Oh well." She slapped Mac on the shoulder. "Lucky

you."

As they made their way to the other end of the building, Mac muttered, "Yeah, lucky me is fucking right. Thank you, Master."

"You honestly think I'd let her play with you again after the last time?"

"I hope not."

"What happened?" Clarisse asked.

Mac stepped to her other side. Keeping his voice low he said, "I had to pee sitting down for a week. That psycho bitch makes Sully look like Santa Claus. She's one of the few times I've ever safeworded for pain. She makes the Marquis de Sade look like a sweetheart."

"She knows Mac's a pain slut," Sully quietly added, "and she was eager to see how far she could go. Mike can't take heavy impact play, and she wanted to try it." He looked at Mac. "You're the one who agreed to play with her. I told you it was your choice. I also gave you the option of letting me red light the scene, if you'll recall, but you said you wanted control of it."

"Yeah, and next time I insist on that, feel free to smack me in the balls and remind me of Yvette."

Clarisse shivered. "You won't let her do anything to me, will you?"

Sully stopped and turned her to face him, his face dark, his voice serious. "No one *ever* touches you but Mac and me. That's a promise."

As they walked, another man stopped Sully to ask him a question. Clarisse leaned in to Mac. "What's a spit roast?"

He laughed as he nuzzled her ear and whispered, "One of my favorite fantasies starring you as the center, watching Master fuck you while you suck my cock."

She gasped, her knees nearly melting out from under her at that mental image.

Mac chuckled. "You okay, sweetie?"

"Yes," she squeaked.

Question answered.

"You okay? You wanted an honest answer, right?" His evil, playful grin told her he knew exactly what effect his words had on her.

"I'm okay." *Just hornier than hell.*

Sully finished talking to the other man and they continued their walk to the end of the building.

The men, Ray and Oot, rummaged through two duffel bags. A nearly-naked woman, wearing only a leather harness, knelt nearby waiting on them. Sully introduced Clarisse to the men. Ray had gorgeous hazel eyes and apparently natural blond hair from the looks of it. Oot's coal black hair was spiked, and his light blue eyes sparkled with good cheer. From the collar around Oot's neck, Clarisse suspected Ray called the shots.

"Are you sure you packed it?" Ray testily asked.

Oot rummaged through another bag. "I know I did, Master. It's got to be here." He started emptying the bag, pulling out riding crops, canes, floggers, and other assorted items.

"Oh, here it is," Ray said, pulling a small device out of his bag. "Sorry about that, buddy. It got caught inside a towel."

Oot sat back on his heels. "I thought I'd lost my mind for a minute there."

Ray grinned. "You mean you haven't?"

The men laughed. Ray stood while Oot repacked the duffel bag. Ray motioned for the woman to stand.

"Come here, kitten." He fitted the device into what looked like a ready-made place on her harness…right between her legs. When it started humming, Clarisse realized it was a vibrator.

"Don't you come until I tell you to, or I'll redden your ass. Daddy Saul gave me carte blanche with you this weekend, girlie."

The woman moaned and shifted from one foot to the other as she struggled to comply.

Ray turned back to Sully and Mac and shook hands with them and Clarisse. He stood a little shorter than Sully.

When his eyes landed on Clarisse, they skirted up and down her body, the obvious questions in his gaze remaining unasked. Instead he said, "Any plans for the evening, or just here to socialize tonight?"

"Going to play it by ear for a while. My girl's never been to a play party like this before."

A ball of heat rolled through Clarisse at Sully's words, the possessive tone in his voice.

His girl.

Sully and Ray chatted for a few minutes before Sully led her and Mac away. He handed her over to Mac. "Go get her changed." Then he walked off to talk with someone else.

Put-up or shut-up time. She looked up at Mac, although with her heels, their height difference wasn't as pronounced.

He smiled and slipped his arm around her waist. "Let's get you changed."

The changing room was mostly empty. Clarisse felt heat redden her skin again as he led her to their locker and pulled out one of their bags.

"Keep the shoes on and slip your skirt off," Mac said.

Easier said than done. She tried not to wobble as she worked to wiggle the snug garment off. He knelt in front of her and tugged on the hem, then let her use his shoulders to brace herself as she stepped out of it.

He laughed. "What's this?" He hooked a finger under her plain cotton panties and tugged a little.

Her face had to be a dark shade of magenta by that point. "Underwear," she shot back. "What do you call them?"

He waggled his eyebrows at her. "Off."

"You can't be serious!"

His face softened. "I won't force you. It's your choice."

Her heart raced as he stared at her. If she wanted a chance to do things their way, she'd have to do things their way. She still wore more clothes than over half the other attendees anyway.

He stood and leaned in, his mouth near her ear. "Master and I promise no one will touch you but us. I swear it."

It wasn't just that, although that made up a large part of it. Then again, after seeing some of the party attendees she actually fell in the middle of the range in terms of body types. There were women—and men—much larger than her wearing much less and apparently completely comfortable with it. From the way they walked around, they obviously didn't feel self-conscious, so why should she?

She closed her eyes, hooked her thumbs in the elastic waistband, and pulled them down. Mac knelt again, letting her brace herself on him. She didn't open her eyes until he'd pulled the other skirt up her legs and into place. She felt a cool draft of air touch her admittedly damp sex.

When she dared open her eyes, Mac had stood and was smiling. "You're beautiful, sweetheart," he whispered. He helped her out of the corset. When she moved to cover her breasts with her hands, he gently grabbed her wrists and pulled them away, bent in, and licked her right nipple, then her left.

He smiled. "Worth every fucking stroke and then some."

He helped her with the halter top, fastening it for her. Then he stepped back and admired her. He grabbed her hand and placed it on the front of his jeans. She felt his large, rigid cock clearly outlined against the denim and straining for freedom.

"That's what you do to me, babe," he whispered. "No other woman here tonight does that to me. Next time you think about putting yourself down, you think about this." He squeezed her hand, molding it around the shape of his stiff member. Then he let her go, grabbed both duffel bags, and led her back to the play space.

Sully was chatting with Alex when Clarisse emerged from the changing room with Mac. She couldn't read the look that passed across Sully's face, the mask that dropped into place.

Tottering across the floor on Mac's arm, she nervously stood in front of Sully and tried to decipher his expression. He held out his hand to her.

"Let's go play, girl," he softly said.

After an anxious glance at Mac, she put her hand in Sully's and let him take charge of her. She stepped away from the safety of Mac's side.

"Can you trust me?" Sully softly asked.

She didn't have a choice. "Yes, Sir."

He smiled as he stroked her cheek. "Good girl. Your safeword is red. If you say that, everything stops immediately. Understood?"

"Yes, Sir."

He laced his fingers through hers and led her to what looked like a long trapeze bar. He nodded to Mac, who walked over to the wall and flipped a switch. A motor hummed to life and the bar descended a little, but still hung almost two feet above her head.

Sully stood in front of her. "Slave, bring me the suspension cuffs." His eyes never wavered from hers.

"Yes, Master." Mac rooted through one of the bags and found what Sully had asked for, then presented them to him.

They didn't look like the leather wrist cuffs she'd seen Mac wearing. They were different, heavily padded and with an attached, short metal bar running the width of the cuff.

As he strapped the first one onto her left hand, she realized the metal bar was a handhold built into the reinforced restraints. She could wrap her fingers around the bar and hold on.

"Suspension cuffs," Sully said, answering her unspoken question. "I had to order a smaller pair. I figured Mac's would be too large."

He strapped the other one on her and had her check the fit.

While Sully did that, Mac clipped two straps to the bar. They dangled from the bar, ending in unusual-looking snaps.

"Take her shoes off, slave," Sully quietly ordered. He wrapped his arms around her and kissed her as Mac complied. She closed her eyes and enjoyed his gentle kiss, soft and sweet, not as passionate as Mac's had been at the store, but taking her focus off her nerves and anxiety.

When she stood barefoot in front of him, he lifted her left arm and clipped it to the bar, then tightened the strap to remove the excess slack. He repeated the action with her right.

Her heart thrummed in her chest.

"Reach up with your fingers. Feel the snaps."

She did. What felt like no slack was actually just enough she could easily wrap her fingers around them.

"Pull down on the snaps," Sully ordered.

When they came loose, it startled her. Mac put his hand in the center of her back to steady her. Good thing she wasn't in the heels or she'd have tipped over.

Sully smiled and reconnected her. "Panic snaps. They release even if under tension. I wanted you to see that."

It did settle her a little to know she wasn't totally immobilized. She trusted Sully and Mac to stop if she used a safeword, but knowing she had the power to get out if she wanted reduced her nervous tension.

The concrete floor felt cool under her feet. Sully stood before her and grabbed her chin, tipped her face to his. "Do you want to play, girl?" he softly asked.

She nodded.

His grip tightened. Not painfully, but authoritatively. "Say it."

"I want to play with you, Sir."

He leaned in and brushed his lips across hers. "If I ask you how you are, you say green, yellow, or red. You call yellow or red at any time you need to, understand?"

"Yes, Sir."

"Good girl." He stepped away for a moment, then moved behind her. Mac took Sully's place in front of her, standing so close she felt heat radiating from him even through his clothes. His brown eyes smoldered with passion.

Then she felt Sully's hands on her waist, his fingers gently raking her bare flesh between the skirt and top. Over her hips, across her ass, along her thighs. On the upward journey, he caught the hem of her skirt and pulled it up to her hips, exposing her.

She blushed.

Mac touched her chin. "Look at me," he whispered.

She did, unable to look away if she wanted to.

Sully slowly caressed her legs, her ass, and traveled up to her hips. When he pressed his body along her back, she knew she didn't imagine the hard bulge she felt through his jeans. His hands skimmed around her waist, to her belly, and pulled her tightly against him.

"I'm going to play with you, girl," he rumbled in her ear. "I want you to trust me. There will be a little pain, but I promise you a lot of pleasure in return if you take it for me."

She shivered in his arms. "Okay."

"Rest your head against my shoulder and close your eyes."

She did.

"Keep them closed unless I tell you to open them."

His hands skimmed up her tummy to her breasts, where he cupped his hands around them over her halter. His lips feathered along her neck, teeth gently nipping and grazing her skin. She felt a second set of lips brush across her collarbone, down her neck to between her breasts.

Mac.

Sully's hands lifted from her breasts. She felt the halter being unlaced and opened. Sully's hands returned, his fingers finding and tweaking her nipples, pinching them between his fingers, rolling them until they were hard peaks. Her hips involuntarily gyrated against Sully, wanting more as tingles of heat shot straight to her clit.

She softly moaned when Sully stepped back, allowing cool air to brush against her flesh. He slipped a blindfold over her eyes as Mac's fingers replaced Sully's on her nipples.

Sully gripped her ass in his hands and squeezed. "I'm going to start here, girl," he said. Then he smacked her with his bare hand. Not hard, but enough to make her jump.

Mac stepped up his efforts in front of her as Sully spanked her. Her body struggled to make sense of the conflicting messages, the pleasure of Mac's fingers on her nipples dueling with the sting of Sully's hand on her ass as he gradually increased the force of his strikes.

Then, both men stopped, almost shocking her system back to reality. Mac stepped in, cupped his hand around the back of her neck, and tipped her head forward so it rested against his shoulder. He left his hand in place as he whispered to her.

"How are you, girl?"

"Green," she gasped.

She felt something hard, flat, and cool touch her ass. Then a stinging slap.

She realized it was a paddle. As she instinctively twisted her hips away from it, Mac's other hand slid between her legs and played with her clit.

She moaned as the strokes from the paddle increased in severity and Mac's fingers plunged deeper into her sex. She gyrated her hips, trying to get closer to Mac, to draw him in even deeper.

"Does that feel good, baby?" Mac whispered in her ear.

"Yes!"

After a moment, Sully stopped and Mac withdrew his hand. She moaned in disappointment. Sully grabbed her hair and gently tugged so she had to tip her head back.

"You want more, girl?" His voice had dropped in tone, deeper, serious.

"Yes!"

"I give you more pleasure, you have to take more pain, too. One doesn't come without the other tonight."

Fuck yeah. So far, he hadn't actually hurt her, the sting from the paddle already dissipating.

But dammit, her clit throbbed almost painfully, begging for relief. "Yes!"

He nipped her earlobe. "That's my good girl." He stepped away.

With the blindfold on, she couldn't tell where either man stood. After a moment, she jumped when she felt something touch her clit. Sully spoke in front of her. "I'm having slave deliver these blows." He kissed her, then whispered in her ear, "If you want to be with us in all ways, you will have to get used to us both topping you."

"Yes!"

She felt Mac stroke her ass with his hand, lovingly, tenderly. Then he laid something she suspected was a riding crop along her backside.

"Now," Sully said. Her world lit up behind the blindfold as a powerful vibrator kicked on and Mac simultaneously smacked her ass with something much more stingy than the paddle.

Sully whispered in her ear. "Do not come, girl."

She whined, wanting it, needing it, and felt another stingy blow across her ass. The pain tempered her pleasure just enough she could gain a foothold on her climbing orgasm, but as she tried to twist her hips away from the vibrator, Mac smacked her ass again and pushed her back onto it.

"Do not come," Sully warned again, louder, deeper.

She felt her tears starting, more from frustration than pain, from desperation for relief and even more desperate to obey Sully.

Mac alternated the strength of the blows, ones that barely made contact with stinging, painful swats that made her yelp and pushed her harder onto the vibrator Sully pressed against her clit.

She couldn't take it anymore. "Please, let me come!"

"Beg me."

"Sir, please! Let me come! God, let me come!"

Mac smacked her harder, then stroked her ass with his hand.

"No," Sully whispered, one hand teasing her nipples, alternating from one to the other. "You cannot come yet. You haven't begged enough."

"Please!" She sobbed, desperate. "Please!"

The pain and pleasure melded into one as she struggled to obey. Just as she knew she couldn't hold on any longer, Mac stopped and stepped closer. He wrapped his arm around her waist.

"Come, girl," Sully commanded.

She screamed, the strongest orgasm she'd ever had in her life exploding within her, her knees unhinging, but Mac holding on with both arms around her.

Just as she started to come down from that, Sully pressed the vibrator more firmly against her. "Again. Come now, girl!" he ordered.

She sobbed as she felt another one hit her, not as powerful as the first, but almost, robbing her of strength. Her oversensitive clit screamed in protest as he wiggled the vibrator against her at the same time Mac pinched her nipples. "One more, girl. Come now!"

Clarisse went limp in Mac's arms as the climax washed through her. Then Sully shut off the vibrator and unclipped her arms. He took her from Mac and carried her to a nearby chair. There, he cuddled her to his chest as he sat and soothed her. Mac removed her blindfold and draped a blanket over her. Sully tucked it tightly around her.

He kissed her forehead. "Very good, girl," he murmured. "That was my very, very good girl."

Clarisse felt like she'd been ripped apart at the seams. She closed her eyes and cried, with relief, with happiness, with emotions she couldn't even begin to identify. It felt cathartic, a release she'd never experienced before, beyond the physical, beyond the emotional.

Sully gently rocked her in his arms. "It's okay," he whispered, his face buried in her hair. "Let it all out, baby. It's okay."

She stayed curled into a tight ball in his arms, not wanting to move, not wanting the moment to end, not wanting to think, wanting just feel and enjoy the avalanche of emotions flooding through her.

To let him take care of her.

Mac reached under the blanket, found her wrists, and removed the cuffs. Then he rubbed her wrists. She suspected she'd be sore there tomorrow, and her arms, not to mention her ass, but…

Damn. Well worth it.

She looked at Sully. She read worry in his grey eyes.

"Are you okay, sweetheart?" he asked.

"Yeah."

He kissed her forehead again and snuggled her more tightly to him. "I hope you still like me in the morning."

She smiled. "I will." Mac also looked worried, but she crooked her finger at him and he leaned in for a kiss. "Thank you. Both of you."

He smiled as he laced her halter top for her. "I'd say my pleasure, but I think you had the most fun."

Letting her head rest against Sully's firm chest, she closed her eyes. "That was…wow."

"Wow's a common reaction," Sully joked.

After she felt comfortable enough to sit up, Sully turned her over to Mac. "Go clean her up and let her put her underwear back on."

At her startled look, Sully laughed. "I saw the panty lines, sweetie. Get her something to eat, too." He squeezed her shoulder as he stood and walked over to a man trying to get his attention.

Mac had apparently gathered their gear while she recovered with Sully, because someone else now occupied the bar. Nestled snugly under Mac's arm, Clarisse tightly wrapped the blanket around her and let him lead her through the dressing room to the private bathroom.

"Do you want to take a shower?"

"No, I'm okay." He had her bend over the counter as he slathered lotion onto her flesh. The cool feeling of the lotion, combined with his gentle fingers, stirred her need again.

Then she winced as he went over a sore spot.

"Sorry, sweetie. I didn't cut you, thank God. A couple of those strokes I was afraid were too hard."

She turned to look in the mirror after he finished. Her pink ass was marked by darker red and purple stripes. Mac followed her gaze.

"You'll be sore in the morning," he said with a teasing smile.

He helped her change clothes and put her shoes back on. "Now what?" she asked.

"You need to get some water in you so you don't get dehydrated. And some food."

"After that?"

Hugging her, he playfully waggled his eyebrows. "I get the shit beat outta me."

Chapter Seventeen

Mac let her lean on him for support as they returned to the main play space. By this time, more people were using various pieces of equipment. With her experience out of the way and her nerves settled, Clarisse now had peace of mind and more than a heaping bucket of curiosity. Yvette had Mike kneeling on the floor, apparently free of his humbler but wearing wrist and ankle cuffs and a full hood. She'd attached a leather leash to his collar.

Doreen flounced over as Mac helped Clarisse get food from the buffet. "How are you feeling? Did you have fun?"

Not wanting to be rude, but not really wanting to talk yet, Clarisse settled for a nod.

Doreen grinned. "You're a lucky girl! I get to play next." Alex called to her from across the room. Doreen slapped a hug around her before heading off.

Clarisse followed her progress. Sully and Alex stood next to a bench.

She felt her mellow harshing as Doreen stripped and eagerly took her place on the bench while Sully and Alex worked to bind her.

Sensing her discomfort, Mac guided her over to chairs lined along the walls, near the buffet. "You need to eat, sweetie."

Jealous? *Hell*, yes. The thought of Sully talking to some other woman the way he'd talked to her, touching her...

Stupid. He's not yours to be jealous over. That didn't stop her from feeling jealous.

Mac couldn't distract her no matter how hard he tried. Bless his heart, he tried damn hard, too. Sully and Alex tormented Doreen,

Sully spanking her with his bare hand and implements for a while before breaking out the vibrator. After nearly a half-hour, Doreen begged her head off, pleading, crying.

Clarisse finally looked away when Sully leaned in and whispered something to Doreen, and she cried out as her climax hit her.

She couldn't stand seeing Sully with her like that. The warm fuzzies she'd felt after her session with him disappeared like dandelions in a hurricane.

"I need to go to the bathroom," she said to Mac. He helped her stand and walk to the bathroom, then stood outside waiting for her.

She had promised herself she wouldn't do it, would try to play by their rules, but she cried anyway. The bubblegum and daisies upside to this arrangement—two sweet, hunky men who would let her spend the rest of her life with them—had a dark and thorny underside. She could accept the BDSM aspect of it. If what she'd experienced was as bad as it got, no problem.

But if she wanted to be a part of them, she couldn't share them. Not like that.

Mac knocked on the door. "You okay, sweetie?"

"Yeah, I'll be done in a minute." She used the bathroom, splashed cold water on her face, and tried for a smile she hoped appeared genuine. When she emerged, Mac looked concerned.

Sully walked over. "You okay?"

"Yeah."

He frowned, but didn't press her for more. He stepped around her and into the bathroom, closed and locked the door behind him.

Probably washing his hands.

That thought nearly drove her to tears again.

Mac sensed her change in mood. "Honey, talk to me."

"I'm okay."

"Please?"

"Mac, I'm fine!" she snapped. "Quit asking."

He shook his head. "You don't look fine."

Alex had Doreen wrapped in a blanket while he talked to her and held her. Mac probably felt okay with it because Doreen was a woman. She wondered if he'd be as accepting of it if Sully played with other guys.

Over the next hour, Sully took part in several scenes with people, helping out the way he had with Alex and Doreen. Each time he touched someone else, Clarisse felt her stomach knot in an ugly way. Mac tried to keep her talking and laughing, but he finally fell silent when he realized she wasn't in the mood for his playful commentary.

After the last scene, Sully disappeared to the bathroom yet again. Clarisse stood and perused the buffet under the pretense of looking for a snack. She jumped when Sully touched her shoulder.

"What's wrong?"

"Nothing!" She pulled away from the men and tottered over to the large cooler where bottles of water had been put on ice. Mac swooped in and opened the cooler for her, fished one out of the icy water, opened it and handed it to her.

"Thank you."

He didn't ask again. When she glanced at him, and at Sully, they wore nearly identical expressions—concern. Sully didn't turn his focus from her. "Slave, go get our things and get ready."

"Yes, Master." He walked off with one last look at Clarisse.

Sully guided her over to the seats and sat with her. "Talk to me," he softly commanded.

Her eyes flicked over to Doreen and Alex before returning to him. "I'm fine."

"You're lying."

"I'm not lying. I'm just tired, that's all."

"Do you want to leave?"

No, I just want the image of your hand up Doreen's twat bleached from my mind. "Not until after Mac gets to play."

He studied her for a moment. "Okay. Would you like to help me with him?"

That little nugget was enough to surprise her out of her funk. "Help?"

His lips curved into a smile. "You'll be the first person I've ever had help me top him. It's going to be intense for him tonight, regardless. You won't get safeword rights. All you can do if you can't take it is step away out of the scene. I owe him a big one though, and I want him to enjoy it."

Her mouth dried. "What do I have to do?"

"What I tell you to do."

It would take her mind off her jealousy. "Like what?"

He shrugged, his face clouding for a moment. That's when his gaze dropped to his hands. "There are things I don't do for him, even under boat rules." He looked at her. "If you want to, I'll let you."

For someone who normally acted pretty straightforward, his waffling behavior was starting to piss her off. "Just say it."

"I'm not going to lie to you. I'm going to savage him pretty brutally. He needs it. He expects it. It would make it even better for him if you'd go down on him. He loves you. It would send him into orbit. I'm not gagging him tonight, so he's going to cry, and he's going to scream."

Her heart pounded. Sully's eyes focused on her, trying to read her reaction.

She nodded.

"Good." He stood and offered her his hand. "Let's take care of our boy."

The trapeze bar, as she thought of it, lay vacant again. Mac emerged from the dressing room with their duffel bags. He'd changed clothes.

Well, clothes being a relative term because he was naked except for his collar, suspension cuffs like the ones she'd worn, and a leather harness around his waist that ran between his legs.

Clarisse stood leaning against the wall where Sully had left her. Mac's eyes held hers as Sully adjusted the bar height and hooked Mac to it. She realized he used different straps with Mac than he had with her. They still had panic snaps, but configured differently, where Mac couldn't reach them to release himself. Sully also cranked the bar much higher than he had for her, so Mac's arms were tightly stretched high over his head.

Mac didn't look away from her until Sully put a blindfold on him. He whispered into Mac's ear. She watched as Mac's cock, fitted through a ring in the harness, slowly inflated. He rotated his left wrist, the whole cuff twisting.

Sully continued talking to him as he slid a hand across Mac's chest. He twisted first one nipple ring, then the other.

Mac's cock stood fully erect.

Letting his hand slowly trail down Mac's abs, Sully gripped Mac's cock and squeezed, hard. Mac winced, but nodded. "Yes, Master," she heard him say.

Sully stepped away from Mac and unbuttoned his shirt, then draped it over a nearby chair where he'd laid out several vicious looking implements. He motioned Clarisse over to him.

He leaned in and whispered, "Take off your shoes, sweetie."

She gratefully kicked them off.

"You stand in front of him. I want you to play with his nipples, rake your nails over him, but don't go near his cock and balls until I tell you to. You can kiss him too, if you want. When I'm ready, I'll point at the floor, and then you can go down on him. Don't do it sooner." He reached over and tucked a stray hair behind her ear. "You don't have to do this if you don't want to."

"I want to."

"Do you want a towel to spit in?"

Time to dish a little back at him. "I'll take a towel, but I'm a good girl. I swallow."

Sully's lips pressed together before he burst out laughing and hugged her. "I love you, sweetie. You're adorable."

She stood in front of Mac and waited for Sully to get into position.

Sully leaned forward and softly spoke in Mac's ear. "I have a surprise for you, slave. You get punishment and a reward tonight."

Mac cocked his head toward Sully's voice but didn't ask questions. Clarisse heard Sully's bare hand strike Mac's ass. Mac's jaw tensed, but he didn't make a sound.

When she reached out and gently brushed her fingers against his nipple rings, he gasped, startled. "Clarisse?"

She leaned in and kissed him. Sully stepped up the tempo and strength of his blows as he reddened Mac's ass with his hand. As she twisted Mac's nipples harder, he softly moaned.

Sully switched to a heavy flogger, striking Mac's back and shoulders as well as his thighs. She drew her nails across his flesh, not hard, but enough to coax noises out of him that Sully's strikes didn't.

Even though she was aware of people standing around watching, her eyes never left Mac's face. His mouth parted, his tongue occasionally flicking out to lick his lips during a lull in Sully's strokes. At one point Sully stopped. He stepped behind Mac, tightly grabbed his hair and yanked his head back.

"Where are we, slave?"

"Green, Master," he gasped.

Sully bit his neck, hard, leaving a mark behind. Then he took a bottle of water and held it to Mac's lips, let him have a sip before he started in on him again. He switched to a paddle, the loud strikes making Clarisse wince in sympathy. Next came a riding crop. Mac couldn't help but respond at this point, twisting against the blows, mixed sounds of pain and pleasure flowing from him. Sully switched to a cane. That's when Mac's cries turned anguished even as his cock throbbed hard between his legs, drops of clear pre-come coating the engorged head.

"Do not come, slave," Sully firmly commanded as he savaged Mac's ass with the rattan cane. "Do not come or I will use this on your fucking cock."

Mac jerked against the restraints, the equipment rattling, his fingers tightly wrapped around the bars inside the suspension cuffs, but he didn't call red.

"Who do you belong to?" Sully barked.

"You, Master."

"What are you?"

"I'm your slave, Master. I belong to you."

"Who does this ass belong to?"

"You!"

Mac's face twisted in pain with each stroke. When Clarisse rubbed her thumbs over his nipples, Mac gasped with need.

Sully took several hard strokes with the cane, harder than the others, before he stepped close again.

"How are we?"

Mac panted for breath. He rotated his left hand.

"Say it."

He finally did, even though his voice sounded low and slurred. "Green, Master."

Sully immediately started on him again with the cane. She pressed her lips to Mac's, surprised when he eagerly kissed her back, fiercely, as if she offered safe harbor and relief from the onslaught.

She felt his moans against her tongue even as he kissed her, until Sully finally ended the set with the cane.

Sully spoke again. "Girl, do not step to either side of him without raising your hand first to let me know you are." That was all the warning she had before she heard the loud crack of a whip. Mac screamed, jumping, straining against the restraints and rattling the entire bar again.

Sully stepped in and pushed Mac's feet farther apart with his. "Do not move, slave. You earned punishment, remember?"

Another crack, and Mac screamed again, his head dropping to Clarisse's shoulder.

"Safeword if you have to, slave," Sully commanded.

Mac rotated his left hand.

Sully grinned. "I didn't think you would." He struck him four more times. "Safeword yet?"

Mac rotated his left hand even as his hips thrust in empty air, his cock rigid and nearly purple.

Sully adjusted his position and started regularly timed strokes. Mac cried out, cried, shivered. Clarisse cupped the back of his neck with her hand, cradled his head on her shoulder as best she could, tried to soothe him as he screamed with each stroke.

Sully stopped after a few minutes. "Step back, girl," Sully softly ordered.

Reluctant to let Mac go, she did. Sully walked around the front of Mac and grabbed his chin. "Surrender yet? Want me to continue?"

He rotated his wrist.

"Say it!" Sully yelled at him as he released Mac's chin.

Mac's head hung, sweat dripping from him. "Green," he muttered, his voice slurred.

Sully grabbed Mac's hair and pulled his head up. "Tell me what you want."

"Fuck you! Green!"

Clarisse gasped, worried. Mac's answer seemed to amuse Sully though. He ruffled Mac's hair and kissed him. "Have it your way, slave." He returned to his position behind Mac, waited for Clarisse to resume her position, and viciously started in on him again. Mac screamed, strained against the restraints as tears ran down his face. Each blow ripped another ragged howl from Mac. Before long, he was swearing at Sully and calling him every filthy name in the book and then some as he yanked on the restraints.

But he didn't safeword. Sully dished the insults back to him as good as he took them, interspersed with taunts to safeword.

Mac's standard response to that: "Fuck you! Green!"

He was still screaming when Sully stepped closer and, almost without missing a beat, switched to a riding crop and locked eyes with Clarisse.

He pointed to the floor.

Still stunned from what she'd witnessed, she dropped to her knees in front of Mac and swallowed his cock, wanting to give him some measure of enjoyment.

Sully yelled, "Come *now*, slave!" He savaged Mac's ass with rapid-fire blows.

Mac's hips bucked against her face as his cock swelled and his hot juices exploded from him, pouring down her throat almost faster than she could keep up. When he went limp in the restraints she worried he'd passed out, but Sully was already there with a blanket, wrapping it around him, supporting him. He pulled Mac's blindfold off.

Sully face was an unreadable mask, his voice hoarse. "Good girl," he whispered. "Help me unhook him."

She jumped to her feet and ran over to the switch to lower the bar so she could reach the straps. Mac cried, sobbing in Sully's arms. When the bar was low enough for her to reach, she unhooked the straps. Sully draped Mac's arm over his shoulders and his own around Mac's waist and half dragged the larger man away.

"Bring our stuff," he called over his shoulder.

She quickly gathered their things and ran after them to the dressing room.

Sully had Mac seated on one of the benches. He was slumped over, his head in Sully's lap, no longer crying but he shivered.

Clarisse hadn't put her shoes back on yet. Sully glanced at her. "Please bring me a bottle of water." She ran for one and brought it to him. Sully twisted the top off and cupped Mac's head in one hand, lifted it enough he could place the bottle against Mac's lips. "Drink, buddy," Sully ordered, his tender tone the polar opposite of the one he'd used during the vicious beating.

Mac took a small sip.

"No, Brant," Sully said. "More. You need to drink."

Mac finally did, then rested his head in Sully's lap. He still didn't open his eyes.

Sully nodded toward one of the duffel bags. "There should be a pair of shorts and a T-shirt in there. Get those, please. And a towel, and the zip-top bag with the ointment and stuff in it."

She found them. "Where do you want them?"

"Bathroom." Once she placed the items on the counter in there, Sully carefully nudged Mac to his feet and guided him into the bathroom.

He closed the door. She felt her heart fall at being shut out.

Sully called out. "Clarisse?"

"Yeah?"

"I thought you were right behind us. Come here."

Her soul lightened as she stepped in with them and locked the door behind her. Mac stood, albeit dangerously swaying on his feet and leaning on the counter for support. His eyes were still closed.

"Get the harness off him, babe," Sully quietly ordered.

She did, working by feel under the blanket and trying to be careful of his back. Sully peeled the blanket up and let out a low hiss.

"Fuck, Brant. Why the hell didn't you safeword?"

"I didn't need to," he replied, his voice still sounding slurred.

Clarisse started to look. Sully touched her shoulder and shook his head. "Not tonight, babe. Sit on the counter and let him lean on you. Keep your eyes closed."

She did. Mac wrapped his arms around her waist and put his head in her lap. She buried her face in his hair and didn't look as Sully removed the blanket from him and did something. Mac grunted in pain a couple of times. She guessed Sully was dressing his wounds.

Sully grabbed her hand. "Hold this." He placed her hand against Mac's back. She felt something under her fingers. "It's safe to look."

He'd draped a large nonstick dressing across Mac's back and affixed bandage tape to hold it in place. Angry welts and red marks were visible around the outer perimeter of the bandage.

"So his shirt doesn't stick to him," Sully explained as he secured the dressing. "The ointment will help prevent infection." He grabbed the T-shirt, carefully pulled it over Mac's head, and she helped him get his arms in it. Then Sully slowly rolled it down Mac's torso, being careful not to dislodge the dressing.

He picked up the shorts and tapped Mac's right leg. "Lift."

Mac obeyed. Sully repeated it with his left and gingerly slid the shorts up Mac's legs and into place. "Stay here with him. I'll be right back." He left the door open as he rummaged through the bag and found the cane, crop, and whip he'd used. He wiped them with antibacterial wipes and then put them away in the bag and packed the rest of their gear.

He looked through the bathroom door. "Can you handle the bags, sweetie?"

"Yeah." She brushed her fingers through Mac's hair.

Sully shoved her shoes into one of the bags, put his own shirt back on but left it unbuttoned, then grabbed the blanket, and draped it over Mac again. "Come on, Brant," he said. "Time to get you home."

Mac finally opened his eyes. Sully helped him straighten up and supported him while he walked. Clarisse followed them. She grabbed the bags on the way out the door and they made their way through the dewy field to the Jag.

Sully led Mac around to the rear passenger door. "Shit. Honey, the keys are in my left front pocket. Can you get them?" His left arm was hooked around Mac's waist.

She fished around, found them, and unlocked the car. "Put the bags in the trunk," he said. "Get your purse out so you have your license." He helped Mac into the backseat and slid in beside him. Mac immediately leaned over, put his head in Sully's lap, and fell asleep.

Sully buckled his seatbelt. "You okay driving?"

"I'm fine."

He pulled the back door shut as she opened the trunk to get her purse. A moment later, she was adjusting the Jag's seat, mirrors, and steering wheel. When she glanced in the rearview mirror, she could make out Sully's form in the darkness. He had his arms around Mac and leaned over to kiss him.

Without another word, she started the car and slowly made her way down the driveway.

She thought she was nearing the interstate when Sully spoke. "Do you remember how to get home?"

Her hands tightened on the wheel. "Yeah."

He was quiet for a few minutes. "Are you okay?"

"Yeah."

More silence. Then, "You had to see us at our worst."

"Worst?"

"Rarely do we play harder than that. Very rarely." He let out a clipped laugh. "Usually when we play that hard it ends with me fucking him. I normally beat him like that bent over a spanking horse or bench, not standing up."

"Then why did you play differently tonight?"

"Because I wanted you to be a part of it. For you to see what it's like. To give you a chance to see it from both sides."

"To see if I could take it?"

He fell quiet for a moment. "You could say that."

"Is that why you were so hard on him?"

"Nope. I warned you, sometimes he needs it this hard."

She still had difficulty processing that, but her brain had stepped a little closer to accepting it, even if she didn't understand it. "You weren't that hard on him just because I was there, were you?"

"No." He was quiet for a while longer. "If you want to be a part of us, you have to accept who we are, not just the parts of us you want to accept. Just like we'll accept all of who you are."

"I'll never be able to take a beating like he did."

"I know you couldn't. I would never make you take one like that either. You're not him. I couldn't believe you went as far as you did tonight." More silence. "I'm sorry, by the way."

She glanced in the rearview mirror. In the headlights of an oncoming car, she saw his grey gaze focused on her. "For what?"

"For pushing you so hard tonight. I told you I wouldn't hurt you. But you took the lighter stuff so well I wanted to see how far we could comfortably take you."

"It was okay." She might be sore tomorrow, but well worth it. "I told you, I've got a higher than average pain tolerance."

"I'm still sorry. I hope you don't hate me."

She had to stop for a light in downtown Tarpon. She turned and looked over the seat at him. "I would have safeworded if I couldn't take it. I don't hate you for what you did to me."

"But you do hate me."

Only a moron could miss the regret in his voice. "No, I don't hate you. Quit putting words in my mouth. Did the thing with Mac shock me? Yes. I'm not supposed to lie, so I won't. It shocked the hell out of me. What you did to me..." She shook her head. "I don't have words to describe it.

"Wow?"

She laughed and turned to drive as the light changed to green. "Yeah, *wow* about covers it."

"What upset you later?"

She didn't want to admit it. "Nothing."

He didn't respond.

"Just dealing with it all, that's it," she added.

He studied her, but said nothing.

At the house, Sully roused Mac enough to get him to climb the stairs. Clarisse brought the bags in and hesitated in the living room. Finally, she left them on the couch, returned to her room, and changed clothes.

Too tired to do anything else, she was ready to fall into bed when Sully softly knocked on her door.

"Yeah."

He opened it. He'd changed out of his jeans and wore only a pair of boxers. "I wanted to say good night, and you did good."

She blushed. "Thanks."

He pointed at her neck. "Want that off?"

The collar. She'd forgotten about it.

She nodded. He removed it for her, then he stepped in and pulled her to him for a long, strong hug. "You don't have to try to make sense of things tonight or tomorrow or even a month from now. There is no expiration date on this offer. I've already told you what would make me ask you to leave. If you stay a year or a lifetime, as long as we're the only men in your life, we're fine with that."

"Thank you."

He pressed a kiss to her forehead. "I'd ask if you wanted to sleep with us tonight, but he'll wake up horny."

She snorted. "I doubt that."

"No, seriously. The next morning, he's..." He smiled. "One of those things you'd have to learn about us." He turned and quietly shut the door behind him as he left.

Clarisse stared at the closed door. *Horny?*

She guessed she had a lot to learn about the men. The question was, could she take the risk to agree to their insane proposition?

Or could she risk *not* taking them up on it?

Chapter Eighteen

The next morning, Clarisse slept late. Her arms felt a little achy, and she had a few bruises on her ass, but otherwise, she felt good. Mac was already awake and cooking breakfast. He grinned when she walked into the kitchen. She didn't miss the fact that he wore a T-shirt and shorts.

"There's our sleepyhead. Pancakes?" He pulled her in for a long, strong hug.

He acted like he'd already had three pots of coffee.

"You're certainly chipper."

"Feeling good."

"How is that possible?"

He gave her a peck on the end of her nose. "Slept like a rock, had a nice morning wake-up, and life's good."

His infectious smile made her smile. "Despite last night?"

"Because of it. And because a certain someone figured prominently in my sexy dreams last night." He waggled his eyebrows at her before turning to the stove again.

Sully didn't make an appearance. "He went back to sleep," Mac explained with a sly grin. "I wore him out this morning." He sat at the counter with her and wolfed his food.

She stared, incredulous. "How can you even walk this morning?"

"Just the way my body is. Yeah, I've got some pain, but that's cool. Except it's making me damn horny." He laughed.

She quit trying to figure it out.

* * * *

The next afternoon, nearly six weeks after Clarisse had first met them, Sully announced arrangements for Mac to take her to Columbus the next day to meet with the investigating officers and get her things…and Bart. Mac took her to the mall to pick her up a few new items, including a nice dress that he insisted looked great on her.

Clarisse found she couldn't eat, her nerves one hugely painful knot that threatened to rapidly return to sender any food she tried to swallow.

Sully sent Mac instead of going himself because Sully had a conference to prepare for and would be leaving for New York in two days. He drove them to Tampa International. Because of TSA rules, Sully couldn't continue with them past the main terminal. He hugged Mac and whispered something in his ear before releasing him. Mac smiled, nodded, and brushed one last kiss across Sully's lips. She noticed the ID bracelet on Mac's wrist. His other day collar, worn in conjunction with the silver chain collar around his neck.

Clarisse watched the men's interaction, startled by the melancholy pang that flashed through her own soul.

Sully smiled at her before his expression grew serious. "Be safe." He took her hands in his. "Listen to him, okay? Do what he says. Let him protect you. He'll take care of you."

She nodded, blinking back tears. She would miss Sully a lot more than she'd anticipated.

Then he surprised her—he wrapped his arms around her and hugged her tightly. "I'm going to miss you," he whispered in her ear.

"I'll miss you, too."

"I've given him orders to behave himself, just so you know. Nothing personal. I don't want any confusion for either of you. When we're all home next week, we'll talk." He pressed a kiss to the top of her head before he released her.

If only she could let go of that last little stupid, stubborn fear and jealousy and totally trust him the way she trusted Mac.

Mac grabbed their carry-ons and led the way through the first checkpoint to the airside terminal monorail. He caught her eye and winked. "It'll be okay, honey."

She wished she could be so sure. Mac was a big guy, obviously able to take care of himself. Bryan was huge, beefy.

And owned a gun.

Thirty minutes later, they made it through security and sat at the gate while awaiting their flight. By the time their flight took off, she felt more than ready for a drink to steady her nerves even though she knew it wasn't a good idea. Besides, she didn't have any cash on her and suspected Mac wouldn't buy her alcohol even if she asked for it.

He brushed his fingers along the back of her hand on the armrest. "I know you're scared," he softly said. "But this will be okay. You probably won't even see him."

She nodded and stared out the window.

They switched planes in Atlanta before continuing to Columbus. The closer they got, the more nervous she felt. If it weren't for Bart, she'd seriously consider leaving it all, even pictures of her parents. It was just stuff, not worth risking her life, or Mac's, over.

Of course Bryan would go free if she didn't go back to talk to the police and prosecutors again.

Mac laced his fingers through hers as the plane circled for its final approach. He didn't speak, sensing her ever-growing tension.

She'd let the men make the plans, willing to go along with whatever they decided. Mac wanted to grab her stuff first thing the next morning so they could leave town immediately after talking to the cops if necessary. They rented a car, then drove to the U-Haul lot where Sully had already reserved a truck for Mac. Clarisse felt jumpy, on edge as they drove to the motel Sully had picked out. Mac got them checked in. She relaxed only after securely locking and deadbolting the door behind them.

While Mac called Sully, she collapsed on her bed and closed her eyes. She jumped, startled, when Mac touched her shoulder what felt like seconds later.

"You hungry?"

She started to say no, but then the smell of pizza hit her and her stomach growled. "Holy crap, where'd that come from?"

He held two pizza boxes and sat on the end of her bed. "You've been out for two hours."

"No way!"

"Way. It's after seven." He handed her some napkins. "I'm sorry. I couldn't wait any longer. I'm starving. I hope you don't mind I ordered."

She sat up and scrubbed her face with her hands. "I can't believe I passed out like that. I even slept through the delivery guy?"

He opened the boxes. "Yep."

He'd ordered everything she liked. "Thanks, Mac."

"We told you we're taking care of you. Sully and I mean it." He took a bite.

She knew they meant it. Part of her felt guilty that they were willing to take care of her indefinitely, without her taking things any further in their relationship. Asking nothing of her in return except for her trust, honesty, and fidelity.

Why could she trust Sully to whip her ass, to not to kick her out on her ass, but she couldn't trust him to own it?

As exhausted as she'd been, at midnight she still tossed and turned in bed. Mac had fallen asleep in his bed and she couldn't help but lie on her side and watch him. Flickering light from the TV caused shadows to dance across him. He slept on his side, facing her.

She thought about the play party, the things they did to her, the things she helped Sully do to Mac. The blow job.

She could have him. Both of them. Clarisse closed her eyes as Sully's words rippled through her memory. She'd have to learn to fully trust him if she wanted to really become part of them.

She remembered the nasty jealousy. That pushed her beyond her limits.

When she opened her eyes again a few minutes later, Mac was staring at her. "Hey," he whispered.

She blushed, glad for the dark room. "Hey."

"Can't sleep?"

"No. I'm too nervous."

He scooted farther away from her and patted the mattress next to him. He wore a pair of boxers and a T-shirt. "Come here."

"You'll get in trouble."

"Not much. He gave me a little leeway. It's okay."

Her need and nerves shoved her guilt to the side. She threw back the covers, changed beds, and cuddled next to him. His familiar scent comforted and soothed her as she snuggled against him.

When he wrapped his arm around her, she felt safe and secure. "Go to sleep, sweetheart. This'll be okay. We'll be leaving for home the day after tomorrow at the latest. Once we're on the road, you'll feel better."

She had to admit calling the men's house her home felt right.

It could be her home forever.

They could be *her* men.

She wasn't sure she'd sleep, but when she opened her eyes again she lay alone in bed and grey light crept around the edges of the motel curtains. She heard Mac in the bathroom, talking. Probably on the phone to Sully. A few minutes later the shower started. She swung her legs over the edge of the bed. She'd wait to take one until after they finished moving her stuff, but she had to call Raquel to confirm their plans. She'd called her after settling in at Mac and Sully's, to let her know she'd arrived safely and what had happened.

"Girl, I'm so glad to hear from you! Are you okay?"

"Yeah. Has he bothered you?"

"He called once, and I think maybe a drive-by or two, but nothing in the past several weeks. You ready to get the peewee pup?"

"Yeah. We'll call you in an hour where to meet."

"That's perfect, because I've got to get him from Tonya's

anyway. He tried to eat John. Tonya's single."

Clarisse closed her eyes and tried not to cry. "I'm sorry I've dragged you and John into this."

"Listen to me, this was a long time coming. I wish you'd stood up to him the first time. He'd be in jail, and you'd be free already."

Clarisse heard the shower shut off. "I know. I'll talk to you later." She was hanging up when Mac emerged, a towel wrapped around his waist.

He smiled. "Good morning, Sleeping Beauty. I'll be ready in a few minutes." He tossed her his phone. "Call Master and say good morning to him, okay?" He returned to the bathroom and shut the door. The marks across his back from the previous weekend were already healing nicely.

Apparently waiting for her call, Sully answered almost immediately.

"Did you sleep well?"

She blushed, started to say yes, then opted for the full truth. "Not at first. Mac offered to let me cuddle with him." She waited for a disapproving tone, but once again, he surprised her.

"Good."

"You're not upset?"

He laughed. "Is your question, are you going to punish Mac?"

"Yes."

"Of course I am, but not for what you think. Thank you, by the way."

"For what?"

"For telling me the truth. As Mac will be the first to tell you, telling me the truth, especially if you know there will be punishment, will always earn you a reward."

The way he almost purred the last word stirred a ball of molten heat between her legs. His voice sounded like it had at the play party.

She closed her eyes and tried to focus. "Thank you for letting him come with me."

His tone grew serious and firm. "If you honestly think I would have let you return alone, you have a ways to go in terms of learning to trust me, don't you?"

She didn't want to answer, but felt his gaze even through the phone. "Yes," she softly admitted.

His soft chuckle stirred her. "Good girl. At least you admit it. Be safe, I'll talk to you later. Love you." Then he hung up before she could reply.

She stared at the phone.

* * * *

Mac drove the U-Haul truck while Clarisse quietly sat in the passenger seat and stared out the window. Familiar sights passed by, and all she could do was concentrate on what she didn't see. She obsessively glanced in the side mirror at traffic behind them.

"It's okay, sweetie. We're not being followed." Surprised, she looked at him. "I'm not a mind reader, but it doesn't take one to see how upset you are."

She nodded.

They called Raquel again when they reached the storage unit. It wouldn't take long for both of them to empty the unit. Only two pieces of furniture, the rest of it boxes, along with garbage bags full of her clothes. She hadn't bothered trying to keep them neat, opting for fast and easy.

Mac took the padlock key from her and opened the door, studied the load. "You weren't kidding that there's not a lot."

"I didn't have time to screw around. I knew I had to be out before he came after me. There's a few things I wish I could have taken, but it's not worth my life."

"Smart girl." They worked fast. Less than thirty minutes later, he clipped the padlock to the truck's back door before he pocketed the key. "Where are we meeting your friend?"

She gave him directions. He circled the block twice while Clarisse nervously looked for any sign of Bryan. She didn't think Raquel was there at first until her phone rang.

"Is that you in the U-Haul?"

"Where are you?"

"I took Tonya's car. I wandered around for a while before I got here. He couldn't have followed me. I left the baby with her and my car at her house. She keeps this in the garage, so I wore a different shirt and a hat." The driver side window rolled down on a blue Honda Pilot parked in the shade in a spot far from the discount store. A hand emerged, waving at them.

Clarisse squealed. She grabbed Mac's arm and pointed. "There!"

Mac pulled the truck in next to the Honda. Clarisse jumped out and Raquel gave her a huge hug. He stood a few feet away, constantly scanning the area, as the women embraced.

"This is Mac?" Raquel asked with a grin.

"Yeah. My hero. One of them."

Clarisse noticed Mac actually blushed. He stuck out his hand and they shook. "Nice to meet you."

"Ready to get the peewee pup back?"

"Am I!" Clarisse followed her around to the back of the SUV.

Still on edge, Mac kept close watch for anything suspicious. Sully had drilled into his brain what to look for, patterns of behavior indicating that they were being observed. It was with some surprise when he noticed the tiny ball of fur Clarisse cuddled. Clarisse was crying.

"Where's the dog?" he asked, confused, sure that must be one of its chew toys.

Raquel laughed as she lifted a wire crate out of the back of the Honda and handed it to him. "That *is* the dog." It couldn't weigh more than three pounds.

"No, seriously. That's not a dog. That's a dog's hors d'oeuvre."

Clarisse laughed even as she sniffled. The ball of fuzz eagerly licked her face. "Bart's a miniature Yorkie. I told you he was small."

"I thought you meant cocker spaniel small. That's not small, that's a cotton ball."

He loaded the crate and a box of dog supplies way too large considering the size of the dog into the back of the truck.

"I hate to rush you guys," he said, "but we need to move."

Clarisse hugged Raquel again. "I'll give you more info when I can. Use that phone number. It's a disposable phone. I'll let you know if I change it."

Raquel gave her a handful of mail. "Your bank stuff's in there too. It all came to the PO box."

Once inside the truck and on their way again, Mac looked at Clarisse. She wore a bright, happy smile, perhaps the first genuine smile he'd seen from her since they'd met. The little dog seemed totally entranced by her, his mini tail wagging. He looked like a real life teddy bear.

No way would Sully ever object to her keeping him. He'd been worried about that, knowing Sully wasn't much of a dog person because of allergies, but Bart was barely a dog.

Bart settled in her lap and stared at Mac at a stop light. Mac reached over but Clarisse shook her head. "He bites. He hates guys."

Mac hesitated. "Bites?"

"I think Bryan did something to him when he was a puppy, even though he never admitted it. He despises all men. I have to take him to a female vet."

"He's not growling."

"He won't. He just bites."

Then, as if to make a liar out of her, Bart jumped from her lap and bounded out of her arms and across the seat. Mac prepared to be bitten, which would hurt a hell of a lot less than pretty much everything Sully did to him considering the size of the dog. But the ball of fuzz instead crawled into his lap.

A horn honking got his attention. The light had turned green.

Clarisse looked stunned. "He...he's never done that before!"

Mac tried to drive without mashing the little critter. "Okay, can we figure this out in a few minutes? Take him, please, before he gets hurt."

She leaned over and grabbed Bart, who immediately wiggled and whined and tried to get back to Mac.

"I don't believe it!"

Mac smiled. "Don't they say dogs are good judges of character?"

Back at the hotel, Mac unloaded the things she'd need for Bart while she unlocked the room. She had to take her shower and nervously set Bart on the floor.

He made a beeline for Mac. He sat at Mac's feet and looked at him, his tail wagging.

He scooped the dog up and scratched him on the head. Bart promptly rewarded him with a lick on the hand. "Okay, see? He's not going to turn into psycho piranha dog. Go grab your shower. It's after nine."

Twenty minutes later, she emerged from the bathroom to find Mac stretched out on his bed and watching TV, with Bart curled up on his chest.

"I still don't believe it."

"Save the disbelief, sweetie. We need to get going. Come take him so I can grab my shower."

She walked over and picked the dog up. "Why didn't you wait to take one?"

He started to speak, hesitated, then looked at her. "How many details you want? I had a little business I had to take care of, so to speak."

She blushed. "Sorry. Is that part of the punishment Sully mentioned?"

He grinned. "For you, worth every stroke. He gave me a choice. Everything has a price, you know."

"Couldn't you have done it anyway and not told him?" She

wouldn't have minded helping him.

Mac slowly shook his head. "Never. I won't do that. Ever. He trusts me, I trust him." He reached out and stroked her cheek. "That's something you'll have to decide if you can live with."

"Even when you know you'll get punished?"

"Ah, but don't forget, he rewarded me in a way too, by allowing me the choice. If I'd jerked off without permission, I'd feel guilty. I won't do that. I'll take the momentary sting of the cane over feeling guilty until I confess. It's not worth Sully not trusting me."

Maid service had already cleaned their room. When Mac emerged from the bathroom, Clarisse had Bart's crate sitting on her bed, the dog inside, and Food Network on the TV.

"What's that for?" he asked, pointing at the TV.

"He likes it. It's his favorite channel. He thinks Bobby Flay's the shit. He won't bark while we're gone."

Mac shook his head in disbelief but got them moving out the door.

* * * *

Mac had put on a suit, and damned if he didn't look gooood in the obviously expensive and custom-tailored outfit. He could easily pass for an attorney. Sully hadn't spared any expenses there. Forget a tall drink of water, he looked like a lush tropical oasis in the middle of a bone-dry desert. He drove them in the rental car, following her directions, to the police station in Maxwell.

She started to get out when he caught her wrist and waited for her to meet his gaze. "No, you wait for *me* to open the door."

Clarisse felt another of those molten waves sweep through her. She nodded, unable to speak.

Another playful smile from Mac. "Good girl." Then he kissed her hand before releasing it and getting out. He walked around, opened her door, and held out his hand. When she took it and stepped out, he leaned in to speak low in her ear. "You let me take the lead. If they ask to speak to you alone, you don't let them kick me out. Don't lie and tell them I'm your attorney, just stick to your guns. Okay?"

Speech escaped her. She nodded.

"Good girl," he repeated. He locked the car. With his hand gently resting on the small of her back, he walked her into the lobby.

Momentary nausea swept through her. Fear. Nerves. She wanted to bolt outside and beg Mac to take her out of there before Bryan spotted them. He apparently sensed it and pressed his hand against her back, just enough to remind her he wasn't letting her go.

When Mac explained to the desk clerk why they were there, she directed them to take a seat in the waiting area while she called the detective. Ten minutes later, they were seated in Detective Calvert's office. Clarisse immediately sensed from the look on the man's face that there was a problem.

Apparently, so did Mac. "What's going on?" Mac asked, getting the bullshit out of the way.

Calvert shook his head. "Miss Moore, we're having trouble locating your case file—"

"Goddammit! I knew it!" Clarisse screamed. She started to stand, but Mac snagged her wrist and gently pulled her back into her chair.

"Stay here," Mac calmly ordered, then looked at the detective without releasing her wrist. "What do you mean, trouble locating the file? Doesn't all of that end up in the computer?"

The detective got on the phone and made several calls, the last of which sounded very angry. He slammed the phone down and looked at them apologetically. "We're working on it. IT is going through the server backups to retrieve the files, but it's going to take them until at least tomorrow—"

"Tomorrow?" Clarisse practically shrieked. She wanted out of there ten minutes ago. She tried to pull her hand from Mac's firm grip, but he wouldn't budge. "We need to leave! I don't want to be around and have that asshole get a second shot at me!"

"Clarisse." Mac's quietly stern, firm voice immediately focused her attention. It was identical to the tone Sully used with her at the club. He caught her eye. "Wait." Without releasing her hand, he pulled his cell out with his other and dialed Sully. After a quick moment of updating him, he nodded. "Right. We'll see you."

Clarisse trembled in Mac's grip as he put his phone away. "He's flying out and will be here in the morning."

"Sully?"

He smiled. "Well, sure as hell not the Tooth Fairy, sugar." He looked at the detective. "What time do you want us here in the morning?"

* * * *

Ten minutes later, after more apologies from the detective, they were back in the car and speeding away from the station. She slumped in the passenger seat and sobbed while Mac constantly checked the rear view mirror. He spent thirty minutes bobbing and weaving around eastern Columbus before finally heading to their motel. Now well past noon, he was starving, but she'd been too nervous to eat breakfast. Once he'd safely locked them in their room, he ordered subs from a nearby shop that delivered.

Clarisse curled into a tight ball on the bed, a glassy stare on her face and Bart tucked against her chest. "He's going to kill me," she whispered. "He's going to find me and kill me. That money meant more to him than anything. He's going to kill me. He's fucking crazy."

Mac stroked her leg. "He's not going to kill you. We will not let that happen. You can't let him have a pass on this. We have to follow through with filing charges."

She nearly screamed at the knock on the door a few minutes later.

"It's okay. It's the food." He checked to make sure it was, in fact, the food before he opened the door and paid for their lunch.

Sully called from Tampa International with his flight info before boarding. His plane would arrive in Columbus at two a.m. local time. Clarisse barely spoke, only picked at her lunch.

He was going to offer to walk Bart for her, knowing the little fuzzwad had to be ready to go, when he noticed a small metal pan, like a brownie pan, in his crate. Filled with cedar chips. "What's that?" he asked, pointing.

"His litter pan."

"His what?"

Finally, a ghost of a smile. She stroked the little dog. "He's litter trained. Like a cat. I had to do it because Bryan told me when I got him that if he had accidents in the house he would kill him." She protectively cuddled him closer. "I thought if you could do it for cats, why not dogs? I dump the cedar chips in the flowerbed after I scoop the poop out and flush that."

"Son of a bitch. Now I've seen everything." He'd changed into shorts and stretched out on his bed. Bart squirmed out of her arms and ran to the edge of the bed. Too little to jump down, he stood there and barked.

Mac rolled over, reached out, grabbed the dog, and brought him over to his bed. There, Bart curled up on Mac's chest and stared at Clarisse.

She laughed, then a frown crossed her face.

"Why the storm clouds, sweetie?"

"Is Sully really going to be okay with me having him?"

Mac smiled. "Yeah. One way or another, I'll make sure of it." *Even if I have to volunteer to take the strokes for him myself.*

They watched TV, talked, and she napped. He ordered Chinese food for dinner, and then she fell asleep again. He set the alarm to wake him at midnight. Clarisse slept right through it. He hated to wake her, but at twelve-thirty, he gently shook her shoulder. "Hey, sweetie, we need to go to the airport and get Master."

She tried to roll over. "Can't I stay here?" she mumbled.

He sat next to her. "Honey, no way in hell will I leave you alone here. Even if I did, Master would beat the crap out of me in public at the fucking airport for doing that."

Clarisse studied him. "Is it hard to live like that? Knowing he can punish you?"

He smiled and shrugged. "It's not much different than when I was in the Army, only it's a lot more fun, I get laid pretty frequently, and I get to live with the man I love who loves me. He only punishes me when I break the rules."

"But he beats you!"

"I know it's hard for you to wrap your head around, but I get off on that. If he let me slide on things it would piss me off. Obedience is only one facet of our relationship. You know that. You've seen it." He stroked her chin. "We'll talk more about this later."

He started to stand but she caught his arm. "If I...if I decide I do want to do this with you guys...does it always have to be like this?"

Mac kept an eye on the clock. They had a little time for this. He sat again. "Sweetie, you've seen how we are. It's give-and-take, not one-sided. He knows what my needs are, and what we do fulfills them. When we go out, we're vanilla. Almost." He smiled. "Why do you think he won't fuck you, baby? He doesn't want to give you his heart unless he knows he's got your trust, love, and a commitment from you. Not after what he went though with Cybil."

"His heart?"

"Didn't you understand what we were telling you? We love you. *Both* of us. We're *in* love with you. What did you think he meant?"

"He's *in* love with me, too?"

He slowly nodded. "You didn't realize that?"

Clarisse's thoughts reeled. She didn't realize it, too caught up in the fact that Mac had confessed his feelings to her. She'd totally missed the true meaning in Sully's quiet confession.

"I thought me meant he...loved me. Not that he was *in* love with me."

He smiled. "He loves you as much as I do." He stood. "Wear

sweats, honey. No need to dress up." She realized he wore jeans and a button-up shirt, the ID bracelet on his wrist. He never took that off.

"Can I bring Bart?"

"Might as well."

Twenty minutes later, they headed for the airport. Mac made her wait for him to open her door again, and she cuddled Bart under her jacket as they walked into the terminal. Protectively, possessively, Mac kept his hand on the small of her back as he had at the police station. He consulted the arrival boards and found the gate number and where they could wait outside the security checkpoint. Ten minutes after Sully's flight arrived, they spotted him. He used his cane and had his laptop case slung over his shoulder.

Clarisse's heart thumped. He *loved* her. Mac's clarification had changed her world.

Still, that niggling doubt remained. Trust him? He hadn't asked her for her love, only her trust. In some ways, that was an even bigger request.

Sully spotted them. They stepped off to the side as Mac greeted him. Sully cupped his hand around the back of Mac's neck as Mac's forehead rested against Sully's shoulder. Sully whispered something and Mac nodded. Then Sully pulled him in for a tight hug.

Her heart thumped even harder. Something about the gesture, both tender and authoritative at the same time, drew her in. She wished he'd greeted her like that.

When the men stepped apart, Sully handed his laptop to Mac and turned to her. He looked tired, but he smiled. "Are you okay, sweetheart?"

Her throat felt dry. She nodded. She had Bart cuddled under her jacket, and he picked that moment to poke his head out.

Sully's eyes widened. "*What* is that?"

Mac laughed. "That's Bart."

"*That's* your dog?"

She nodded again, very nervous.

"Oh," Mac added, "guess what? He's litter trained."

"You're kidding."

"Damnedest thing you ever saw."

Sully stared at the little dog. Clarisse felt his tail wagging under her jacket. She unzipped it a little so she could pull him out and show him to Sully. She couldn't be lucky twice, could she?

"Be careful. He usually bites men," she warned.

Sully arched an eyebrow at her. "Usually?"

Mac laughed again. "I'm apparently the first guy he's never bitten. He loves me."

Sully held up his hand, palm open, in front of the dog. Bart sniffed him as his tail increased in speed. When Sully reached for him, he willingly went and licked his chin.

Clarisse shook her head. "I don't believe it."

Sully lifted the dog to eye level. "You like to protect your lady, don't you, buddy? You only trust her with guys she trusts."

He said it playfully. Bart's stubby little tail wiggled so fast it was barely visible. But his words slammed into her. Trust. Honestly? Since she'd gotten Bart, she didn't trust any men.

Except these two.

Yes, she did trust Sully.

Sully scratched the dog on the head and returned him to her. As they walked toward baggage claim, Sully kept his arm around Clarisse's waist while Mac filled Sully in. She couldn't resist leaning into his warm embrace while they walked.

When Mac finished, Sully said, "Well, if they aren't the most sophisticated of agencies, it's possibly a glitch, though I doubt it. Case files can get mislaid, accidentally stuck inside other files. To also lose the digital version at the same time is bullshit. Especially considering Bryan's job duties." He turned to Clarisse. "We'll get this taken care of. Didn't you say Raquel took pictures of you, too?"

"Yeah. I stored them online."

"Digital pictures aren't as good as film, defense can claim

Photoshopping went on. I brought the pictures and copies of the negatives of the ones I took when you arrived. Those were a few days old, but they will be consistent enough with what Raquel took to lend credence. And she can testify. Jason will swear an affidavit and come testify if we need him. We might have to hire an attorney in Columbus to pursue this if we can't get it resolved through the state attorney's office."

She gasped. "I can't afford that!" When both men looked at her, she realized what their looks meant. "I can't let you do that, spend that kind of money on me."

"There's no 'let' involved here, Clarisse," Sully said. He pointed at his bag as it emerged onto the luggage carrousel. Mac grabbed it, then shouldered the laptop case and led the way to the parking garage.

Sully helped her into the backseat. Mac opened and held the passenger door for Sully before he slid behind the wheel. Bart sat on her lap, his tail still wiggling, vainly trying to see over the seats to look at the men. Two new friends for him.

"I'm sorry you're going to miss your conference," Clarisse said. "Thank you for coming."

"I'm not missing it," he said. "I sent another bag to New York already. It'll be waiting for me at the hotel. That'll give me at least two days here if I need it. You guys will drive home, and I'll stay in touch with the detectives. If it's not resolved by then, I'll fly back here next week from New York and work on it with an attorney."

She tried to absorb that. He'd said it in a calm, matter-of-fact tone, as if planning arrangements for a small dinner party.

"But...I can't ask you to do that!"

Sully turned to look at her over the seat. "Bryan is *not* going to skate on this if I have anything to say about it." The dark, dangerous tone of his voice didn't scare her. It made her want to lean forward and kiss him. He settled back in his seat, breaking the spell. "As I told you, all I ask is you do what we say when it comes to this. I don't want you spending the rest of your life looking over your shoulder."

At the hotel she thought she might not be able to get back to sleep, but she found herself drifting. Sully lay next to Mac, on his side, his arm draped possessively over Mac the way Mac's had been draped over her. She'd never seen them exactly like this before.

What would it feel like to be the one cuddled with Sully? Or better, between the men? Like the night of her nightmare, to sleep feeling safe and protected?

* * * *

The next morning, Clarisse's nerves had stretched to the breaking point before they even left the room. She set Bart's crate on the bed. After they'd all had showers and dressed, Mac hung the Do Not Disturb card on the doorknob before they walked across the street to a restaurant.

When she insisted she wasn't hungry, Sully ordered for her anyway. Sully talked with Mac about what had happened and how he planned to approach things. When their order arrived, hers a small meal of scrambled eggs and toast, Sully looked across the table at her.

"Eat," he softly, firmly commanded. "I don't expect you to finish it, but pick at it, at least. You'll get sick if you don't."

She thought she wouldn't be able to get through more than two or three bites, but by the time the men had finished eating, she was surprised to realize she'd finished most of hers, too.

Sully paid for their meal and they rode to the station in silence. He scanned the parking lot as they pulled in and directed Mac where to park.

"Do you see his personal car anywhere?" Sully asked Clarisse.

"No, but that doesn't mean anything."

"True."

Mac walked around and opened Sully's door, then hers. The men flanked her as they walked into the station. Mac wore his suit. Sully was also well-dressed in slacks, a dress shirt, and tie. Between the two of them, she felt fat and frumpish even in the nice dress Mac had purchased for her.

The detective immediately ushered them back to his office where Sully took over. Clarisse quietly sat between the two men, nervously twisting her hands together in her lap. Mac reached over and took one of her hands, gently stroked the back of her knuckles with his thumb.

She gave up trying to listen to the detective. It was all she could do not to cry. Bryan would try to kill her, hurt her men, and her life was basically over. That's what it boiled down to.

The detective's phone rang. He excused himself and answered, then asked the caller to hold on.

"It's IT. They've got the data retrieved. They're restoring it and printing a hard copy for me."

Sully nodded. "Excellent."

Clarisse burst into tears.

Sully grabbed her hand. "Detective, do you have a private room?"

"There's an empty conference room, take a left out the door, fourth door on the right."

Sully looked at Mac. "Take her and calm her down. Stay with her."

Mac immediately stood, pulled Clarisse with him, and led her out of the office.

* * * *

Bryan stood at the end of the hall, talking with his cousin, Ed. When he saw the guy walk out of Calvert's office, holding Clarisse's hand, it was all he could do to not beat the shit out of her and him both. The guy was big, but he knew he could take him. When the guy glanced his way, Bryan got a good look at the son of a bitch's face. He wouldn't forget him.

She never looked his way, didn't see him.

Ed noticed the direction of his gaze and forced him back into the break room. "Don't do it," he warned. "Don't go there. You're in enough fucking trouble if they figure out what happened to the damn files," he whispered.

"That bitch owes me ten-k."

"Yeah, well she didn't break the law by taking it. Joint account. You, however, will end up in fucking prison if they find out you tampered with evidence, which they probably will. I am *not* going to jail for you, asshole. If I were you, I'd strongly suggest getting your affairs in order, because those two guys she's got with her look like no-nonsense kind of guys."

"Who the fuck are they? She can't afford an attorney."

"I don't know, and I don't care. The blond one came in with her yesterday. The other guy I saw, the one still in Calvert's office, he wasn't here." He got in Bryan's face, no easy feat considering Bryan stood three inches taller.

"I always warned you your fucking temper would get you into trouble, asshole. Your first mistake was hitting her, you stupid fuck. Your second was to leave her like nothing happened and then lie about it. Don't give me any bullshit about she was fine when you left. You and I both know you hit her. You should have apologized and groveled, fuckhead, and maybe she wouldn't have pressed charges. Go home. Get the hell out of here."

Bryan shoved him out of his way and stormed out the back door. He got in his car, pulled out, and parked across the street from the public lot.

And waited.

* * * *

Ed fought a battle of conscience—and a surge of adrenaline—as he watched Bryan leave. He couldn't believe he stood up to the fuckwad.

No, what had happened in the system couldn't be traced directly back to him. He used an open terminal on someone else's desk to log in to the system. Thank God for their old and archaic computer system. It was due to be upgraded in three months. Otherwise, there's no way he could have pulled it off. Bryan giving him a back-end access code didn't hurt either. He'd stuck the physical file in a stack of other files heading to archives. It probably wouldn't be found anytime soon. But he didn't want to see Clarisse get hurt. Again.

After more deliberation, he stuck his head in Calvert's office. "Hey, Bryan Jackson was just here." He looked at the dark-haired man talking with Calvert. Ex-cop immediately flashed through his mind.

The man frowned. "Is he gone?"

"Yeah."

"Mr. Nicoletto," Calvert said, "we'll make sure she safely gets out of the station, but we obviously can't give you an armed escort back to Florida."

"Don't say anything to her about him being here," the man said. "She's upset enough as it is."

Ed left them and walked out to his patrol car. He'd been thinking about moving to Texas, his brother said the department he worked for there was hiring. He could be close to his brother, away from Bryan.

Maybe it was time to take him up on the offer.

* * * *

Sully opened the conference room door and tilted his head to Mac, indicating he wanted him to step out for a moment. Clarisse still sniffled, a handful of used tissues piled on the table next to her.

Sully closed the door behind Mac and whispered into his ear what happened. "Keep her here until I come back for you. Don't let her out of your sight."

He grimly nodded. "Let the fucker try something."

Sully returned to Detective Calvert's office. The reconstructed file was brought in and they discussed the case. A half-hour later, they were able to leave. Sully's mind raced. He needed to get her out of the station safely and without Bryan following them back to the hotel. Bryan was on administrative leave, so he shouldn't have access to any resources to track them.

Theoretically. Depending on how loyal his buddies were.

Calvert walked with him. "I don't know Bryan Jackson well, but I've heard he's got a vicious temper. IA's looking into him too, now."

"He tries to mess with us, he'll find he's got a fight on his hands. How do we get out the back door?" The detective gave him instructions. He left the detective in the hallway and got Clarisse and Mac. The detective had shown him a picture of Bryan, so he knew what he looked like, but had Bryan seen him with Clarisse?

He got the keys from Mac. "Wait with her by the back door. I'll bring the car around. Be ready to jump into the backseat with her and get down," he whispered.

Clarisse was too out of it to pay attention, her fear in control, flight instincts ready to trigger at any second.

Sully paused at the front entrance before walking out the door. He scanned the parking lot, noticed no other cars nearby with people in them. Walking quickly, he got in the rental and pulled out of the parking lot. He drove a few blocks away from the station, noticed no one following him, then doubled-back from a different direction and pulled into the official lot. Mac and Clarisse hurried out and jumped into the backseat. Mac pushed her down while Sully quickly headed in the opposite direction of the hotel.

They were two miles from the station when he told them to sit up. Clarisse looked near tears again. "He was there, wasn't he? He saw us?"

Sully glanced in the rearview mirror. "I don't think he saw us."

"But he was there?" she asked again, near hysterics, her voice tight.

Mac pulled her close. "Honey, listen. He's not getting you. Don't worry."

"You guys are leaving," Sully said. "As soon as we get back to the hotel. I want you to take the long way home."

* * * *

Two hours later, Bryan realized they'd managed to leave without him seeing. He swore and hit his steering wheel.

Fuck it.

He returned to the station and entered through the back door. Calvert frowned when he saw him.

"What are you doing here, Jackson? You're on leave."

"I have a right to know what's going on."

"You get your ass out of here before I find something to throw you in jail for. You want to know what's going on? Have your attorney find out." He glared. "I don't know what happened to the original file, but thankfully we retrieved the data. I'm sure you and your cousins had something to do with that. Believe me, once this case is handled, we will be looking into that. I personally don't give a shit who your father is."

Bryan fought the urge to slug the guy. He'd been a cop for ten years. This guy had only been with the department for two years after moving from Pittsburgh. A goody-two-shoes who did everything by the rules.

He turned and left. Now he had to find out where she was. He called his attorney.

Chapter Nineteen

They packed fast. Clarisse's heart raced, terrified. Mac went to use the bathroom, leaving her alone with Sully. He caught her hand and pulled her to him.

"You'll be okay," he said in that soft, firm voice. "Do you trust me?"

She nodded.

"Do you? Really? You didn't trust me for the longest time."

Sully had given her every reason to trust him. "Yes," she whispered. "I trust you."

"Do you love me? Honestly?"

"Do you love me?"

He smiled. "Answer my question."

"Answer mine first."

His face softened, looked sad. "I love you very much. I would die for you, sweetheart. I would do anything to make you happy, to keep you safe, to protect you. Now you answer *my* question. Honestly."

She draped her arms around his neck, her heart racing. "I love you very much."

"You understand what I'm asking of you?"

She took a deep breath. "I understand, Master."

She didn't miss the surprise in his face, although he tried to mask it. He kissed her, long and deep, passionately, possessively, nothing like his other kisses had felt. She closed her eyes and savored it, enjoyed the feel of his body molded against hers, something to finally take her mind off the panic threatening to wash over her.

She gave him all control, his lips first pressing, then his tongue carefully insisting she give up all resistance.

Sully slowly tasted and explored her, gently nibbling and nipping and giving her more than a glimpse of what the future held in store.

He eventually broke their kiss, still holding her close. He cupped his hand around the back of her neck, much the way he had Mac's at the airport. "We'll talk once we're all safely home," he said. "Nothing changes for now, okay? If you still feel like this then—and I hope you do—we'll discuss what comes next." Then he stroked her hair and kissed her forehead. "I love you, sweetheart. I really do. I think I fell in love with you when I first met you."

She wanted to cry, only happy tears this time. "I love you, too."

"Obey Mac as if he's me. Don't worry about titles. Let him take care of you. That's his job."

"Yes, Master."

His low chuckle warmed her. For a moment it was easy to forget she felt scared witless in a hotel room in Columbus with her psycho ex-boyfriend wanting to do much more than rip a strip out of her hide. "That's a good girl," he whispered. "You're *my* good girl, aren't you?"

She pleasantly shivered as his arms firmly held her, his fingers tightening against the back of her neck. "Yes, Master."

She heard his breath catch, and he pressed another kiss to the top of her head. "Lean on Mac if you need to. Don't let fear eat you alive, pet." He chuckled and tipped her face to his. "My pet." His eyes searched her face. "I think that will be my name for you. *My* pet."

Clarisse shivered again. The deep, possessive tone in his voice branded her heart.

She *was* his.

She knew that she loved Mac too, but she also understood that from this moment on, she would belong to Sully first and foremost.

In any way he desired.

She also knew Mac would insist on it being that way.

He released her and stepped back. Bart whined and wagged his tail. Sully sat on the bed and held the little dog at eye level. "Listen to me. You help Mac take care of her, okay?"

Clarisse didn't know whether to laugh or cry with relief.

Bart squirmed with pleasure as Sully cradled him against his chest and scratched the back of his head. As Mac emerged from the bathroom, Sully winked at Clarisse.

She couldn't help but smile as a bolt of heat shot straight through her core.

"We ready to go?" Mac asked.

"Yeah. She's all packed."

Sully's eyes held her, captivating her.

Mac glanced at Clarisse, then Sully. A knowing smile crept across his face. "Everything okay, Master?"

Sully smirked as he handed Bart back to Clarisse. "Everything's fine, slave." He stood and crooked his finger at Mac, then pointed at the floor in front of him.

Without hesitation, Mac knelt in front of Sully and bowed his head. Sully placed his hand on Mac's head and tightly knotted his fingers in the man's hair. Clarisse suspected it had to hurt, but Mac never even winced. "Slave, I'm charging you with taking care of my pet. And I don't mean Bart."

"Yes, Master."

"Bring her home safely for me. I hold you personally responsible for her safety and well-being. Do you understand?"

"Yes, Master."

Sully's fingers relaxed in Mac's hair. He lovingly smoothed Mac's hair back into place and gently trailed his fingers down the other man's cheek, over his ear.

Mac clasped Sully's hand, kissed it, nuzzled it against his face. "Please have a safe trip, Master. I love you."

Clarisse wanted to drop to her knees in front of Sully, too.

"I love you too, slave."

Clarisse needed one more bathroom trip before they left. When she returned, both men were smiling. Mac handed Bart to her and kissed Sully good-bye. Then Sully kissed her good-bye, another passionate kiss that curled her toes. He helped her climb into the truck cab and handed Bart to her.

Before he closed her door, he winked at her. "Be safe, pet. Obey slave."

She smiled. "I will, Master."

* * * *

Before dark, they arrived at a small motel in Memphis. Despite leaving Ohio on an up-note, she'd barely spoken to Mac during their drive because of her nerves. Sully had specifically instructed Mac to take it easy, take his time, and pay close attention to any vehicles that appeared to be following them. Even to take exits in populated areas and to drive around for a minute before getting on the interstate again if he had to.

Overkill, sure, but the men wouldn't risk her safety.

Clarisse was surprised to see the room only had one bed, not that she was complaining. Mac set up Bart's crate. "Master said a couple of rules could lapse." He looked at her. "Unless you want me to get a room with two beds?"

She shook her head.

They talked to Sully on the phone before they walked across the street for dinner. "What's on your mind, sweetheart?" Mac asked. "You've been quiet all day."

"Did you talk to Sully before we left Columbus?"

Mac grinned. "Yep. Why do you think he relaxed a few rules?"

"That doesn't make sense. Why would he relax them instead of making them stricter?"

"Ah, the irony inherent in the lifestyle," he joked. "Because you've seen us strict. You know what that's like. But will you like us vanilla too?" He winked. "I told you, it's not all about the kink. That's just one part of it."

"A big part of it."

"Depends on who you ask. Some would call a lot of what we do nothing special. Some would think we're total pervs. It's all relative."

They hit the road before nine the next morning. She'd slept well cuddled against Mac, but nothing sexual happened between them despite the new status of their relationship. Sully called them after he talked with the detective and the state attorney's office. He also hired an attorney to coordinate things on that end for them. That evening, Sully was in New York and they were south of Atlanta. Mac had taken his time, frequently taking smaller roads.

"Not much longer, sugar," Mac said. "We're pushing home from this point."

It would be good to be home. But the closer they got, the more her nervous tension increased. There was still time to back out, take her words back.

Not that she wanted to, if she was totally honest with herself.

They rolled into their driveway a little before two a.m. the next morning. Mac helped her carry Bart's things inside and then headed straight for his bedroom. He didn't close the door, but he didn't ask her to sleep with him either.

She waited for any hint of an invitation, then went to her own room. Despite how sexually frustrating it had been for her to sleep next to Mac, she'd behaved herself. Although she suspected Sully's commands to Mac would have kept him honest regardless.

Clarisse went to her bedroom, but she left her door wide open. An invitation if he wanted to take her up on it. Bart spent a few minutes sniffing around their new digs before curling up on his bed in his crate.

Upset and not quite sure why, she crawled beneath the covers and tried to sleep. When the house phone rang a few hours later, she rolled over and answered it without thinking. Sully.

"Did I wake you, pet?"

She glanced at the clock. Almost ten. "That's okay. Want me to get Mac?"

"No, I wanted to talk to you anyway. I'll be home in three days. Have you thought more about what we talked about?"

Sleep evaporated from her system. "Yes."

"And?"

"I still want to, Master."

"Very good. Good girl. Tell slave to call me when he wakes up. Love you."

She swallowed hard. "I love you, too."

He hung up. She couldn't contain her smile.

She also couldn't go back to sleep. So she made a pot of coffee and took Bart downstairs to the backyard to let him run around. It was a peaceful morning, a few boats in the bayou heading out for the day. This could be her life forever.

That was a good thing, she realized. Why fight it?

The mental image of Sully playing with Doreen spoiled her perfect picture.

She heard the back sliders open a little later. "You down there, kiddo?"

"Yeah. Sully said to call him."

"Okay." He walked back into the house.

She called Bart to her and carried him upstairs. She was hungry. Mac would probably want something. His bedroom door was closed and she heard him talking, too low for her to hear. She was cooking pancakes for them when he opened the door and walked into the kitchen. He wore shorts, but no shirt. The ID bracelet and necklace were gone, but his locking leather collar was in place. He carried something in his hand.

She couldn't read his serious expression. Her heart skipped with fear. "What's wrong?"

"Nothing. I talked with Master. He wants me to work with you before his return. To give you a taste of what life will be like with us.

Are you ready?"

"Yes." She hesitated. "Master?"

"No. You never call me Master. That title is reserved for him only. For the time being, when I'm topping, you can call me Sir, just like you called him Sir at the party."

She nodded, too nervous to speak.

"I don't know what he's going to have you call me when he's home and we're together. For now, he said boat rules until he comes home. Except for one small thing."

"What?"

He smiled. "I'm not allowed to fuck you. He gets the honor of being first." He held up what was in his hand. A lightweight, silver chain collar with a small, silver decorative lock, similar to the discreet formal collar Mac wore when out in public with Sully. "But Master gave me the privilege of being the first to collar you. Among other things."

This made it real. Her pulse thrummed.

He stepped across the kitchen. "Are you sure you want this? You can back out. You can live with us as long as you want without being involved with us, you know that."

She couldn't take her eyes off the length of silver chain and the heart-shaped silver lock. "I want it," she whispered. "I love you."

"I love you too, pet." His face and voice grew stern again. "You have to abide by the rules I set down for you. Including punishment. Do you understand?"

"Yes."

He arched an eyebrow at her.

"Yes, Sir," she corrected herself.

"Very good, baby. Hold up your hair." She did while he fastened the collar around her neck. It felt cool at first, then quickly warmed to her skin.

"Strip."

Her skin flushed. She waited for him to break into a smile or joke or something, but he stood there, watching, waiting.

Blushing, she did as commanded. He held out his hand for her clothes and once she stood totally naked, he carried them to her room.

Not sure what else to do, she continued cooking breakfast. It made her self-conscious, and she felt weird to be totally naked, but she also realized it made her more than a wee bit horny.

He returned a little while later and sat at the table with the paper and started reading. He still wore his shorts and sat where Sully usually sat.

Without any further direction, she fixed him a plate and placed it in front of him before fixing her own.

"Thank you, pet," he said, but he didn't look at her.

She sat in his normal seat, on the towel. After a few minutes, he glanced at her. "You okay?"

"This is weird."

He grinned. "You'll get used to it a lot faster than you think." He shifted in his chair. "This fucking thing, however, is murder."

"What thing?"

"The CB." He stood and pulled down his shorts enough she could see the clear plastic cage-like device he wore over his cock and balls. Padlocked shut. Then he sat and continued eating. "Master trusts me, but only so far." He laughed. "It's probably better this way," he said with a wicked grin. "If I had half a chance, I'd be fucking you all day. It'd be worth a hundred strokes from the cane. More, even."

She gasped as a flood of heat pooled between her legs. She knew her face reddened.

From the look on Mac's face, he noticed. "Babe, you ain't seen nothing yet." He grinned.

She gulped.

* * * *

He returned her clothes after they finished breakfast and cleaned the kitchen. She followed him downstairs where they started unloading the truck's contents into the downstairs storage room. An hour later, they'd both had showers and she rode with him to return the truck.

When they returned home, he stopped her inside the front door. "Strip, sweetheart. When you're inside the house, unless Master's said otherwise or we have guests, you'll be naked."

This time, she was brave enough to meet and hold his gaze as she removed her clothes and handed them over. When she stood naked before him, he smiled.

"Damn, girl. I'm *never* gonna get tired of seeing you like this. You're beautiful."

She blushed as she dropped her gaze and fought the urge to say something self-deprecating. Sully's admonishments rang in her ears.

Then again, getting spanked by Mac might not be a bad thing.

"Thank you."

He gently tipped her chin up. "You're gorgeous, baby." He leaned in and kissed her, gently, slowly. She savored the feel of his lips against hers. She didn't resist when he gathered her in his arms and his tongue swept over her lips, tasting, exploring. They parted before him. Time expanded, slowed, passed them by. When he lifted his face and tightly cuddled her to him, he let out a ragged sigh.

"Jesus, I could do that with you all day." He buried his face in her hair as his hands slipped down her body and pulled her hips tightly against his. She felt the hard plastic of the chastity device through his shorts. "Fucking good idea he ordered me to wear this damn thing," he growled. "I'd have you on your back in bed and be fucking you right now, you realize."

Hot desire coursed through her, a dull throbbing ache between her legs holding her attention. Then he scooped her into his arms and carried her to his bedroom. She stared into his sweet brown eyes, captivated by the blatant passion there. Bryan had never looked at her like that.

No one had ever looked at her like that. Except Mac and Sully.

He gently laid her on the bed and stretched out next to her. "Master said I'm not allowed to fuck you or use my mouth between your legs. He has the right to take you first like that." He leaned in and slanted his lips over hers, kissing her, taking her breath away.

A sultry smile curved his lips. "He didn't say I couldn't make you come. In fact, he told me I could and should."

His eyes never left hers as his fingers slowly trailed down her cheek, between her breasts, over her belly, through the downy tuft of hair between her legs. "This," he whispered, "will have to go." He leaned in and kissed her before lifting his head again.

His fingers trailed lower before they curved, teasing, pressing for entrance.

She closed her eyes, her back arched, encouraging him.

He withdrew his hand. "No, baby. Keep your eyes open. Look at me."

Clarisse forced her eyes open. Liquid, molten need pulsed in his gaze. Nestled in his arms, she'd never felt safer or more loved.

Except when nestled in Sully's arms after the scene at the party.

"Good girl."

His gaze never wavered from hers as he returned his fingers to her mound, slowly teasing, finding her wet. She let out a soft gasp as he slid one finger deep inside her and slowly pumped it before his hand fell still.

"If that was my tongue, I would have it buried so deep inside you," he whispered.

Her breath came in short gasps, her body afire.

He withdrew his hand and traced her mouth with his finger, then crushed her lips with his. He let out a soft moan as he plunged his hand back into her sex.

"Jesus, you taste good," he moaned. The hungry sound of his voice only served to fire her own need as she squirmed on the bed, her body impaled by his fingers.

When he withdrew his fingers again, he slipped his hand lower between her legs and found her rosette.

She froze, but didn't look away.

"Are you a virgin there?" he asked.

She nodded.

He lowered his mouth to hers and gently traced his finger around the puckered ring of muscle, never attempting to breach it. After several minutes of this, she relaxed. When he felt that, his thumb slipped inside her wet sex as his other fingers massaged her rim.

"Don't come," he softly ordered, his voice firm.

The very order propelled her body closer to release as she squirmed harder on his hand, wanting more.

He nipped the base of her throat. "If you come before I tell you, I will give you five strokes with the cane."

Clarisse forced her body to lie still, tried to think of any and everything but what his hand did to her body.

Mac played dirty. He sucked her right nipple into his mouth and teased it, nibbled and bit at it, then repeated the action with her left.

"I...can't hold it..."

"You can," he said, his voice stern. His fingers worked harder, teasing, his thumb slowly fucking her.

Desperation vied with need. Was it worth five strokes to not fight harder to obey? She trembled from the stress of trying to comply.

"Are you close?" he asked.

"Yes!"

He sat up. With his other hand, he grabbed her chin. "Don't come yet. Look at me."

She tried to focus on his eyes, on his voice, not on what his other hand was doing between her legs. When she thought she couldn't take any more, he sternly ordered, "Clarisse, come for me now!"

Her body obeyed, the explosion ripping through her as his hand continued fucking her. She struggled to keep her eyes on him, his gaze stern and unreadable. Just as the first wave began subsiding, he rolled her clit between two of his fingers. "Come again, pet. Now."

Apparently her body didn't need her brain's assistance in the matter. A second wave of pleasure ripped a cry from her lips. This time, her eyes dropped closed as she ground her hips against his hand. When she couldn't take it anymore and tried to pull away, his hand followed.

"Again. Now."

Pain and pleasure wrapped into one as he pinched her clit between his fingers and another climax punched through her conscious. Then her body gave out as she sobbed.

He lay next to her and pulled her into his arms, soothing her, one hand stroking her hair. "That's my good girl," he murmured. "That's my very good girl. That was so good. I'm very proud of you."

She cried harder, relief and things she couldn't begin to explain tumbling through her heart and soul. Mac didn't question it, let her cry herself out in his arms as he continued to whisper to her what a good girl she was and how much he loved her.

She didn't realize she'd dozed off until she opened her eyes a while later.

Mac smiled. "Feeling better?"

She nodded, not knowing what to say. One thing for certain, now she knew why people enjoyed scening. She'd never understand the need for pain, but if their cathartic release was a fraction as good as hers, that *was* something she understood.

He leaned in and kissed her again, tenderly, sweetly. "You were perfect, sweetheart," he said. "Absolutely beautiful. I wish Master had been here to see that."

She blushed, which prompted a playful grin from Mac. He touched the tip of her nose. "What's with the red face?"

Clarisse shrugged.

He sat up, pulling her with him. "You'll get over that pretty quick. Come on, let's take a bath." He led her by the hand into their bathroom and had her sit on the counter. "First, we need to take care of something." He grabbed a small pair of scissors and knelt in front of her.

She blushed again as he pushed her knees apart to expose her to him. He wore a playful grin. "Don't move, sweetie." He carefully trimmed her close, then cleaned up the hair on the floor. He scooped her into his arms and kissed her as he carried her over to the huge sunken tub and set her on the low edge. "Wait right there."

When he shucked his shorts, she got a better look at the devious device keeping her from his cock. Actually, Sully was probably pretty smart to order he wear it. Given half a chance, she'd be riding him.

Mac grabbed a new disposable razor and shaving cream, then proceeded to finish the job. He ran warm water into the tub and rinsed her, smiling as his fingers traced every fold and curve of her sex. "That's much better, darlin'." He filled the tub and pulled her in with him, nestled her between his legs, her back against his chest.

When he settled against the back of the tub, he wrapped his arms around her and let out a content sigh. "I could easily turn into a prune like this."

She let her head fall back onto his shoulder. "Me too." She closed her eyes as he stroked her arms, his hands tender and gentle on her flesh.

He kissed her temple. "When Master gets back, we'll talk. You understand Master will own you too, right?"

"Yeah." The thought thrilled her.

"You won't be mine to do whatever I want with."

"I know."

He nuzzled the top of her head. "I love him, babe. He's my life. I'm not going to lie to you and say that you and I will run away together one day. If you want to be with me, you have to be with him, in whatever way he dictates. That's the rules."

"I'm okay with that. Two hunks who love me and who would kick the crap out of my ex to protect me? Tell me how that's a bad thing."

Mac smiled. "Yeah, absolutely. You'd better believe it. That shithead shows up here, he's a fucking dead man." He prompted her to sit up and washed her hair for her, lovingly, massaging her scalp as he lathered her head. Then he took a long time running a washcloth over her, kissing his way across her shoulders after he rinsed the soap from her.

She turned around and took the wash cloth from him, kissed him as she repaid the favor. Their interlude was interrupted by Mac's shorts ringing on the floor next to the tub.

"Dammit." Mac reached for them, fished his phone out of his pocket, and answered as he hung over the edge of the tub. "Hello, Master."

Clarisse draped herself over him, her arms around him.

Mac listened for a moment. "Yes, Master…We're in the tub…No, I'm wearing it…Yes, hold on." He handed the phone to her. "He wants to talk to you, sweetie."

She blushed and took the phone, careful not to get it wet. "Hi, Master."

"Hello, pet. How are you?"

Her hand slid between Mac's legs, her fingers running over the plastic cage. "Trying to figure out how to pick a lock."

Sully laughed, the sound thrilling her. "I bet you are. All the more reason slave has to wear that thing. Too much temptation for you. Did slave shave you?"

She blushed. "Yes, Master."

Sully's voice dropped, sexy and low. "So your sweet pussy is totally bare for me?"

It was also throbbing with need again. "Yes, Master," she whispered.

"Good. Love you. Put slave back on."

"Love you, too." She handed the phone back to him.

Mac's eyes twinkled. "Yes, Master?" He listened for a moment, then leaned in and kissed her while Sully still talked to him. "Yes, Master. Love you, too." He hung up and put the phone down, then pulled her on top of him. "Okay, where were we?"

She straddled him, feeling the hard plastic bump against her bare mound. "Isn't that thing uncomfortable?"

"Fuck yes it is. It's practically cutting into me. That's sort of the idea, it keeps me from being able to do anything about my hard cock, but it doesn't stop my cock from trying." He kissed her again, then took her hand and placed it between his legs. "Play with my balls, babe."

"Won't that make you hurt?"

He grinned. "Masochist, remember?"

She stroked her fingers along his sac, where the plastic had them corralled and swollen. That was as hairless as the rest of him. Mac closed his eyes and bucked his hips against her.

"Don't stop," he said, lacing his fingers through her free hand. "Master said I was allowed to come if I could while wearing this thing."

"Is that possible?"

"I don't know. I damn sure want to find out."

She stroked his balls, traced the shape of the plastic cage, and gently raked her short nails over his flesh. After a few minutes of this, he opened his eyes. Without a word, he grabbed her hand and pushed it down lower in the water, pressed one of her fingers against his rim.

"I don't know what to do," she nervously said.

He smiled. "You'll figure it out." He spread his legs further, hooking one over the edge of the tub. She gingerly pressed against his dark hole. "Don't I need to use lube or something?"

He nodded to a small bottle on the edge of the tub. She erred on the side of caution and used a huge dollop of the goop, then slowly pressed for entrance.

Mac let out a low groan. "That's it," he gasped. "That's the spot." He pulled her close and kissed her as she wiggled her finger around, paying attention to his responses to determine what worked. It wasn't long before he grabbed her tightly and loudly moaned as he kissed her, his hips bucking against her hand.

When he relaxed against the back of the tub, she popped the stopper open on the tub to let it drain and curled up in his arms. "Good?" she asked.

"Yep. Not as good as the real thing, but at least it's not pinching as badly."

She snickered. "I thought you said you like pain."

He waggled his eyebrows at her. "Even I have my limits, sugar."

Chapter Twenty

He sent her to her bedroom to get dressed, with orders to wear something nice. When she emerged, she found him sitting on the sofa, wearing slacks, a dress shirt, and a tie.

Handsome and gorgeous and all hers for the evening. He stood when she walked in. He'd taken off the locking collar, but he'd put on the ID bracelet and necklace.

"You're gorgeous, sweetheart."

She blushed again but fought the urge to talk herself down. "Thank you, Sir."

He pulled her to him for a long, deep kiss. That's when she felt something different, a long, firm shape poking against her instead of a hard plastic bulge. She grabbed his crotch, but he gently pulled her hand away. "Where is it?"

"I called Master. He said since I came that if I promise to behave, I can keep it off for tonight."

She wiggled her hips against him and felt his cock stiffen more in his slacks.

He swatted her on the ass, hard enough to sting a little through her skirt. "Stop, pet. He also told me I have permission to lock you up if you misbehave. I'll play with you later if you're a good girl."

They took the Jag. He drove them over to Tampa, to a fancy steakhouse. They had a wonderful dinner, great conversation, and it suddenly hit her halfway through their meal that this was how normal relationships were supposed to feel. She'd never been allowed an opinion with Bryan Jackson. He preferred eating in silence unless he was the one doing the talking.

Mac noticed. "What's wrong, babe?"

"Sully really loves me too?"

He reached across the table and squeezed her hand. "Yes, you'd better believe it. As much as I do. Is that what's got you all worried?"

"No. I realized I don't really know what normal is. I have to figure it out. I didn't have it for so long."

He grinned, playful. "I wouldn't exactly call this normal, babe."

"I mean..." She chewed it over. "Healthy. Happy. Fun."

He rubbed his thumb over her knuckles before releasing her hand. "It'll be all that and more. I promise."

When they returned home around eleven that evening, Bart met them at the door, his tail wagging and ears perked. Mac scooped him up and played with him before letting him down. "You're on your own for the evening, puppy. I've got plans for your mom." He pulled Clarisse to him and kissed her while pinning her wrists behind her back. "Go get naked, sweetie." When he let her go, he turned to watch her walk through the living room.

That's when he spotted something laying in the middle of the living room floor. Before he could investigate, Bart streaked over to it, grabbed it, and dragged it behind him as he took off for Clarisse's bedroom.

"Pet, what does Bart have?"

She turned around to intercept him, but the dog zipped under the couch, where he growled at them. "I don't know. It was bigger than him."

They both got onto their hands and knees to pull him out, but he streaked out the other side, without his prize, and headed for Mac's bedroom.

Mac felt under the couch and came up with a riding crop.

They stared at it for a moment before bursting into laughter. "Where was that at?" she asked.

"In my closet."

They heard a noise in the master bedroom and went to inspect.

They caught Bart in the middle of the room, one of the rattan punishment canes in his mouth. He dropped into a play bow over the cane and growled at them.

Mac laughed so hard he had to sit on the bed. He roared, long and loud, until tears rolled down his cheeks.

"It's...Dom Dog," he finally choked out before laughing even harder.

Clarisse hoped he'd still find it funny. She found the stand tipped over in the closet and breathed a sigh of relief that nothing appeared to be chewed.

"Hey, Mac? How many of these were there?"

Still laughing, he stood to join her in the closet doorway. "Holy crap, there's several missing."

They turned, but Bart had snuck off with the cane. "That fucking thing's bigger than he is!" Mac said.

They caught sight of him disappearing into Clarisse's bedroom. In his crate, they found the missing implements.

"I don't understand," she said as she handed them out to Mac. "He's never done anything like this before."

Mac grinned and picked the little dog up. "Hey, he's expressing his dominant side, that's all."

Clarisse finally allowed herself to laugh again after examining the other implements, which were also tooth mark free. She took Bart from Mac. "I think it's time puppy goes to bed." She turned Food Channel on for him, put him in his crate with a bowl of water and food, and pulled the bedroom door mostly closed. Mac leaned against his bedroom doorway, smiling, his arms crossed over his chest.

"What?"

He waggled his eyebrows at her. "Where were we?"

She smiled. "I think right about here." She started unbuttoning her blouse.

"Yeah, that's a good place to start."

She seductively stripped for him. When she stood naked before him, he crooked his finger at her. She willingly stepped into his arms and enjoyed his long, deep kiss. He slowly maneuvered her into his bedroom and onto the bed.

"Don't move." His eyes never left her as he slowly removed his tie and unbuttoned his shirt. "Master gave me permission to play with you in a few ways. I plan on taking full advantage of it." His erection tented his dress slacks. He kicked off his shoes and removed his slacks before kneeling beside her on the bed. "Stroke my cock, babe," he hoarsely ordered.

She did, wishing he'd let her do a lot more than that.

"Spread your legs."

When she did, he teased her wet opening with his fingers, smiling when he found her slick. "Did I do that to you?" He plunged two fingers deeply inside her and held his hand still.

"Yes, Sir."

He withdrew his fingers and touched them to her lips. "Open."

She did, and he gently pushed his fingers into her mouth. "Pretend that's my cock, pet. Show me what you would do."

She closed her eyes and as her hands stroked the real thing, she simulated with her mouth how she wished she were running her lips and tongue over his silky flesh. Her thumb caught a bead of clear pre-come at the tip of his cock. She slicked it over his shaft, which made him moan.

He withdrew his hand from her mouth and plunged it back into her wet sex. This time he used his thumb to stroke her clit while he pumped in and out. She moaned when he withdrew his hand again.

Mac smiled. "You want to suck my cock, pet?"

She nodded.

Mac's brown eyes smoldered with passion. "You have to ask, pet. Tell me what you want."

"Please let me suck your cock, Sir!"

"Very good, pet." He changed position so his cock brushed her lips. "Open."

Her lips eagerly parted. She engulfed him, using one hand to stroke his sac and the other on the base of his shaft.

Mac let out a long, loud groan. "Oh, fuck! Baby, that's great!" He held still for a moment before he started rocking his hips against her.

Clarisse laved his cock with her tongue, tracing the veins, exploring the ridge and mushroomed head, tasting his slit. She closed her eyes and enjoyed every second.

"Make me come, pet," he hoarsely ordered.

She eagerly sucked him deeper, harder, wanting to please him. He cupped one hand under the back of her head, tangled his fingers in her hair, and fucked her mouth as his release approached.

"Get ready," he grunted.

She dug her fingers into his ass, pulled him tighter, swallowed him deeply as he came. After a moment, he pulled out and collapsed on the bed. He wrapped his arms around her and held her. "Holy fuck, that was great," he whispered. "Jesus, that was fantastic."

Despite how horny she felt, she enjoyed being curled up next to him. Before she stopped herself, the comment popped out. "Sully told me he doesn't do that for you."

Mac chuckled as he kissed her. "No, he doesn't. Lots of other things, but not that."

"Why?"

Mac shrugged. "He never has. I've never forced him to do it, and I wouldn't force him any more than he'd force me to do something I didn't want to do. You're better off asking him the whys, babe." He stroked her shoulder. "He told me until he comes home, as a reward for working with you and for wearing the CB like he told me to, I can let you do that."

"What about after he gets home?"

"That's for him to decide." He patted her ass. "And now that I can think again without my cock screaming bloody murder, it's time for a little training. You still horny?"

"Duh."

He lightly slapped her ass. "What was that?"

"Duh, Sir."

He grinned and rubbed noses with her. "That's better. You've got a bratty streak in you, don't you?"

"Is that bad?"

"Naw, just don't embarrass Master in front of others. Some people are real pricks for protocol and look at a bratty sub as a bad thing. Some people, it doesn't matter. You'll learn when it's okay to be bratty." He lifted his eyebrows. "A little bratty. Not a lot." He stood and walked into the bathroom. He returned a moment later with a bottle of lube and a large towel. He motioned for her to move. "Roll over."

He spread the towel out and had her lie on it.

She felt a little nervous but tried to relax.

He opened a dresser drawer, took out a few things, then dropped them onto the bed.

Oh, boy. One was a large dildo. The other...

Boy, oh boy. She was pretty sure it was a butt plug. At its widest point, it was larger than Mac's cock.

Then he added one more item to the mix, a large vibrator with a cord. "The Hitachi Magic Wand," he said with an evil grin. When he plugged it in and flicked it on, she jumped as it hummed to life.

He laughed and shut it off. "Not yet, pet. It'll soon be your new best friend."

Stretching out next to her in bed, he leaned in and kissed her. "Spread your legs, babe." He kissed her again as she felt the dildo make contact with her pussy. He didn't try to push it in at first, just teased her with it, running it up and down from her clit to her sex and back again. Slowly, gently, he started pressing for entrance.

She gasped.

His hand froze. "You okay?"

"Don't stop!"

He chuckled and resumed his motions, slowly fucking her, going a little deeper with each stroke until he could almost fit the entire thing inside her slick passage, fucking her with it, gently twisting it and plunging it into her.

Then he pushed it in as far as he could. Holding it in place, he lightly brushed his thumb along her clit, making her squirm on his hand.

"How's that feel, baby?"

She eagerly nodded. Not as good as having the real thing inside her, sure, but with Mac's hard body holding her, it wasn't a bad substitute.

"Roll over."

She did.

Then she felt something cool and wet against her virgin rim. "Relax. I'll take it slow."

She tried to relax, but that was damn hard as horny as she felt and with the dildo buried inside her.

He gently massaged her tightly puckered ring for several minutes before pressing one finger against her. "Push, baby."

His finger slid inside, which made her gasp.

"Oh, and pet?"

"Yeah?"

"Do not come," he growled.

She whined, nearly desperate. Until he'd said it, she hadn't been close. Now knowing she couldn't, it pushed her nearer the edge.

He slowly worked one finger in and out of her, then added a second, and finally a third. The alien stretching sensation felt like an erotic burn against her muscles, one she wanted extinguished, and soon.

He withdrew his hand and replaced it with something firm and cool. "Push."

She did, gasping as she felt the butt plug slide into place with a slight pinch of burn as her muscles stretched to accept it before clamping down on the silicone toy.

With his hand firmly pressed between her legs and holding the dildo in place, he ordered her to turn over onto her back again.

Clarisse rolled, feeling stretched, full, desperately horny.

He grinned. "You okay?"

"No!"

His grin changed to worry. "Does it hurt? If it ever does, say red immediately—"

"No! I've got to come!"

He laughed, relieved. "Oh, baby, you will do that. I promise." He picked up the vibrator and with an evil grin he flicked the switch. It hummed to life, her heart hammering nearly as fast as the electric motor.

He stretched out next to her again. "Do not come, pet. Not until I say so." He lowered his mouth to her right nipple and bit down, not hard, but not gently either.

The action sent another bolt of liquid fire straight to her clit as the dildo and the butt plug caressed her secret places.

Then he brushed the vibrator against her clit, making her jump, but not enough contact to make her come. He tortured her for nearly an hour like that, not letting her come, making her lay perfectly still at times until her body calmed down. By that time, his cock had grown rock hard again and she was nearly in tears, begging him to let her come.

He turned off the vibrator and knelt over her on the bed. He stroked her hair. "Take care of me first, pet, and then I'll take care of you."

She practically inhaled his cock, eagerly, desperately. He closed his eyes and slid his member deep between her lips.

"I can't wait until Master lets me fuck you, babe," he said. "I can only imagine what it'll feel like sliding my cock into that sweet pussy of yours."

She moaned around his member, wishing it was right the hell then, because her desire had hit a fevered pitch.

He fisted both hands in her hair and thrust his hips. "Take me deep, babe." She matched him stroke for stroke, lifting her head to swallow his entire cock. She grabbed his balls and lightly raked her fingernails along his sac, sending him into orbit.

"Fuck!" He pumped his cock into her as he came, his body going rigid until he finally swung off her and collapsed next to her on the bed, breathing heavily.

Clarisse squirmed. "Please, Sir!" she begged. "Please!"

He chuckled as he reached for the vibrator. "You were a very good girl. You may come." He flicked it on and pressed it to her clit.

Clarisse squeezed her eyes shut and screamed as her muscles contracted around the toys, coming harder than she ever had before, even harder than the night of the party. Mac didn't relent, making her come two more times before he shut the vibrator off and pulled her trembling body into his arms.

"Good girl," he cooed. "That's my very good girl."

She tucked her damp forehead against his chest and cried.

Worried, he clung to her. "You okay?"

"Oh, fuck yeah! Good tears."

He laughed. "Yeah, I've had those a time or two myself."

She was almost asleep when she felt him reach between her legs and gently remove the toys before leaving the bed. The sound of water running reached her, then he returned a moment later with a warm, damp washcloth. He swabbed her clean and dried her before shutting off the light and climbing into bed with her.

He pulled her into his arms. "Sleep tight, sweetheart."

Exhausted, sated, and happier than she'd felt in a long time, that's exactly what she did.

* * * *

Mac set a steaming mug of coffee on the bedside table next to her before sitting on the bed and brushing the hair from her forehead.

"Good morning, sweetheart."

She blearily opened her eyes. It looked like late morning outside. "Holy crap, what time is it?"

He smiled. "After ten. Master said I could let you sleep." She noticed he wore shorts. He correctly interpreted her look and he tapped the front of his shorts. She heard a plastic noise. "Master said I need to wear it this morning as a reminder. I can take it off later when I have you take care of me."

She heard a playful growl. Mac looked down. "Hey, pup." He set Bart on the bed. "I already took care of him this morning," Mac said. "Get up when you feel ready. Master said today's a free day for us."

"Free day?"

He lovingly kissed her, trailing his fingers down her cheek to her chin. "Whatever you want to do today, we will. He said for us to take the day off and have fun."

She grinned. "What kind of fun?"

"Vanilla fun." Lacing his fingers through hers, he brought her hand to his mouth. He feathered his lips along her knuckles. "He doesn't want you overwhelmed. We're just Mac and Clarisse for the day."

Out came the pouty lip. "But I like Sir and pet."

He grinned and rolled on top of her without squishing Bart. "I know. I do too. We can play Sir and pet later."

Bart started running around the bed, playfully growling. Mac grabbed him and carefully set him on the floor. Mac kissed Clarisse again. "What would you like to do today?"

"Seriously?"

"Yeah."

She thought about it for a moment. "Can we go over to Howard Park?"

"Yeah." He rolled over, pulling her on top of him. "You want to go out for lunch?" Out of the corner of his eye, he caught sight of Bart running from the bathroom and out the bedroom door.

"Oooh, Plaka's?"

"Sure." It was her favorite restaurant. "Let's go see Tad," he suggested.

"Can we take him to lunch?"

"Yeah. Let's get our shower."

"Soap my back?"

He grinned. "Don't have to ask me twice." He climbed out of bed and walked into the bathroom. As he reached into the shower and turned the water on, he glanced over at the tub.

The dildo he'd used on her last night sat on the edge, where he'd left it. But the butt plug was missing.

"Hey, honey?"

"Yeah." She walked into the bathroom while sipping her coffee.

He looked around. "Did you do something with the butt plug?"

"No."

"It's missing."

She playfully grinned. "Want to search me?" She turned and wiggled her naked ass at him.

He rolled his eyes. "No, seriously, where is it? I left it on the side of the tub to dry after I washed it last night."

She helped him look. It hadn't fallen into the tub and wasn't on the floor anywhere.

"That's weird," he said.

Bart ran into the bathroom and raced past them. As they watched, he stood on his hind legs, grabbed the dildo off the side of the tub, and started dragging it across the bathroom floor.

"Hey!" Mac and Clarisse both lunged for him. He dropped his prize and ran from the bedroom.

"I think that answers that question," Mac said as he picked the dildo up and put it safely on the counter, out of the little dog's reach. Mac searched for the missing butt plug in Bart's crate. Nothing. He sat up. "Where the hell did he stash it?"

They turned and saw Bart standing in the doorway. He took off running. Before they could make it to the doorway, he'd disappeared.

Mac started laughing. "So he's a kleptomaniac?"

Horrified, Clarisse shook her head. "No, I swear, he's usually not like this!" She started crying. What if Sully didn't let him stay now?

"Hey, what's wrong?" Mac pulled her to him. "Why are you upset?"

She managed to get it out between sobs. "He's my baby! What if Sully doesn't let me keep him if he won't stop doing this?"

"Listen to me," Mac sternly said. "Master's already said he can stay. I bet little Mr. Dom Dog is happy to be somewhere he doesn't have to be afraid all the time. He's back with his mom, and he's just feeling his oats, that's all."

She sniffled. "Okay."

"Let's go find him."

They finally located him in Sully's office, under the desk.

With the missing butt plug.

Bart grabbed it and backed away from them, until his hind end nearly touched the wall. He growled at them even while his little tail furiously wagged.

Mac laughed. "Guess he's got a new chew toy. Won't hurt him, will it?"

Clarisse tried to take it away from Bart, but he ducked out the other side of the desk and ran for the door. "As long as it was clean, it shouldn't. He doesn't destroy chew toys, just chews on them."

He patted her on the ass. "I left the water running in the shower. Let's go."

When they emerged from the shower, Bart was under the dining room table with his new toy. As soon as he saw them, he grabbed his prize and ran for Sully's office.

Mac laughed. "Guess we need to make a stop by the toy store and get us a new butt plug while we're out today. Remind me we have to take it away from him when vanilla guests drop by."

* * * *

They had a nice, normal afternoon. Lunch with Uncle Tad, then a trip to the beach where they sat on a retaining wall and stared out at the Gulf. Safely nestled in Mac's arms, she closed her eyes and deeply inhaled the sweet salt air.

"Whatcha thinking?" he mumbled into her hair.

"I could spend the rest of my life like this."

"So could I."

She stayed quiet for a long time, deep in thought. "When Sully's home, will he let us do stuff like this?"

"Yeah. He'll want to do stuff like this with you, too. I told you, it's not all about the Master/slave dynamic. Is that always in the background? Sure. It's just not always in the forefront."

Wrapping her head about the future dynamic still puzzled her. "You won't be jealous?"

"Will you?"

"I…" Her mouth snapped shut. "No, I guess not."

He chuckled and hugged her closer to him. "Remember, there will be times you're the one sitting there watching him with me. Or on the boat, you'll see me ordering him around and having my way with him."

Clarisse honestly hadn't thought of it like that. Framed that way, it did make perfect sense.

* * * *

Sully spent the trip home from the airport with his eyes closed, trying to rest. His leg had tuned up again. Mac would chew him out for overdoing it.

He called Mac when he knew he was about thirty minutes from home.

"We'll be ready, Master," Mac said.

Sully hung up and stared at his phone, a smile breaking through the pain.

We.

He closed his eyes again and thought about Clarisse, if she really would go through with it. He hoped she would, but he wouldn't, couldn't force her. He would hold back and let her make the decision to take this to the next level.

He'd swore he'd never again put himself in a position to be vulnerable like he was with Cybil. Taking their relationship to a new level wouldn't happen unless Clarisse wanted it.

When they arrived, he had the driver put his bags in the utility room. He wouldn't need them until tomorrow, and then Mac could take care of them. With his laptop bag slung over his shoulder and cane in hand, he slowly ascended the stairs. The front door was unlocked, and when he walked through, he stopped at the sight.

Clarisse and Mac knelt on the floor.

Both naked.

Sully stared, still not believing his eyes even though he knew to expect it. His cock stiffened in his pants as he fought the urge to order her to bed so he could fuck her brains out.

Not yet. Too soon.

Mac looked up, smiling. "Welcome home, Master."

"Hello." He set his laptop case down. "Do I get a hug and a kiss from you two?"

Both of them rushed him, practically throwing themselves at him. Sully laughed. "Jesus, you two are like a couple of puppies."

That's when Bart ran in, dragging his newest toy.

The butt plug.

Sully stared. After a moment he asked, "Is that what I think it is?"

Mac ran a hand through his hair. "Um, yeah, about that. I had to buy a new butt plug."

Sully noticed Clarisse's horrified look. He pulled her to him and kissed her again. "What's wrong?"

"Please don't be mad!"

He frowned. "Why would I be mad?"

"He's never stolen stuff before. I don't know why he's..." She burst into tears.

Mac sighed. "Sul, we need to drop formal for a minute."

Sully nodded as he tried to soothe her.

"Would you please reassure her you won't make her get rid of Bart? She's been in a near panic over it."

He peeled her off him. "Why would I make you get rid of him? I know how much you love him."

She sobbed. "He's stealing things! He never used to do this! I'm so sorry!" She dissolved into tears again.

Sully sighed and pulled her close as he stared over her head into Mac's brown eyes. "Sweetheart, I promise, I will never make you get rid of him."

"Really?"

He stroked her hair. "Really. Please stop crying. It's okay."

Bart dropped into a play bow over the butt plug and growled at Sully. Sully smiled and tried to mask his pain as he lowered himself to the floor. "Come here, Bart."

Bart's tail sped up and he put his mouth on the butt plug, but he didn't move.

Sully grinned and patted the floor in front of him. "Bring it."

Bart grabbed the butt plug and brought it to Sully, where he played tug-of-war with him.

Sully gently pulled it away from him and tossed it across the living room. Bart streaked after it and brought it back for another round. After five minutes, Sully scooped Bart up and scratched his head.

"Enough, pup. I need to get to bed. I'll play with you tomorrow." He handed the dog and the butt plug to Clarisse. "Go ahead and put him to bed for the night. Move his crate into our bedroom if you want."

She froze. "You mean it?"

He held his hand up to Mac, who hauled him to his feet. "I wouldn't have said it if I didn't mean it, babe. Or you can put it outside the bedroom door if you think he might be better off there. Your call. I mean, that's presuming you want to sleep in our bed with us."

She threw her free arm around Sully and hugged him. "Thank you!" She raced into her bedroom.

As soon as she left, Sully dropped the façade and slung his arm around Mac's waiting shoulder. "Help me to bed. Quick."

"That bad?" He helped Sully into their room and carefully lowered him to the bed.

"Yeah. Didn't want her to see. She seemed upset enough."

Mac fetched the ointment from the bathroom, then dropped to his knees, and removed Sully's shoes. "Why didn't you say something as soon as you got home?"

"The naked slave greeting sort of distracted me."

Clarisse walked in. "I put his crate outside the door."

"Go bring Master a pain pill and a glass of water, please," Mac ordered. She raced to do it. After she took care of Sully, Mac crooked his finger at her and pointed to the floor. "I want you to learn this." He helped Sully remove his slacks, then started working on Sully's bad leg.

Sully closed his eyes, lay back, and let Mac take charge. They didn't need him. His pain had almost reached critical mass. He didn't listen to their words as much as he focused on the comforting sound of their voices and the feel of their hands. Mac, his firm, warm touch, kneaded his flesh, going through the range of motion exercises. Clarisse, more tentative, afraid of hurting him.

"Harder, honey," he grunted. "It's okay."

A half-hour later, he felt some relief as the meds kicked in and Mac's magic touch loosened the muscles. Sully removed his shirt as Mac shut off the lights. Mac quickly climbed into position as Sully relaxed against him. Sully patted the bed in front of him.

"Come here, pet," he softly said.

She cuddled against Sully. As tired as he felt and as much as he hurt, it wasn't difficult for him to keep his cock under control. He kissed the back of her neck. "Sweet dreams, baby. Love you."

"Love you, Master."

He reached behind him and patted Mac's thigh. "Love you, Brant."

He nuzzled the back of Sully's head. "Love you, too, Sul."

That night, the drugs had no influence over Sully's dreams.

Chapter Twenty-One

Sully pleasantly awoke from sleep the next morning to a pair of soft, warm lips engulfing his cock. He opened his eyes. Mac lay propped on one elbow next to him, smiling.

"Good morning, Master."

"Morning." Sully lifted his head and spotted Clarisse between his legs. He dropped his head before reaching down and burying his hand in her hair. "Good morning, pet," he said.

She mumbled something around his cock that sounded like, "Good morning, Master." The humming vibration resonated through his body.

"I told pet she could have the honor of waking you this morning," Mac said with a grin. "Hope that was okay?"

Sully closed his eyes and nodded, enjoying it, his cock pleasantly throbbing against her eager tongue despite the pain in his leg. She was good. *Damn* good.

Not as good as Mac, ironically, but good enough that in a few minutes he felt his release boiling deep inside him. He cupped his hand around the back of her head. "Now, pet," he gasped.

She deep-throated him as he came. As he lay there recovering, he felt Mac's stiff cock brush against his thigh. When he looked again, Mac still wore a playful smile.

He crooked his finger at Mac, who leaned in for a kiss. "Pet," Sully said, "take care of slave."

Mac's eyes rolled back in his head as she sucked his cock between her lips. Sully shifted to his side and watched his lover's face. He'd always felt a little guilty that in this one way he'd never reciprocated.

Clarisse certainly didn't have any qualms about it.

Sully played with Mac's nipple rings. "Hold it, slave. Don't come until I tell you."

Mac groaned, his bottom lip caught under his upper teeth as he tried to maintain control.

"You come before I tell you," Sully growled, "I'll whip your fucking ass."

Sully looked at Clarisse. Her hair spilled around her, a beautiful sight. He'd always worried about Mac lacking for this despite the other man's assurances to the contrary. With eyes closed, she eagerly serviced Mac's cock.

"Did you want to sink your cock into her sweet pussy while I was gone?" Sully murmured in his ear.

"Yes, Master!"

"I bet you dreamed about it, didn't you?"

"Yes!"

Sully smiled. He'd had more than his own fair share of those sorts of dreams about Clarisse.

"Is she beautiful when she comes?"

"Yes, Master!"

"Were you obedient while I was gone?"

"Yes, Master!"

"Very good." He twisted Mac's nipple rings, hard. "You may come."

Mac tensed as he cried out. Sully continued tormenting Mac's nipples until he knew Mac had finished climaxing. After Mac finished, Sully reached over and gently tapped Clarisse's head. "Very good, pet. You're done."

She lifted her head. The sexy smile on her face nearly hardened his cock again.

"Come lie down between us. Slave, I want a demonstration of the other night."

Mac grinned and jumped out of bed to fetch the toys. Sully stared into Clarisse's blue eyes. He leaned over and deeply kissed her. "I want to hear you scream as hard for me as you did for him, sweetheart."

Mac returned and slipped a towel under her. "Do you want to do the honors, Master?" He held up the new butt plug.

Sully smiled. "I want to watch." He kissed her as Mac slowly fucked the dildo inside her until it was fully buried. When she rolled over, Sully stroked her ass. "You are beautiful, sweetheart."

She softly moaned as Mac prepared her, then slid the new butt plug home. When she rolled face up again and Mac held up the vibrator, her eyes darkened with passion.

Sully rolled her left nipple between his fingers. "Don't come until I say so, pet," he warned.

Wordlessly she nodded as Mac flicked the vibrator on and pressed it to her clit.

She jumped and moaned, squirming under it as he tormented her.

Sully alternated from one nipple to the other as her skin flushed and she grew desperate.

"Please, Master!"

"Please what, pet?"

"Let me come! Please!"

He winked at Mac, who lifted the vibrator for a moment to let her cool down. "No, pet. I want to watch you squirm for slave. He apparently took very good care of you while I was gone. He brought you home safely. His reward is he gets to torment you. I don't want to deny him that."

Mac laughed. "Oh, baby, you're so fucking screwed." He pressed the vibrator to her clit again and tormented her for a few minutes.

After twenty minutes of this, and her tearful begging to come, Sully took pity. "Let her come, slave. Go for two."

"With pleasure, Master."

Sully caught and pinned Clarisse's wrists to the mattress above her head as Mac held the vibrator against her clit. Squirming, she cried out as the first orgasm rocked her.

Wishing he could fuck her right then, Sully leaned in and kissed her. "Again! Come now!"

Despite thrashing her head and moaning, she couldn't, she did. Once certain she'd finished, Sully nodded to Mac, who withdrew the vibrator and shut it off.

Sully gathered her into his arms, where her moans turned to sobs that shook her whole body.

"My good girl," he whispered. "Very good. Did that feel good?"

She nodded as Mac crawled up the bed to snuggle next to her.

Sully brushed the hair from her forehead. "When you feel up to standing, we'll all go take a shower, and then we can eat."

She nodded again.

Mac caught his gaze, a sultry smile lighting his face. Sully leaned over and kissed him. "Excellent job, slave."

Mac waggled his eyebrows at him. "Any time, Master."

* * * *

After breakfast, they sat and talked at the dining room table. "So what do you want, exactly?" Sully asked her.

She shook her head. "I don't understand the question, Master."

"What do you expect to get from this relationship? What do you need?"

"I love you. I want to keep loving you. Both of you."

"You can keep loving us without becoming my slave, I told you that."

She struggled to think. She'd never tried to put it into words. "I want to belong to you."

"Security?"

"Not like that." She thought. "I don't want to lose you. I want you to love me as much as you love Mac."

"You realize I will always love you differently than Mac. You're not him. He's not you. Differently doesn't mean less or more, however. I love you, and I love him."

"I know."

"Do you want me to fuck you?"

Her heart raced. "Yes, Master!"

He captured her chin and gently tilted her head so she had to look at him. "I won't do that without a lifetime commitment from you. You know that. Not unless we're married. I know that sounds stupid and old fashioned, but it's what I want. You need to think long and hard if you're really ready for that."

"I have."

"That won't give you carte blanche to fuck Mac any time you want when I'm not home, either. I own his cock the same way I'd own you and your body. He understands that. There might be times I tell him he can't make love to you when I'm not home. Will that be a problem?"

She glanced at Mac. "No, Master. That's not a problem."

Sully studied her. When he next spoke, his voice sounded low and soft. "Clarisse, I know you'll need us to be vanilla for you sometimes. I understand that. It's a need you'll have, and we will do that for you. But most of the time, it's going to be like this to a certain extent. The Master/slave dynamic. There will be protocols, obedience, and discipline."

"As long as you're fair, Master."

He leaned in to kiss her. "I am always fair." He looked at Mac. "Do you think I'm fair?"

"Yes, Master. I do. You don't hear me complaining."

Sully grinned. "But you enjoy getting the shit beat out of you."

Mac laughed. "True. Still, you are always fair. You've never been punitive. I might not always agree with you, but you're always consistent."

"I'll be right back." Sully walked to his office and returned moment later, a legal pad and pen in his hand.

This made it real. She was really going to do this.

The thought thrilled her.

Sully studied her for a moment before speaking. "If we ever divorce, there will be no second chances. I will never force you to stay with me, as Mac will be the first to tell you. If you ever decide you can't do this and want to leave, I will help you go, but you cannot come back. Ever. I won't play games."

"I understand."

He paused, gathering his thoughts. Clarisse spotted the old pain and betrayal in his eyes. "I would allow counseling, working on the relationship if you felt it necessary. I would do whatever it took to try to help you through any issues. I will not, however, stop this aspect of our relationship. You will be my wife in name and legal designation, but you will always first and foremost be my slave, and I will be your Master."

"Yes."

"Mac and I started out with a lot of negotiated limits. Over time, we dropped most of them. Now we safeword. I know what he doesn't get off on, and I rarely push him past his limits."

Mac nodded in agreement, but didn't speak.

Sully continued. "Our hard limits. Total honesty, even if it's uncomfortable. Never lie. I'm sure you had to lie to Bryan as a survival tactic to keep him from coming down on you. You do not have that fear with me. You can always approach me to talk and negotiate. Always. Do you understand?"

"Yes, Master."

"Lying will always be punished. Severely. Usually more than if you'd simply told the truth. Because I always reward honesty."

Mac smiled. "That's for damn sure."

"That's another thing—you will on occasion receive punishment. That punishment is up to me. Sometimes, it will include things you will not enjoy, like caning. Sometimes it might be something like kneeling for a set amount of time. Or whatever I deem appropriate for the infraction. There are times I will trade you the option to do something in exchange for punishment. Other than those situations, punishment receives no negotiation. Punishment will also never violate a hard limit. Understand?"

Fear set in. "But I don't get off on pain like he does."

"Let me clarify. Mac gets off on pain. I also use it for punishment for him. If you decide you cannot tolerate caning, for example, it might not be used as punishment. It would never be used in play unless you were willing to push the edge. I might have to find things other than corporal punishment that you hate enough I can use them as punishments. Back to hard limits. We do not have sex or intimate contact with others. No one will ever be allowed to touch you but Mac and myself."

From fear to confusion. "What about what I saw at the play party here and at club that night? You and those other people?"

"I was assisting with a scene. They used me like they might use a vibrator or a flogger. I was just helping them out."

She remembered her nasty flood of jealousy when she watched him do that. "Total honesty?"

He nodded.

"I can't handle seeing you do that with others. Not even just to help. I couldn't handle Mac with anyone else either."

He made a note on the legal pad. "What are you comfortable with? What if someone needs advice or help rigging?"

She thought about it. "If you're helping them set up a scene, or they need help with equipment, that wouldn't bother me. Honestly? It made me really jealous seeing the way you touched Doreen, even if it wasn't sex for you. I don't want either of you being involved with anyone else, even just for play. I want to be the only person you touch like that, besides Mac."

"Is that why you were upset at the party?"

She finally nodded. "Yeah," she quietly admitted. "It was."

"Good. See? That wasn't difficult, was it?"

"What?"

"Negotiation. It's as simple as that."

Could it be that easy? "No fighting?"

"Not about something like that." He smiled at Mac. "Doreen will be disappointed, but she'll understand."

Mac laughed. "She'll get over it."

Clarisse stared at them. "Really? You mean it?"

Sully put down the pen. "I love you. I'm willing to spend the rest of my life with you making you happy. If that means I have to give up something that's not important to me, I'm okay with that. I'm not one of those pricks who puts principles over the people they claim to love. If you don't want us having intimate contact with others like that, then we won't do it. Period."

"Thank you."

"What else is a hard limit for you?"

She shrugged. "I don't know."

"Knife play?"

She shivered. "No. Definitely not."

He made a note. "Negotiable in the future?"

She hesitated. "I don't know. For now, no."

"I'm guessing no on needle, fire, and blood play as well."

She shivered again. "Definite no's."

"Good, because they're not my kink either." More notations, then he looked up. "You will be expected to participate in impact and percussion play. Obviously, I won't be nearly as hard on you as I am with Mac. Especially in the beginning."

"I understand."

"You will always have a safeword. We will always respect it."

She nodded.

They went through a grocery list of things, neither man objecting to her hard limits. The talk made her totally wet.

Sully went over the list again. "Anything else you want to add?"

"Like what?"

"Like what you want. Not just limits of what you won't do, but what you need from us. I want to make you happy."

"Cuddle time."

Both men smiled. Sully noted it in a different column. "Any specific times?"

"I...I don't know. I never thought about that before."

"We'll leave it flexible." He winked. "I'm sure we won't have any problems meeting your needs there. Anything else?"

"Can I get back to you as I think of things?"

"Of course. You know our non-negotiable limits."

"If I ever decide I want to change things?"

"We talk, like this. It's possible in a few years you might be on a total safeword protocol like Mac is."

A few years. She hoped for forever, if she got her way.

"What happens if you get tired of me and want to get divorced and I don't want to? Or if one of you gets tired of me and the other doesn't? Will I automatically lose both of you?"

The men exchanged a look. "I seriously doubt that will happen," he said. "I am going to draw up a pre-nup. To protect you and me. Do you have a problem with that?"

Hell, she was negotiating her life as a slave. A pre-nup was easy. "That's fine."

"Regardless, even in the unlikely event we were to split, I would still take care of Tad. That's never something you have to worry about, never something you should ever allow to influence your decisions. I will put that in writing for you."

Unlikely event! Her heart soared at that. "I appreciate that."

"You will be expected to perform sexually as you are told. Your body will belong to me. And on the boat, to Mac by proxy." He leaned forward, his eyes intense. "As Mac's already demonstrated to you, you will be expected to submit regardless of what we ask of you. What we do privately is different from what we do at a party or club. Sexually, there will be no limits, except that we will never share you with anyone and we will never violate a hard limit. There will be times we fuck you at a party in front of people, or require you to sexually perform with us in front of others."

His voice dropped, deepening, tinged with desire. She suspected his cock had hardened in his pants. "I may choose to fuck your ass, or use your mouth, or even both of us fuck you at the same time. We will always love you and take care of you, but you *will* belong to me."

Her mouth had gone dry again. "Yes, Master." Frankly, the thought of both of their cocks fucking her at the same time weakened her knees in a good way. She survived the double penetration of the dildos, and they were both larger than the men. Her head had nearly exploded, but she'd survived it.

Loved it.

She was dying to try that with them.

"Does that scare you?"

"In a good way," she confessed.

He smiled and sat back in his chair. "When you're not feeling well, when you've got cramps, you're free to wear clothes as you feel comfortable. I don't want you to be miserable, and I understand we need to work around that. You will always be collared, and you would have to stick to other protocols we have. There will be times I expect you to perform certain sexual duties regardless."

She nodded.

"We can negotiate on the fly on that. I don't ever want sex to be painful or unpleasant for you. Making love in private and playing a scene are two totally different things, even though there will be times I incorporate sex in a scene. Do you understand?"

"Yes."

"Mac will take you to the doctor again. You need another round of STD and HIV testing, just to make sure. I'll get our medical paperwork so you can see it, that we're clean."

"I don't need to see it."

He frowned. "Yes, you do. I want you to know we're telling the truth."

"I trust you."

"Don't ever trade trust for your life if you don't have to." He consulted the list. "Mac needs to go over boat rules with you. That's his domain."

Mac laughed. "Do what I tell you to do. It's that easy. I don't violate our hard limits."

She stared at the two men as reality hit her. She was really doing this. Not lost on her, the irony that she felt like she had more control and voice now than she ever had with Bryan.

"Do you want me to stay on the Pill?"

Sully's face softened as he reached across the table and stroked her hand. "Sweetheart, that is one thing that is *always* in your control. I will never demand that from you one way or another. Your health takes priority to anything."

Mac nodded in agreement, but didn't say anything.

"What do you two want?" she asked.

Sully shook his head. "Oh no you don't. You don't pass that decision to us. I mean it, it's always your decision."

"Do you want kids?"

He shrugged. "It was never an option for us, so it's not anything I ever thought about before. No chance of him getting pregnant any time soon."

Mac snorted with laughter.

She'd never wanted kids with Bryan. "If I decide I want children?"

"Then we talk about it. It's safe to say it's an issue we don't need to worry about for a while. We've got a lot of craziness to get through, including the trial and you getting used to how we do things around here." He shrugged again. "After that, if you want to talk about it, we will."

"That's not an answer."

"Neither of us hate kids, if that's what you're getting at."

Clarisse nodded. "How long before we get married?"

He playfully arched an eyebrow at her. "I haven't even proposed yet."

Embarrassed, heat flooded her face again. "Sorry."

He smiled and stroked her hand. "I don't want to rush things. I don't want to pressure you. As much as it's going to kill Mac and me to wait, I want to give you at least three months to try this arrangement before we discuss taking things further. I don't want you to change your mind and feel like you're trapped."

"I won't change my mind."

"Good. Then the wait will be torture on all three of us. Regardless, you and I will talk again in three months, see if you still want to go through with this, see if you still feel the same way. Or if you need more time, we can do that, too. Or make changes. I'm willing to negotiate as much as I can to keep you happy." He glanced at the time. "You both need to get dressed. Your doctor appointment is at one."

Mac stood immediately, but she hesitated. "Can I ask one more thing?"

Both men nodded.

"Can I call him Brant when we're not playing?"

Sully smiled. "That's up to him."

Mac looked at Sully, who apparently sensed what he wanted. Sully nodded. Mac kissed her, a simple brush of his lips across hers. "I would like that very much, sugar."

* * * *

She was surprised when later, after dinner, all they did was sit and watch a movie on TV. Mac took up his usual position on the floor. Sully patted the couch beside him. Clarisse lay next to him, resting her head in his lap.

The movie received absolutely none of her attention. Despite being naked, it felt right, totally normal to relax like that with them. She draped one arm over Mac's shoulder, and he laced his fingers through hers. Sully rested one hand on her waist and played with strands of her hair with the other.

Closing her eyes, she imagined living like this years from now. Easy to do, until reality intruded into her thoughts.

"I'll have to get a Florida driver's license," she said. "My name and information will be on file when we do all the paperwork." Unbidden, her tears flowed. With the men, she'd been able to shut herself off in a little fantasy bubble of invisibility and safety and let them protect her. "He'll be able to find me."

Sully pulled her into his arms. "Hey, it's okay. Don't worry. He'll be on his best behavior since he knows he's royally fucked. His lawyer will try to show that if he really was guilty, he would have been trying to hunt you down and he hasn't. Weak defense, but all he's got at this point."

She forced a smile she didn't feel. Sully waved Mac onto the couch and the men held her between them. "Honestly, sweetheart, if he was determined to find you, he would have. The prosecutors have the case, and with IA up his ass, he'll behave."

Clarisse didn't feel so sure about that, but she was willing to trust Sully. "Okay."

* * * *

The next morning, Sully closed himself in his office and called Ohio for a progress report. Twenty minutes later, he hung up, smiling. The asshole had accepted a plea deal. Sully hadn't honestly thought he would, but he was offered probation and immunity from an IA investigation if he ended it now. It also meant Clarisse wouldn't have to return to testify. No, the asshole wouldn't do jail time, which Sully had hoped he would. It also meant the guy could never be a cop again, would lose his retirement and bennies, and he would agree to a permanent restraining order.

He found Mac and Clarisse in the kitchen, working on a shopping list. Sully scooped her into his arms and spun her around. The ultimate test of will—feeling her naked flesh under his hands and not giving in to the temptation to make love to her right there. Mac looked on, amused.

"Guess what, pet?" Sully asked her as he set her back on her feet.

"What?"

He lightly smacked her ass, which she met with a smile. "I said guess, pet."

"Animal, vegetable, or mineral?"

"None of the above. News."

A slight frown crossed her face. "News?"

He nodded. "Big news."

Her eyes widened. "Bryan swallowed a bullet?"

Sully laughed. "No, not quite. He took a plea bargain."

She stiffened in fear. "Will he do jail time?"

"No, but he'll have five years of probation, lose his job and benefits, and he agreed to a permanent restraining order against him."

She pulled away from him and wrapped her arms around herself. "But no jail?"

"No. The prosecutor said if they took it to trial, the most he'd probably get would be two years with time off. If the lawyer didn't get him off. I'm sorry, babe."

She studied the floor for several minutes before looking at him. "Is this good?"

Sully gathered her into his arms again. "It's very good. You don't ever have to see him again. It means you can quit hiding."

"Really?"

"Yeah." He tipped his head, motioning Mac over. He stepped behind her and put his arms around her too. "It means you don't have to worry about him anymore."

"Does it mean we can end the three-month wait thing early and get married?"

He rubbed noses with her. "No, it doesn't, smarty. Nice try, though."

* * * *

True to his word, Sully wouldn't let her rush him. Although he fucked Mac more frequently over the next several weeks than he normally did.

Enmeshed in the men's dynamic, it was easy for Clarisse to let go and trust. Sully soon discovered she hated kneeling for long periods, so the few times he had to punish her for an infraction, he used that instead of strokes.

With Clarisse a part of their relationship, Sully dropped many of the rules they'd had before that got Mac in hot water. When Sully felt the need to punish Mac, he discovered it was extremely effective to lock him in the chastity device and then let Clarisse give him a lap dance.

"You *are* a fucking sadist," Mac groaned one night as the device painfully dug into him.

Sully sat back on the couch and laughed as he watched Clarisse wriggle her naked body over Mac's. "As you yourself have said before, 'Duh.'" He took a swallow of his beer. "But damn, this is a fine-looking sight. Make sure to get him nice and hard, pet."

Mac closed his eyes and winced. "Fuck!"

Sully grinned. "You won't talk back to me again anytime soon, will you, slave?"

"No, Master," he painfully grunted.

After twenty minutes, Sully felt reasonably sure Mac had experienced a fair amount of agony. "Pet, go get the small vibrator."

She ran to do it. He didn't fail to spot her evil grin. When she returned, he ordered her back into Mac's lap, facing him. "Are you horny, pet?"

"Yes, Master," she said, giggling.

"Slave, help pet come." He smiled as she turned on the vibrator and pressed it to her clit.

Mac moaned as he cupped her breasts in his hands and played with her nipples. He would feel a little of the vibrator through his shorts and the chastity device, adding to his torment.

Clarisse threw back her head as she raced toward her climax. Sully rose from the couch and, standing behind her, supported her. He unzipped his shorts and brushed his cock against her lips. "Take me, pet."

Mac licked his lips as Clarisse swallowed Sully's cock. Sully held her hair out of her face. "Come for me, pet."

She did, deeply swallowing his cock as her own orgasm exploded inside her. He fucked her mouth as she came, his own climax not far behind.

He took a deep breath to steady himself, cuddling her head against him. Mac's face twisted in pain as he struggled to will his cock soft.

"You okay there, slave?" Sully asked.

Mac glared but didn't reply.

Sully smiled. "Go take a cold shower. And stay locked up."

Muttering under his breath, Mac helped Clarisse stand and went to take his cold shower. Sully lightly swatted her ass. "Go clean up, and then get dinner started."

"You're going to torture him all night?"

Sully winked. "Until bedtime, but don't tell him that."

* * * *

By the end of the second month, Clarisse knew without a doubt that she was deeply in love with both men. They'd taken her to two more play parties where both men topped her. They had two private parties at the house as well. In addition to the slave aspect of her relationship with them, they made sure to spend plenty of time as a "normal" family.

If Tad suspected there was more going on between the three, he didn't let on.

Sometimes Sully went out on the boat with them, sometimes he didn't, depending on his work schedule. When Sully traveled out of town and they needed someone to watch Bart, the facility where Uncle Tad lived let him dogsit, much to her uncle's delight. The other residents enjoyed it too.

When Clarisse and Mac returned from one boat trip, Sully had returned home before them and already picked up Bart. When she walked into the living room, she stopped. "What's that?"

Sully sat on the sofa and watched TV. Bart lay in his lap while chewing on the butt plug. It had become his favorite toy. Sully looked at where she pointed. "It's a doggy ramp. So he can get up on the couch by himself. I got one for our bed, too."

Clarisse hugged him. "Thank you, Master!"

Sully scratched the dog's head. "I saw them in the pet store today when I was getting him more food and I thought we could use them."

Mac laughed. "See, pet? I told you he'd be okay with Bart."

She couldn't pull her gaze away from Sully's grey eyes. "I love you so much."

He arched an eyebrow at her. "I love you, too." He spanked her, once. "Why aren't you naked?"

"Uh-oh," Mac said from the bedroom doorway. He'd already stripped off his shirt. "I think you're in trouble."

She smiled. When she tried to stand, he pulled her back. "Missed you guys."

"Missed you too, Master."

He released her and did a mental countdown. One more week. While she had talked to him several times for clarification about some of their terms, she'd expressed no desire to end or modify their relationship, except she constantly hinted at wishing the three months were up already.

* * * *

Sully kissed Mac and Clarisse good-bye the next morning. "I need to run some errands," he cryptically said. Mac had enough sense not to question him. Clarisse looked curious, but reined it in. He suspected she'd ask Mac for information as soon as he walked out the door.

In the Jag, Sully drove to a jeweler's in Tarpon Springs before heading to Tad's. He located Tad in a common room, arguing over a poker hand with a fellow resident.

When Tad spotted Sully, he raised his hand in greeting. "Probably a good thing you're here. I'm about ready to break out the shootin' irons on this varmint."

"Fuck you, Moore," the other elderly gent said.

Sully didn't bother hiding his smile.

"Yeah, bet you'd like to fuck me more, Mickey." He grabbed his crotch. "Go read your goddamned rule book and get back to me when you feel like playing honest." He led Sully to his room.

"I thought you and Mickey were friends."

Tad grinned. "Oh, we are. Same old bullshit every time. What's up?" His face clouded. "Is Risse okay?"

"She's fine." Sully fought a bout of nerves. This plan seemed like a good and noble idea at the time, but now he wasn't so sure. "I need to talk to you about something."

Tad lowered himself to his sofa with a grunt. "Sure. What?"

Sully reached into his pocket and withdrew the ring box before he sat. He opened it and showed it to Tad."

Tad smiled. "I love you, boy, but I'm not marryin' you. Don't think Mac would agree. Besides, you're not my type and you're too damn young for me."

Sully laughed, then grew serious again. "I wanted to ask your permission to marry Clarisse."

Tad stared at him for a long moment. "Risse?"

"Yes, sir."

The older man blew out a long, haggard breath. "What happened with you and Mac?"

Sully reddened. Now for the hard part. "Well, see, that's the thing. We both love her."

"Only one of you can marry her."

Sully nodded.

Tad stared at the ring. "Mac's okay with this?"

"It was his idea."

"Well, fuck me. No shit?"

"No shit."

"But do you love her?"

"As much as I love Mac. We both love her. I promise we'll take good care of her."

"I have no doubt you will." Tad's face broke into a lopsided grin. "So she gets a two-fer-one deal?"

"Yeah, you could say that."

"She's been kinda quiet on that topic lately. I was wondering what was going on." He looked at the emerald and diamond ring. "It's beautiful. Looks expensive."

Sully closed the box and returned it to his pocket. "Yes."

Tad smiled and stood. "Wait here." He tottered into his bedroom and returned a moment later holding something. He handed it to Sully before he sat again. It was a beautiful engagement ring, rubies and diamonds in an antique setting. "That was my Karen's ring," he softly said. "I saved a long time to afford it."

He held up his left hand, where he wore a wedding band on his left ring finger, and a more delicate mate to it on his pinky. "I'll wear these until the day I die. Then Risse can have them and do what she wants with them. But I'd be honored if you'd give that one to her. I know Karen would have loved it."

Sully slipped it into the ring box with the other for safe keeping.

"I'm the one who's honored." He smiled. "So does that mean you're okay with this?"

"Hell yeah, I'm okay with it. Means she won't be gallavantin' all over the place and end up with some abusive jerk." He grinned. "Don't worry, I won't be asking to move in and cramp y'all's style."

* * * *

The only problem Sully had with accepting the ring was that he'd promised Mac he could pick out his own ring for Clarisse. Now he had one ring too many. Clarisse was at the vet with Bart when Sully returned.

Mac immediately crossed his arms, his face dark. "What's wrong?"

Sully showed him the ring box and explained. "I need to take the one back I picked out and get a refund or a credit toward the one you want to get her."

Mac fingered the rings. "What's wrong with this one? It's beautiful."

Sully took the box back. "Because I want you to pick a ring out for her."

He pointed at the box. "I like that one."

"Brant, I mean *you* need to go to the store and pick one out you want her to wear."

He stepped forward. "Can we drop formal for a minute?"

Sully nodded.

Mac grabbed Sully's hand and opened the ring box again. "Sul, I like the ring you picked out for her. It's something I would have picked out. I'll pick out my wedding band for her. I think she should wear Karen's ring. It's gorgeous."

Sully studied him. "You're not upset?"

Mac smiled. "No, I'm not upset, dude."

"How about I let you pick out my wedding band for her to make up for it?"

"Jesus, Sul, quit worrying about it."

"Okay, then at least go with me and give me your input. I'd feel better about it."

Mac snorted. "You're really worried about this, aren't you?"

"Dammit, I want to be fair!"

Mac pulled Sully to him and kissed him, hard. "You *are* fair. Be honest. You'd whip my ass if I danced around an issue like this."

He sighed and took a moment to compose his thoughts. "I don't want you to hate me in a few years for being married to her and you aren't."

Mac rolled his eyes. "Fuck. Me." He poked Sully in the chest. "You, Master." He pointed at himself. "Me, slave. Duh."

"It's not funny."

"No, it's not fucking funny. Jesus, Sul, grow a set for crying out loud!"

"How can you be so okay with this?"

Mac's expression softened as he seemingly grasped the crux of Sully's unease. "Because," he said, his tone gentle, "you're my Master, and I'm your slave. If you'll recall, that's the way I wanted it. It's still the way I want it. It's the way I'll *always* want it."

"I couldn't be as generous about this as you are."

"I know you couldn't." He gently poked Sully in the chest again. "That's why you, Master. Me, slave."

Sully stared at him for a long moment before bursting into laughter. He let Mac pull him close and wrap his arms around him as he rested his head on Mac's chest. "What the hell would I do without you, Brant?"

Mac closed his eyes as he held Sully and rubbed his chin across the top of his head. "Let's not ever find out, okay?"

* * * *

The men took Clarisse out for a sunset beach picnic dinner at Howard Park on Thursday. Mac knew Sully would go first, as was his right. As they snuggled on the blanket, Clarisse between them, she stared out at the horizon.

"This is beautiful, guys." Sully had told her it was a vanilla evening. "Thank you for doing this."

Sully swallowed back his nerves and slipped the ring out of his pocket without her seeing it. He laced his fingers through hers and leaned in to kiss her. "Anything for you, you know that."

"Just don't ever get rid of me."

"No chance." He slipped the ring on her left hand. "I'm hoping you'll be ours for life. If you'll marry me."

Her eyes widened as she stared at the ring. She threw her arms around his neck. "Yes!" she whispered. "For life."

He smiled and kissed her, then pointed at Mac, who also wore a smile. He took her right hand in his and slipped the other ring on her finger. The emerald and diamond ring looked beautiful on her hand. "Two hands, two husbands, two rings." He folded his fingers around her hand. "If you'll marry me, too." He laughed. "Well, you know what I mean."

Her eyes brimmed with happy tears. "Yes, I'll marry you, too."

He kissed her, then brushed her tears away. "For better, for worse, for boat rules?"

She laughed. "Yes, even for boat rules." Mac had taken great pleasure enjoying her on the boat, although his catch yield had suffered as a result.

Sully changed position so he sat in front of both of them. He put an arm around each. "If you need more time, it's okay. You can say so."

She shook her head. "No. I don't need any more time. I don't want any more time."

He caught her chin and tilted her face to his. "I can be a very harsh Master at times," he dangerously growled. "Have you considered that?"

Her gaze never wavered. "But you're always fair, Master."

His lips curled into a smile as he kissed her. "Yes, sweetheart. I am always fair."

"Then that's all that matters."

* * * *

Bryan bought a disposable phone and called the PI he'd hired. "What do you have for me?"

"I found the boat. The Coast Guard has it listed as being registered to Sullivan Nicoletto. PO Box."

"That doesn't help me."

"He's a writer and a former cop. He got shot almost ten years ago, retired from the sheriff's office. Guy must be loaded, traced several properties to him and some other guy through a trust."

"I paid you to get me a fucking home address."

"Calm down. I found the marina where he keeps the boat." He read off the address. "I should have the home address later today. It's a pain to sort shit out when there's a trust involved."

"I want it as soon as you have it." Then again, maybe barging into a cop's house wasn't the smartest way to go. He didn't even know if Clarisse had gone to the boat.

The boat. How many fucking lame stories had she whined about how much she missed her uncle and that fucking boat? Enough that he couldn't wait to beat the living crap out of her for the mess she'd created. He'd tossed the letters she'd received about Tad's stoke. The last thing he'd needed was her heading to Florida to move some old feeble geezer into his house.

He'd hoped the bastard would have died by now.

It'd taken him years to get her damn parents out of the fucking way, thought he had her firmly in hand, and then she finally grew a set of balls when he least expected it. What a pain in the ass that had been. He never thought she'd file a report. He thought he'd gotten her trained well enough to just take it.

Fuck. Another three months and he would have married her and gotten life insurance on her, waited a little while, then took care of her, too. Oh no, the little mouse couldn't shut the hell up and stick to his plan.

He cracked open another beer. Only two in the afternoon, but not like he had a job to go to. His thoughts turned darker as he took a long pull on the bottle.

Tad Moore would be one way to get a pound of flesh out of Clarisse. She fucked his life all to hell?

She hadn't seen *anything* yet.

Chapter Twenty-Two

The next morning, Friday, the three of them drove to the clerk's office to get the marriage license. Clarisse wore the silver chain collar under her shirt and enjoyed the feel of Sully's firm grip on her hand as they stood in line and awaited their turn. While they filled out the paperwork, he whispered, "You can still back out, sweetie."

She looked at him, then Mac. "You're stuck with me for a long, long time. You're not getting cold feet, are you?"

Mac laughed. "Oh, man, are we in for a wild ride."

Sully grinned and kissed her. "I wouldn't have it any other way."

Due to state laws, they had to wait three days to get married since they didn't take the premarital course. Monday afternoon, they stopped by Tad's and picked him up. He grinned as Mac helped him into the passenger seat of Sully's Jag.

"This'll give me something good to talk about at bingo tonight," he teased.

Clarisse blushed in the backseat. When Mac climbed in with her, he laughed and kissed her. "Talk of the town."

Sully caught her gaze in the rearview mirror and winked. "They'll talk because they're jealous."

At the clerk's office, they met their attorney and filed the paperwork before they were escorted into a small anteroom for the ceremony. Mac and Tad served as official witnesses while the attorney looked on. The clerk didn't bat an eye when Clarisse slipped the wedding band on Sully's left hand where Mac's already lay.

He had told her Mac's would stay on his finger first. She was more than okay with that. In fact, she liked the idea that they were both tied to Sully in a tangible way. Considering she knew there would be times Mac would top her, she preferred it that way.

"You may kiss the bride," the smiling clerk told Sully.

Clarisse couldn't pull her gaze from Sully's grey eyes. Her husband. How had she gone from barely able to trust him to totally giving herself to him?

She didn't care. She loved him, and he loved her.

His gentle, tender kiss wrapped her heart and soul around him. The clerk didn't notice how he slipped his hand up the back of Clarisse's head, fisted her hair, and gave one quick, firm tug that nearly melted her knees right out from under her.

He lifted his head. "Forever, pet."

She smiled. "You'd better believe it."

The clerk stepped out. The attorney followed so he could file Clarisse and Mac's name change paperwork. Clarisse would take both men's names, to become Clarisse MacCaffrey-Nicoletto, although she would use Nicoletto on a daily basis. They took the opportunity to hyphenate Sully's last name to Mac's.

Sully put her hand in Mac's. "Well, kiss our bride, Brant," he said.

Mac smiled, gathered her into his arms, and planted one on her that nearly finished her already rubbery skeleton. By the time he lifted his lips from hers, she wanted to drag both of them into the nearest lockable room and let them fuck her brains out. He released her, but not until he gently stroked her chin with his thumb. "I love you," he whispered.

She wiggled her hips against him, feeling his hard bulge pressing against her. "I love you, too."

He waggled his eyebrows at her, sending her into a giggle fit.

Tad laughed. "I always did think of you boys as sons. Now you really are part of the family."

* * * *

Sully and Mac took great pains to secretly tease Clarisse all through their celebratory dinner at Plaka's with Tad. By the time they dropped him off, she was ready to jump her two men in the backseat of the car.

At home, Sully scooped Clarisse into his arms and carried her up the stairs and through the front door as Mac held it open. Once inside, Mac closed and locked the door and started stripping.

Sully set Clarisse on her feet and stood back, his arms crossed over his chest, not speaking.

She glanced from Mac, already down to his slacks, to Sully. She realized what he waited for.

A seductive smile played across her face as she unbuttoned her blouse. Sully nodded. "Good girl." A moment later, both Mac and Clarisse knelt before him, heads bowed.

Sully stood over them. "Hold hands."

Mac's fingers wrapped around Clarisse's hand. He gently squeezed.

Sully placed a hand on each of their heads. She had no doubt he had a tighter grip on Mac's hair than he did on hers.

"I have plans for you tonight, pet. You are going to cross the line, take the final step your training has prepared you for. Are you ready for that?"

"Yes, Master."

"Slave, are you ready to do whatever I command to add pet to our family?"

"Yes, Master," he replied.

"I am laying down the law. In this house, I am Master, and slave is my Alpha slave. Do you understand, pet?"

"Yes, Master."

"When I am not around, you will follow his orders as if he was me. There may be times I allow him to punish you."

She shivered in a good way. "Yes, Master."

He gently stroked her hair. "Tonight, I am officially claiming you as my slave, to wear my collar. Do you understand and agree to this?"

"Yes, Master."

"Go get her collar, slave."

Mac released her hand and went to comply. He returned a moment later, wearing his leather collar. He handed something to Sully before retaking his place next to her and lacing his fingers through her hand.

"Look at me, both of you."

Clarisse saw it was a new collar, custom made, similar to Mac's but smaller, more delicate, complete with a small padlock. It could pass for a piece of Goth neckwear.

"I take this even more seriously than I do the vows we spoke earlier," he said. "As we've already discussed, there will be no coming back if you leave. I won't play that game. You must talk to me, keep communications open, discuss things with me if you are ever unhappy or find yourself needing something. Do you understand?"

"Yes, Master."

He squatted in front of her. "Hold her hair, slave."

Mac gently swept her hair off her neck as Sully removed the silver chain collar and replaced it with the new one. Her breath caught as she felt the soft, supple leather touch her flesh and heard the lock click into place.

Sully smiled and stroked her cheek. "My sweet, beautiful pet," he softly said. "Tonight I finally get to make you mine in all ways. You have no idea how long I've wanted to make love to you."

He stood. "Both of you meet me in the bedroom. I want slave's wrist cuffs on him. Help him with that, pet."

"Yes, Master." Mac flashed her a smile as they hurried to comply. Sully entered the bedroom a few minutes later, carrying a glass of water.

Clarisse felt like every nerve ending in her body had caught fire, her senses on edge. She knew Sully would follow through on what he'd said, and all she had to do was go along for the ride.

And be ridden.

Sully crooked his finger at Mac. "On the bed, on your back. Head at this end." Mac quickly complied. Sully clipped Mac's wrist cuffs to the chains at the foot of the bed. He leaned over and placed a long, deep kiss on his lover's mouth. "You'll be swearing at me by the end of the evening," Sully teased.

Mac smiled. "Of that I have no doubt."

Sully turned and swatted her ass, not too hard, just a little sting. "On the bed. Next to him, on your back. Ass right here at the edge."

Nervously, she complied. The way Mac was trussed didn't give her a lot of room, but she managed.

Sully grabbed her legs and pulled her closer to the edge, slung them over his shoulders. Then he looked at Mac. "Watch me while I taste my pet."

Mac softly moaned and licked his lips. Sully lowered his head to her bare mound and gently swiped his tongue from her ready entrance all the way up, over her clit.

Clarisse loudly moaned.

Sully laughed and lifted his head. "Do you like that?"

"Yes, Master!"

"Hold slave's cock while I do this, but don't let him come or you'll get five with the cane."

When she wrapped her fingers around Mac's cock, he worked his hips against her hand.

Sully leaned in to him. "If you come, remember *she* gets the strokes, not you. Is it worth it to watch her take them for you?"

His hips stilled. "No, Master."

"Very good." He lowered his head to her sex again and repeated his earlier motion. "By the way, pet, you may come."

She gasped, not close yet but the fact that he was allowing her to climax unhinged her body's need in a pleasant way. She wiggled her hips and enjoyed how he'd clamped his hands around her thighs, the feel of his hot mouth on her flesh.

Sully swirled his tongue around her clit, slowly, drawing it out, teasing her mercilessly.

Mac watched and licked his lips.

Sully pushed two thick fingers inside her, pumped them a few times. He pulled them out, then pressed his hand to Mac's lips. Mac greedily sucked Sully's fingers inside his mouth.

"See how she tastes?" Sully asked. "When you next get to taste her, it will be only after I've fucked her. Then you'll taste me, too." He tightly gripped Mac's chin. "Who do you belong to?"

"You, Master!" he gasped.

"And who does pet belong to?"

"You!"

Sully leaned over and kissed him, hard, crushing Mac's lips. "All of her belongs to me—her body, her name, everything. Just like all of you belongs to me. You don't get to kiss her lips or suck her clit or fuck her unless I say so. Do you understand?"

"Yes, Master!"

"Do you love my pet?"

"Very much, Master."

Clarisse was caught in an emotional high not quite subspace, fired by her sexual need. She wiggled her hips, trying to get Sully to continue his oral explorations, but he hadn't finished with Mac yet.

"You may love my pet as much as you want with your heart and soul. You will protect her and care for her, just as she'll love and care for you. But you only get to have sex with her when I say it's okay. If you disobey me, you'll find yourself wearing a CB for years without relief. Do you understand, slave?"

"Yes, Master!"

"I will make sure your needs are taken care of as long as you obey me. I will be generous with my pet, but under my terms. Do you want to fuck my pet tonight?"

"Yes, Master! Please!"

"Then you keep behaving yourself and you'll get to." He looked at Clarisse. "Where was I?"

"Between my legs, Master," she breathlessly gasped.

He chuckled. "Very good, pet." He laved her clit with his tongue, then wrapped his lips around it and sucked, hard. The bite of pain, combined with the explosion of pleasure, quickly drove her over the edge with a scream. At the last second, she realized she had to release Mac's cock or she'd risk jerking him off, and beyond that, coherent thought escaped her as she bucked her hips against Sully's face.

Relentless, he continued working her swollen clit with his mouth until she whimpered and shivered on the bed. Only when convinced he'd wrung every last ounce of pleasure out of her did he release her with a final kiss to her clit.

"Very good, pet. Your performance earned slave a reward." He looked down the other man's body. Mac's cock stood rigid, the thick veins well-defined against the engorged surface. "How did you enjoy that, slave?"

"She sounded wonderful, Master."

Sully rolled Clarisse over, pulled her to her feet, and repositioned her at the end of the bed so her feet were on the floor and Mac's head lay directly between her legs.

"Lean forward. Can you reach slave's cock with your mouth like this? Don't take him in yet."

"Yes, Master."

Sully rubbed her shoulders, slowly trailed his fingers down her back, gently stroking. "Slave, watch me fuck my pet. You will lick my balls and cock, but you may not lick or kiss pet between her legs. Incidental contact is allowed. Do you understand?"

"Yes, Master." Mac's voice sounded low, almost slurred. Clarisse realized he'd slipped into subspace at some point. Her eyes were firmly fixed on his cock, her mouth practically watering in anticipation of wrapping her lips around the large head.

Sully suddenly grabbed her ponytail and pulled her head back, not roughly but not gently, either. "After I slide my cock inside you, you will go down on slave. If you do not make him come before me, he will not get relief and will not be allowed to fuck you tonight. You will keep sucking him until I'm done regardless of how many times he comes. You will swallow every drop."

"Yes, Master."

His hands slowly skimmed her back, to her hips. He used his feet to spread her legs a little more, and then she felt his stiff cock press against her entrance. "Ask me to fuck you, pet."

She closed her eyes, "Please fuck me, Master! I want your cock inside me!"

He rammed home, deep, stretching her, drawing a gasp out of her. But he didn't withdraw.

Pressure from Sully's hand on the back of her head reminded her of his command. She lowered her body on top of Mac's and sucked his cock into her mouth as deeply as she could.

Mac groaned.

Then both of Sully's hands tightly gripped her hips, his fingers digging in as he slowly fucked her. "Okay, slave. Lick my balls."

Clarisse felt movement beneath her. From the way Sully's breathing changed, she knew Mac was complying. "Very good, slave," Sully gasped. He took his time fucking her, long slow strokes combined with short jabbing ones that stole her breath in a good way. As she greedily sucked Mac's cock, she realized for the first time in her life she felt totally wanted, desired.

Sexy.

She closed her eyes and enjoyed the moment, even when Sully occasionally swatted her ass with his hand while he fucked her.

Mac's cock throbbed against her tongue. Then at the same time he let out a loud, low moan, she tasted his hot seed as he climaxed.

Within a few minutes, Mac had grown hard again in her mouth.

Sully's pace changed, increased speed, the tempo more steady. "That's it, slave," he panted. "Suck my balls. You know what I like."

Clarisse gave up trying to help. She let Sully have total control of her body, using her.

Owning her.

She shivered, feeling the start of her own climb again. Before she could get there, he let out a loud cry and plunged deeper than before. He wrapped his arms around her and pulled her up against his chest and off Mac's cock.

She felt his heart race against her flesh, both their bodies slick with sweat. Then he pressed his lips to the side of her neck and mumbled, "I love you, Clarisse. I love you so much, baby. I swear to God, we'll make you happy."

"I love you too, Master." She looked into Mac's face. "And I love you."

"You will call him Sir," Sully whispered in her ear.

She grinned. "I love you, Sir."

Mac's smile lit the room. "I love you too, pet."

Sully, his cock still buried inside her, nudged her to the side and face down onto the bed. Then he withdrew and straddled Mac's face again. Mac's mouth automatically opened. Clarisse rolled onto her side and watched, turned on beyond belief at the sight of Mac eagerly taking Sully's cock like that.

She wanted to nose in there and help.

Sully stroked Mac's cheek. "Do you like how she tastes? I think you'll spend a lot of time tasting pet on my cock, won't you?"

Mac nodded, but didn't release Sully's cock.

"Very good. Get me hard again." Mac worked at him with his lips and tongue. Clarisse watched, her mouth gaping. A few minutes later, Sully tapped Mac on the head. "Very good. Stop, don't make me come." He stood and unclipped Mac's wrist cuffs, then pulled them off him. "Wait here." He retrieved something from the bathroom. Clarisse realized it was a bottle of lube.

He stood at the end of the bed and studied them. "Pet, scoot up the bed. On your back, legs spread. Let slave taste you."

She quickly changed position, her heart racing and sex throbbing as Mac knelt between her legs. Sully sat on the bed beside her where he could watch. "Make her come, slave. Make sure you stick your tongue deep inside her."

Mac dove for her and she moaned at the sensation of his hot, eager mouth between her legs. Sully tangled his fingers in Mac's hair, getting a good grip on him. "Do you taste me inside her, slave?" he growled in Mac's ear.

He lifted his head. "Yes, Master."

"Remember, she is my pet, and I am allowing you to taste her."

Mac nodded but didn't lift his head.

Clarisse felt another rapidly approaching climax spin through her core. She'd come damn hard the first time, and this one felt like it would be just as big.

Sully didn't release Mac's head. He sucked her nipples, nipped at one, then the other, alternating, just enough pain to enhance the pleasure Mac gave her.

"Come hard, pet," he coaxed. "Scream again. I want to hear how hard slave makes you come. He doesn't get to fuck you until he makes you come."

Mac's tongue dipped deep inside her, fucking her, then alternating with flicks against her sensitive clit. She was aware of her climax starting, an amazing flood of pleasure exploding inside her, driving the breath from her.

The world went black.

When she opened her eyes, both men anxiously hovered over her, worried looks on their faces. Sully gently patted her cheek.

"Clarisse, honey, come on. Wake up."

She took a deep breath. "What happened?" She tried to sit up, felt woozy.

Poor Mac looked horrified. "You passed out. I think you hyperventilated. You okay, sweetie?"

The men steadied her. "Yeah...I think. How long was I out?"

"Just a few seconds," Mac said, sounding relieved. "I think you've had more than enough for one night."

She shook her head. "No, because I haven't had my turn with you yet." Both men's cocks had gone limp, probably from fear over her blackout.

"Honey, I think Mac's right," Sully said. "You scared the crap out of us." Gone was his low, dominant tone. He was back to Sully, her concerned friend.

Her loving husband.

"Master, I don't think that's very fair to Sir." She set her jaw and stared him down.

Stunned, he looked at her a long moment before laughing. "Jesus, you're going to wear us out, aren't you?"

She wanted back into the game. Dammit, this was her wedding night and the boys were harshing her mellow. "Master, that's my job, isn't it?"

"She's not giving up, Sul," Mac said. His cock twitched, slowly inflating.

Sully slowly shook his head, but in resignation, not denial. "I dunno. I think I should make slave pay for doing that to you and scaring the crap out of me."

"Please don't do that, Master." She leaned in and kissed him, long and deep. "It felt so good." Better than fucking good, it had topped the previous orgasm by a country mile, and the first one had been her best ever.

"Hmph. Well, okay, I won't punish him this time, but only because you asked very nicely." He was finally getting back into the game, his voice lowering, deepening.

"Thank you, Master," Mac said.

She lay back and smiled. "I'm ready when you are."

Mac grinned and pounced on her, kissed her. "I'm going to fuck you so good, baby."

Sully slapped his ass, hard. "What did you call her?"

Mac laughed even though his cock had fully hardened again.

"Sorry, Master." He nuzzled his nose against hers. "I'm going to fuck you so good, *pet.*"

"That's better." Sully changed position, knelt behind Mac.

Clarisse wrapped her arms and legs around Mac. "Please fuck me."

He pressed for entrance, slid home, stretching her. "Jesus you're wet!"

"Well considering what you did to her that's no surprise," Sully snarked.

Mac rolled his eyes. Clarisse giggled. Then she heard the slap and felt Mac jump.

"What was that for?" she asked.

Sully looked over Mac's shoulder. "Because he rolled his eyes, didn't he?"

She gasped. "How did you know?"

"From the way you giggled after I made that comment."

She stared into Mac's sweet brown eyes, loving him, loving both men. From the different angle of approach, his cock filled her, stroking her and hitting different spots than Sully's had.

"Do you think you can come for me like this, pet?" he asked.

She shook her head. She was tired, rapidly approaching exhaustion. "Maybe another time."

"Okay." He pressed his face against the side of her neck and slowed his strokes, his breath hot against her flesh. When he stopped moving, she knew Sully was up to something.

Then Mac moaned and flexed his hips against her. "Oh, you weren't kidding when you said I'd be swearing at you," he mumbled.

She lifted her head and realized Sully had sunk his cock inside Mac. He skimmed his hands down Clarisse's legs, where they were wrapped around Mac's waist, and grabbed her thighs.

"I never kid about something like that, you should know that. Don't stop what you were doing on my account." She felt the bed shake, hard, and knew Sully had to be pounding into Mac's ass.

Mac moaned louder, his cock throbbing inside her. "Jesus," he whispered, "that's so good!"

"Get moving. I come before you, you're done for the night." He stroked Clarisse's legs and met her gaze.

Her heart thumped. Maybe a different night it would be her sandwiched between them. The thought made her shiver in a pleasant way.

Mac started thrusting again, but his movements were jerky, hard.

"You can come any time you want, slave," Sully growled. "Don't wait too long."

Mac's thrusts gained strength and speed until he soon pounded into her. Clarisse held on for the ride.

"Oh, God that's fucking good!" Mac groaned.

Sully started slapping his ass. "Then show me how good. I'm letting you fuck my pet. You'd better show your appreciation."

Mac cried out, his body going rigid as Clarisse tightly held him. When he went limp, Sully grabbed his hips and quickly finished in a few strokes before collapsing on top of them.

"You okay, sweetie?" he asked as he rolled off Mac.

"Who you calling sweetie?" Mac mumbled.

Clarisse heard another loud slap, but Mac chuckled.

"Her, dumbass," Sully clarified.

"I'm fine," she said.

She felt the bed move, then heard water running in their bathroom a moment later. "I love you, Brant," she whispered as she stroked his back.

He lifted his head and kissed her. "I love you too, sweetie. So much, you have no idea."

"It doesn't bother you I'm married to him?"

He grinned. "Nope. Because I know I'm not going anywhere. Now I know you're not either." He kissed her again. "Besides, this makes you my wife too, in a way."

Sully walked in with something in his hand. As he knelt behind

Mac, she realized it was a washcloth. He cleaned Mac and tossed the cloth into the bathroom, then stretched out next to them. "You okay, sweetie?"

"I'm okay, Master."

He smiled and kissed her. "Don't need to be formal." He brushed the hair from her damp forehead. "Besides, Brant has something for you."

Mac smiled and reached over to the headboard where he retrieved a small ring box. The set of matching his and hers gold bands were different from the ones she'd exchanged with Sully.

Mac took her right hand. "Clarisse, I love you. Legally, only he can be married to you. I want you to always know that I'm your husband too, in heart and soul. That's what matters." He then slipped the band on her right ring finger.

She cried and threw her arms around him. "I love you guys so much!"

Sully hugged her from behind, wrapping his arms around both of them. "Still one more."

She sat back, wiping her face and sniffling as Sully handed her the other ring. He held up Mac's right hand, and she slipped the band onto his finger.

On Mac's left hand, Sully's ring would remain alone. Mac's only master, his lover.

His husband.

"Just because we do this," Mac said, indicating the three of them in bed, "doesn't define the core of our relationship." He kissed her. "We love you. We promise we'll always take care of you. That's what our relationship is really about, not sex or scenes. Understand?"

She nodded.

Sully kissed her. "A double set of rings is as good as we can do unless they ever change the law." He laced his fingers through hers. "Remember, not every night is like this, okay? You can and should always talk to us if you need something."

"All I need is the two of you."

Mac grinned. "That can be taken more than one way." He playfully waggled his eyebrows at her.

"Maybe I meant it more than one way."

Both men laughed.

Mac turned out the lights, and the three of them cuddled in bed. Clarisse spooned against Sully while Mac cuddled close in front of her, his arm draped around her and Sully.

As she drifted to sleep, she had no thoughts whatsoever about Bryan Jackson.

* * * *

The next morning, Clarisse awoke a little after seven, firmly snuggled against Mac. When she reached behind her to feel for Sully, she realized the bed was empty.

"He'll be back in a little while," Mac mumbled without opening his eyes.

"Where'd he go?"

"To make coffee and work for a while."

"Work?"

One of Mac's eyes slid open. "He wanted me to have some alone time with you." He kissed her and ran his hand through her hair. "You know, like normal newlyweds." A playful smile teased his lips.

"Nothing normal about the three of us."

"Got that right." He nuzzled the crook of her neck. "We told you, it's not all about the slave stuff, that's only part of what we do and who we are. Yeah, he's my Master. More important, he's my friend, my partner and my lover. My husband. He was all those things to me before he was my Master. If he weren't all those things first, I never could have trusted him enough to give myself to him like that."

It did make sense to her. In just a few months, she had come to understand without a doubt the truth of that statement. She had more love and faith and trust in Sully and Mac in their short time together than she'd ever had in her years with Bryan Jackson.

He skimmed his hand down her tummy, left it resting over her navel. "Because he's always my Master, that takes precedent, because that's the way I want it. There have been plenty of times he's been hurting or tired, or I'm tired or busy with the boat, or he's preoccupied with a book, and then we're just Sully and Mac, not Master and slave. Why this works is because even if one of us is in 'formal' mode and the other can't be for whatever reason, that's okay. He might be slammed with work and I can still bring him his coffee and take care of him. I can be busy trying take care of things with the boat and still submit to him in ways that don't interfere with what I need to get done. That'll happen with you, too."

"So what are we doing right now?" she asked as she rolled over on top of him.

He smiled as his cock hardened against her. "I'm making love to my wife, that's what I'm doing." Splaying his hands across her ass, he shifted his hips and his cock slid home. "Mmm, that's what I wanted," Mac said.

She slanted her lips across his and, kissing him, met every slow thrust of his hips. He rolled them over without breaking contact and slowed his strokes even more.

His eyes searched her face. "I love you so much," he said. "I can't believe I get to wake up next to you every morning for the rest of my life. You give me good dreams, baby. You make my bad dreams go away."

Sully had told her a little about that, not wanting to spill all Mac's secrets and confidences, but wanting her to know more about the man. She wrapped her legs around him and dug her heels in. "I hope you're only dreaming of me. And Sul," she quickly added.

He rubbed noses with her. "Of course." He took long, languorous strokes inside her. "Can you come for me like this, baby?"

She ran her fingers through his hair. "I want to."

Mac stilled his movements and lifted himself. He reached between them, found her clit, and gently stroked the sensitive nub of flesh.

As her eyes dropped closed, he lowered his mouth to her left breast and gently sucked her nipple between his lips.

A breathless, wordless gasp escaped her as her hand tightened in his hair. "Yes!"

He lifted his head. "Right there?"

"Yeah!"

He latched on to her other breasts and teased the nipple into a similar taut peak as his fingers gently drew her closer to release.

"Come for me, baby," he whispered, gently coaxing, not commanding.

With her muscles gripping his warm, stiff cock, it felt different from all the other times. The men had figured out how to damn near make her head explode from passion, but this felt even better. This was a connection to her men. Well, to one of them, at least.

His eyes held hers as she felt her climb begin. He touched his forehead to hers and kissed her. "Give it to me, baby. Don't tease me."

Unlike all the other orgasms he'd given her, this one was gentle, coasting, and even sweeter because he was inside her.

"That's it, sweetie." He started stroking again, trying to prolong her pleasure.

She kissed him, muffling her soft moan with his lips on hers. Matching him thrust for thrust, she urged him harder, faster.

With both hands on the bed for leverage, he took hard, strong strokes as she held on to him, her rock, her man. Then his eyes closed as he cried out, thrusting even deeper before holding himself still inside her.

Clarisse dug her heels in even more, never wanting him to leave.

He kissed the base of her throat. "Oh, Jesus, that's amazing."

"It sure was."

Sully's voice in the doorway startled them. They looked to find him standing there, naked, leaning against the door frame with a smile on his face, his arms crossed, and his cock rigid.

Mac laughed. "How long you been watching?"

"Not long enough." He walked over to the bed and climbed in with them. "That was...beautiful."

A moment of fear passed through Clarisse. Would he be mad? Jealous?

Sully leaned in and kissed Mac, then her. "I could watch the two of you together all day long." His smile softened his face. "You're gorgeous together."

"New spectator sport for Master's amusement?" Mac quipped.

Sully arched an eyebrow at him. "Don't give me too many ideas, buddy."

He looked at Clarisse and stroked her cheek. She slipped her hands down Mac's back, around his waist, hoping he wouldn't move just yet. She enjoyed the feel of his body on top of hers.

"If our girl isn't too tired," Sully said, "there's one more thing I'd like to do."

"What?" she asked.

"If we can get His Royal Horniness hard again, there's still one place I get to lay claim to."

Mac grinned and rolled over, taking her with him and surprising her, making her laugh. "How about that?"

Sully laughed and reached over to the bedside table for a bottle of lube. "Yeah, that's good."

"Kiss me, babe," Mac said. "I get fucking horny just looking at you."

She kissed him, his tongue gently sweeping across her lips, parting them, tasting and exploring her.

Carefully, so she didn't dislodge him, she started a slow grind against his hips. A moment later, she felt him start to stiffen inside her again.

Sully caressed her ass, his fingers gently working cool lube into her. Technically she was still a virgin there, if you didn't count playing with toys.

To have both her men taking her at the same time...She pleasantly shivered in Mac's arms.

Mac tenderly stroked her back, brushing his fingers up and down her spine as Sully prepared her. When she felt his warm cock press against her back entrance, she wiggled her hips.

He laughed and gently swatted her ass. "Who's in charge here, kiddo?"

"Just trying to help out."

He slowly slid inside her and waited for her to adjust to the feeling.

Mac softly moaned beneath her. "Oh...fuck! I can feel you, man."

This was way better than playing with toys. She didn't know if she'd come again like this, as tired as she already was, but it felt fantastic.

Sully took his time, slowly, gently thrusting, until his cock was tightly sheathed inside her. "Sit up, baby," he coaxed.

Mac played with her nipples while Sully wrapped his arms around her waist. "Lean on me," he said.

She let her head relax against his shoulder as the men found a slow rhythm, deep alternating strokes that felt so fucking good, better than any toy ever could.

Her men.

Sully dropped one hand between her legs and started playing with her clit. "I want another one from you, baby," he said, his tone growing deeper, dominant. "I want you to let us feel you come with both our cocks inside you."

She found her own place in their rhythm, slowly rotated her hips as Sully's fingers teased her closer to release.

"Be a good girl, pet," Sully coaxed. "Come for us." He rolled her clit between his fingers as he bit her shoulder.

Clarisse came unhinged as one more climax spiraled through her.

Sully's fingers clamped onto her clit as his voice grew stronger. "That's it, pet. Keep coming for us." He fucked his cock deep as Mac drove his hips into her from below.

She reached behind her and held on to Sully as her back arched, sensuous explosions arcing through her.

Sully lowered her to Mac's chest as the men quickly thrust, harder, faster, until they both came. Panting, Sully stroked her back, kissed her spine. "You all right, sweetie?"

Beyond speech, she raised her arm and rotated her wrist.

Both men laughed.

"Guess that means she's okay, Sul."

Sully carefully withdrew and walked into the bathroom. Mac rolled them over so he could untangle himself from her, then carried her into the bathroom where Sully was drawing a warm bath.

The men climbed into the huge sunken tub with her, cradling her between them. She snuggled against Sully as Mac massaged her feet.

Sully brushed a wet strand of hair out of her face. "You all right?"

She didn't open her eyes as she smiled, held up her hand, and rotated her wrist again.

"Green's good, baby. Green's real good."

Chapter Twenty-Three

Clarisse didn't try to keep track of time. Sully went light on protocol, and the three of them spent most of the week in bed. Until Saturday afternoon, when Sully told Mac to help her get ready for the play party.

The men had kept most of the details from her, but she had an idea that something special would happen that night. Mac massaged her feet and painted her toenails. Her leather collar was exchanged for a new silver necklace, similar to Mac's, with a small, delicate silver charm hung from it. Engraved on it were Sully's initials, with Mac's in lowercase letters beneath them.

She looked at Sully questioningly.

He smiled. "Because at least one thing in our lives can accurately tell people you belong to both of us, pet."

Sully instructed Mac what to dress her in, and as they prepared to leave, Sully laced his fingers through hers. "For the rest of the evening, unless I say otherwise, we are back to Master, Sir, and pet. Do you understand?"

Her heart raced. Thrilled, she enjoyed this part of their routine. She felt cherished and protected, even more than when they were just vanilla together. "Yes, Master."

"Very good, pet."

The men helped her navigate the stairs in her high heels. They safely tucked her into the backseat of the Jag and Mac drove. When they arrived at the party a little after nine, she felt a different tone from the men, caught hints of shared glimpses between them.

It might have made her nervous...before. Now, she understood they would do anything to protect her.

If whatever happened was too much, she could always call red.

Somehow, she didn't think that would happen. Not with these two men.

At least, not tonight.

Sully carried her across the grass to the barn where the dungeon lay waiting. Their friends had already arrived, and they applauded when Sully and Mac walked in with her, each holding one of her hands.

Clarisse blushed at all the attention and bashfully accepted their congratulations. As the party steamed into full swing her anticipation grew.

She saw Sully whisper something in Mac's ear. Mac smiled, nodded, and disappeared into the dressing room. He returned a moment later with their bags.

Sully gently squeezed her hand and led her to the center of the space, where Mac laid out a towel. After getting everyone's attention, Sully motioned Mac to stand next to him. Sully looked at Clarisse and pointed at the floor.

She knelt on the towel and assumed a formal kneel as Mac had shown her.

Mac handed something to Sully. "We had a ceremony this past Monday," Sully said to those gathered. "As you all can well guess, although it did mean a lot to all three of us, there were two things lacking. Well, three, if you count all of y'all." The audience laughed.

Sully continued. "One, it didn't allow us both to rightfully claim this woman we love. And two, it didn't allow me to lay rightful claim to her as her Master."

He placed his hand on top of her head. "My sweet pet, we both love you. Tonight, I swear to you in front of all these witnesses that as your Master I will protect you, care for you, cherish you for the rest of my life. Do you swear to obey me, respect me, and give me all that you are?"

"I do, Master."

He held up her leather collar. "This collar is, to me, even more important than the ring upon your hand. It is the symbol of your willing submission and service. Do you wish to wear it?"

"I do, Master."

He handed it to Mac and directed his next comment to him. "I swore to you when I collared you in front of some of these very same people that you would be my partner for life. And tonight I swear to you that is still true. As your Master, I bring pet into our household to serve not just me, but to also serve you in any and all ways I deem fit."

Mac nodded. "Yes, Master."

"Do you promise to love and care for and cherish and protect her?"

"Yes, Master."

"Pet, do you promise to obey slave as you would me?"

"Yes, Master."

"By accepting this collar, you are accepting both of us."

"Yes, Master."

He leaned over and swept her hair from her neck. "Slave, collar our pet."

Mac smiled as he leaned in and carefully buckled and locked it around her neck. He kissed her. "Our sweet pet," he whispered.

Sully helped her to her feet and kissed her. "Do you trust me, pet?" he whispered.

She nodded.

She did.

He led her to a nearby trapeze bar where he kissed her again. "Strip, pet."

With her eyes locked onto his grey gaze, she did, until she stood naked before him except for her collar.

Mac, still dressed in jeans and a black button-up shirt like Sully's, fastened the suspension cuffs to her wrists. After her wrists were hooked to the bar, Mac raised it enough to take up the slack.

Tonight, the panic straps were not within her reach. Sully used the straps he usually used with Mac.

Both men took their time massaging her, slow, sensual strokes that relaxed her and sent her mind swirling into subspace. She'd deeply experienced it at the last play party they attended and longed to feel it again.

When Sully slipped the blindfold over her eyes, she knew he was preparing to start in earnest. He leaned in and whispered in her ear, "There will be no pleasure this time, pet. I will never be as harsh with you as I am with slave, but do you want to feel my mark on you tonight?"

"Yes, twice."

"Twice?"

"Once for each of you."

He kissed her, as did Mac. "Then you shall." He warmed her up with the flogger first, while Mac stood in front of her, maintaining contact with her, kissing her, playing with her nipples, whispering to her as Sully stepped up the play.

He switched to the riding crop, gentle at first, increasing his strokes as he brought her deeper into subspace. Mac slipped two fingers between her legs and slowly stroked a few times before pressing them to her lips. She sucked them in and laved his fingers with her tongue.

"Good girl," he whispered as he kept repeating the gesture, bringing her close to orgasm each time he stroked her with his fingers before withdrawing them again.

Sully switched to a cane. He wasn't as hard on her as she thought he might be, but as her conscious spun into that happy place where the endorphins kicked in, she wiggled her ass, encouraging him.

Sully laughed. "Playful pet."

He increased the tempo and strength of his strokes, until she thought she couldn't take it anymore.

The briefest thought of calling red crossed her mind when he stopped and stepped in close, his body pressed against hers. "How are we, pet?"

She rotated her left hand.

He grabbed her hair and pulled her head back. "Say it, pet."

"Green, Master."

He kissed her and tenderly stroked her hair. "Do you still want our mark?"

"Yes!"

"Two strokes, that's all I'll give you. You have my word."

He stepped away. Mac cupped his hand behind her neck and pulled her head forward against his chest, supporting her.

"Good girl," he whispered. "Take a deep breath."

She heard the crack of a whip. She jumped, but it didn't make contact.

Sully stroked her ass with the handle. "I'll mark you here"—he traced a line on her right ass cheek—"and here." He traced a matching line on her left.

He took a few more practice throws, making the whip crack each time.

"Who do you belong to, pet?" Sully asked.

"You, Master!"

Before she finished the last word, the whip cracked. A fraction of a second later, she felt the whip bite into her flesh.

Mac held her. "How are you, pet?"

She rotated her left hand.

"One more, pet," he whispered.

Before the sound died on his lips, the whip cracked again. As the feel of the whip striking her made it to her brain, Sully was already behind her, holding her while Mac unclipped her wrists. Sully scooped her into his arms as Mac tucked a blanket around her. She knew her ass would be sore in the morning, but the brain buzz was well worth it.

Sully carried Clarisse into the dressing room, where he sat on one of the benches with her protectively cradled in his arms. Mac joined them a moment later, carrying their things. He removed her cuffs and knelt in front of Sully so she was supported by both men.

"Such a good girl," Sully softly said. "I'm so proud of you. I will never be that hard on you again."

"Why not?" She cracked an eye open. While the two places he'd nailed her with the whip still stung, the rest of it had faded into a dull ache she knew would be fine by morning.

Sully's face broke into a wide grin. "Because you aren't into pain, pet. I know that."

"I trust you not to take me too far."

He kissed her. One of his hands snuck under the blanket and caressed her between her legs. Mac reached under as well, pressing two fingers inside her.

She shivered, her desire still hovering, incomplete from before.

Sully pressed his lips to the top of her head. "Come for us, pet. You more than earned it."

Clarisse went limp in their arms as she enjoyed the feel of their hands on her. It didn't take long for them to bring her to orgasm. She buried her face against Sully's chest and cried out, letting go as her body welcomed the pleasure she'd been denied earlier.

While she recovered from that, Sully let Mac take her. "Let's get her cleaned up and take her home."

"What about slave?" she mumbled against Mac's chest. "We just got here a little bit ago."

Sully laughed and brushed the hair from her face. "Tonight was all about you, sweetheart, not him. We're going to take you home and tuck you safely into bed and sleep late. Then we're going to spend tomorrow pampering our very sweet pet."

Mac carried her into the bathroom. Between the two men, they took care of her, pulled an oversized T-shirt over her head, put a pair of shorts on her, and then Sully carried her out to the Jag and crawled into the backseat with her.

As she dropped into a deep sleep, she felt him weave her hair around his fingers and rest his hand against her shoulder.

Chapter Twenty-Four

Clarisse helped Mac unload the groceries and supplies from the Bug at the marina. "I'm going to run Bart over to Uncle Tad."

He hooked an arm around her waist and pulled her close, kissing her deeply. "Hurry." He nipped her bottom lip. "I've got a collar with your name on it, and I'm in a mood to play." He ground his hips into hers, making sure she felt his stiff cock. "I'm in a mood to play hard."

She grinned. "I'd say you are."

He swatted her ass before releasing her with a final kiss. "Love you."

"Love you, too." She climbed back into the Bug and drove off.

Mac smiled as he watched her go. A four-day weekend alone with her was a special treat. Sully could have taken her with him to the conference, but wanted them to have time together.

He returned to the boat to finish his trip preparations. In the three months since the wedding, life had hit a happy plateau he never wanted to come down from. He hadn't had a single nightmare, and neither had Sully. Clarisse also slept like a rock every night.

Sully smiled more than Mac ever remembered him smiling before. It tickled Mac when Sully would be the stern, unyielding Master, yet turn around later the same day and drop protocols to privately ask him if he wanted alone time with Clarisse.

Sully had started to accept that Mac really wasn't jealous. Mac had tried to explain it to him one evening after dinner while Clarisse cleaned up the kitchen. "Could you honestly see her trying to beat or dominate me?"

A cloud passed through Sully's face, darkening his expression.

"No."

"You and I go back further than our relationship. You know that. I *need* that from you. I need the things you do for me that she can't do. Let's face it, you redlight every other scene with her when she's begging you not to stop. You don't do that nearly as often with me."

A slow smile crept across Sully's face. "You could spend all day with your cock in her mouth."

"Duh." He grinned. "So could you."

"You're better at than her. Just don't tell her I said that."

Mac hugged him. "Yeah, like I'd be stupid enough to do that."

He came back to the present and looked around. Lots to do before they pulled out, including a couple of minor honey-do projects. He rummaged through the tool box and found the wrench he'd need for one, the hammer he'd need for another, and laid them on the dash. He waved to Dan and Elise in the next slip over before heading into the wheelhouse.

* * * *

Across the marina, under the shade of a dry-docked sailboat and still feeling the three beers he'd drunk earlier, Bryan Jackson watched the man who'd kissed Clarisse good-bye. The same guy he saw with her in Ohio.

He wasn't sure if he was the ex-cop Nicoletto or not, but the guy would definitely never forget Bryan Jackson. The PI had confirmed Nicoletto had bucks, and obviously Clarisse was someone special to him.

He didn't care who he got his money from, but he would get that as well as a pound of flesh for fucking up his life.

He glanced around to make sure no one had spotted him, then quickly strode across the yard. The man was below decks when he walked down the dock. Without hesitation, Bryan jumped to the deck and ducked through the open wheelhouse door. The man had his back turned to him.

Bryan attacked.

* * * *

Dan heard noises from the Dilly Dally's slip, and not good ones. Mac screaming, crashes, and another man's enraged voice.

He didn't have a weapon, but he yelled at his wife to call 911 as he raced off their boat. As he ran up the dock so he could circle back to the Dilly, he saw a man bent over, raining punches on someone crumpled on the deck.

"Hey! What the hell's going on?"

The man looked up, startled, then dropped a hammer and bolted for the dock. Dan didn't have time to go after him because he spotted Mac, still and bloodied, lying on the deck.

"Shit!" Elise had stuck her head above deck. "Mac's hurt bad! Have them send a cop and ambulance!" he screamed.

Heads popped up from boats around the marina, but the guy had already disappeared among the dry-docked boats. Dan didn't get a good look at him.

He jumped onto the Dilly's deck to help Mac. Next to him lay a bloody hammer.

Mac moaned. Dan grabbed his hand. "Hey, buddy, hang on. Please, Jesus, hang on."

His face battered almost beyond recognition, Mac turned toward the sound of Dan's voice. "...Jackson."

"It's Dan, Mac. Stay with me." He screamed over his shoulder. "Where's the goddamned ambulance?"

Mac spit up blood. "Bryan Jackson...did it. Tell them I love them."

"Jesus, Mac, don't you fucking die on me!" In the distance, he heard the wail of a siren.

* * * *

Mac's world began and ended with pain. He remembered feeling the boat rock, the sound of someone jumping onto the deck, assumed it was Clarisse. He had time to catch a glimpse of the man's face as he sucker punched him, enough to recognize Bryan Jackson.

As his vision greyed, he tried to focus on Dan one more time. "Sully...Risse...I love them."

"You can tell them yourself, buddy. The ambulance is almost here."

His world went black.

* * * *

Clarisse spent some time talking with Uncle Tad and the nurses. "You have no idea how cool this is," she said as she handed Bart over to her uncle.

One of the nurses laughed. "We love Bart. He's so cute and no trouble. The residents love him. This works out great for everyone, seriously."

She kissed Bart and her uncle and headed for her car. She'd spent more time there than she'd meant to. It'd been over an hour since she'd left the marina. When she pulled in and saw the deputy cruisers and yellow crime scene tape, her heart hit her feet.

Dan and Elise intercepted her, looking grim.

"What happened? What's wrong? Where's Mac?"

Dan tried to hold her back. "Honey, he's not here. They already took him to Harborside."

"What happened?" she screamed.

Elise had been crying and looked like she'd start again any moment.

A deputy and a detective approached her. She recognized the detective as Jason Callahan. From his equally grim look, it couldn't be good.

"Jason, please, what's going on?"

He pulled her to the side and nodded to the deputy. "We're going to take you to him."

Her eyes widened. "Oh my god. It was Bryan, wasn't it?"

Dan took her hands. "He told me Bryan Jackson did it."

She sobbed as Dan and Elise hugged her. "Is he going to die?"

"They airlifted him to Harborside," Jason said. "I don't have an update on his condition."

Dan kept her on her feet as her knees gave out. He guided her to a bench. Elise flanked her on her other side. "He told me to tell you and Sully he loves you."

Numb, she nodded.

"Give me your keys. Elise and I will drive your car, meet you there, okay? Where's your cell?"

"My purse. Car."

Dan had to cup her hand in his to take the keys from her trembling fingers. Elise brought Clarisse's purse, and Dan and Jason Callahan carefully guided her to the passenger seat of Jason's unmarked car. With the deputy leading the way in his marked cruiser, lights and sirens blaring, they left for Harborside Hospital in St. Pete.

Emotional numbness had set in. "We've got to call Sully," she said as they pulled out of the marina parking lot. "His plane leaves in an hour."

"Do you want me to do it?"

"Please." She broke down crying again.

* * * *

Sully sat at the gate, reading, when he felt his BlackBerry vibrate. He pulled it from the holster and answered without looking at the screen. "Nicoletto."

"Sul, it's Jayce."

Maybe it was instincts, maybe it his cop training, maybe it just recognizing the tone of his friend and former partner's voice. He sat bolt upright in his seat, his heart freezing into a hard, cold ball. "What happened?"

"The fucker nailed Mac on the boat."

"How is he? How's Clarisse?" *Please, please, please let him be alive! Let her be safe!*

"I've got her. She's okay. She wasn't here when he attacked Mac. They airlifted Mac to Harborside. We're on the way there in a cruiser."

Sully numbly gathered his carry-ons and raced toward the security checkpoint where he'd catch a shuttle to the main terminal. "What happened?" His voice broke.

"Jackson jumped him. Mac ID'd him before he passed out and the EMTs took him."

"What'd he do to Mac?" Jason didn't want to answer. "Dammit, tell me!"

Jason's voice quieted. "It happened quick. He ambushed him on the boat, nailed him in the head with a hammer." He dropped his voice even lower. "It's bad, Sul. I know he made it to Harborside alive, but I don't have any other news."

Sully felt the tears on his face as he ran for the shuttles. "You find that fucker. You find him before I do, Jayce. Because if I find him first I'm killing the son of a bitch, do you hear me?" He managed to catch a shuttle to the main terminal, pushing through the doors before they could slide shut.

"Calm down, Sul. Don't say anything—"

"I'm not saying—I'm promising. Put Clarisse on."

There was a pause as Jason handed the phone over. Sully angrily brushed his tears away on his sleeve, ignoring the other passengers in the shuttle with him. Then Clarisse's voice, haunting and flat, came on the line.

"Master?"

Formal meant she wasn't doing well at all. That she had used formal speech without hesitation in front of someone else told him not only how upset and in shock she was, but how much it comforted her.

He had to stay calm for her. She needed him. Brant needed him. He forced a strength he didn't feel. "I'm here, pet. I'm leaving the airport and heading straight for the hospital. I'll be there in about forty-five minutes."

"I'm scared."

"I know, pet. You listen to me, stay with Jason until I get there, do you hear? You do not leave his side, not even to go to the bathroom alone, understand?"

"Yes."

He hated himself, but said it anyway. "Yes, *what*, pet?"

"Yes, Master."

"That's my good girl. You stay with Jason. He'll keep you safe until I get there. I love you."

"I love you too, Master."

"Put Jayce back on, pet."

There was a pause, then Jason's voice. "Yeah."

Sully dropped his voice to an angry growl. "Don't you *dare* let her out of your sight, do you hear me? That fucker will track her to the hospital. Swear to me you'll personally stay with her."

"Jesus, Sul, you know I will."

He reached the taxi stand and grabbed the first one that would take him to St. Pete. He jumped into the back and let the driver handle his bags. "I'm on the way. Keep her safe for me."

"I'll see you soon."

Sully hung up, laid his head back on the seat, and allowed himself to cry. It would be the only luxury of time he'd have. Because once he knew Brant was okay and he could get Clarisse to a safe house, he wouldn't have any more time to cry.

He'd only have time to kill.

Chapter Twenty-Five

Jason and the deputy escorted Clarisse into the hospital and handled the talking for her. She clung to Jason's arm while the deputy carried her purse. Mac was already in surgery, and they couldn't give her an update because they were still trying to determine the extent of his injuries.

He was alive. That's all they could say.

"Did they find Bryan yet?" she asked during the walk to the waiting room.

Jason grimly shook his head. "Not yet, sweetie. But we will."

He'd found her. Worse, he'd hurt Mac. Now Sully would be in danger, too. If Mac died because she'd led Bryan Jackson to them, she'd never forgive herself.

A horrible thought struck her. "What about Uncle Tad?"

"I already sent a deputy there to watch him. The facility has been notified. We'll keep him safe, I promise."

She wrapped her arms around herself and slowly rocked back and forth in her chair. *Please be okay...please be okay.* She silently chanted it over and over again. Dan and Elise arrived to sit with her and she barely noticed. She focused on Mac's sweet face in her mind, praying he'd pull through.

When Sully arrived, he dropped his bags by the waiting room door, raced to her, and engulfed her in his arms as she broke down sobbing. He sank to the floor with her, holding her.

"Shh, pet. I'm here. It's okay."

* * * *

Time blurred for them. Despite using Sully as an emotional crutch, Clarisse refused to leave the hospital, didn't want to leave Mac's side to go home. No masterly orders or husbandly suggestions would change her mind, either.

Sensing this, Sully didn't force the issue. He stayed with her, getting a room at a hotel a few blocks away where he would force her to go at shift changes so she could take a shower and lie down to sleep. The few times he knew he had to take a nap or risk collapse, Jason would come in and sit with her in the ICU to ensure she was safe. Because of the circumstances of the situation, and that Mac needed twenty-four hour armed protection until Bryan was in custody, they loosened the rules to allow Clarisse and Sully round-the-clock access to the ICU instead of the normal limited visitation.

By the fifth day after the attack, Mac's condition hadn't changed. They'd listed him as critical, but stable. Until the cranial swelling went down, they wouldn't begin to reduce his medication and bring him out of his coma.

Sully watched Clarisse's face grow more gaunt. It was hard to stay strong for her when all he wanted to do was lay his head on Mac's bed and sob himself to sleep. He didn't dare cry in front of her. She needed his strength. If this was a fraction of the agonizing grief Mac felt when their positions were reversed, then he felt guilty as hell for putting Mac through that.

Jason stepped into Mac's ICU cubicle a little before noon and tipped his head at Sully, wanting to talk privately with him. Jason had told the uniformed deputy on duty to take a few minutes to go eat since he was there.

Sully leaned over and kissed Clarisse on the forehead. "Baby, I need to talk with Jayce for a few minutes, okay?"

She nodded, the deep hollows under her eyes adding to his grief. There was nothing he could do, no comforting words he could offer.

They had to wait and see.

He tenderly tucked a stray strand of hair behind her ear. "When I come back, we'll go downstairs and eat."

"I'm not hungry," she whispered. Her eyes never strayed from Mac's face, willing him to wake up, to rise and be healed.

If she'd taken in more than two thousand calories in the past few days, he was Richard Nixon. It was all he could do to get her to drink water. Hating himself, he hardened his voice. "Pet," he softly said, "you have to eat. Sir wouldn't want you making yourself sick, you know he wouldn't."

After a long moment, she finally nodded. "Yes, Master."

"Good girl." He kissed her temple and gently squeezed her shoulder before leaving the cubicle and sliding the door shut behind him.

* * * *

Bryan watched the ICU corridor. Hospital security was amazingly lax, even the uniformed deputy on watch tended to ignore anyone in hospital garb and bearing an ID badge. Walking around wearing a pair of scrubs and a white lab coat while carrying a small tote full of phlebotomy supplies and a clipboard practically guaranteed access to any area without question, especially the hectic ICU wing. Harborside, being a regional trauma center, wasn't exactly a quiet place.

He'd snagged an employee's ID clipped to an unattended sweater left hanging over an office chair in admissions. It hadn't taken him long to create a bogus ID on his laptop, make a quick stop by a automated photo printer machine at a drugstore, and then glue the fake to the top of the existing badge. A carefully trimmed sheet of laminating film over the top made it good enough for government work and would stall people long enough.

Long enough for him to get Clarisse.

He'd shaved his head bald. A throw pillow belted around his

midsection added at least thirty pounds to his appearance, and a careful slouch enhanced the illusion.

Inside the pillow, he stashed the gun.

He slipped inside the cubicle, relieved to find her alone and knew that he wouldn't have long before the uniformed deputy and the other two men returned. She never glanced at him, why would she? She was used to seeing medical personnel come and go.

He couldn't deny the satisfied thrill when he pressed the gun's muzzle to her temple and she stiffened.

"Hello, Clarisse."

She didn't speak. He pressed harder. "Aren't you going to say hello? Where the hell are your manners?"

"Hello, Bryan."

"Here's how this works. You come with me, quietly. Otherwise, I kill you and him and that other guy when he shows up. You've totally fucked my life. Well, I'm fucking yours. I want my goddamned money."

"It was my money."

He enjoyed her hiss of pain as he grabbed her arm with his other hand and squeezed, his fingers digging in. "Wrong. It's *my* money. I worked hard for it, and I want it, you fucking cunt. With lots of interest. I need it to start over. Then after I have a final goodbye with you, I'll go and you'll never see me again."

* * * *

Clarisse felt numb. She realized for the first time she wasn't scared of Bryan for herself—she was scared for Mac. And for Sully. "I'll go with you. Just…please don't hurt him."

"I already got my pound of flesh out of him. Give me your cell phone."

She handed it over, and he quickly figured out how to turn it off. He jammed it into his pocket before he roughly dragged her to her feet and propelled her toward the door. Then he pulled an envelope out of the medical supply tote he carried tossed it on the bed. He stuck the gun in his right lab coat pocket, but he didn't let go of it. He carried the tote in his left hand.

When he stepped close behind her, she had to suppress the urge to scream. "Turn left," he quietly ordered. "Walk in front of me, to the first hallway on the right and turn there. There's a stairwell on the left. That's where we're going."

Feeling more numb than scared, she complied, wanting Bryan as far away from Mac and Sully as she could draw him. She didn't care if he killed her. Sully had tried to keep the truth from her, but she'd heard the doctors talking with him. There were no guarantees that Mac would ever wake up. Or if he did, he might be little more than bedridden, barely cognizant, for the rest of his life. They couldn't evaluate the extent of his brain injuries until more healing had taken place from the initial trauma.

But if Bryan tried to kill her, she damn sure would take her pound of flesh in retaliation first, if given half a chance.

* * * *

Sully and Jason returned to Mac's bedside ten minutes later. No news. The asshole had taken huge cash withdrawals on his credit cards in Ohio, a payday advance loan for five hundred dollars, and had disappeared off the face of the fucking planet. None of his family had heard from him. The BOLO had produced no leads, and his car hadn't been spotted.

Sully worried when he didn't see Clarisse sitting next to Mac's bed, but figured she'd gone to use the restroom because her purse still sat on the floor under his bed where she usually left it. He stood in the cubicle doorway with Jason and kept his gaze focused on the bathrooms. When she still didn't return, he walked down the hall. The ladies' room was a single bathroom, no stalls, like the men's room.

He tried the knob and found it unlocked and unoccupied.

Fear twisted his gut. She wouldn't have left without him or without telling him where she went.

Without her purse.

He returned to the cubicle. Jason stared at him. "What's wrong?"

Sully shook his head and looked around for Mac's nurse. "Have you seen Clarisse?"

"Yeah, she left a little after you did. She was talking with a lab tech."

"Lab tech?" Jason and Sully exchanged a glance. To comfort himself more than anything, he walked over to Mac's side.

That's when he spotted the envelope. On the front was printed one word: *Nicoletto*.

Adrenaline spiked his system. His hand trembled as he reached for it. He exchanged another glance with Jason. Fuck protocol, he knew who left it. Fingerprints be damned. The note was printed on a computer.

If you know what's good for you, you'll sit tight and wait for me to get in touch with you. Don't worry, I won't hurt her. Much. Play this lone wolf or you'll never find her body. I'll contact you later. Be ready with one hundred grand in cash if you want her back in one piece. You know the drill. Don't forget, I do too.

Color drained from Sully's face as he handed it to Jason.

Jason scanned it. "Fuck!" He reached for his radio but Sully put a hand over his and shook his head. He grabbed Jason and dragged him from the room into a conference room where he closed and locked the door behind them.

"You can't call in help!"

"Sully, you know the rules. I have to get an alert out on this!"

"He'll kill her."

"He'll kill her regardless! We're wasting time! He's out for blood.

He damn near killed Mac!"

"He *will* kill her, Jayce. He's probably already out of the hospital with her." His hands shook as he sat in one of the chairs. "We can't report this."

"Listen to yourself! This isn't one of your fucking books! You can't seriously think you can handle this."

"You'll help me."

Jason slowly shook his head. "You're not thinking straight, Sul. We have to go by the numbers."

Sully's jaw clenched. "You're two years past vested. What are they going to do, fire you? You can retire. You were going to in a couple of years anyway. You'll still get your pension and bennies. You and me, we can catch this son of a bitch."

"Um, yeah, then the fucker gets off at trial and you and I are cellmates in Raiford with some of our past collars. Great fucking plan. No thanks."

Sully turned a hard gaze on Jason. "There *won't* be a trial."

"Listen to yourself! You're a cop, man! You're sworn to protect and to serve, not play Dirty Harry!"

"Either help me or stay the fuck out of my way, Jayce. There are no alternatives. This guy is a cop, he knows what we know, but we have the advantage of home turf. We can take him out and you know he fucking deserves it. It's not a question of needing DNA for a sure conviction. If we go through channels, we lose time and maneuverability and he'll kill her anyway. He knows he's going down, and he's willing to take as many of us with him as he can."

"Fuck!" Jason paced, running a hand through his hair. He stood for a long moment at the far end of the room, then turned on Sully. "You're asking a lot."

"I'm not asking anything. Help me, or forget you know anything. You won't hurt my feelings unless you get in my fucking way."

He studied Sully's face, knew the look well, the resolute determination.

Sagging, he nodded. "I'll help, only because I don't want to be a pallbearer at your funeral."

Sully stood. "Then let's go. We'll need your vest."

* * * *

Clarisse huddled in the passenger seat. She refused to cry, refused to sniffle or beg or plead. He'd gone totally shithouse rat crazy. She sensed if she lost her composure it would only egg him on and get her killed faster.

When she shifted position, her feet bumped against several empty beer bottles littering the floor of the front seat. Great, he was drinking again, too. She didn't know where he picked up the beater car with Virginia plates, but it sounded like it wasn't too far from its final date with a junkyard. He wove through traffic in downtown St. Pete. She thought he might take I-275, but he stuck to secondary roads, constantly checking his mirrors. He didn't speak and she didn't bother trying to reason with him.

He headed north, to an old motor court-style motel two blocks west of Alternate U.S. 19, in Palm Harbor, south of Tarpon. He pulled into a parking space in front of the room on the far end and looked at her.

"Nice and easy. Get out and wait for me, then follow me. I will shoot you and drive off if you don't. Then I will go kill your boyfriend."

She slowly opened the door under his watchful eye and stood waiting beside the car after closing the door. He grabbed a tote bag from the car and she followed him to the very last room where a Do Not Disturb sign was hung on the door.

He locked the door behind them and drew the gun from the lab coat pocket. "Empty your pockets." He put her cell phone on the dresser.

She couldn't delay. Slowly, she pulled out a couple of bills and change. She'd left her rings at home as she usually did before a boat trip, locked in the gun safe, not wanting to risk losing them or getting them caught on something.

Thank God she had.

"That's it?"

She nodded.

He grabbed a chair from the small table and dragged it to the back of the room, near the bathroom. He waved the gun at it. "Sit."

She did.

He used a roll of duct tape to secure her legs and arms to the chair. She felt marginally relieved that he wasn't going to rape her, at least not right then.

If he tried to touch her like that, she would fight him. No one touched her like that except her men. Even under risk of death she wouldn't let him do that to her.

When he was satisfied with her bonds, he reached out and slapped her, hard, across the face. "You stupid fucking cunt. You had to go crying to everyone that I hurt you."

He studied the venom in her eyes when she didn't respond, didn't cry. He slapped her again, harder. "What the fuck? You go stupid and forget how to talk?"

It stung, and if he used his fists on her, she didn't doubt she would cry. But considering his slap didn't hurt nearly as much as Sully's riding crop on her ass, she'd be damned if she'd give him the satisfaction. "I don't have anything to say to you."

"I bet you'll be saying a lot if I'm cutting your fingers off one at a time while your asshole friend is listening." He grabbed a beer, cracked it open, and took a long, deep swallow from it. Then he reached for her cell phone.

* * * *

Sully kept hitting refresh on the tracking software as Jason hovered over his shoulder. Dammit, the bastard must have shut her cell off. Once he had a location, depending on what cell towers her phone hit, it should get him close, at least within a few blocks of her location if the phone could firmly lock on the satellite signal for the GPS coordinates.

Then the first ping as the system found the phone. Not her exact location, he'd have to call her to triangulate. But he had too many programs and windows open on his laptop, and it froze before it could pick up the signal.

He swore and grabbed his phone as he rebooted the computer.

* * * *

Clarisse realized it had to be bugging Bryan that she wasn't pleading and crying and groveling like she normally would when he went after her.

That she showed no fear for herself.

He set down his bottle of beer and leaned in close. Grabbing her chin, he dug his fingers into her cheeks. "You'll have plenty to say to me later, bitch." He always got more angry when he drank, which frequently happened when they were together. On his third beer, he was on his way to getting very drunk.

And very angry.

He released her after slapping her one final time. That one, harder than the first two, rocked her head and left her seeing stars. Nevertheless, somehow she managed to choke back her smile.

"You slap like a girl, asshole." Okay, not the smartest thing to say, and she knew the second she uttered it she'd regret saying it.

He drew back his fist to hit her when her phone rang the *Mission Impossible* theme. Mac's phone.

Sully. It had to be him, because he had Mac's phone.

"Is that your other boyfriend?"

She forced the lie. "No." Well, technically not a lie. He wasn't her boyfriend, he was her husband.

He stepped back, grabbed her phone, and looked at it. She couldn't believe it when he flipped it open and held it to her face. The beer must have fogged his judgment. Thank God she'd set the caller ID to read Sir B instead of Brant.

She didn't cower, didn't drop her eyes from Bryan's. "Hi there, Sir. How are you doing?"

"Pet, it's me. How are you?" Clarisse tried to read Sully's voice, knew he must have found the note Bryan had left at Mac's bedside, but she didn't know what the note had said.

"I'm fine, Sir. It's nice to hear from you. Thanks for calling. We're getting along okay. It's been rough."

Sully paused, and when he spoke, his voice sounded soft. "Good girl, pet. I'm rebooting my computer. It's going to take a minute. Keep talking. He's right there?"

She thought fast. "I decided to alternate with Sully. He told me to come back at nineteen-hundred hours, give or take, after shift change in the ICU. I might go back a little early though."

Another long pause from Sully. "Understood. Where does he have you? Give me a clue in case I lose you."

"That's okay. It's been a long few days. I didn't feel like going all the way back home so I'm at the motel. You can call his cell, though."

Another pause. "Seminole?"

"No, that's the number he had before. Call the new number."

Less hesitation. "Largo? Keep talking in case he takes the phone away. My computer's not up yet."

"Not quite, but they're hoping sooner than later." Bryan watched her for any sign of treachery. She refused to look away.

"You're amazing, pet. I'm so proud of you. Dunedin?"

"No, if you come by tonight, you have to park where you did before and keep going, around to the other hospital entrance. It's farther up. You could park in the north garage but you have to pay."

"Holiday?"

"That would take you too far from the hospital. You don't want to walk that far in this neighborhood. The Harborside parking lot where they have all the palm trees, that's the one I mean."

She heard a muffled male voice in the background and the rattle of what sounded like paper. "Palm Harbor? A motel in Palm Harbor?"

"Yes, that's right."

"Good girl, pet. Sit tight. Has he hurt you?"

If she had half an opportunity, Bryan would be the one in serious fucking pain. "No, Sir. I'm getting along okay. Things are very tight right now."

"I love you, pet. So much, you have no idea. I promise I *am* coming for you. I *will* bring you home safe. Just sit tight. Fucking computer, I'm trying to get the air card to log on so I can track you."

Bryan made a slashing motion across his throat.

"Same here, Sir. I'm sorry. I have to go. Thank you for calling. Good-bye."

Bryan didn't drop his gaze as he pulled the phone away and hung up. "Who the fuck was that? Sir B?" He turned it off again. "Your battery's low. We'll call your little friend later."

"I've been taking some...spirituality classes at the Greek Orthodox church in Tarpon. Bill. He's the teacher. We all call him Sir. He's British. He was knighted." She mentally winced, wishing she'd come up with a better story. Lying wasn't easy anymore, not even to Bryan, and not even when faced with death. It felt wrong to lie. Her skills had atrophied with disuse.

She never had a reason to lie anymore. She never had to fear telling the truth.

Clarisse fought back the old fears returning to cripple her, how oppressive life had been with Bryan. Like a thick, nasty slime it wanted to suck away all her hopes.

His eyes crawled over her face, then dropped down her body. "You've changed, Clarisse. I don't know what, but I think I like it. Too bad you didn't find religion before when you were with me. It looks good on you." He turned and dropped the phone on the bed. "I'm taking a shower. I'll leave the bathroom door open." He ripped a piece of duct tape from the roll and slapped it over her mouth. "Just in case." Then he drained his beer, grabbed another, and headed for the bathroom.

* * * *

Sully hung up and studied the map. They'd had Mac's phone on speaker mode and taped the call. Sully used Mac's knowing his own phone appeared as "Master" on her caller ID. He didn't want Jason's phone associated with this.

He hoped she'd come up with a good explanation for "Sir B." Sully worked on his laptop to trace her phone's GPS, then swore when he realized the fucker had shut it off again. He tried to call back, but it went straight to her voice mail.

"She's in a motel in Palm Harbor, on or near Alternate 19," Sully said, studying the map.

"How can you be that sure? I know the Palm Harbor part, but the location?"

"She specifically pronounced it 'alternit' and used military time. Nineteen-hundred. She never uses military time. Alternate 19, in Palm Harbor, but not on Alt. 19, close by." He flipped between windows on the computer, trying to locate any motels that would fit the bill. A minute later, he pointed at the screen. "There." He couldn't believe Bryan hadn't ditched her phone. Even more astounding, that he let her answer it and talk. The trifecta, that he let her keep talking as long as he did.

Thank God for the tracking software. Next time, he'd be ready.

Jason looked over his shoulder. "There's at least six different motels in that area. We don't know which side of Alt. 19 she's on.

"We'll find her." He powered down the laptop and started packing. "Come on."

Jason helped him gather some things. Sully followed Jason to his house, where Jason grabbed a bulletproof vest and another gun. "You gonna help me pay my mortgage if I lose my bennies over this?" Jayce snarked.

"Buddy, I'll pay *off* your fucking mortgage."

* * * *

After his shower, Bryan sat on the bed and looked at Clarisse. "You've really changed. What the fuck happened to you?" He'd viciously ripped off the duct tape and grinned when she glared at him.

"You happened to me."

"Yeah, well, I'm about to shit on your parade. I read in the paper about that guy on the boat. Glad I didn't kill the cash cow. We're going to call your writer cop buddy, and he's going to make a little withdrawal at his bank. By the time I leave, I'll have enough to get to South America and retire. I've got a contact there who needs a computer expert. Easy money, no fucking hassles." He stretched out on the bed. "So what's the deal? You fuck that guy Nicoletto for rent? That's all you're worth anyway."

She clenched the arms of the chair as much as the duct tape would allow. "He's my husband, asshole." Probably the wrong thing to say, but she couldn't stand listening to his mouth.

Bryan's eyebrows arched. "Son of a bitch! You're married to the fucker? How'd you sucker him into that?" He laughed, long and hard. "Poor bastard. Well, maybe I can make him a widower." He glared at her. "So you're married to him, but you're obviously close to that other asshole. I saw you kissing him. What's the deal with that?" A slow, evil grin twisted his face. "You screwing around on your new hubby already? Or are you fucking both of them? Is that what the problem was, I didn't share you with my buddies? Kinky bitch. You're a little fucking slut whore, aren't you?"

Clarisse struggled against her bonds. "I'm gonna kill you, you son of a bitch!"

He laughed and raised the gun, the sight of which stilled her movements. "No, I don't think so."

* * * *

Three hours later, Sully and Jason were set up in a motel in Palm Harbor. Sully used a fake name and paid cash for the room. They scouted all the nearby motels close to where the last tracking signal had pinged. When Bryan's call came in an hour before dark, Sully had the GPS software loaded and logged on, ready to trace the phone's location.

"Is this Nicoletto?" the man asked.

"Yes. Where's Clarisse?"

"She's okay. She's alive, for now. So, she's your wife, huh?"

Sully winced. He'd hoped that wouldn't come out, knowing it would make Bryan want to get more than money out of her. "Yes."

"I think that ups my price. I don't mind keeping her safe for a few more days. Two hundred thou, cash. I know it'll take a couple of days for you to get it together. I also know you'll want to talk to the Feds. If you do, she's dead. Lots of wetlands around here to dump a body, lots of Dumpsters."

Sully tried for a scared tone of voice so he didn't sound maliciously pissed. "Please, don't hurt her."

"You're not so tough now, are you?" Sully heard a loud slap. "What the fuck did you do to her? I slap her and it's like she's a fucking deaf mute."

In the room, Clarisse glared up at Bryan. That did it. She *would* kill the fucker if she had the chance. If he put the gun down, she would get it, somehow. He had to sleep sometime. He'd cut her free once to let her use the bathroom but kept the gun trained on her the entire time. When he rebound her, he only taped her legs to the chair. He handcuffed her hands in front of her, in her lap. He'd put more duct tape on her mouth and ripped it off so she could tell him the number to dial on her phone to call Sully.

"No! Please, don't hurt her!"

"Then get me the fucking money, asshole." He hung up, shut off the phone, and threw it onto the bed. "You're going to make me a rich man, baby."

"Don't fucking call me that!"

"Well then, how about I call you a cocksucking whore? You prefer that?"

Clarisse watched him, engaged in a staring match. He finally blinked first and shook his head. "I'll fuck that attitude outta you before I get my money. Just not right now. I might have to move us someplace else tonight after it gets dark. I've been here too long."

Her heart raced. If he moved her, Sully wouldn't be able to find them as fast. At least she had a fighting chance here. She could only hope Sully understood her clues as well as he seemed to.

Chapter Twenty-Six

Sully and Jason ran out the door and down two blocks to stand across the street from another motel. On a quiet side street, the old nineteen-sixties vintage motor court had twenty rooms. Four cars sat in the lot, two with Florida plates, one from Michigan, and one from Virginia.

The men sat on a bus stop bench down the block and looked around like they were waiting for the next one.

"See anything?" Sully asked.

"Nope," Jason said. "We sure this is him?"

"Pretty sure. We need to know which car." They watched and waited. Fortunately, no bus came by. As dusk descended, they spotted lights on in four of the rooms, pinpointing where the occupants were in relation to their cars.

"How you want to handle this?" Jason asked. They'd moved to another bench, not visible from the motel, but they could still watch.

"I'm working on it." They stood to walk toward their motel when a car bearing a lit pizza parlor sign on top pulled in to the motel. The driver went directly to the last room and knocked. They watched as a large man carefully opened the door and stepped out, not allowing the delivery guy to see inside the room.

Sully's heart pounded, but he forced himself to keep his feet steady as he continued walking. "That's him. That's the son of a bitch."

"You sure?"

"Yep. He's shaved his head, but that's him."

"Let me call in a SWAT team—"

"No, fuck that. He'll kill her, won't give a shit then. She won't have a chance."

"Then what?"

Sully gritted his teeth. "I've got an idea."

Once out of sight, they raced to their motel and climbed into Jason's car. The small independent pizza parlor that delivered the pie to Bryan lay three blocks away in the other direction. A different delivery man stood outside smoking a cigarette.

Sully left Jason in the car and walked up to the guy, spoke with him for a moment. Sully reached into his wallet and passed him a few bills. The guy nervously looked around, then took the money before he disappeared inside. He returned a moment later and handed Sully a set of keys, a pizza box, and a shirt.

Sully jumped into another delivery car. Jason followed him back to their motel, where Sully wasted no time returning to their room.

"What the fuck?" Jason demanded.

Sully grinned, devoid of mirth. "I told the kid I wanted to play a practical joke on a friend to get back at the guy. Hey, shit happens. Accidental double order." He stripped off his shirt, donned the bulletproof vest, then pulled the pizza shirt on over it. He'd brought in a windbreaker from the car. It bore the pizza shop's logo. When he pulled it on and zipped it, it hid most of the bulk.

"Go to the motel, check around the back, make sure there's no rear entrance and that the bathroom window's too small for a guy to get out."

Jason raced to do it, returning a few minutes later. "Check. I couldn't see through the window, it was frosted, but I heard a guy ranting and swearing."

Sully's gut clenched. "Could you tell if she's there?"

"No, sorry."

"Fuck." He loaded the 9mm, chambered a round, and checked the safety. He looked at Jason. "When I get there, I'll go in. You leave your car around back, keys on the floor, and drive the other car back to the pizza joint. Park it around back, leave the keys in it, and meet me at our motel. Have everything packed and be ready to leave."

"When do we call in reinforcements?"

Sully glared at Jason.

"Oh, fuck, man. No, come on. Neutralize him, get the hell out with her, and then we call for backup."

Sully shook his head. "You with me or against me?"

"Fuck!" Jason ran a hand through his hair as he paced the room. "It's fucking murder! I can't go along with that!"

"What do you call what he did to Mac? He tried to kill him. You saw what he did to Clarisse. You also know he probably had a hand in her parents' deaths. His car gets stolen the night they're killed in a hit-and-run? Come on, you can't tell me that's not hokey."

Sully refused to cry despite the overwhelming emotion threatening to take him under. "It's personal, Jayce. We don't know for sure Mac's gonna make it. He might not be able to live a normal life after this. You tell me what the fuck you'd do if it was your wife or daughter lying in that hospital bed!"

Jason stared at the wall for a long moment. "I don't want to know what happens in there," he quietly said.

"You grab the pizza guy's car and leave. If it makes you feel better, you come back here and drive my car to Harborside and wait for me there. It'll be there on surveillance video, give me an alibi. In fact, that's for the best. Go sit with Mac for me."

"My choices are to be a fucking pussy coward asshole or an accomplice to murder. Not very good."

"You're not a coward. You helped me find her. I can do the rest. Your hands are clean, and I'll still respect you in the fucking morning." His face hardened. "I'm not letting this asshole get away with this. I won't let him take the people I love away from me. Besides," he said with a smile, "a body means less fucking paperwork and no goddamn trial or IA investigation to sit through."

That finally pulled a smile and laugh from Jason. "Jesus, Sul!" He shook his head. "All right. You call me within twenty minutes after you go through the door, or I'm placing an anonymous call to 911 that there's a violent domestic disturbance in progress. Deal?"

"Deal. Let's go."

* * * *

Sully kept the gun on the seat under the pizza. The pie had gone cold, but Sully didn't care. It was only for show.

The kid at the parlor had looked up Bryan's order. Bryan had used the name Smith.

Of course.

Paid cash.

Sully parked at the end of the building where Jason could easily get the car. Before he stepped out, he pulled a baseball cap also bearing the pizza parlor's logo down over his head and slumped his shoulders. He pulled on a pair of gloves and balanced the pizza on top of the gun, which he held flat against the bottom of the box.

When he knocked, he heard an angry male voice swear. "Who's there?"

Sully put on a fake Bronx accent. "Antonio's Pizza. Got an order for Mr. Smith."

"What the fuck?"

Sully heard the door unlock, and then Bryan opened it a little. Sully couldn't see past him into the room, but he saw all he needed. The fingers of Bryan's right hand were curled around the edge of the door, and the fingers of his left were pressed against the doorjamb.

No gun in his hands.

"I already got my pizza."

Sully jammed the gun against Bryan's chest. He pushed him inside the room and kicked the door shut behind him. "Special toppings, this time, asshole." He didn't dare take his attention off Bryan to look at Clarisse as he let the box drop to the floor. Outside, he heard the car start and pull out.

The clock was ticking.

Bryan drew away from Sully. Sully was prepared and kicked out, knocking the larger man off balance. Bryan fell backward and started scrabbling toward the bed, where Sully saw the gun lying on the bedspread.

Fully aware Bryan couldn't look like he was beaten to a bloody pulp for his plan to work, Sully hauled off and kicked him between the legs, nailing him in the balls. He didn't get him as hard as he wanted. Bryan flipped over and kicked out, catching him in his bad leg.

* * * *

Clarisse watched in shock as Sully and Bryan battled near the door. She couldn't walk, but she could hop. She leaned forward and caught the far side of the bed for balance. Stretching, she couldn't reach the gun. She let out a muffled cry as Sully went down and Bryan grabbed for Sully's gun. She yanked on the bedspread, her maneuverability severely hampered by the handcuffs, and started pulling the bedspread toward her.

The gun inched closer to her hands as Sully and Bryan battled on the floor on the other side. She finally got it, fumbled it, then managed to find and release the safety.

Hobbled and trying to maintain her balance, she edged around the bed. She couldn't even scream at Sully to get out of the way, and she was not a good enough shot, especially with adrenaline coursing through her, to not hit him.

Then Bryan managed to roll over on top of Sully and, sitting up, drew back to punch him.

She fired.

The gun kicked back and flew from her hands. She watched in horror as Bryan looked at her, then slumped to the side as Sully pushed him off.

Sully scrambled to his feet and managed to catch Clarisse before she fell. He eased her and the chair back into position, then gently pulled the tape from her mouth.

"Are you okay, baby?"

She couldn't speak, the adrenaline crash hitting her hard and fast, sending her spiraling toward shock.

He ripped the tape off her legs and pulled her to him. They wouldn't have much time. He rained kisses on her face as he tightly clutched her to him. "It's okay, baby. It's over. He's dead."

"Check him," she whispered. "Now. Check him."

He left her on the bed and limped over to Bryan. Her shot had hit him in the chest, near his heart. Not dead yet, but the wound was sucking. He should bleed out pretty soon.

"Not yet."

"Kill him," she managed. "Kill the fucker."

They didn't have time for this. His plan had been to stage it to marginally look like a suicide. Considering what Bryan had done, crime scene techs would have overlooked any inconsistencies with Jason smoothing the way.

This, however, wasn't good.

"We can't. We need to get out of here."

She vigorously shook her head. "Kill him, or I will."

"Just a minute." He ripped the duct tape remnants from the chair and returned it to its place at the table. He checked Bryan—still breathing.

He found Clarisse's phone on the dresser, scooped it into his pocket along with the change. Then he rummaged through Bryan's pockets until he found the handcuff key. He freed her and rubbed her wrists. "Baby, are you okay?"

She couldn't take her eyes off Bryan's still body. "Is he dead?"

He cradled her face in his hands and forced her to look at him. "Pet, listen to me. Focus on me." He felt her trembling, and her color didn't look good. "Did he hurt you?" Some bruising already shadowed her left cheekbone, but not bad.

"No. He just slapped me around. Fucking pussy coward asshole!" she angrily shot over Sully's shoulder at Bryan.

Despite the situation, Sully had to bite back a laugh. If all he'd done was slap her, then he'd only pissed her off, not hurt her. "We have to go. Now."

"I want him dead!"

Sully checked Bryan again. He stripped off his right glove and touched his fingers to the man's carotid artery. His pulse felt weak, thready, his breathing shallow. He wouldn't last long. Sully didn't see where the bullet had struck the wall or door. It must not have passed through him.

He pulled the glove back on and found Bryan's gun, wiped it clean on the bedspread and then put it in Bryan's hand to get the prints on it before placing it on the floor near him. He retrieved his gun and both pizza boxes, the duct tape remnants, handcuffs, and quickly wiped her prints off the chair and in the bathroom. As a final thought, he found Bryan's wallet and took his laptop, along with the fake hospital ID he found laying on the table. It could look like a robbery. He then stood in front of Clarisse.

"Pet, we are leaving."

She defiantly looked at him. "Is he dead?"

"He's dying." He held out his free hand. "Come, pet."

She shook her head like a stubborn child and crossed her arms over her chest. "Not until he's dead."

Sully silently swore. He didn't have time for this! "*Now*, pet. We have to get back to Sir and check on him."

At the mention of Mac she started crying. He scooped an arm around her waist and pulled her to him. "It's okay, pet. He's going to make it. We have to go in case anyone called the police. Pet, you must obey me."

She finally nodded and allowed him to guide her from the bed. He gave wide berth to Bryan's body. At the doorway, she stared back at him and shuddered. Sully started to open the door when Bryan let out a rattling gasp. Clarisse stifled a cry.

Sully knelt over him again. No pulse.

"Okay, he's gone. And so are we." He pulled her close and despite his heavy limp from where Bryan kicked him, he quickly led her from the room and around the back of the building to Jason's car.

Inside, he stripped off his gloves, jacket, and hat. The kid could easily replace the jacket and hat with the grand he'd given him for the information, use of the car, and to "lose" Bryan's original ticket. Sully would wait to throw all the stuff away in different places on the way to the hospital, but not this close to the scene. He buckled Clarisse's seat belt around her and drove away from the motel. He drove north on Alt. 19 for several blocks before turning east and heading for U.S. 19. He pulled into a shopping center and called Jason with barely minutes to spare.

"Well?"

"Done. All clear. She's safe."

Jason breathed out a sigh of relief. "I'm on the way to the hospital. I'll see you there. I cleared out the room already, so head straight back. I've got all the stuff in your trunk. Don't risk going back." He paused. "And ditch that gun, it's not traceable."

Sully closed his eyes. "Thank you, but I didn't use it."

"No problem." He hesitated. "What's the story going to read?"

"That's for the papers to decide. Random robbery, most likely. Housekeeping will find him in a day or two."

"I'll see you soon."

Sully hung up, and that's when his own shakes hit. He shut off the car, pulled Clarisse to him, and allowed himself to cry into her hair as she desperately sobbed against him. A half-hour later they composed themselves after her trembling stopped.

"I'm so sorry I didn't protect you, baby. I'm so sorry."

"I killed him," she whispered.

He nodded. "You did good. You saved me."

Her eyes widened as she looked into his eyes. "I killed him. I killed someone!"

He cradled her chin in his hands again and gently pressed a kiss to her mouth until she started responding. "Self-defense. We didn't leave evidence they can tie to you for this." He hoped. He sniffed gunpowder on her clothes. "We need to get you to our room and I have to throw those clothes away. You have to have a shower."

"Do we call the cops?"

He shook his head. "No." He took a deep breath, played dirty, told her what Jason had uncovered about her parents' deaths. "Pet, this is an order. You are to not feel guilty about this. It was self-defense."

She finally nodded and collapsed against him again, sobbing.

He took his time driving to St. Pete, threw out the various things in different locations. At their hotel, he helped her strip and held her as they both sat in the shower. She sobbed against him while the water washed the smell of gunpowder off her. After she regained her composure he helped her stand and thoroughly scrubbed every inch of her flesh and his, hoping to remove any residue. Incidental residue could be explained away by their regular target practices, but lots of fresh residue couldn't.

It was nearly eleven when they returned to the ICU. Sully nodded at the armed deputy standing guard. He'd forced a little soup into Clarisse, and her shocky tremors had stopped. Jason looked up from where he sat reading a book at Mac's bedside.

Without a word, she walked over to Jason when he stood. She hugged him, then whispered, "Thank you."

He let out a deep sigh. "I'm glad you're safe, kiddo."

They stayed for another hour before Sully coaxed her back to their hotel where they crashed, tightly clinging to each other in bed and sleeping until well past dawn.

Chapter Twenty-Seven

Mac opened his eyes for the first time nearly a month after the attack. His doctors had gradually reduced his sedation as the brain swelling decreased and his injuries healed. It was a beautiful afternoon. Jason had stopped by to visit and chat with Clarisse. Sully had gone to the house for the day to check on things, to run through a list Clarisse gave him to make sure the Dilly was okay, and to visit Tad. Bart stayed with Tad at the nursing home, one less worry on Clarisse's plate.

They had rented a small furnished apartment near the hospital, closer than the hotel room and cheaper in the long run. It was on the ground floor and accessible by wheelchair.

They hoped it wouldn't be long before they could bring Mac to their temporary home. They didn't want to talk about what-ifs, if their home in Tarpon Springs would be impractical, or if they'd have to install an elevator and convert a bathroom for him.

They didn't want to talk about a future where they might have to sell the Dilly.

They didn't talk about it at all. They talked about *when* Mac got better, not if.

Clarisse stood at the end of Mac's bed, massaging his feet and running through his range of motion exercises while Jason talked. Over the past weeks, Mac had seven surgeries for his brain injury and facial reconstruction to fix the damaged bones. The last had finally healed, somewhat. His hair, now longer than he normally wore it, had grown in choppy and uneven over his surgical scars.

She was focused on Jason when she noticed his expression. When she followed his gaze, she realized Mac's eyes were open. Her happy yell alerted the nurse.

Jason hooked an arm around Clarisse's shoulders and gently guided her out of the cubicle while the nurse called in a doctor and they checked Mac. Twenty minutes later, one of Mac's doctors walked out, smiling.

"It's a good step. He's not really awake, but it's a good step."

Jason held her while she cried. They let them back in a few minutes later to be with him. His eyes were still open, and he blinked occasionally, but he showed no signs of comprehension. She held and stroked his hands, whispering to him, begging him to respond while Jason called Sully.

By the time Sully returned to the hospital, Mac had closed his eyes again and wouldn't open them.

Clarisse didn't want to leave him. It took Sully whispering a stern order in her ear and Jason's help to pull her from Mac's bedside. That night, when she refused to eat because she wanted to return to the hospital and visit Mac, Sully pulled her over his lap and spanked her, hard, until her tears flowed.

As she sobbed in his arms, he held and soothed her, hating himself, knowing she was barely holding things together. He hadn't had the energy to give her the structure he knew she needed and craved now more than ever, most of his energy diverted to keeping a façade of strength together for her. But tonight, she needed that from him.

"You can't make yourself sick, baby," he murmured. "He'll wake up really pissed at me if I let you do that."

That elicited a snurfly snort and a lopsided smile from her. When she sat up, he handed her a tissue. "I want him back," she said. "I want him back *now*."

He tucked her hair behind her ears. He remembered his own recovery. While not involving brain trauma, it had still been long and hard and he expected that to be a walk in the park compared to Mac's journey. "I know, sweetie. Me too."

* * * *

The next morning, Mac's eyes were open when they walked into the cubicle. Mac hadn't been on the respirator in over a week, and Sully choked back a sob when he saw Mac's sweet brown eyes staring into space.

He leaned over the bed and pressed a kiss to his lips, then whispered in his ear. "I'm ordering you to come back to me, slave. Our life is empty without you."

Clarisse took up her position next to the bed on Mac's left side. She laced her fingers through his hand and waited.

Mac would blink on occasion. He closed his eyes again around ten that morning. Sully didn't try to push Clarisse's limits at lunchtime. He left her with Mac and went downstairs to eat. He brought her back a sandwich and a bottle of juice, which she reluctantly ate without too much prodding. At four, when the nurse checked Mac's vital signs, he opened his eyes again.

Sully watched Clarisse's hopeful look. He'd finally found a comfy position in the hospital recliner chair he occupied. He could watch Mac's face without moving and twisting his already sore leg any more than necessary.

Then Mac's eyes shifted position, falling on Sully and staying there.

Sully's heart seized. There was something…there. Or was he deluding himself with wishful thinking?

After several minutes, Mac's gaze still hadn't left Sully. The nurse left. Not wanting to get Clarisse's hopes up, he said, "Sweetie, my leg is killing me. Can you run down to the gift shop and get me some Tylenol or something and a cup of coffee?"

"Okay." She stepped around the bed and kissed Sully before leaving.

Sully watched Mac's eyes shift, following her departure before they returned to him. With his heart pounding in his chest, he leaned forward and clasped Mac's hand. "Brant?"

Mac stared at him, then slowly blinked twice.

Sully choked back his own tears. "Blink again, two times."

He did.

Sully looked around, saw the nurse was tending to another patient. Sully leaned even closer, brushed Mac's hair away from his face and left his hand on Mac's cheek. "Once for no, twice for yes. Answer me this. Do I call you my pet?"

One blink.

Gripping Mac's hand a little harder, he smiled. "Are you my slave?"

Mac blinked twice.

Sully's composure shattered as he dropped his forehead to the bed and sobbed. That's where Clarisse found him five minutes later.

* * * *

The neurologist came in and spent an hour evaluating Mac while Sully and Clarisse huddled in the waiting room. When the doctor finished, he found them there and sat with them, a smile on his face.

"This is good. Very good. He's showing a lot of improvement, the brain scan shows cognitive function. He's also responding appropriately to yes-and-no questions. We've talked about this. He's going to need therapy and lots of it. He might have issues with his verbal and motor skills. He might have memory or cognitive impairment. But this is a step in the right direction."

Sully clutched Clarisse to him and cried with her as they celebrated the news.

* * * *

For the next week, Mac didn't make drastic improvements. He did start following them more with his eyes, and if questions were kept to yes and no, he could hold very simple conversations. Slowly, he regained a little control of his hands, could squeeze when told to. Sometimes he rotated his hand for yes, shook it a little for no.

Seeing the familiar gesture made Clarisse and Sully smile.

Sully sat alone with him one afternoon, having sent Clarisse to the apartment to eat and nap. He would sit and stare at Mac with his fingers laced through Mac's. Mac had drifted in and out of consciousness all day, occasionally squeezing Sully's hand or responding to comments. The nurse had checked Mac's vitals and left Sully with Mac's afternoon feeding dose. Sully and Clarisse had learned how to feed Mac through his feeding tube and insisted on being the ones to do it when they were present.

Sully stood and washed his hands, then hooked up the feeding syringe. He smiled at Mac. "Ready for chow time?"

Sully didn't think he imagined the sudden tilt to Mac's mouth.

Sully laid the syringe on the sheet and leaned in close. "Brant?"

Mac's lips twitched in a faint smile. "…sssster."

"What?"

Then Mac's mouth opened and he slowly licked his chapped lips. They coated them with lip balm several times a day, but some dryness still occurred. "Yesss, Massster," he breathed. Then his lips returned to the faint smile, obviously proud of himself.

Stunned, Sully didn't process what Mac had said for a moment. He whooped with joy and grinned. "Son of a bitch! Please tell me you said what I think you said."

Mac's smile widened a little and he blinked twice.

Yes.

Sully's eyes filled with tears as he started the feeding process. "Jesus, Brant, that was the best sound I think I've ever heard in my life."

Mac dozed during the feeding, but he opened his eyes when he heard Clarisse arrive. The faint smile returned to his face.

Sully noticed his look and grinned, stopping Clarisse in her tracks. "What?" she asked.

He looked at Mac. "You want to try again?"

Yes.

Sully grinned even wider. "Honey, lean in close."

She did, and Mac licked his lips. "Pet."

She gasped as her eyes widened, then filled with tears. "Oh, Brant!"

Mac smiled.

"He said it, all right," Sully said, beaming. He glanced around to make sure the nurse wasn't close by and leaned across the bed. "I asked him earlier if he was ready for his lunch and he said, 'Yes, Master.'"

Her hand flew to her mouth as she tried and failed to choke back her sob.

Mac watched as she leaned in and kissed him. "Sir, I've missed you so much," she whispered.

A tear rolled down Mac's face. He blinked.

Yes.

* * * *

He could speak in short, simple sentences by the end of the next week. It was both a difficult physical effort for him, as well as a troubling mental one, Sully observed. Mac had problems finding, much less saying, the right words. He still used the blinking system, and shaking or rotating his wrist for yes or no. He also used his familiar eyebrow arch to indicate a question instead of speaking at times. A speech therapist came in to work with him, as did occupational and physical therapists. The next week, he was moved to a rehab facility a couple of blocks from the hospital, still within walking distance of the apartment.

After a month there, he'd regained some of his gross motor skills, enough Clarisse and Sully could take him "home" to the apartment. Mac didn't remember the attack, and he hadn't asked what happened.

Sully decided that story could wait until later, if it ever needed to be told at all.

With Mac decidedly on the mend, Clarisse's mood greatly improved. The nightmares that plagued her after the shooting disappeared almost overnight once Mac was safely back with them. Their first night together following the attack, Sully and Clarisse snuggled tightly against Mac, with him firmly sandwiched between them.

The next morning, Clarisse left to pick up Bart from Tad and bring him to the apartment. Sully was dressing Mac and getting him ready for his daily therapy appointments.

Mac still didn't talk much, even though he could. Sully suspected it was an exhausting effort for him. His voice sounded weak, almost forced, nothing like its former rich tone.

He was buttoning Mac's shirt for him while Mac sat in his wheelchair. When Mac weakly caught his hand, Sully looked into his lover's eyes and saw the concern there.

"Tell me."

Sully sat on the bed. "Everything?"

Mac nodded.

Sully told him about the attack. He stopped at Mac being admitted.

"More."

"Brant, you don't need to know that."

"Did he hurt her?"

"She wasn't there. She'd left the marina."

"After."

Sully had never lied to Mac in the course of their relationship. Ever. It was a point he prided himself on.

He owed the man honesty. Hell, he owed him his life.

"He can't ever hurt her again." Bryan's body had been found late the next day by motel housekeeping. As Sully had expected, while there were questions, the fact that Jason caught the case because he was in charge of the investigation of Mac's attack, combined with Bryan Jackson's history, allowed many questions to simply remain unanswered. The car, it turned out, had been stolen. If Clarisse's prints were found in the car, Jason must have taken care of it because it was never brought up, neither of them were ever questioned about Bryan's murder.

As far as Jason was concerned, he ate dinner with Sully and Clarisse that night, before he returned to the ICU to sit with Mac while the other two took a nap and got some rest.

Surprisingly, when Jason searched Bryan's room at the crime scene, he found an ounce of cocaine hidden inside his suitcase.

Sully didn't ask Jason where he'd found that little party favor, but it only stacked the deck against Bryan. The current popular theory was a robbery or drug deal gone wrong because of the surrounding neighborhood being rife with frequent narcotics busts.

He told Mac the rest of the story. Mac listened, his gaze on his hands, which he clenched and unclenched in his lap while Sully softly related what happened.

When he finished, Mac looked up with tears in his eyes. "She okay?"

Sully gently laid a hand on Mac's shoulder. "She's really okay. Her nightmares have stopped."

Mac sniffled, took a deep breath, and let it out. "Okay." He met Sully's gaze. "Love you."

Sully smiled and leaned in for a kiss. "I love you too, Brant."

Mac scowled.

"What's that for?" Sully asked.

Mac arched an eyebrow at him. After a long moment, Sully laughed and hugged him. "Quit pouting, *slave*. Your face will freeze like that."

Mac snickered. "Yes, Master."

* * * *

"I can do it," Mac insisted.

Clarisse hovered behind him, around him, in front of him, worried. "I know, sweetie, but let me help—"

"Let him do it, pet," Sully sternly ordered.

Clarisse shot Sully a dark look, but stepped away from Mac.

With his right hand, Mac gripped the hand rail and slowly lifted his left leg, planting his foot firmly on the riser. It took him ten minutes and three more orders from Sully for Clarisse to leave him be, but Mac climbed the stairs to their house by himself. Once at the top, Sully stepped in and slipped his arm around Mac's waist for support.

"All right, tough guy. That's enough independence for your first day home." He guided Mac over to the couch and helped him sit. In the months since the attack, Mac had dropped nearly thirty pounds, most of that in lost muscle. He'd started using light hand weights, but Sully knew it would take a while to regain his former body tone.

Bart ran into the room, dragging something. It wasn't until he climbed the ramp next to the couch and jumped into Mac's lap that Clarisse realized what he had.

The butt plug.

Mac and Sully started laughing. Sully snickered and grabbed the dog. "What a way to welcome him home, pup. Let's go empty your pan." He carried the dog out of the room.

Clarisse recognized Mac's playful expression. "What?"

He patted his lap.

"I don't want to hurt you."

"Won't break. Come here."

He had her straddle his lap, facing him. He slowly worked to unbutton her shirt, pushing her hands away when she tried helping him.

"Behave, pet," he scolded.

She grinned. "Sorry, Sir." It had been several months since she'd even remotely felt in the mood. But as Mac's planned homecoming loomed and her libido returned, just weeks before Thanksgiving, Sully had denied her release to amp up her anticipation.

Now she understood why.

It'd only been in the past couple of weeks that Mac felt like being intimate. Because of his weakened condition, they kept things simple, usually Clarisse going down on him while Sully held him.

He parted her shirt and pushed it down her shoulders, exposing her bra. He struggled for a moment with the front clasp, then dragged in a long, deep breath when the fabric parted.

"Love you, pet."

"I love you too, Sir."

He pulled her to him and traced circles around her nipples with his tongue. After several minutes, he'd driven her close to the edge.

Sully walked in carrying a laundry basket. "Ah, I see we're really getting back to normal."

Mac arched an eyebrow at him.

Laughing, Sully shook his head. "Carry on. Don't let me interrupt. I've got laundry to do or we'll all have to run around here naked."

Mac's hands settled on Clarisse's waist. "Shirt off," he softly said. "Please."

She shrugged her shirt and bra off and draped her arms over his shoulders. "Like this?"

He smiled, shifting his hips against her. "Yeah. Like that."

She took a cue from him and started a slow, seductive grind against his pelvis. She felt his stiff cock rubbing against her through his shorts. "Want me to lose my shorts?"

He grinned. "Duh."

She stood, slipped them and her panties off, then retook her perch on his lap. "Does Sir want a lap dance?"

"More than that." He pulled her to him and kissed her, slowly, savoring every second. He never asked her about the shooting. The men didn't want her to think about it. Now with Mac home, despite still having therapy once a week that would continue for at least several months, he wanted life to go back to normal.

As normal as it could be for them under the circumstances.

The sound of footsteps racing up the stairs heralded Sully sticking his head through the front door. "Pet, get dressed. Now. Jason and Katie just pulled in."

"Shit!" She jumped off Mac and scrambled for her clothes as Mac let out a long, sad sigh. She leaned in and kissed him. "I'm sorry, Sir. We'll pick up where we left off when they go, I promise."

He grabbed her wrist. As more footsteps sounded on the stairs, he pulled her in for one last long, deep kiss. "No underwear."

Clarisse grinned. "Okay. Let me go get dressed!" She bolted across the living room and closed their bedroom door behind her as the front door opened and Sully walked through, followed by Jason and Katie.

Mac grabbed a throw pillow and pulled it into his lap to hide the pup tent his shorts had become. Katie swooped in to give him a hug and kiss. Jason shook his hand. Sully stood behind them, smiling, and winked at Mac.

Mac smiled and winked back.

Clarisse returned a moment later. After three hours, Jason and Katie finally left.

Unfortunately, so had Mac's stamina. When Sully returned from walking them out, he helped Mac stand. "You worn out?"

"Yeah."

Sully kept an arm around his waist and walked him to the bedroom while Clarisse fixed them all something to eat. Sully helped him onto the bed.

"You okay?"

"Tired."

Sully knelt in front of him and helped him remove his shoes. "It's good to finally have you home, Brant."

Mac arched an eyebrow at him.

"I can call you Brant if I want, slave."

Mac snickered. "Yes, Master."

Sully stared into his eyes. "What the fuck would I have done if I'd lost you?"

"Your own laundry."

Sully laughed. "I'm doing that already." He closed his eyes and rested his head in Mac's lap. "You're not allowed to ever scare me like that again...slave."

Mac snickered again. "Yes, Master."

Sully felt Mac's fingers stroke his head, twine in his hair, rest there. He fought the urge to cry with relief that their nightmare had truly ended. Bryan dead, Clarisse safe, and Mac home for good. Life could finally go on. This man was his strength, his rock. It didn't matter Mac called him Master. Mac had saved his life, kept him sane and whole.

Kept him from putting a bullet into his own brain on more than one occasion when he didn't think he could stand the pain.

"I love you, Sul," Mac whispered.

Sully smiled and lifted his head to look at Mac. His soul felt lighter than it had in months. "Love you too, Brant."

Clarisse brought dinner into the bedroom. They watched TV while they ate. After dinner, she took everything to the kitchen to clean up. Mac snuggled against Sully.

"Collar?" Mac asked.

Sully had let Mac wear his ID bracelet once he'd regained most of his independence, afraid he might catch it on something and hurt himself somehow before then.

Sully propped himself on one elbow and looked at him. "Let's go easy for a while, okay?"

Mac frowned and rolled onto his back away from Sully.

Sully sat up. "Stop it. Dammit, we just got you home."

"Won't break." He wouldn't look at Sully.

"Jesus Christ, you are one fucking stubborn man, do you know that?"

Mac glared at him and stuck out his tongue.

Sully laughed. "Fuck me, you are too much."

Mac flipped him a bird. Sully pinned his arm to the bed. "You want to lose that finger?"

He flipped him off with his other hand. Sully pinned that hand to the bed too, then straddled him. "You're looking for a good caning, aren't you, slave?"

"Duh."

They locked eyes for a moment. Sully leaned in and kissed him, hard, until he felt Mac's cock stiffen in his shorts. Only then did he release Mac's hands as he changed position. He slid Mac's shorts down his hips.

"What're you doing?"

"Shut up, slave." Sully knelt between Mac's legs and grabbed his lover's cock. All these years and he'd never done this for a whole bunch of reasons that he really didn't understand anymore. It didn't matter.

A lot of things didn't matter. Only two things in his life mattered, and one of them was lying in front of him. The other would be back from the kitchen in a few minutes.

He lowered his head to Mac's cock and licked the head.

"Master—"

"I said shut up. That's an order."

Mac lay back and obeyed. Sully explored the head with his tongue, closed his eyes, and slowly engulfed Mac's cock with his lips.

"Ohh, man. I want to help!"

Both men laughed as they looked at Clarisse. She stood in the doorway and wore a pouty face.

"Get over here, pet," Sully ordered. "You can lick his balls while I suck him."

She quickly climbed into position. Mac threw his head back and writhed on the bed as they tag teamed him. After a long time of Mac not coming despite all his efforts, Sully realized his stupid mistake.

He lifted his head. "You can come any time you want, slave." Sully lowered his head to Mac's cock again. A few moments later, Mac's loud cries signaled his release.

Clarisse raised her head and giggled. "I was going to say something, but I figured you knew what you were doing."

He slapped her ass. "Thanks a lot, pet."

"Any time, Master."

They cuddled next to Mac as he lay there with a content smile on his face. "Boat rules?"

Sully laughed. "No, not quite. Something special for your first night home, that's all."

"Thank you, Master."

"I'd say anytime, but you have to earn the next blow job from me."

Mac opened his eyes and arched an eyebrow at him.

Sully smiled. "First time you really get back in the saddle, so to speak, running the boat and boat rules are in effect, feel free to take advantage."

Mac still stared, questioning.

"Hey, I have to give you some incentive to keep working hard in therapy."

Mac lowered his head, closed his eyes, and snickered. "Yes, Master."

Epilogue

It was a chilly March morning, but the clear skies and calm winds promised good seas. Mac sat behind the wheel and looked over the bow. "Go ahead and cast off."

Sully worked the bow line while Clarisse manned the stern. Mac eased the Dilly Dally out of her slip and carefully turned her in the basin. During Mac's rehab, after his homecoming but before he was steady and strong enough to return to his captain's duties, they'd taken the boat out many times with Clarisse in command.

Although Sully never gave her the "boat rules" option, he did defer to her as captain. After seeing her in charge of the boat, he signed her up for Sea School so she could earn her captain's license. Mac enjoyed helping her study for her classes.

Even though Mac felt much better, they didn't want to subject him to the long hours commercial fishing entailed. She suggested converting the Dilly to a dive and deep sea fishing charter, an idea Sully, Mac, and Tad wholeheartedly endorsed. She oversaw the retrofit while Sully managed Mac's rehab and doctor appointments.

They motored down the channel toward the head marker when Mac turned from the wheel with something in his hand. "Come here," he said to Sully.

Clarisse grinned. She already wore her collar, never bothered to take it off that morning since she knew Mac would only be putting it right back on her.

Sully smiled. "Are you sure you can handle me, *Captain?*"

Mac stood. He grabbed Sully's shirt, pulled him close, and kissed him. "I can put you on your ass." He probably could, too. He'd regained his lost weight, mostly in muscle mass since he'd started on a weight training program. He didn't look like a gym rat, but he'd rebuilt his body almost to its pre-attack physique even though his dexterity and balance sometimes faltered.

Sully bowed his head as Mac fastened the collar around his neck and snapped the padlock into place. "Clarisse, take the wheel."

She did. Mac pointed Sully outside.

Sully expected Mac to tie him to the rail like he normally did. Mac surprised him, unzipping his own jeans and pushing them down far enough to expose his cock. Then he leaned against the rail. "Get busy."

Sully arched an eyebrow at him. "Not wasting any time, are we?"

Mac kissed him again. "Fuck, no. You said you'd do it." He hesitated. "I won't make you do it if you don't want to, but why the fuck you think I worked so hard all these months?"

Sully smiled as he sank to his knees. "Maybe I can be a little more lenient from time to time."

"You saw why I enjoy it so much."

Sully had to admit that he was right. There was something powerful about the intimate contact, from the giving end, delivering that much pleasure. "Yeah." He leaned in and sucked Mac's stiff cock into his mouth. Mac dropped his hands to Sully's head and slowly pumped his hips. "Fuck, yeah man."

Sully closed his eyes and worked hard to make it feel as good for Mac as Mac always did for him. He gently squeezed Mac's balls in his hand, massaged his sac, played with his taint.

Mac threw his head back. "I'm fucking close," he hissed.

Sully grabbed the back of Mac's thighs and deeply swallowed, fighting his gag reflex. Mac let out a loud moan as he climaxed. "Fuck, fuck, fuck that's good!"

A strange, warm feeling rolled through Sully. He'd done that to Mac.

Sully had never felt quite like that before.

Mac's grip in his hair loosened. "Fuck, man, that's fucking good."

Sully rocked back on his heels. "Happy?"

"Hell yeah." He tucked himself into his jeans and kissed Sully after helping him to his feet. "Let's get back in the wheelhouse."

Mac took the wheel from Clarisse and slid into the seat. "Pet, suck Sully's cock."

She eagerly complied. Mac locked eyes with Sully. Sully helped her with his jeans and grabbed onto the dash for support as she nearly took his knees out with the power of her blow job.

Mac smiled as he watched. Sully's eyes never left him. "Don't come yet, Sul."

Sully groaned. "You fucker."

"That comes later." He stared at Sully, amused. "She good?"

"Oh, fuck, Brant. You know she is."

That spurred Clarisse and her slightly evil playful streak into working even harder to make him come.

Mac glanced around to make sure their way was still clear, then turned back to Sully. "I think you can hold out a little longer."

Sully's knuckles whitened as he gripped the dash tighter. "No, fuck, I can't."

"I'll make you suck my cock to the Middle Grounds and back if you can't hold it."

Clarisse's head popped up. "Ooh, I'll do it!"

"Get back to work, pet," he growled, trying not to laugh. He knew what she was doing—her interruption had given Sully enough leverage to maintain control.

He leaned over, grabbed Sully's shirt, and kissed him. "Come for me," he whispered in Sully's ear. "Show me how much you love me."

Sully's eyes dropped closed as he came. He cried out and held onto the dash as Clarisse eagerly milked his release from his cock. When he finished, she sat up after placing one last kiss on the softening head.

"Now what?" she asked Mac.

"Go make us lunch, pet."

Sully's eyes opened as he stared at Mac. She left them alone. Mac sat back and crooked his finger at Sully. After zipping his jeans, Sully stood next to him.

Mac wrapped his arms around Sully. "I fucking love you, man. You realize you're stuck with me for life, right?"

Sully smiled. "I hope so."

Mac rested his head against Sully's chest and enjoyed the feel of his lover's arms around him.

"I can't believe you put up with me," Sully said.

"You're my safe harbor," he murmured. "I don't belong anywhere but right here."

THE END

WWW.TYMBERDALTON.COM

ABOUT THE AUTHOR

Tymber Dalton lives in southwest Florida with her husband (aka "The World's Best Husband™") and son. She loves her family, writing, coffee, dark chocolate, music, a good book, hockey, and her dogs (even when they try to drink her coffee and steal her chocolate).

When she's not dodging hurricanes or writing, she can be found doing line edits or reading or thinking up something else to write. She loves to hear from readers. Please feel free to drop by her Web site and sign up for her newsletter to keep abreast of the latest news, views, snarkage, and releases. (Don't forget to look up her "alter ego," Lesli Richardson!)

Website: www.tymberdalton.com
BookStrand: www.bookstrand.com/authors/tymberdalton/
www.bookstrand.com/authors/leslirichardson/

Also by Tymber Dalton

Writing as Lesli Richardson

Siren Publishing, Inc.
www.SirenPublishing.com

LaVergne, TN USA
26 July 2010
190951LV00011B/129/P